ELFSONG

BOOK FIVE OF THE CHRONICLES OF PARTHALAN

JENNIFER ALLIS PROVOST

BELLATRIX PRESS

Bellatrix Press

CONTENTS

CAST OF CHARACTERS

Aeolmar—First Hunter of Parthalan and commander of the Palace Contingent, mate of Latera, father of Mara, Ember, and Tor.

Aldo—caretaker of The Seat and Leran's personal *saffira*.

Alia—commander of the Northern Contingent.

Alluria—mate of Caol'nir, mother of Aeolmar.

Alyon—priestess of Asherah in the mortal realm.

Argent—prior First Hunter. Killed at the Battle of Esguth.

Asgeloth—*mordeth-gall*, Ehkron's whelp. Killed by Latera.

Asherah—Queen of Parthalan and Lady of Tingu, mate of Finlay, mother of Finlay Torim.

Atreynha—High Priestess of Teg'urnan.

Attia—royal *saffira-nell* and Asherah's confidant.

Avinor—King Markham's youngest son, brother to Iruna.

Bron—hunter in the Palace Contingent, brother of Luth.

Caol'nir—mate of Alluria, father of Aeolmar.

Caol'non—Caol'nir's twin brother.

Cerillia—mate of Senan.

Cydia—Moon Goddess, former mate of Olluhm, mother of the fae.

Ehkron—former *mordeth-gall*, Asgeloth's sire. Killed by Elvasla.

Elkin—Second Hunter, mate of Innetha.

Elvasla—former Lady of Thurnda and ancestor of Latera. Killed Ehkron in the mortal realm.

Ember—younger daughter of Latera and Aeolmar.

Esguth—*mordeth* who attacked Teg'urnan. Killed by Aeolmar.

Finlay—King of Parthalan, mate of Asherah, father of Finlay Torim.

Finlay "Finn" Torim—Asherah and Finlay's son.

Grelk—King of the Trolls, master blacksmith.

Harek—former Prelate. Executed for treason.

Innetha—huntress in the Palace Contingent, mate of Elkin.

Iruna—youngest child of Markham, sister of Avinor.

Ish h'ra—The Deliverer. Once leader of the old gods, she was persecuted by Olluhm.

Kemen—hunter in the Palace Contingent, son of Krylle.

Krylle—priest of The Deliver and the old gods. Father of Kemen.

Leran—Lord of Tingu, son of Lormac.

Latera—First Huntress of Parthalan, *deva'shi*, mate of Aeolmar, mother of Mara, Ember, and Tor. Killed the last *mordeth-gall*, Asgeloth.

Lormac—former Lord of Tingu, father of Leran, mate of Asherah. Killed on the Day of Sadness.

Luth—hunter in the Palace Contingent, brother of Bron.

Mallia—matriarch of the palace's healers.

Mara—eldest daughter of Latera and Aeolmar.

Markham—last king of Parthalan directly descended from Olluhm and Cydia, father of Iruna and Avinor. Killed by a usurper who was then killed by Sahlgren.

Mersgoth—*mordeth* who marked Alluria, and went on to kill her, Caol'nir, and six of their children. Eventually killed by Aeolmar.

Natreus—former king of the dark fae. Defeated in battle by Asherah.

Nyshanti—goddess of dawn, lover of Ish h'ra.

Olluhm—Sun God, former mate of Cydia, father of the fae. He cast the old gods from the sky and installed himself as the All Father.

Rahlle—former royal sorcerer, one of Cydia and Olluhm's original twelve children. Hasn't been seen since shortly after Asherah took the throne.

Sahlgren—former king of Parthalan who betrayed his people. Executed by Asherah.

Sarelle—former High Priestess of Teg'urnan who acted in collusion with Sahlgren.

Sarfek—sorcerer, brother of Sarfek. Killed by Latera.

Solon—the child sun, first born of Olluhm and Cydia.

Surya—huntress in the Palace Contingent. Surya's eyesight rivals a hawk's.

Tor—Latera and Aeolmar's youngest child. Named for his grandsire.

Torim—Asherah's companion, killed on the Day of Sadness.

Wren—an herbalist, and Latera's oldest sister.

PROLOGUE

Grelk remembered everything.

He remembered when all the realms were one, and when warring factions of gods split the one realm into three, and then split those three into the nine realms that exist today. He remembered the first people that inhabited Parthalan, and when the elves rose in the north. He also remembered when the Olluhm rose to power and cast the old gods from the sky, decimated their followers, and repopulated Parthalan with his own progeny.

Grelk had never cared for Olluhm. It was a dirty trick he pulled, first usurping the sun god and the whole of the sky, and then laying claim to the land below. Even so, Grelk never held the Olluhm's actions against his descendants, especially his first born, Solon, also known as the child sun. That boy took after his mother, the noble moon goddess, Cydia, and when Solon descended from the skies, he saved not only the fae, but the trolls too. In Grelk's eyes all the fae were descended from Solon, and not the treacherous elder sun.

Many thought the old gods were dead, but Grelk knew better. Olluhm had sent many of the old gods to the underworld, true, but the trolls managed a network of tunnels that ran below Parthalan, Tingu, and the surrounding lands. The trolls helped bring the Parthians out of the underworld, and to a safe haven beyond the Great Southern Sea.

Their forges worked day and night, hammers clanging as the trolls made all manner of things the Parthians might need in their new home. They produced swords and shields aplenty, along with domestic items like cauldrons and axe heads. Grelk wanted the Parthians to build a home for themselves far out of Olluhm's reach, and he gave them the means to do it.

The last of the old ones to go was Ish h'ra, The Deliverer, and her lover, Nyshanti of the Golden Dawn. Grelk worried for them, being that Olluhm hated the pair most of all, but many winters after the last of the old ones went into hiding, Grelk encountered them again. Ish h'ra seemed to have forgotten who she once was, but Nyshanti remembered. Nyshanti, like Grelk, remembered everything.

Now orcs once again raged across the northern plains, and the underground troll dens shook with the thunder of their feet. Grelk remembered when The Deliverer had last saved his people from the orcs, and smiled. She promised she would return if he ever needed her, and Grelk had never doubted Ish h'ra's word. Soon, Ish h'ra would remember, and the goddess would walk Parthalan's soil again.

Soon.

Chapter One

The mountain troll's hide made a thick, tearing sound as Leran's sword pierced its flesh, followed by the wet crack of bone. Leran stepped back from the corpse, then braced his boot against the still-twitching corpse and wrenched his sword free. He looked up from the mess and saw Balthus striding toward him.

"Is that the last of them?" Leran asked.

"There's a few up by the ridge," Balthus replied, "nothing that won't be dealt with by day's end." Leran nodded and looked out across the rocky plain. A few days ago, it had been an expanse of frozen tundra punctuated by the occasional boulder. Now, it was littered with stinking troll corpses.

How did they come upon us so quickly? Leran stepped around a congealed pool of ichor; while the bloodlike substance that flowed from mountain trolls was not nearly as caustic as that which oozed from the orcs, it still left a nasty mark. Mountain trolls had long been an enemy of the elves, mostly because of the alliance forged between Nexa, the first elf, and Grelk, King of the Forge, that allowed the ground trolls to remain their dens beneath Tingu's soil while the elves live above. It was a reciprocal relationship; elves sheltered the ground trolls, and trolls supplied the elves with weapons unequalled in all the nine realms.

Even if the ground trolls offered the elves nothing in return, Leran would sooner die than enter into any sort of agreement with mountain trolls. They were vile, despicable creatures, as likely to war with neighboring lands as eat their own children. Nexa had proclaimed the mountain trolls enemies of the elves, and each of her descendants had followed her edict.

"Let's have at the stragglers," Balthus said. Leran grinned, despite his exhaustion. He was a warrior born, and the thrill of battle was one of the few pleasures he allowed himself. Good thing, too. He'd been fighting for his throne nearly his entire life.

"The elfsong is strong within you," Balthus said as he clapped Leran's shoulder. Leran could not fathom what would have become of Tingu without the steadfast Balthus; not only had he commanded the legions under Leran's father and grandsire, he'd served as Leran's regent until he grew to manhood. True, the lands surrounding Tingu saw Leran's youth as the opportune time to break away from his rule, but that was hardly Balthus' doing. Of the seven lands, four were again under Tingu's standard, and it was only a matter of time before Leran reclaimed the remaining three.

And, I'm still the Lord of Tingu. No matter whom the other lands called leader, it was Leran who was Nexa's last living descendant, Leran who was the ruler of the elves. The Queen of Parthalan, Asherah, still bore the title of Lady of Tingu, but she left the elves to govern their own affairs, and it should be an elf to rule the elves.

Half-elf. Leran's parentage had always been an issue. Some said his mother was a nymph, while others claimed she was fae, but it mattered not what sort of blood coursed through her veins. What mattered was that she was not an elf, and whenever Leran's leadership was called into question, his half-blood status was raised. Normally, he railed at the fool who dared disparage his mother; while she had done very little mothering, she had been good enough for his father, and for Leran, that was enough.

Of course, once the issues had turned to Leran's parentage, someone invariably mentioned Asherah's continued rulership of both the elves and all of Parthalan, and that the only land she had ever expressly given to Leran was Nibika. Never mind that Leran now wore the Sala, or that Nibika was little more than a memory after Leran's thorough razing of it in the wake of Natraeus' treachery, those who would question him claimed Asherah was his faerie mother looking out for her boy. Nothing could be further from the truth, and Leran had spent his life rejecting the only parent left to him in order to prove his mettle.

Such had been Leran's life since his father died, too soon to have taught him the nuances of leadership, too soon to help him become the king he was born to be. Leran's time since then had been a struggle, but he wanted nothing more than to rebuild his kingdom, and preserve his father's legacy.

Leran swept his gaze across the battlefield. The mountain trolls were subdued, for now, and a new, unwanted task loomed on the horizon. He shouted for his men to regroup, then Leran turned to Balthus and uttered the words neither wanted to hear.

"We'd best return to The Seat, and make ready for our journey," he said to Balthus. "If we arrive to Thurnda late, I'd rather face another host of trolls than Senan's new mate."

Chapter Two

Aeolmar and Latera arrived at the corridor leading to Teg'urnan's royal apartments a moment after Elkin and Innetha did. "You were summoned, too?" Elkin asked.

"We were," Aeolmar replied. "Any idea why?"

Innetha shrugged. "With Asherah, it could be anything."

Aeolmar frowned. "More attacks from the north, I assume."

"Of course you assume that," Innetha said. "When have you ever expected good news?"

"Only one way to find out what this is about," Latera said as she stepped between them; it wasn't yet second dawn, she hadn't had her tea, and the last thing she wanted was to listen to her mate and Innetha bickering. The apartment's door opened of its own accord—Aeolmar had charmed it to recognize Latera long ago—and the four hunters entered the chamber.

Queen Asherah and King Finlay stood in front of the hearth, their heads close as they looked over a small square of parchment. Asherah raised her head, and smiled at her hunters.

"Thank you for coming so quickly," she said. "And early," she added, motioning for the *saffira* to begin pouring tea.

"Of course," Elkin said, as the six of them sat around the queen's map table.

"We've received news from the north," Asherah began.

"More attacks?" Aeolmar demanded.

Finlay shook his head and set the parchment he and the queen had been reading in the center of the table. "Not this time. Senan of Thurnda is taking a mate, and he has invited us to the feast."

"All of us?" Elkin asked, as Latera added, "The full seven-day feast?"

"Apparently so, and yes, it will be the full ritual," Asherah replied to each in turn. "The invitation specifically names myself and Latera, and we're to bring our families, households, and whatever others we deem necessary and proper."

Aeolmar drew the parchment across the table and scrutinized it. "Are we to move all of Teg'urnan, then?"

"They can't mean that," Latera said. Now that she'd had some tea, her head was clearing. "I'm sure Sibeal only worded it that way so she wouldn't overlook anyone."

"Yes. Well." Asherah folded her hands together and glanced at Finlay. "My question to you is this. Should any of us attend this gathering?"

Latera opened her mouth to speak, then she felt her mate's presence in her mind. She raised her bowl to her mouth instead.

We should go, Aeolmar said to Latera.

You, of all people, think we should go on holiday while demon attacks are worse than before Asgeloth fell?

The library in Thurnda is vast, and much older than Teg'urnan's. Perhaps it contains information about the old gods.

Latera bit her lip; the mates dared not speak of the Ish h'ra, not even via their mindtouch, not until they were certain Asherah wasn't her. And if their queen was one of the old gods, well, Latera had no idea what they would do.

"What are you two discussing?" Finlay asked. He was well aware of a bound pair's ability to communicate mind to mind, mostly because it was something he'd never shared with his own mate.

Perhaps they cannot mindtouch because she is a god, Latera suggested, then she smiled at the king. "Are you sure you want to hear about our most intimate thoughts?" she asked. Elkin laughed as Finlay's ears pinked.

"We were discussing Sibeal's invitation," Aeolmar said, pausing to bring Latera's hand to his mouth and kiss her knuckles. "I was telling Latera that I think we should go."

"Do you?" Asherah leaned forward. "Go on."

"What is the common bond between all our enemies?" Aeolmar asked. "The north."

"Elves are in the north," protested Latera, while Asherah pointed out that demons have always bled up from the underworld in Parthalan's south and east. Once they'd both said their piece, Finlay spoke.

"Aeolmar's right," said the king. "Where did Ehkron go? North. Where were the dark fae? North. Before she served in the Great Temple, Sarelle was from the north."

"I am from the north," Innetha said.

"And why did you leave?" Finlay asked pointedly. Innetha scowled at the table, but Finlay didn't make her admit to her curse. "I agree that there must be some great evil in the north. One must wonder if demons aren't being used to distract us from our true foes."

Aeolmar leaned back in his chair, rubbing his chin. "Interesting. When I was in the north, Grelk's dens were nearly overrun with demons and orcs. Once I'd eliminated the orcs, the demons all but disappeared."

"Oh, not the orc story again," Innetha grumbled.

Latera's glare silenced Innetha. Not bothering to hide his satisfied smile, for he did enjoy it when his mate defended him, Aeolmar continued, "It takes sorcery to create an orc, and to control them. Demons, too, can be put under a mage's thrall." He looked pointedly at Asherah. "What do you know of the lands north of Tingu?"

"Leave Leran out of this," Asherah warned.

"But he is hiding something," Finlay said. "He is secretive in all things, never sharing his plans, or even allowing Parthians more than a few leagues past his borders. Why?"

"Oh, you know why," Asherah muttered, shoving away from the table and pacing before the hearth. "As for the Northern Waste, it is as the name implies, a waste. A frozen, barren wasteland."

"Yet the mountain trolls flourish there," Aeolmar said. "One must wonder how they manage, with no fertile soil for crops, and nothing to burn for warmth. There is a secret in the north, Asherah, and Leran is keeping it from you. Perhaps at this gathering in Thurnda—"

"Perhaps nothing." Asherah stopped pacing and leaned her elbows on the back of her chair. "Even if Leran bothers to attend, he won't tell us anything. Hells, he can hardly stand to be in the same room with me. If I order his compliance, he'll likely leave and build a wall around Tingu, keeping me away forever."

"He'll talk to me," Latera said. "He and I have always gotten on well, even before we knew of our kinship."

"How are you related to him again?" Aeolmar asked, his dislike of the Lord of Tingu plain. It was Asherah who answered.

"L'hirre was Lormac's father... and L'hirre's mother was the Lady of Thurnda. She in turn bore Latera's ancestor, Elvasla." The queen was silent for a moment, fingering a length of her pale hair. "They strive to keep their bloodlines intermingled, those of Tingu and Thurnda do. Why, before Elvasla perished, there was talk of Lormac taking Sibeal as a mate." Asherah uttered a mirthless laugh. "That certainly wasn't how things worked out." Then ensuing silence was heavy, so the queen cleared her throat and changed the subject.

"Elkin, you've been quiet," she said, fixing the Second Hunter in her gaze. "What do you think of Aeolmar's theories?"

Elkin leaned back and rubbed his chin, mimicking his commander's posture. "His thoughts may have merit," he murmured. "While I led the Northern Contingent, we were under constant attack from the first day of winter straight through to spring. We never did determine where the demons were coming from." He leaned across the table and pulled a map of the elflands before him.

"What I do know is that none ever approached us by way of Thurnda, and as we know Tingu is the land beyond. I believe, my queen," he continued, raising his gaze to meet Asherah's, "that if there is an evil person or persons in the north, your boy might be the one holding it at bay."

Elkin's words effectively silenced the lot of them, a far heavier silence than Asherah's ruminations about her once-mate Lormac had created. "He's not my boy," Asherah muttered at length. "He keeps to himself because elves take care of elves, because..." The queen took a deep breath, then she raised her head and regarded the five who gazed intently back at her.

"Because he is his father's son," she finished. "Lormac never would have let anything, bet it a demon or an orc or... or any sort of monsters overrun his borders and into the lands beyond. He would have held them back, even if it meant his death."

Asherah dropped her gaze; ever since she'd been bespelled by Mallia and forgotten her mate's face, Finlay bristled when she mentioned Lormac, or Tingu at all. He laid his hand on hers, but his voice was hard when he spoke.

"You believe you can garner something intelligible from Leran?" the king asked Latera.

"I can try," she replied. "Even if he refuses to answer me, I can learn much from his reactions."

"But this is only half the problem," Innetha burst out. "If Leran turns out to be our hero, well, so what? We still won't know who is responsible."

"Perhaps Leran knows," Latera said.

"He doesn't," Aeolmar said with a shake of his head. "If he did, he would have dealt with them by now. No, if he's involved, it's on the battlefield, no more."

"Then it is settled." Asherah moved toward the garden windows, her hair reflecting silver in the early morning light. As was her habit, she was attired in a white gown, her pale hair restrained by nothing more than a golden fillet. The rich glow of the suns made her appear as a creature of light and air, a true faerie queen.

Or a goddess.

Latera blinked, unnerved by her own thoughts, and paid attention to what the queen was saying.

"We shall go to Thurnda, and enjoy ourselves at Senan's feasts," Asherah declared. "Latera will endeavor to glean whatever bits of information Leran deigns to share. I suppose the rest of us will drink Sibeal's wine, and see what comes of it. Elkin, the messenger waits in the lower hall. Please give him our response."

The Second Hunter bowed and left the chamber. Latera watched as Asherah sighed and closed her eyes, and asked her mate, *If she really is who we think she is, would she feel everything so heavily?*

I wish I knew, beloved.

Chapter Three

Asherah Speaks

Aeolmar and Latera left my chamber shortly after Elkin did, him to begin preparations for our journey while she was on her way to the archive yet again. Latera had been spending a great deal of time in the archive, and in the Great Temple with Atreynha, and for the life of me, I didn't understand why. When I asked Latera what she was looking for, she said she was researching Parthian history, but I knew that wasn't the entire answer. Since I trusted Latera implicitly, I made no move to halt her research. However, I was curious.

I was also curious about Innetha, who'd remained at the table lingering over her tea. She held her bowl tightly while she looked over a map of Thurnda. A drop of tea splashed onto the map, and I realized she was trembling.

Finlay glanced at me. When I nodded, he excused himself and left the room. I sat across from Innetha and took the bowl from her hands.

"Forgive me for spotting the map," she began.

"Don't worry about a drop of tea." I set the bowl aside. "Talk to me."

"Thurnda, that's where this gathering is to be?" Innetha looked away, appearing to study the far wall rather intently. "The *doja* where Olwynn was held was only a few days' ride from Thurnda's palace, wasn't it?"

Olwynn was Innetha's former mate. A brave, brave man, he died during our confrontation with Natraeus and the dark fae, during the same battle that nearly killed Finlay. To my shame, I hadn't even thought of the former *con'dehr* in many, many winters, much less his relationship with Innetha. Based on Innetha's sudden interest in my decidedly uninteresting wall, she still thought of him often.

"Yes. He was imprisoned at the *doja* Lormac and I liberated together." I pointed to a mark on the map. "It was here. Olwynn helped us burn it to the ground."

Innetha nodded, pursing her lips as she stood and turned her back to me. She and Olwynn hadn't known each other for very long, and they hadn't bound themselves to one another. Of course, I knew better than anyone that a binding has nothing to do with how much you love another. Nor does time, or death, dampen that love.

"I think not," Innetha said suddenly, loudly. I ignored the waver in her tone. "I think I'll stay here with Elkin, and assist him with running Teg'urnan. You'll need someone to say behind, what with you and the king and Aeolmar gone, and Elkin's the best choice. He can be quite foolish, you know, and I'd hate to see the palace suffer in your absence."

I am a babbler, Innetha is not. I placed my hand on her shoulder, startling her though I didn't mean to. She smiled tightly when I caught a glimpse of tears. "Forgive me, my queen. I am not as strong as you," she murmured as she wiped them away.

I squeezed her shoulder and said nothing, letting her have her grief. I didn't even bother to tell her that she is mistaken, and that I am not strong at all. What I am is stubborn; too stubborn to die, or stay defeated, or let Parthalan be anything but the greatest land in all the nine realms. According to the legends, the only one ever to be as stubborn as me was Ish h'ra, The Deliverer, she who defended her people until her last breath.

I wondered if we would encounter any of Ish h'ra's ruined shrines in the north.

"I will miss your company, but I understand," I said. "Innetha, do you recall any shrines to The Deliverer near your old home?"

Innetha's brow pinched at the abrupt subject change. "There are many, but the ones that remain are mostly in Tingu." She shuffled the maps, and indicated a far-off point beyond the Northern Ridge. "I've heard that there's one near Grelk's forge, too. Are you planning on visiting them?"

"Perhaps," I said, tracing a route from one shrine to another with my fingertip. "Perhaps I shall."

Chapter Four

"Really, Ember, how many dresses does one person need?" Mara looked around their sitting room, which was heaped with gowns in every style and color imaginable. "I don't think Asherah will bring so many."

"I'm not bringing them all," Ember retorted. "But we will be in Thurnda for ten nights, so I will need at least ten dresses, and two or three special gowns for the high feasts, and riding dresses to wear there and back…" Her voice trailed off as she counted on her fingers, only to quickly run out of digits. "So really, I only need a trunk or two."

"Two very large trunks," Mara commented. She fingered an orange silk sleeve from the "possible" pile and remarked that only her younger sister could get away with such behavior. On the whole, faerie women wore light-colored, diaphanous garments reminiscent of the blue and white robes worn by priestesses before the Great War. The queen favored this style, and most followed her example, with the notable exceptions being their mother, Latera, and the rest of the female hunters. They dressed in their usual riding gear, though Latera occasionally wore a gown cut in the elfin fashion. Ember, however, had a style all her own.

In a hall filled with faerie women clad in white and silver gowns, Ember was a riot of color in her jewel toned gowns topped by her head of flaming curls. That, coupled with her infectious gaiety, ensured that she never wanted for a companion.

"Father will never allow you to bring all of this," Mara continued, though she knew he would. The First Hunter would allow his daughters to drag Teg'urnan itself to Thurnda if they could devise a way to do it. "You know, you can wear a dress more than once while we're there."

"And I will wear this one at the welcome feast," Ember announced, effectively ignoring her sister as she produced an emerald green frock. The sleeves were a sheer, pale green, and the skirt was layered in the same fabric. The bodice was embroidered with green and blue crystals, and edged in gold thread.

"It's lovely," Mara murmured, for it was a lovely gown. "You certainly will outshine the queen."

"Oh, Mara, that's not my intent," Ember said. She draped the gown against her arms and danced about the chamber, no easy feat considering the heaps of clothing she needed to avoid. "I just want to be a girl, not the First Hunter and *deva'shi's* daughter. For once, I just want to be Ember."

Mara understood what her sister meant; it was difficult to forge one's identity when every Parthian already knew that your parents were the saviors of the realm. Indeed, Mara had never met anyone who didn't already know who she was, and been aware of most, if not all, of her parent's exploits. Some of them even knew about her past with Kemen, and had the audacity to ask her when she would reconcile with him. As if her private life was any of their business.

For the most part, Mara didn't mind, and contentedly sat to the side while her parents were the ones immortalized in story and song. Her brother, Tor, felt much the same, but not Ember. She was determined to have ballads sung about her exploits, and not be a supporting character in someone else's story.

"Ember, if anyone can transcend our parents, it is you."

Before Ember could respond, there was a knock at the chamber door. Mara opened it, and found Kemen waiting across the threshold. Mara stared at him, wondering if he'd somehow known she was thinking about him. Then again, she thought about him all the time.

"Are you well?" he asked, when she remained silent.

"I'm fine," Mara said. "Can I help you with something?"

"I've come to help you," Kemen replied. "We're making up the baggage lists for our journey north. How many trunks will each of you be taking?"

Our journey. "Are... are you going, too?" Mara asked.

"Yes. Your father requested it just this morning."

"Hello, Kemen," Ember said, as she sailed past the entrance with an armful of clothing. "What brings the most handsome man in Parthalan to our door?"

"I've come to assist with your luggage," Kemen said as he smiled. Everyone smiled at Ember. "How many trunks will we have between the two of you?"

Ember dropped the clothes onto a chair and joined them at the door. "One trunk for Mara," Ember said, tapping her chin. "Would it be terrible if I brought two?"

"Of course not," Kemen said. "I'll have them make space for four trunks, two for each of you, just in case. Good day, ladies."

With that, Kemen turned on his heel and left the sisters. Mara watched him walk down the corridor, but he didn't look back.

"Really, Mara, just go after him," Ember said.

"No." Mara shut the door, pausing with her hand over the latch. It wasn't necessary to lock the door; not only was their chamber in the heart of the palace behind soldiers and hunters alike, those who lived in Teg'urnan would never dare enter the First Hunter and *deva'shi's* chamber unannounced. "It didn't work out with us. No reason to dredge up old, hurt feelings. He's moved on, as have I."

Mara steeled herself for Ember's questions—why not try again, is there anyone else, aren't you lonely—but she remained silent. Mara turned and saw her sister packing and repacking her trunks, concentrating on her brightly colored clothes rather than her sister's lack of a mate.

It's not Kemen's fault, Mara told herself. *After what happened, I can hardly imagine anyone touching me. And when I do have the nerve to imagine it, it's Kemen. Always Kemen. But, I don't know if I could go through with it.*

Mara closed her eyes and leaned against the door, and silently asked Cydia if she'd be alone forever.

CHAPTER FIVE

EMBER SPEAKS

After a flurry of activity over the next two days, we set out for Thurnda. It seemed that this Senan was in a rush to take his mate, which made me wonder why he was bothering with these elaborate rituals at all. Why not just declare the woman in question his mate and be done with it? It's not like anyone in Thurnda had ever sought Asherah's approval for a mating before, or anything else, for that matter.

My thoughts about Senan's motivations were interrupted by Kemen. He melted out of the throng of people assembled in the Great Square leading my horse.

"Here you are," Kemen said as he handed the reins over to me. "Are you and your sister ready to travel?"

"We are." I mounted up, and accepted the blankets he passed up to me. I was told it was much colder in Thurnda, and it was best to be prepared. "Thank you."

Kemen nodded, then he was off to his next task. As soon as he was out of sight, Mara appeared on her own horse.

"Were you waiting for him to leave?" I asked as I gave her one of the blankets. "Avoiding him won't do either of you any good."

"I'm not avoiding anyone," Mara snapped.

"Of course you're not," I said as I turned toward the gates. There, in front of the statues of the stag and doe, were Asherah and Finlay. They looked so different that one would hardly assume they were mated, much less that they ruled together. The queen was slender and pale, while the king was stocky with dark hair and warm brown skin. Disparate appearances aside, when their eyes met, it was plain how they adored one another.

I want to be loved like than someday. Movement next to the pair caught my eye. Astride a magnificent honey colored horse was Asherah and Finlay's son, Finn.

His name was really Finlay Torim, but he'd gone by Finn for many winters. Why he'd decided to shorten his perfectly good name was beyond me, since no one had ever confused him with his father, the king. What with Finn's pale hair and black eyes, he looked more like a male replica of the queen. With the exception of his tightly curled hair, he hardly resembled his noble father, which was a shame. We did have a handsome king. I hadn't considered Finn handsome, or anything at all for a very long time.

Finn caught me staring at him and raised his hand in greeting. I smiled in return—perhaps it was more of a grimace—and turned back to Mara.

"Who's avoiding people now?" Mara asked. She waved and smiled at Finn, while I stared at my pommel. Of course, the Prince of Parthalan was attending this ridiculously important celebration in Thurnda. We wouldn't want to leave him out of anything, now would we?

"Is he bothering you?" Tor demanded as he rode up beside us. Never mind that he was the youngest of us, Tor had fancied himself my and Mara's protector since he'd been old enough to hold a sword. It had been a tiny wooden sword carved by our father, but it was a sword, nonetheless.

"No one is bothering us," I said. "Mara is just waving hello to Finn."

Tor grunted, not bothering to hide his dislike of Finn. Finn, on the other hand, absolutely adored everyone he encountered, and had kindly overlooked Tor's bad manners for almost his entire life. Good thing, too. If Finn decided otherwise, Tor would be in a great deal of trouble, so much that even Father might not be able to help him.

"Do you know why Father asked Kemen to accompany us?" Mara asked Tor.

"It's got something to do with the old gods," Tor replied.

"What in the nine realms could Papa want to know about the old gods?" I wondered.

Tor shrugged. "I have no idea, but I heard him talking about it with Mama. They also want to spend some time in Thurnda's archive."

"Wonderful." I couldn't think of anything I'd like less than spending time in a dusty old archive. This excursion to Thurnda was becoming less pleasant by the moment. Before I could ask any more questions, Luth blew his horn, and we got ourselves assembled for our journey away from Teg'urnan and into the cold north.

I couldn't wait to start this adventure.

Chapter Six

Latera Speaks

"You're sure you know what to look for?" Wren asked me, again.

"Yes, Wren," I replied, also again. Wren was one of only two people Aeolmar and I had confided in regarding Asherah's possible godhood. The other person was the High Priestess of the Great Temple, Atreynha. Being that Wren had one of the sharpest minds in Parthalan, she helped us look for clues and analyzed whatever evidence we uncovered. As for why we'd also confided in Atreynha, she was the resident expert on gods.

Both of them thought Asherah being The Deliver was a real possibility. That was both amazing and terrifying.

"I'll send a messenger back with anything I find," I continued. "That way, you and Atreynha won't have to wait for us to return before—"

"And when are you planning on returning?" Wren asked, rather loudly. I glanced over my shoulder and saw Bron approaching us. He and his brother, Luth, were hunters, and had been assigned to the palace contingent since shortly after Aeolmar had been made First Hunter. Luth was accompanying us to Thurnda, but Bron had elected to stay behind. Wren insisted that his remaining in Teg'urnan had nothing to do with her. Perhaps my sister isn't as sharp as I thought she was.

"Bron knows," I whispered. He had been present when Sarelle, in her guise as Mallia, revealed to Aeolmar and the rest of the hunters who were present her suspicions that Asherah was The Deliverer.

"Aeolmar told him not to mention it, and he's effectively shut the facts away," Wren said. "He won't even think about it until Aeolmar says otherwise."

"He does follow orders well," I murmured, then both Bron and Aeolmar descended upon us.

"Between myself, Innetha, and Elkin, we'll keep the palace running smoothly," Bron declared.

"Keep an eye on Elkin," Aeolmar said. "Question his every order."

Bron paused. "I thought you trusted Elkin?"

Aeolmar smiled and clapped Bron's shoulder. "I do, but we don't want him getting complacent, now do we?"

"He's teasing you," Wren said. "Aeolmar is an awful man."

Aeolmar laughed. "And you are a wonderful sister, Wren. I trust your watchful eye will keep Bron out of trouble, except for whatever mischief he finds with you?"

At that, Wren went scarlet. "Come on," I said, tugging Aeolmar toward our horses. "Let's go before you cause an incident. Wren, I'll write as soon as I can!"

"I'll be waiting," she called.

I slid my arm around Aeolmar's waist as we walked toward the horses. "What do you think we'll find in Thurnda?" I asked.

He squeezed my hand. "Honestly, I've no idea. Something good, I hope."

I spied Asherah, standing before the gates with Finlay. If she was a god, what would that mean for our king? "I hope so, too."

CHAPTER SEVEN

ASHERAH SPEAKS

By the second day of our journey, I was thoroughly enjoying myself.

Though I'd been hesitant to accept Sibeal's invitation, the journey to Thurnda was exactly what I needed. I hadn't been outside of Teg'urnan since I'd recovered from Sarelle's awful, evil magics. At first, I'd kept to my chambers in order to allow my eye to heal, then to heal my relationship with my mate. Finlay claimed he didn't hold me responsible for forgetting him, since I had been under a spell and therefore not acting as myself. While that was true, it didn't make me feel any less shamed.

So I stayed inside the palace and acted as the dutiful mate and queen, and while my life got a bit more boring, it was also good. We watched Finn grow from an inquisitive boy into an intelligent, thoughtful man, and handled matters of state, and presided over the court. Together, just as the king and queen should be.

Now that I was outside again, atop a horse and breathing in the sharp air of new places and experiences, I didn't know if I could ever go back.

"Asherah," Finlay called, and I turned to smile at him. Of course, I would return to Teg'urnan, if for no other reason than Finlay would be there. My man from the desert, he would remain by my side no matter what life decided to throw at us. He truly was my rock, and I loved him more every day.

"Yes?" I urged my horse closer to his. "Have you discovered some revolutionary new stockings of unrivalled warmth?"

His eyes narrowed; being that Finlay was born and raised in the desert, the weather he considered cold was considerably warmer than what I considered cold. "You won't be laughing when my warm clothes save you from frostbite. Look, between those trees."

I did, and saw a tall, slender waterfall cascading down a mountain. "It's lovely, isn't it? The fall is called the Maiden's Veil."

"You've been here before?"

"Yes, when—"

And I fell silent, feeling the words in my throat that refused to leave my mouth. I brought my hand to my neck, gasping as the words collected in my windpipe and threatened to choke me.

"Sher? Asherah!" Finlay said my name so forcefully those nearby craned their necks to see what sort of predicament I'd gotten myself into this time. I raised my hand, and forced a smile.

"Just a cough," I said, which everyone believed, except for Finlay. Once the rest had gone about their business, Finlay reached over and rubbed my arm.

"You're all right?" he asked, and I nodded. When I opened my mouth, he continued, "Don't speak, not for a moment. You've never been on this road before, yet you've been to those falls?"

I was about to dispute his claim about me traveling this road, when I remembered that this was an old route that had fallen into disuse in Sahlgren's day. It had only been refurbished ten or so years ago, which meant that if I had indeed traveled this road, it was before I was queen.

Long before.

"I have," I replied. "There was once a grotto at the base of the falls, and it was customary for maidens to bathe there before they went to their mates. That's how it got the name Maiden's Veil."

Finlay nodded. "What else do you remember?"

"Bits and pieces," I replied. "I remember the hawkers and their carts, selling cheap veils that would tear in a sennight's time. I remember a temple filled with kind priests. And I remember that while the falls were cold, the water in the grotto was deliciously warm." I glanced at him. "You would have found it freezing."

He smiled, and I smiled in turn. I hated worrying him, but I'd long ago learned that I needed to tell Finlay about these random memories as soon as I had them, lest I forget any details. We were solving a mystery, my mate and I, though neither one of us were sure of what the prize might be.

"Would you like to stop at the falls?"

I shook my head. "The temple was destroyed long ago, and the grotto must be an overgrown mess by now."

"Perhaps, after we've returned from Thurnda, we can look into restoring the grotto."

"*Yes. That would be a good thing.*" Finlay squeezed my hand, and I turned back to the falls. They really were lovely, an ideal spot for whiling away a day. It was no wonder men took their lovers there.

"*Sher?*"

"*Mmm?*"

"*How was the temple destroyed?*"

"*Olluhm destroyed it,*" I replied, the words falling out of my mouth. "*He got into a terrible row with Cydia, and the priests fled in terror. It's said that the moon first went red that very night, but that's only a story. The moon had gone red long before that.*"

"*You remember when the moon went from red to white?*"

I gasped, my gaze swinging from the falls to Finlay's face. "*Yes. I think I do.*"

"*Do you remember why she changed colors?*"

I tilted my gaze skyward, though it was too bright to see Cydia during the day. Olluhm had seen to that long ago. "*She was sad, but more than that, she was angry,*" I replied. "*She was angry he claimed her, angry he kept having her bear child after child. It was all she could do to be rid of him.*"

"*How was she rid of him?*"

"*She...*" I shook my head. "*I don't know, not yet.*"

"*Will you tell me when you remember?*"

"*I will.*"

Chapter Eight

On the fourth day of the journey to Thurnda, Mara was up before the rest of her family. She was usually the first one awake; her mother liked to sleep past second dawn, and while her father frequently bemoaned his mate's late rising, he slept just as long as she did. As for her siblings, they also followed their mother's example.

Mara had never minded being the first to wake. She loved the quiet time just before first dawn, when she could settle her thoughts and plan out her day. Once the others were up and milling about, the press of bodies and constant chatter threatened to overwhelm her. On some days, it was all she could do to keep from screaming.

She slipped outside the tent and inhaled the crisp air. She'd just decided to take a walk around the perimeter of the camp, when she heard footsteps approaching. Mara was about to flee to the safety of her family, when Finn appeared.

"Finn! You gave me a fright," Mara said, and immediately wished she could bite back the words. She hated that she was still skittish when so much time had passed since her abduction, and she especially hated that she was skittish here, surrounded by hunters and soldiers, all of whom would protect her against any foe, real or imagined.

"Forgive me. I didn't mean to," Finn said, then he held a bowl toward her. "I heard you walking early yesterday, and the day before, and it gets very cold before first dawn, so I thought you might like some tea."

Mara accepted the clay bowl. "You made this for me?"

He smiled and blushed at the same time, just like he'd done when he was younger. "I did. I hope it's to your liking."

Mara sipped the tea. It had cooled down, and was a bit over steeped. "It's wonderful. Thank you." They stood staring at each other for a moment, then Mara said, "Would you like to walk with me?"

"Surely," he said, and they picked their way among the tents. The only others awake were a few weary soldiers; Mara wondered if they'd sleep on the luggage carts once they were moving again.

"Are you excited about going to Thurnda?" Mara asked.

"I am," Finn replied. "Unlike you, I've never been far from Teg'ur-nan." Mara grimaced; it was well known how Asherah coddled her only child, and kept herself between him and the rest of the world.

"Well, a trip to Thurnda is an excellent way to begin your travels," Mara said. "My parents have been, and many of the hunters. They all say it's a lovely land. We should be there by noon tomorrow, if the weather holds."

"Do you know the best way to ensure clear skies?" When Mara shook her head, he continued, "By drinking all of your tea, so you don't catch a chill."

Mara dutifully finished her tea. "Will you dispense more of your wisdom later today, or are you saving it for the elves?"

"Perhaps I am," he replied, with a wink. "I am interested in meeting the elfin rulers, and especially Leran." Finn frowned, and added, "I suppose he and I are brothers, of a sort."

"I suppose you are," Mara said. "I hope you two get on well."

"So do I," Finn replied, but Mara hardly heard him. Striding across the open area in the center of the camp was Kemen.

He really was handsome, and despite what Mara always said to Ember, she'd never gotten over him. Sometimes, she thought he wasn't over her, either; he still went out of his way to talk to her, and every so often he brought her flowers or other small gifts. But, those talks and tokens were all that passed between them, and for the life of her Mara couldn't think of a way to turn those instances into something more without humiliating herself. She'd already suffered ten lifetimes' worth of humiliation, and would like to avoid any further incidents.

"Mara?"

Mara blinked; she'd forgotten all about Finn. "Forgive me," she said. "I must still be sleepy. What were you saying?"

"I asked if you were with Kemen again."

"Oh, no," she demurred. "And what of you, Finn? Surely you have suitors."

Finn blushed again, so brightly his cheeks all but glowed in the gray morning light. "I suppose I do, but..." He sighed, and looked away. "It will be light soon. Would you like me to walk you back to your tent?"

"That would be lovely," Mara said, then she looped her arm with his. "Careful, Finn. If you keep treating me so well I'll chase all your suitors away and keep you for myself."

"If I had any sense, I'd let you do just that."

Mara laughed, and after a moment Finn joined her. "Remember when it was always the four of us?" Mara asked. "You and me and Ember and Tor. I miss those times."

A shadow moved across Finn's face, and Mara regretted her words. "Finn, I didn't mean to make you feel badly."

"You didn't," he said, and forced a smile. "Memories, though, they can be persistent."

Mara looked toward where she'd last seen Kemen. "Yes, they certainly can be."

Chapter Nine

Leran strode into Thurnda's great hall, pleased that those within bowed when they saw him. Long ago, Sibeal had wrested control of Thurnda from his grasp, and had done it in such a cunning manner he could only hold respect for the sly old vixen. She had been painfully young when she ascended to power—not as young as Leran had been when he became Lord of Tingu, but not much older, either—and many had doubted that someone so young would make an effective Lady of Thurnda. Sibeal went on to prove herself many times over.

No matter who ruled Thurnda, Leran was the Lord of Tingu, and all elves respected the title. As the direct descendant of Nexa, the first elf, Leran was their king by blood if not by politics. Yet none outside of Tingu knew of his greatest triumphs, which were the keeping of mountain trolls and orcs at bay. He was fighting a silent, secret war, all because he refused to ask the aid of Parthalan, and Asherah.

Lately, he'd begun to wonder if he was losing that war.

"My lord!"

Senan, Sibeal's youngest son, approached Leran, and greeted him by bowing so low his forehead nearly grazed the floor. *I wouldn't bow so low before Nexa herself,* Leran grumbled inwardly, but he recalled that Senan had always been a bit of a bootlicker.

"Allow me to present my mate—intended mate, that is," Senan continued, "the Lady Cerillia."

Cerillia stepped forward and demurely bowed her head. Rumor had it that Senan believed once he took a mate Sibeal would step down as Lady of Thurnda, thus handing the land over to her youngest and only living child. It was unusual for an elfin ruler to remain unattached—except for Leran, only Sibeal also eschewed taking a mate—and Senan hoped that this mating would hurry his mother along.

Senan's chosen companion, Cerillia, was lovely enough, with long golden hair and clear blue eyes widely set in her brow, but Leran detected no spark behind them. The most interesting thing about her was the ornate necklace she wore, a heavy collar decorated with hammered gold leaves. No, here was a woman who would be obedient on pain of death, and never contribute an original thought to the most basic of proceedings. Sibeal would never let her land be handled by such a person, and Senan was a fool if he thought otherwise. Besides, that was not how the Thurndian rule of succession worked, either.

But then, these were Senan's problems, not his. "My lady," he greeted as he kissed her hand; Cerillia flushed and looked to her ladies, who were all chittering away that the Lord of Tingu had so favored their mistress. Leran smiled at them, though he couldn't imagine sharing his life with such women, or anyone else, for that matter. Leran's sole companions were battle and solitude.

"Where's our Lady?" Leran asked, referring to Sibeal.

"She will be here shortly," Senan replied. "We've had an unscheduled visitor, and she's dealing with him."

Leran wondered who this visitor could be, but was confident that Sibeal could handle them. Hells, Sibeal could rout a company of mountain trolls if needed. For a woman who rarely touched a weapon, her fierceness was legendary.

On and on the introductions flowed, and Leran reacquainted himself with the varied members of elfin nobility, until a familiar voice caught his attention.

"Balthus!"

Leran turned to watch Asherah enter the hall, closely followed by the rest of Parthalan's delegation, and felt a pang of sympathy for Cerillia. This event was intended to celebrate her mating, yet when the Faerie Queen entered a room it was difficult to look elsewhere. Asherah was tall and slender, with blond hair so pale it was nearly white, eyes as black as a moonless night, and alabaster skin. Her beauty was the stuff of legend and song, and her presence filled a room and drew others to her. Cerillia would be lucky if anyone remembered her name.

"My queen," Balthus said as he kissed Asherah's hand in greeting. "How was your journey?"

"Swift and dry, as all good journeys are," she replied. Balthus stepped aside, and Asherah's gaze settled upon Leran. "And I trust you are well?"

"I am," Leran replied, then he noticed her clouded left eye, and the scars on her cheek.

"What happened," he demanded, reaching toward her. "Battle?"

"Ah, no." Asherah ducked her head, letting her hair fall across the left side of her face. "There was a sorceress, and the short of it is my eye was compromised."

"I'll kill her," Leran declared.

"Latera already did," Asherah said. The two regarded each other for a moment, the Lord and Lady of Tingu. Leran had spent much of his life avoiding Asherah, but after she'd sent Latera and Aeolmar to return the Sala to him, he'd gone to Teg'urnan to lend help when it was attacked by the *mordeth-gall*. That was the first time he'd journeyed to the faerie palace, and it had somewhat repaired the rift that existed between him and the mother of his heart.

He'd made a second journey for Asherah's jubilee, and found her heavy with child. Knowing that she was about to have another son—a true son, not her former mate's child, as Leran was—undid nearly all the repairs the last journey had made. Now, as he stood a few paces from her and learned of her injuries, and that she'd fought a sorceress that was strong enough to injure her, all of his rash decisions came crashing back to him.

I was a fool for pushing her away.

"I'm glad she's dead," he said at length.

Asherah cleared her throat, then she graced him with a wry grin he remembered from his youth. "As am I," she said, then she waved over her new mate.

After all this time, I still consider him Asherah's new mate. In Leran's mind Asherah would always be mated to his father, and he their only son. But Asherah had moved on, found herself a new companion and had a son that didn't avoid her, while Leran fought alone in the frozen north. He wondered how his life had gotten so far away from him. Nevertheless, he exchanged a formal yet friendly greeting with the King of Parthalan, then he spied a length of fire-bright hair.

"First Huntress," Leran said as he bowed before Latera.

"Leran!" she admonished as she grabbed his hands. "If anyone should bow, I should!"

"Never, dearest cousin," Leran replied. "The *deva'shi* bows to no one. Tell me you are well."

"I am," she replied. Aeolmar and a younger man strode up to Latera's side. After he and Aeolmar exchanged greetings, she said, "And this is our son, Tor."

Leran nodded to the young man, remarking to himself that he'd never seen a child so unlike his parents. Tor had Aeolmar's height and large frame, but that was where the similarity ended. His lion's mane of hair was straw colored, his eyes a pale green, and his wide, smooth features must have been the relic of a long-ago ancestor. If Aeolmar hadn't been there he'd have asked Latera if she'd found Tor as a babe abandoned on a hillside, but the First Hunter was as humorless as the night was dark.

"Our daughters have taken to their rooms," Latera continued. "Preparing for tonight, and such."

"How many children do you have now?" Leran chided. "Are you raising a clan of warriors in the south?"

"My daughters are no warriors," Aeolmar said, his tone wistful. "I'm afraid neither will hunt like their mother. Luckily, Tor is nearly my equal in swordsmanship."

"Nearly?" Tor asked with an arched brow, and Leran saw the same wicked grin that Latera often wore. "Care to wager on that?"

"I'll take that bet," Leran said. "A troll sword to the victor."

Tor's eyes widened. "You can't be serious!"

"Tingu's coffers can afford a sword or two," Leran said. "Besides, Grelk owes me at least a score of blades."

Aeolmar snorted. "Good luck collecting on those debts. Grelk once owed me a sword for decades. He worked so slowly I assumed it would be used as my grave marker long after I'd turned to dust."

"But it was worth the wait, wasn't it?" Latera asked, lightly touching the pommel of Aeolmar's sword.

"It was," Aeolmar agreed, then he turned toward his son. "What do you say? Should we take Leran up on his offer and show him how the fae fight?"

"Absolutely," Tor said.

"Tor is half elf," Latera reminded him.

"In that case, we already know who will win," Leran said, and Tor and Latera laughed at Aeolmar's expense.

"Enough," Aeolmar said good-naturedly. "It looks like it's time to sit."

Latera gave her mate a look, but didn't call out his abrupt subject change. "Then we'll sit. We'll talk later, Leran."

"That, we shall," Leran said, and he watched his cousin and her family take their seats at the main table. The initial feast was to welcome all to Thurnda, and the seven nights of revelry to celebrate Senan and Cerillia's mating would begin tomorrow. If the pair held to custom, Senan would declare Cerillia his mate at this evening's conclusion, but Leran doubted that they had followed the old ways so closely. He could hardly remember the last time he had attended a mating feast, never mind one where each of the old tenets were held.

Actually, he did remember. It had been when his father and Asherah were mated.

Leran shook his head, and moved to his own assigned place. As he approached the table, he passed by Senan as he greeted Latera.

"Cerillia, this is my cousin, Latera," Senan said. "Her ancestor was Elvasla, who was the Lady of Thurnda before Mama."

Cerillia's eyes narrowed. "Does that mean you're here to reclaim Thurnda?"

Leran paused, and waited for Latera's reply.

"Me? No," Latera said, shaking her head. "I have no interest in ruling Thurnda. Besides, you have Sibeal as your Lady."

Cerillia sniffed. "For now."

Latera looked toward Leran, but Senan made his apologies and moved on to greet the other guests. "What was that all about?" she asked. "As if I want or need another title."

"I'm sure it's just Senan letting his ambitions get the better of him," Leran replied. "I don't think Sibeal has any intention of giving up her position."

Leran had no sooner said the words than Sibeal herself entered the hall. She had been Lady of Thurnda longer than Asherah had been Queen of Parthalan, though her many years of ruling weren't apparent. Her hair, which had been blonde in her youth had long since gone snow white, but that was her sole mark of age. Sibeal moved as gracefully as ever, and her eyes were clear and bright and her mind as sharp as her sword.

Now, those sharp eyes scanned the hall and immediately found Asherah. Sibeal approached the queen, and a moment later the two of them left the hall.

"Interesting," Leran said. "I wonder what that could be about."

Chapter Ten

Asherah Speaks

While everyone else took their places at the table, I stood in the center of Thurnda's great hall, my mind still reeling from my encounter with Leran. I don't know why his simple greeting had affected me so; he was polite, and calm, and perhaps even happy to see me, yet when he showed concern over my eye my throat had closed up and my hands shook. I dealt with things better when he outright shouted at me.

If our past interactions were any indication, he would be shouting at me soon enough. No matter what I did or said, Leran would always blame me for his father's death. While I knew in my head that Lormac's death was Harek's doing—may Harek's soul rot for all eternity—my heart agreed with Leran. And so I stayed away from Tingu and its king, as I'd promised him long ago. It was the least I could do.

I saw Leran speaking with Latera, and smiled. The two of them were so alike, each feeling they had no family to speak of, and both had been overjoyed to learn of their connection. Perhaps Latera was right, and she could get Leran to divulge what was happening in the wasteland north of Tingu. She had a better chance than I did.

"Asherah. My queen."

I turned around and saw Sibeal standing behind me. "Sibeal. It's good to see you."

A curt nod. "I must bring you to someone right away."

With that, Sibeal put her hand on my elbow, and we left the hall. Her behavior was highly unusual, beginning with how she'd never before addressed me as the queen of anything. I supposed she was offering a polite greeting in public, and hoped she wouldn't remain so formal for the entire time we were her guests.

We hurried down the corridor, coming to a stop at her private chamber door. "Asherah, I must warn you. You will not be expecting the person inside this room."

"Who's in there? Nexa? Olluhm, perhaps?" Sibeal frowned, which worried me. "Sibeal, is something wrong? Do you need my help?"

"If anything, you may need mine." Sibeal opened the door, and on the far side of the room stood a man. His back was to us, but I noticed he was tall and broad shouldered, with blond hair caught up in a braid that reached his belt. His boots were well-worn, and a sword hung in a sheath across his back. A warrior, then, or perhaps a mercenary?

"Has he threatened you?" I asked, my hand traveling to my own sword.

Sibeal shook her head. "He hasn't." She cleared her throat, and said, "The queen is here. Asherah."

The man turned around, and I felt the room swirl with him. For a moment I thought Mallia had again bespelled me to see only dead men, because Caol'nir was standing in front of me.

"How are you here?" I demanded. "Does Aeolmar know?"

"Aeolmar?" he repeated, and took a step toward me. Once he was closer, I noticed his eyes, which were blue instead of green.

"Caol'non," I said, and he nodded. The only difference between the twin brothers was their eye color. "I haven't seen or heard of you since the day you walked out of Teg'urnan."

"I've been away," he said. "Who is this Aeolmar?"

"He's Caol'nir's son," I replied, and Caol'non's face darkened. "Didn't you know?"

"I'd heard they all perished in the fire," he replied.

I chewed my lip. Caol'non knew his brother's family had perished, but it hadn't been in a fire. Aeolmar had found them all murdered by Mersgoth. "Who told you about the fire?"

"I saw the remains myself when last I went to see them."

Caol'non took a step toward me. I took a step back. "When were you last in Caol'nir's presence?"

Caol'non's shoulders slumped. "Some time ago. Too much time, in fact. I helped him and Alluria build their home, and I remember their son's birth, then Father and I moved on." Caol'non's brow wrinkled. "Their son wasn't called Aeolmar."

"Where have you been? Where is your father?" I demanded, then I then I held up my hand. "Wait, don't answer yet." I opened the door and beckoned the guard stationed in the corridor. "Please, fetch the First Hunter and Huntress. Immediately."

The guard bowed and left on his task. I turned toward Sibeal.

"When did he arrive?" I asked.

"Only hours ago," she replied. "At first I thought he was a ghost."

"I assure you, I am no shade," Caol'non said.

"But you haven't exactly been among the living, have you?" I asked. Before Caol'non could respond, I heard footsteps behind me. I turned to the corridor and faced Aeolmar and Latera, blocking their view of the room behind me.

"What's wrong?" Aeolmar demanded.

"Is it Sibeal?" Latera asked.

"Sibeal is fine," I replied. "Aeolmar, this is strange. Whatever happens, I am here for you."

Sibeal came to stand next to me. "I am sorry this is happening in my halls."

"What is happening?" Aeolmar demanded, again.

I glanced at Sibeal, then we stood aside. Aeolmar stormed into the room, but his footsteps halted almost immediately.

"Father?"

Chapter Eleven

Leran stood in the great hall, idly wondering where some of the guests had gone. He understood that most were readying themselves for the feast that would begin soon, but that didn't explain why Asherah had disappeared, yet her mate still lingered in the hall. And where was Sibeal?

Since this first night's gathering was informal, Leran motioned to his commanders, Balthus and Belenos, and the three of them left to walk the battlements. They circled the palace twice before the rain started up. When they reentered the hall, Leran saw Sibeal and Latera standing together near the greater hearth. Sibeal wrung her hands, while Latera kept looking over her shoulder toward the far entrance.

"Sibeal," Leran said as he approached the Lady of Thurnda.

"Leran," Sibeal said as she took his hands. "I'm glad you're here."

"You know I'm not one to pry, but what is happening?" he asked.

"What makes you think anything is happening?" Sibeal countered.

"The two of you are nervous, and nothing unnerves the Lady or the *deva'shi*," he said. "Is there anything I can do?"

"If only there was." Sibeal frowned at the fire. "Do you remember Caol'nir?"

"The fae warrior?" Leran asked. "He and his father stayed at The Seat while the *Ish h'ra hai* prepared to march on Teg'urnan."

"*Ish h'ra hai?*" Latera repeated. "There were followers of the Ish h'ra in Tingu?"

Leran shook his head. "They were those liberated from the *dojas.* They took to calling Asherah the Ish h'ra—The Deliverer—and themselves the *Ish h'ra hai.*"

"Followers of Ish h'ra," Latera muttered.

"That doesn't mean anything," Sibeal said, squeezing Latera's forearm.

"What doesn't mean anything?" Leran asked.

"Caol'nir's brother is here, and his presence is most unusual," Sibeal replied. "No one—not I, nor Asherah or anyone else—has heard tell of Caol'non since the old fae king fell, yet today he walked through the palace gates and asked to see me."

"I never knew Caol'nir had a brother," Leran said.

"He had two," Latera said. "One was killed in the Great Temple during the Battle for Teg'urnan. The other left Teg'urnan with Caol'nir and their father, and disappeared. Until today, that is." Latera glanced toward the eastern exit and frowned. "This Caol'non didn't even know who Aeolmar was."

"Should he have?" Leran asked.

"Caol'nir was Aeolmar's father," Latera replied.

"Then the First Hunter was sired by Parthalan's greatest warrior," Leran said. "Greatest warrior until the *deva'shi*, that is. By your words, I assume Caol'nir has perished?"

"Yes," Latera replied. "Some time ago."

"And this brother picked today of all days to make himself known," Leran said. "Why here? Why not in Teg'urnan?"

Latera frowned. "I wish I knew."

"Asherah and Aeolmar are with him now," Sibeal said. "Asherah's one of the few still living who has met Caol'non."

Leran understood what Sibeal left unsaid: Asherah was one of the few that could prove Caol'non was—or wasn't—who he claimed to be. "You never met him?"

Sibeal shook her head. "I never spoke to him. I remember seeing Caol'nir with him, but that's all. Perhaps Balthus would remember him? Or Belenos?"

"I will ask them," Leran said, then Aeolmar entered the hall and strode directly toward the hearth. Once there, he wrapped his arms around his mate.

"Where is he?" Sibeal asked.

"Retiring to his room," Aeolmar replied after he kissed Latera's hair. "He said he didn't want to cause a disturbance."

"Too late for that," Latera said. "Mar, Leran knew your father."

"Did you?" Aeolmar released Latera and faced Leran.

"Knew may be too strong a word," Leran said. "I was very young, but I do remember your father, and his." Leran realized something. "Your son is named after your grandsire."

"In a way, yes," Aeolmar replied. "What were they like? Tor, and... my father?"

"Kind," Leran replied. "Tor was very serious, but whenever no one was watching, he would pass me sweets. Caol'nir asked Grelk to make me a quarter-sized sword, and he and I would spar in the snow." Leran's face darkened. "Is this man whom he claims to be?"

"Asherah thinks so," Aeolmar replied.

"That doesn't explain why he is here," Sibeal said. "Neither Caol'nir nor Tor, and certainly never this Caol'non, ever set foot in Thurnda before today."

"He claims it was time for him to reenter the world," Aeolmar replied. "Supposedly, we will learn more from him tomorrow."

Leran nodded. "One way or another, I'm sure we will."

A *saffira* approached them and spoke quietly to Sibeal. "Our meal is ready. Please, let's relax and put this afternoon out of our minds, at least for now," Sibeal said.

"A splendid idea," Latera said, and she led Aeolmar toward their son.

"Their boy looks like Caol'nir," Leran said.

"He does," Sibeal agreed. "I must say, when things like this happen, it makes me grateful that my family tree isn't the only one with a few oddities in the branches."

"What oddities could there possibly be in Thurnda's first family?" Leran extended his arm to Sibeal, and they walked to the center table. As Lady of Thurnda and Lord of Tingu, theirs was a place of honor. Across from them were Thurnda's most honored guests, Asherah and Finlay. After they were seated, Sibeal smiled toward the room, then she leaned close to Leran.

"My son and his intended mate, for one," Sibeal said. "He's got this notion his mate will someday be Lady."

"That's not how the succession works," Leran said. "The next Lady would be one of your daughters, or Senan's."

"I know. He disputes the truth." Sibeal paused as a *saffira* filled their goblets. "No matter that he's wrong, he has decided Thurnda is his to rule."

Leran shook his head. "That will never come to pass. His mate will have no claim to Thurnda. Hells, the only living woman I'm aware of with a possible claim is Latera."

Sibeal glanced at him, then she looked over the hall. "Who mentioned that?"

"Cerillia did, to Latera," Leran replied. "Latera was shocked."

"Latera would be." Sibeal paused, and added, "Her daughters also have a claim."

Leran rubbed his chin. "Yes. I suppose they do. What of Priya?" No one had heard any news of Priya, Elvasla's daughter, since she returned from the mortal realm to tell those who remained of how her mother had killed the *mordeth-gall* but died in the attempt.

Sibeal frowned. "Priya abandoned Thurnda long, long ago. As far as I know, she returned to the mortal realm, and there she has stayed."

"Interesting." Leran wondered where Senan had gotten such ideas, and where he'd met Cerillia. However, he wasn't about to ask these questions during a celebration.

"To family," he said, and clinked his goblet against Sibeal's. "They do keep life interesting."

Sibeal smiled, and drank from her own goblet. "They certainly do."

***

While long and uneventful, Leran admitted that the meal itself wasn't unpleasant. Once the remains of the meal were cleared away, the hall was rearranged for dancing and other entertainment. Leran decided against finding a partner, choosing instead to indulge in more of Sibeal's wine. He quickly drained his goblet and sent a *saffira* off to refill it; while he waited, he found himself standing next to Asherah's son.

"Finlay, is it not?" Leran asked. He'd never met Asherah's son, unless he counted the time he had journeyed to Teg'urnan and Asherah had been heavy with child. Now here he was, a man grown.

"Just Finn," the younger man corrected. "It got confusing, me and the king having the same name." Leran nodded; he'd never had the problem of being confused with his father. *If only he'd been here,* Leran thought, and deliberately shoved the thought away. As he returned his attention to Finn, Leran remarked that no one could mistake who his parents were. He had the same tight curls and broad shoulders as the elder Finlay, along with Asherah's pale hair and dark eyes.

"So, you're the heir?" Finn said, rousing Leran from his thoughts.

"I am the scion of Tingu," Leran replied. Why was it that all these functions ever did was remind him that he was parentless? "I am no one's heir."

"You're the heir to Parthalan," Finn stated. "Didn't you know?"

Leran remembered Asherah declaring him her heir long, long ago, right after she had taken the old king's head and been crowned Parthalan's queen. It was nothing more than a formality, done so if she died childless neither Parthalan nor Tingu wouldn't be pitched into war over the search for a successor, though he'd never thought much about it. He had enough trouble in his own lands, and the last thing he wanted was to rule Parthalan as well.

"That was a long time ago," Leran said. "Things change."

"This hasn't," Finn said, smiling. "It is clearly noted in the royal archives—archives that are updated every five winters, mind you—that you're my mother's heir. It only makes sense, since you're the elder of us."

"Elder?"

"I've always thought of you as my older brother," Finn continued. "We're so alike, both of us being alone. Well, not any longer, since we've met one another."

The *saffira* returned with Leran's wine, but he set the goblet aside. He had the impression that wine had loosened Finn's tongue somewhat more than was advisable, and he didn't want his own tongue loosened as well.

"I suppose you've a point, Finn," Leran said, though he'd never consider the fae prince any sort of a sibling. "But, rest assured that your inheritance is safe from me. The last thing I need is to watch over you lot."

Finn stared dumbfounded, and Leran wondered if his annoyed tone had taken him by surprise. Well, why wouldn't he be annoyed by this boy who assumed that Leran was his brother, of all things?

Finn said something further, but Leran had had enough. He excused himself and left the hall, and exited to the adjacent balcony. It offered fresh air as much as solitude as one could muster in the center of Thurnda's palace. As he stepped out of the oppressively warm and noisy hall, the cold mountain air struck him all at once, making his lungs contract even as he inhaled deeply. The brisk air settled his mind, and cooled his anger.

He heard a small movement, and turned to see Latera's daughter standing on the opposite end of the balcony. Leran briefly contemplated leaving, being that he had no reason to act as the gracious host since Thurnda was not his land, but he was Lord of Tingu. He would not give a faerie cause to disparage the hospitality of elves.

"My lady," he greeted. "Are you enjoying the celebration?"

"So far, yes," she replied. "You're the Lord of Tingu, are you not?"

"You fae have short memories. I am he, and we have met before."

"Have we?" she asked, arching a delicate brow. "I didn't think you'd been to Teg'urnan in my lifetime."

"I attended the celebration of Asherah's one thousandth winter as queen. You were very young," he added.

"Then we only met if you spoke with my mother's belly," she said, then laughed at his confused face. "You remember my sister, Mara. I wasn't born until three moons after the celebration."

Leran looked closely at her, reconciling the image in his memory with the flesh and blood woman before him. Yes, the girl he had met in Teg'urnan had had darker eyes, and while both sisters had red hair, the elder did not have the wild, corkscrew curls that were obviously passed down from Latera.

"Forgive me, I'd forgotten that Latera was blessed with two daughters," he murmured.

"You are forgiven," she said, then resumed gazing at the World's Spine.

"May I have your name?" Leran asked, a little impatiently.

"Ember," she replied.

"Ember," he repeated, taking in her fiery red hair. He found her name a trifle obvious. "Is this your first time in the north?"

"It is, and I love it here," she replied. "The cold air, the mountains, the snow, all of it. I think they speak to my elf blood."

Leran snorted. "You're only half an elf, if that."

"So are you." He spun to face this girl who dared to question his heritage, and was met by Ember's level gaze. "Don't give me that grouchy face. It's true and you know it. Your heritage is well documented in Teg'urnan's archive."

She called me grouchy. "You read about me in your archive?" he asked. It seemed that his heritage was required learning for all faerie children.

"I wanted to learn about elfin customs before I came here. It's what my mother did, before her first journey north." Leran remembered well how Ember's mother and the First Hunter had turned up at his keep, and how he had dismissed Latera as nothing more than another fickle faerie woman. Then, she had turned out to be not only an elf but Elvasla's descendant, the long-awaited *deva'shi*.

"Everyone in Teg'urnan followed the same tactic," he grumbled.

"You've met Finn?" she asked, and he affirmed he had. "Pleasant, isn't he?" Leran did not mistake her sarcasm.

"He seems to think we're brothers, and that I'm to inherit Parthalan."

"I don't believe our gracious queen plans to relinquish her throne to him or anyone, so we are safe from Finn arguing with you over his legacy for the time being," she said lightly.

Leran nodded, then wondered again why he was still Asherah's heir. He cast his memory back to when Asherah came to Tingu to advise him of his father's death, and of the many heaps of parchments she had written in her own hand with only him and Balthus present. Many of the proclamations were to cement Leran's place as Lord of Tingu and Lormac's heir, but now that he knew Asherah had made him the heir to Parthalan, as well, he questioned what she'd really intended.

"Asherah may have named me as heir once, but I imagine her son is now the true heir," Leran said.

"I believe she still considers you her eldest child."

Leran squeezed his eyes shut as he clenched his fists; he remembered those days as if it was only yesterday, of his father alive and hale, and Asherah filling the role of mother, replacing his true mother who could not be bothered with him; and of riding before Asherah on her saddle and sleeping nestled between her and his father. He also remembered how his somber father had become the very picture of happiness once Asherah had come into their lives, not that he cared to admit that to Ember, or himself.

"I... She is not my mother," Leran said slowly.

"Whether she is or not, it is an honor nonetheless, so perhaps you should accept the kindness the queen has offered you."

"What do you know of such things?" he demanded. "You're nothing but a girl. Have you ever lost one you loved? Have you ever had to fight to reclaim what was rightfully yours?"

Most would have apologized to Leran after such an outburst, and scuttled from his presence in fear of their lives. The Lord of Tingu's volatile emotions was the stuff of legend, and he took any comment about his family or his birthright as an insult. Ember neither backed away nor offered a hasty apology. Instead, she acknowledged his anger.

"You're right. No one I love has ever been taken from me, and I've never fought a battle in my life. Once, we had reports that my father and sister had perished, which proved false, but I remember well the feeling of dread and loss." Ember turned away from him, her eyes fixed upon a far-off point as she spoke. "I wouldn't wish for anyone to know such pain, not for a single moment. I wish I could make things right for you, but as you say, I'm but a girl."

As Ember stood upon the balcony, the icy wind blowing her hair back from her face, she reminded Leran of her mother, who had spoken to him from her heart so long ago. It had been Latera's words that made him travel to Teg'urnan for the first time, to offer Asherah his aid against Asgeloth, and while he did not go so far as to call Asherah his mother again, he no longer ignored her when she spoke.

"You're much like your mother," he said at length.

"Is that a good thing?" she asked with a sidelong glance.

"Yes, I think it is." Leran found himself smiling at her, and he could not recall the last time he smiled with such sincerity. He also could not recall the last time a woman had such an effect on him.

"Forgive me, for how I spoke," he said. "I didn't mean to offend you."

She smiled, and her effect on him deepened. "You are forgiven, my lord."

"Leran. Call me Leran." Hesitantly, he extended his arm. "Will you accompany me back to the hall?"

"You're not ashamed to have a half-elf on your arm?"

"I walk with whom I like," Leran replied. None of the women in his own court would dare to be so forward with him, not even the few he took to bed. He had initially found Ember's teasing words an annoyance, but he was now intrigued by the woman beside him. Then she took his arm, and the slight pressure of her fingers against his skin somehow made everything right in his world.

"Your father and I don't get on very well," he felt the need to tell her. Why he felt that need, he could not explain.

"That's just his manner," Ember replied as they stepped back into the hall. "He's not nearly as awful as he pretends to be."

"Good to know," Leran said. "I'm sure he's occupied by this family member of yours that arrived earlier."

Ember's face darkened. "Apparently, he's an uncle of mine. Why he's chosen today to appear is anyone's guess."

"He didn't say?"

"He was hardly given a chance. Asherah was more interested in determining if he is who he claims to be." Ember glanced across the hall. "I wonder if he's here now."

Leran followed her gaze. "I don't see him," he said, though he meant he didn't see anyone who looked like Caol'nir. Leran did see Ember's sister at the far end of the hall, surrounded by elfin suitors. Now that he could see and compare them, he noted that Mara was the taller of the two, and her hair more of a dark auburn. He glanced at Ember, and decided that he preferred her bright hair and petite frame. "Your sister is quite popular among the elfin lords," he said.

"For all the good it will do them," Ember muttered. "Mara is destined to be the next Virgin Queen of Parthalan."

"She'll take vows in the temple?" Leran asked. Ember waved away his confusion.

"No, nothing like that. She has this notion that she will encounter her perfect mate and be swept away by him, much like our mother was by Papa. She won't even look in a man's direction unless she suspects him of being her soul's true mate." Leran looked back to Mara and her suitors, and noticed that she seemed to ignore most of them.

"And you, sweet girl?" he asked, hoping that Ember did not share her sister's penchant for chastity.

"Sweet girl?" she asked as that lovely brow arched once again. "Are all elves so forward?"

"We are," he replied. "And we enjoy happening upon lovely maidens in the midst of boring feasts." Ember's cheeks darkened, but her voice held steady.

"Luckily for you, I was on the balcony." They had reached the mid-point of the hall, and Leran realized she was still holding his arm. He was about to ask her to sit beside him, when he spied Balthus glowering in the distance. Before he could act, Ember's sister beckoned to her.

"I'm being summoned," Ember murmured, and slipped free of his arm as gracefully as a cool breeze. Leran watched her bright hair as she made her way across the hall, and only turned to address Balthus when she was out of view.

"Have you heard about this Caol'non?" Leran asked. When Balthus nodded, he added, "Think he is who he claims to be?"

Balthus shrugged. "He looks like Caol'nir, but that's all I can say. Mark my words, Leran, the fae are nothing but trouble."

Leran's gaze moved to where he'd last seen Ember. "Not all of them, I hope."

Chapter Twelve

The welcome celebration was meant to last long into the night, but Finlay had had enough of the event after the main meal was served. Asherah also wished to retire early, and while the musicians set up for the night's entertainment, the King and Queen of Parthalan slipped away to their rooms.

"Today was certainly interesting," Asherah said, once they were alone.

"Most of it was good, too," Finlay said. "I saw Finn speaking with Leran."

"Did you? Gods, I do hope they get on well." Asherah sat at the dressing table, and tapped her fingers on the polished wood. "Do you ever feel like your past is trying to speak to you?"

Finlay halted with his shirt halfway over his head. The last time Asherah had gotten wrapped up in her memories, she'd forgotten nearly everything about her life, including who he was. "Did Caol'non's appearance upset you?"

"Upset? No, not at all. His presence is confusing, but not upsetting." Asherah faced her mate. "Caol'non said that where he's been holed up these many years, the old gods are still worshipped."

Finlay's brow pinched. Asherah hadn't mentioned the old gods since they stood before Olluhm's shrine at the Golden Knoll. The estate had been owned by Iruna and Avinor, who were the only living children of King Markham, the last of Parthalan's rulers from the original royal bloodline. Then Iruna committed treason, and her lands and estates, including the Golden Knoll, were seized by the crown.

The shrine in question, while currently dedicated to Olluhm, was an oddity. Unlike the other shrines to the elder sun, this one had a roof. Olluhm himself had decreed that all of his shrines should be open to the sky, so he could look down and see his followers. This out-of-place roof led Asherah to deduce that the shrine at the Golden Knoll had originally been dedicated to one of the old gods: Ish h'ra, The Deliverer.

"And why are you thinking about who worships which gods?" Finlay asked.

"I don't know," she replied. "But ever since we've been traveling, I keep catching bits of memory, like I did at the waterfall. The farther north we go, the stronger they become. It's as if these memories are trying to tell me something, but they're so jumbled I can't understand them."

Finlay dragged a chair over to his mate and sat in front of her. "And Caol'non's mention of the old gods stirred another memory?"

"Yes," she replied. "It stirred up many memories, and again I cannot make sense of them."

He took her hands. "We could write them down, maybe make a few sketches of what you do understand."

"Maybe." She stroked her thumb across his knuckles. "Did you know that I was once called The Deliverer?"

"I did. It was before you were queen, yes?"

"Yes." Asherah let out a breath, and continued, "Caol'non said it was time for the old gods to return."

"And you think the Ish h'ra will return, as well?"

She shook her head. "No. I think she's already here. And I think the key to finding her is locked in my memory."

Finlay tucked a length of Asherah's hair behind her ear. "If that's the case, all we need to do is find you a key."

"You will help me?" Asherah asked. "You'll make sure I won't lose myself, like I did before?"

"Of course I'll help you," Finlay said. "And you didn't lose yourself. Sarelle locked part of you away. It wasn't your fault."

"Yes, well." Asherah looked at her lap. "I don't want to forget you again."

Finlay gathered her in his arms and kissed her hair. "I don't think you will, but even if that happens, I'll be right here to remind you."

Chapter Thirteen

The next morning dawned bright and clear, and Leran walked the battlements between sunrises. While he would never admit to preferring any aspect of Thurnda's palace over his home in Tingu, he did enjoy how all the battlements led into one another in one continuous path. Whenever he stayed in Thurnda, he made a point of walking the looping route at least once per day.

During his last tour, he heard a commotion in the training yard. He descended to the ground level and found Latera standing next to the training field, frowning.

"Cousin," he greeted. "Training so early?"

"This is all your doing," Latera said, with an amicable scowl. Normally he wouldn't stand for such talk, but he liked Latera. As his kinswoman, and the *deva'shi*, she was entitled to speak her mind.

"Exactly what am I responsible for?" he inquired.

Latera nodded toward the training field. Leran followed her gaze and saw Aeolmar sparring with his son. "I seem to recall you promised the victor a troll sword."

"So I did," he said. "The boy seems to be doing well. He must take after his mother." Indeed, Tor was holding his own, and Aeolmar wasn't pulling any of his strikes. The sheer force of the First Hunter's blows were enough to flatten most men, yet Tor either evaded or parried them all. Tor was fierce, no doubt about it, though Aeolmar had yet to break a sweat.

Latera shook her head. "He takes after his father in that he's too stubborn to know when to stop."

Leran nodded and was about to offer Latera a few words of encouragement, when a gentle laugh floated to his ears. Standing at the far end of the field were Cerillia and her ladies, Ember among them.

They must have been out for an early ride, Leran deduced, since the women weren't attired in their usual gowns but dull brown gear. Then Ember made her way to the forefront of the group, ostensibly to watch the bout, and Leran saw she was clad in a dress rather than more practical leggings. *Foolish faeries.* The dress was plain green, but did nothing to detract from her beauty; in fact, Leran imagined he would enjoy a short ride from the palace with her, listening to her gay laugh, watching the sunlight reflect gold upon her hair. He didn't realize he was staring at her until she gasped and covered her eyes, then Latera grabbed his arm.

"Tor is going to get himself killed," she said. Leran looked to the field; Tor was on his knees, blood trickling down his neck while Aeolmar looked aghast, but Latera was right; the boy refused to surrender. Tor got to his feet and rushed at Aeolmar, the clang of metal on metal ringing out across the spectators.

"Tor, I'm begging you! Yield," Latera yelled.

Ignoring his mother's plea, Tor pressed his attack. Leran observed, wishing the boy would ease up but intent on remaining silent; it was not the Lord of Tingu's place to meddle in who spars with whom, and faeries at that, when he caught sight of Ember. Her hand was balled into a fist before her mouth, her delicate ginger brows knit together. He couldn't let this match go on, not if it was distressing her in any way.

"I'm stopping this now," Latera said.

Leran halted her with a hand on her shoulder. "I'll do it," he said, then he turned to the field.

"Enough," he bellowed. Leran strode out onto the field, heedless of the flying blades. *Let them try to strike me.* Aeolmar immediately put down his sword and backed away; after a moment, Tor reluctantly lowered his weapon.

"Why are you stopping us?" Tor panted. Leran suspected that if Tor hadn't already been exhausted from the match, it would have been a shout.

"I need give no reason," Leran replied; he may not be the king of all elfland as his father was, but the Lord of Tingu was the ultimate authority in all matters related to battle. "However, this bout is upsetting my kinswoman, and I'd rather not have that."

Both Aeolmar and Tor's gazed flicked toward Latera, who stood at the sidelines with her arms crossed over her breast, lips pursed and bloodless. Leran's gaze returned to Ember, whose face was paler than her mother's was. Leran believed he'd discerned why: in Tor's quest to prove himself a worthy opponent to his father, he would have pushed until one of them was seriously injured. He understood what it was like to grow up in the long shadow of one's father, and sympathized with the younger man.

"I declare Tor the winner," Leran called out, and watched the indignation bleed from Tor's face. Leran gave no reason for his decision, and nor did anyone question him. "Give me your specifications for whatever weapon you'd like, and I will personally deliver them to Grelk. I will warn, it may be a century before you claim your prize."

"Thank you, my lord," Tor said, and Leran merely nodded. He turned away, narrowly avoiding Latera as she rushed toward the bleeding Tor, and again caught sight of Ember. She crossed her hands over her heart and smiled, and Leran offered her a shallow bow.

I've involved myself in faerie matters, and I'm indebted to a sword from Grelk, all over her lovely smile.

Leran had just decided to approach Ember, when there was a commotion near the fence. A moment later, Caol'non strode onto the field.

"Would either of you care to spar against me?" Caol'non asked.

"I've already given away one troll sword," Leran said. "Perhaps tomorrow I'll offer a second."

"No need. I've a troll sword of my own." Caol'non drew his sword from a sheath on his back. It was unadorned, which Leran found unusual. Trolls prided themselves on their craftsmanship and attention to detail, and every sword he'd seen come out of Grelk's forge was inset with gems or at the very least engraved. Caol'non's sword was nothing but smooth silver metal, polished to a mirror sheen.

"I think not," Aeolmar said, sheathing his own blade. "For all we know, that sword's spelled to render us into piles of ash."

Caol'non looked stunned. "You really think I'd harm my family?"

"You've done little to help," Aeolmar said.

"Not here," Leran said, indicating the crowd with his eyes. He knew well how fast rumors travelled. "Use my apartments if you have things to discuss. The walls are enchanted against eavesdroppers. We can go there now, if you need to."

"Thank you." Aeolmar nodded to Leran, then he and his son joined Latera at the edge of the field. Leran gazed toward where she'd last seen Ember, but she was gone.

Chapter Fourteen

Leran had nothing scheduled for that day, except for the feast that wouldn't begin until nightfall, so he led Aeolmar, Latera, and Caol'non from the training field to his apartment. After Leran shut the door behind them, Caol'non frowned.

"This is a family matter," Caol'non said.

"These are my chambers, therefore I remain," Leran said. "And I am family. Latera is my cousin."

Caol'non glanced between Aeolmar and Latera. "You don't mind if he stays?"

"I would prefer it," Latera said.

"As would I," Aeolmar added. "Leran, should we sit?"

"Yes. This way."

They followed Leran into a larger room filled with benches and tables, and a massive desk set in front of the hearth. Leran sat behind the desk, and shuffled a few parchments while the rest settled themselves. Aeolmar and Latera claimed the cushioned bench to the right of the desk, while Caol'non sat across from them. Once everyone was seated, Leran rang a bell, and his chamberlain, Aldo, appeared.

"My lord," Aldo began, then his gaze alighted on Latera. "I see we have noble visitors. I shall fetch refreshments."

"Noble?" Caol'non asked, as Aldo went to gather the refreshments.

"He means Latera," Leran said. "Now, I understand you've much to discuss with my cousin and her mate. I'd like to start with your sword."

Caol'non frowned. "What about my sword?"

Leran gestured at the wall behind him. Many swords were displayed above the hearth, all of them richly ornamented. "You say yours is a troll sword. I've spent my life surrounded by such weapons, but I've never seen one like yours come out of Grelk's forge."

"My sword didn't come from Grelk's forge."

Leran's eyes narrowed. "Was it forged by mountain trolls?"

"Perhaps. I've no idea." Caol'non unsheathed his sword and laid it across Leran's desk. "Please, examine it if you like. Perhaps there's a marking that will speak to its origin."

"Where did you get it?" Aeolmar asked.

"I found it, and others like it."

Aeolmar shook his head. "Trolls don't give weapons to just anyone. Hells, they rarely even sell them. Yet you happened across a blade worth as much as a castle?"

"I don't know what it's worth. There was an entire armory full of them, covered in dust."

"If you were *con'dehr* like Aeolmar's father, you must have been familiar with what the trolls manufacture, weaponry included," Latera said.

"Both of my brothers and I served in the *con'dehr*," Caol'non replied. "Our father was our commander, and the king's Prelate." Caol'non paused, and asked, "Wasn't Harek named Prelate after Asherah took the throne?"

"Yes," Aeolmar replied.

"Is he Prelate still?"

"He's dead," Aeolmar said flatly. "Execution by beheading."

Caol'non swallowed. "Much has changed in Teg'urnan."

"Yes," Aeolmar said. "Much, indeed."

Aldo returned with his tray of refreshments. Caol'non reclaimed his seat while the chamberlain poured wine and water for his guests, and brought a steaming bowl of tea to Latera. His duties seen to, Aldo retired to a chair next to the door.

"We were discussing your sword," Aeolmar prompted.

"Anything you can say to me, you can say in Aldo's presence," Leran said in response to Caol'non's questioning glance toward the chamberlain. "His loyalty and discretion are beyond reproach."

Caol'non nodded. "As I was saying, the abandoned armories on Ysr are filled with troll-forged weapons."

"Ysr," Aeolmar repeated. "You've been to Ysr?"

"I lived there for many winters," Caol'non replied. "Long before my brother and I were *con'dehr*, we were soldiers in the legion. We spent two winters stationed at the Southern Outpost. Whenever we had the chance, we would go to the mountains above the beach. We could see Ysr at the edge of the horizon, nearly out of sight. Caol'nir always wanted to go to the island, find out if it was abandoned, as the stories claimed. After his and Alluria's son was born, it was plain he wouldn't be traveling for a time, so I went to the island, alone." Caol'non looked away. "And there I stayed, until recently."

"Forgive me, but what is so significant about this land?" Latera asked. "It's only an island. Can't anyone with a boat go there?"

"They could, but no one does," Aeolmar replied. "Long ago, when Parthalan still kept a navy, we went to war against Ysr. By all accounts, we defeated our foes and left a desolate, uninhabited island."

"Why did we go to war against them?" Latera asked.

"It was where the first people of Parthalan retreated to after Olluhm cursed them," Caol'non replied.

"Some say the old gods retreated there as well," Leran said.

Aeolmar frowned and looked pointedly at Latera. She shook her head slightly, then Aeolmar asked, "Why would those cursed by Olluhm have a trove of troll weapons?"

"Ah. I understand that you're closer in blood to Olluhm than most, even closer than my brothers and me," Caol'non said. "What do you know of Olluhm's curse?"

"I know enough," Aeolmar replied.

Caol'non nodded. "Then you also know that the trolls existed long before the other races. For reasons known only to the trolls, they sided with those who came before the fae."

"Did they," Aeolmar said. "Grelk never mentioned as much."

"Grelk is ancient," Caol'non said. "Like as not, he forgot."

"Grelk has never forgotten anything," Leran said. "This has been a wonderful history lesson, but our purpose in retiring here was to learn why you've chosen now, and in Thurnda of all lands, to reappear."

"Very well." Caol'non finished his water and set the cup on a side table. Aldo moved to refill it, but Leran motioned for him to wait. "Were you aware that some of those cursed by Olluhm still live on Ysr?"

"Let me guess, alongside the old gods?" Aeolmar asked.

"I've never seen any god in the flesh, nor do I want to," Caol'non replied. "Those on Ysr still worship the old gods, and claim it's time for one of them to return."

"The Deliverer," Latera said.

"Yes," Caol'non said, nodding. "You've heard the Ish h'ra's call as well?"

"What makes you think she's returning?" Aeolmar demanded. "For that matter, how do you or any of these Ysrians know she's still alive?"

"All of the old gods are alive. Olluhm didn't kill them. He merely banished them. That's why I'm here."

"Have you become a priest?" Aeolmar asked. "Or are you a herald of the vanquished ones?"

"I've returned because I have very little family left, and you will need all the protection you can muster," Caol'non said. "When The Deliverer returns, she will recommence her war against Olluhm."

The four of them sat in silence for a moment. "We should speak to Kemen," Latera said. "His father is a priest of the old gods. His insights may prove valuable."

"Agreed," Aeolmar said as he rose. "I will speak to him. Latera, will you confer with Sibeal?"

She nodded. "I shall. Leran, thank you for allowing us the use of your chamber."

"Of course," he said, though he thought their departure abrupt. He assumed Caol'non's appearance was more distressing than either had let on. "Please, let me know if I can be of further assistance."

Caol'non reclaimed his sword and then stepped into the corridor, followed by Latera. Aeolmar paused, and said, "Beloved, I would like to discuss a few things with Leran. Please give Sibeal my regards."

Latera nodded, and shut the door.

"You leave your mate with this unknown man?" Leran asked.

"Latera can take care of herself," Aeolmar replied. "What do you make of Caol'non's story?"

"I'm not sure," Leran replied. "He has a troll sword of unknown provenance, yet he also thinks Grelk didn't forge it. And if there is an armory full of troll-forged weapons on Ysr, how has no one raided it yet?"

"He also said he had very little family left, but yesterday he'd never heard of me," Aeolmar said. "I had six siblings, but he has only mentioned one of my brothers. That means he's been gone from Parthalan nearly as long as Asherah has ruled."

Leran grunted. "What of his claim that Ysr is inhabited?"

Aeolmar shrugged. "I don't know if it's inhabited. I've never set foot on the island, so I couldn't say one way or another. But wouldn't someone have noticed people living there?" Aeolmar rubbed the back of his neck. "What sort of archives do you keep at The Seat? Is there anything about Ysr, or the old gods?"

"About the old gods, very little," Leran replied. "As for Ysr, there is far more information about the island here in Thurnda. There's a trade route that ran from here to Ysr and beyond." Leran blew out a breath. "Perhaps that's why Caol'non came here, instead of Teg'urnan or anywhere else. He may have followed the old route."

"That would make sense," Aeolmar agreed. "Thurnda once traded beyond Ysr?"

Leran nodded. "They still do. Aldo!"

The elder elf was at Leran's side in a moment. "My lord?"

"I need a map of the trade routes between Thurnda and Ysr, and two, maybe four warriors willing to travel the route—quickly—and report back on what they find."

"Would you like them to travel all the way to Ysr?"

"Yes." Leran glanced at Aeolmar, and continued, "I must also send a messenger to Grelk. Did you hear what Caol'non claimed about the troll weapons on Ysr?"

"I did."

"I need to know if Grelk made those weapons."

Aldo nodded. "It will be done, my lord."

Aeolmar watched Aldo sit behind Leran's desk, and proceed to pull out a few blank parchments and a box of sealing wax from a drawer. "How long will it take your men to reach Ysr?"

"This time of year?" Leran rubbed his chin. "They can reach the coast in four days—"

"I will send Diem and Graun, and they will reach the coast in three," Aldo interjected.

"Three days," Leran amended, "then it depends on the sea. Once they reach Ysr proper..." Aldo produced a map of the island and handed it over without looking up from his work. Leran flattened it across the desk, then Aeolmar stepped forward to look over the map as well.

"The island isn't very large," Aeolmar said. "It should be easy to determine if it's inhabited. They could be back with news in as little as ten days."

"We may be on our way to Tingu by then," Leran muttered, thinking about the trolls that yet harried his border. "I'll likely have Grelk's response waiting for me at The Seat."

"You won't remain in Thurnda until the next full moon?"

Leran closed his eyes, and silently berated himself. Aeolmar noticed every detail, and he knew exactly how long Leran was supposed to remain in Thurnda. "Perhaps not. If my people need me at The Seat, that's where I will be."

His reply satisfied Aeolmar. "Understood. Thank you for your help. I realize this is a fae matter, and it's good of you to help us."

"This isn't just a fae matter," Leran said. "The first alliance elves ever struck was with Grelk. If those weapons were stolen from him, I would like to know by whom."

Aeolmar paused. "Grelk remembers the old gods, doesn't he?"

"Yes. I've heard him speak of them many times."

"Once this business in Thurnda is done, I believe I will pay my old friend a visit."

Chapter Fifteen

Latera Speaks

I shut the door to Leran's chamber and started toward Sibeal's apartments. Unsurprisingly, Caol'non followed.

"Leran said you're nobility?" he asked.

"Do I not appear noble to you?" I countered.

"It's not that. With Leran being the Lord of Tingu, for his chamberlain to make note of your status, you must be someone of some significance."

My gaze slid toward Caol'non. If he was who he claimed to be, he'd grown up in the heart of Teg'urnan in the same halls as kings and princes. Me having a title couldn't be all that interesting, could it? "I'm descended from Ganneran and Thurndian royalty," I replied. "I also killed the last mordeth-gall, *" I added, a bit off-handedly.*

"Asgeloth?"

"Yes."

Caol'non's brows knit together. "The last person who killed a mordeth-gall *was also Thurndian. Her name was Elvasla."*

"Yes. I know of her."

"It's the Lady of Thurnda's duty to kill the mordeth-gall, *" Caolnon, murmured, then he asked, "She was Sibeal's sister?"*

"Why don't you know about anything that's happened recently?" I demanded, rounding on this infuriating man. "If I didn't know better, I'd say you've been asleep since the day you left Teg'urnan!"

He pursed his lips, this man who looked so much like Aeolmar's father and our son that we were both unnerved. "Very little news reaches Ysr," he said. "Most of what we do get is about the elflands. Before I left the island, I hadn't heard anything from Parthalan in many winters, and I have never heard of... Ganneran?"

"Gannera. I am the heir to Gannera's throne."

"And Aeolmar is the heir to the sun." When I remained silent, Caol'non asked, "Haven't you ever heard that saying?"

"I have not. What does it mean?"

"The Deliverer was Olluhm's greatest foe. When she returns, she will wage war not only against Olluhm, but also his children."

I managed to not swallow my tongue at Caol'non's revelation, and after we parted ways, I found Sibeal alone in her chambers. "I heard about the match," Sibeal said by way of greeting. "Leran declared Tor the winner?"

"Tor did win, and then Caol'non arrived and produced a plain troll sword he claimed to have found lying about on Ysr." Sibeal put down her quill and gaped at me. "Yes, it happened exactly like that."

Sibeal fanned the parchment she'd been writing on in order to dry the ink. "Does Leran know?"

"He does." I sat across from Sibeal. "Caol'non also told me that Ish h'ra is returning and that she'll wage a war against Olluhm and his descendants."

"You can't possibly believe him," Sibeal said. "Where on would he have learned such things? Really, Latera, I wonder if Caol'non's not addled."

"What if he's not?" I worried the edge of Sibeal's desk. "What if everything he says is true?"

"Anyone can make claims about the old gods. It's not like they're here to dispute them." Sibeal set down the parchment and folded her hands on the desk. "You saw this supposed troll sword?"

"I did, though whether or not it was troll forged I couldn't say."

"But you say the sword was—how did you put it—plain?" Sibeal asked.

"Yes. It had no engraving or other markings."

"Then Grelk certainly had no hand in making it."

"I agree. But what interests me more is his claim that the old gods are alive and well and living on Ysr." I held my head in my hands. "Could Asherah really be the Ish h'ra?" I wondered.

"If anyone could be a god, it's Asherah," Sibeal said. Aeolmar hadn't been pleased when I told him I'd confided in Sibeal, but I maintained it was the best course of action. Sibeal had known Asherah before she was queen, and might hold valuable clues to her true identity.

Besides, I couldn't very well go skulking about Thurnda's archive without Sibeal's knowledge.

"Even when Asherah was little more than a filthy beggar, people flocked to her," Sibeal continued. "Her followers gladly did anything she asked of them. I daresay she still has that effect on people."

"She does." I recalled the first time I met Asherah. She'd been sitting on her throne, and the combination of her pale hair and dress and the late afternoon sunlight streaming into the room had made her look like the magical Faerie Queen I'd heard stories about from my nursemaids in Gannera. "There is a temple dedicated to Asherah in the mortal realm."

"Humans worship The Deliverer?"

"Not The Deliverer. They worship Asherah, the Faerie Queen."

"Yes. Well." Sibeal folded the now-dry parchment. "This is a writ for the archive's keeper. She will have all volumes that mention the old gods brought here for our examination. I don't know how many volumes there are, but we can at least begin sorting through them."

I reached across the desk and grasped Sibeal's hand. "Thank you."

"Of course. Now, I must ask something of you."

"Anything."

Sibeal exhaled and rubbed her eyes. "Senan thinks his mate will be the next Lady of Thurnda, but the title is passed from mother to daughter. Since my own daughter has passed, I would like to name you, and your daughters, as my heirs."

I felt as if the floor had fallen away beneath me. "I cannot lead Thurnda," I said, eventually. "I appreciate what you're saying, but there must be a better choice than me!"

Sibeal smiled sadly. "There is no other choice, save for any other descendants of Elvasla in your family." She pursed her lips, and looked away. "Elvasla did once have a daughter. Priya, she was called, and she was a delight. After Elvasla met her end in the mortal realm, Priya returned to tell me everything that had happened."

"Shouldn't Priya be the next Lady?"

"She should, but the day after she related her mother's fate, she left Thurnda and no one's seen her since."

"Sounds almost like Caol'non."

"If only she'd been on Ysr with him. After all this time with no word from her, I can only conclude that she wants nothing more to do

with Thurnda, which means I must find an alternative." She placed her hand on top of mine, and continued, "I have no plans of going anywhere or stepping aside, but I also never planned to be Lady of Thurnda. I need to name someone as my heir, if for no other reason than to silence Senan."

I chewed my lower lip. "All right. I accept the honor, and also hope we live a long time and this ends up being something our children sort out many years from now."

Sibeal smiled again, and this time it reached her eyes. "Wise words, cousin. Let's hope it plays out exactly like that."

Chapter Sixteen

Leran strode into the feasting hall, surveyed the revelers, and had half a mind to walk right back out. The last thing he needed was to pretend to celebrate Senan and Cerillia's mating, but his absence would lead to questions he'd rather not answer. After he'd spent the morning dealing with the mysterious Caol'non, and then sending messengers to both Ysr and Grelk's dens, Balthus had arrived with a detailed report on mountain troll activity in the Northern Waste.

"So it seems the trolls continue their destructive ways," Leran had said, once Balthus relayed the information. "Which direction are they moving in?"

"They're headed eastward, for now," Balthus replied. "With any luck, they'll all freeze to death in a blizzard."

Leran had pinched the bridge of his nose, which did little to ease his pounding head. "If only."

Now, Leran linked his fingers behind his neck, tipped his head back, and frowned at the ceiling. These mountain trolls were determined to make him miserable, even when they were leagues away to the north and east. As he imagined his forces rampaging through the trolls, a woman spoke to him.

"My lord?"

Leran looked down, and saw Ember standing in front of him. She took a step back, and he realized he was scowling at her.

"Leran." He put his hand on her elbow to keep her from moving further away. "Please. I'd rather not have formalities stand between us."

Ember smiled, and Leran allowed himself a moment to drink in her appearance. Her red curls tumbled loosely over her shoulders, and she was wearing a many-layered gown of green silks. The shades of green varied from pale springtime hues to the deep cast of emeralds, and tiny green gems were embroidered across the bodice. What Leran enjoyed most about Ember's gown were the sleeves, which were split at the shoulders and allowed him glimpses of her slender arms.

"Is there something I can do for you?" he asked.

"I wanted to thank you for earlier," Ember continued.

"Earlier?" he asked. "Exactly what did I do earlier that warrants thanks?"

"For me, nothing," she began, "but when Father and Tor were sparring, it was very good of you to intercede on Tor's behalf. After Father drew blood—"

"Aeolmar made contact with the boy?" Leran asked.

"Father slapped him with the flat of his sword," she replied. "That's always been his signal to ease up, but Tor ignored it and ended up with a cut to his neck." She cocked her head to the side, her brows peaked. "You didn't see that?"

"I did not," he admitted. "I was watching how the morning sunlight turned your red hair to gold." He caught a lock of her hair, drawing it between his fingers. "You're not spoken for?"

Surprisingly, she laughed. "You elves and your silly customs. Everything you do is entrenched in so many layers of meaning. Did it ever occur to you that not all follow such a strict regimen?"

Leran smiled, since he often found those customs stifling. "Tell me, little flame, what does it mean when a faerie maiden wears her hair loose?" He knew well that only an unclaimed elf maiden would let her hair hang unrestrained about her shoulders.

"Only that it is loose." Ember laughed at his consternation. "My mother's hair is often loose, and you cannot find a more claimed woman than she." Leran was forced to agree; one would be hard pressed to find a pair more devoted to one another than Latera and Aeolmar.

"You haven't answered my question," Leran said.

"I did," she replied, "unless you have a second." Leran moved to draw Ember closer, but the announcement was made for all to take their places. Ironically, Cerillia was about to have her hair ritually bound for her mating night. *If I ever take a mate, I will not suffer such nonsense.*

"Find me afterward," Leran murmured, then he squeezed her elbow and took his place beside Sibeal. All the while, his eyes tracked Ember's every move.

Chapter Seventeen

Aeolmar Speaks

I entered Thurnda's great hall, and frowned when I couldn't find Latera.

Beloved?

I'm with Sibeal. I'll be there soon.

I smiled, since Latera's presence in my mind was almost as comforting as having her in my arms. Why some mates could speak mind to mind, as we often did, and others couldn't was a mystery to me. I was just glad I got to converse with Latera that way.

My gaze moved around the hall again, and this time I smiled. I remembered the first time Latera and I were in Thurnda, sent by Asherah on a diplomatic mission; we'd entered the hall separately then, too. I could only hope tonight turned out as wonderful as that night had.

Since I didn't want to rush Latera's time with her cousin, I looked around the room for other ways to amuse myself. I saw Tor surrounded by youths and maidens alike, all of them hanging on his every word as he told them how he bested me and won a troll sword. When we get home to Teg'urnan, I'll show him who's the better swordsman. I left him to his storytelling and spied Kemen nearby. Caol'non had brought up many questions about the old gods, questions Kemen may know the answer to, so I made my way toward the hunter.

"Are you enjoying yourself?" I asked him.

"I am," Kemen replied. "Been too long since I was in the elf lands."

"Agreed. Life is different in the north." A saffira approached us bearing mugs of ale. After we'd each accepted one, I asked, "What do you know of Ysr?"

"The island? Not much. I don't know if anyone does, these days."

"Are the old gods there?"

"Some say they are. Why? Are you looking for them?" Instead of answering him, I drank more ale. "Does this have anything to do with what Mallia, I mean Sarelle, said, when we were in the west?"

"In a way, yes." I glanced around, but no one appeared to be in earshot. "I was told that there are followers of the old gods living on Ysr. Apparently, these followers believe that Ish h'ra will soon return."

"That's the cornerstone of what my father preaches," Kemen said. "The Deliverer will return and save us all." He looked about the room, his gaze lingering on Asherah. "You don't really think the queen is a god, do you?"

I had no intention of answering that question. Luckily for me, Latera picked that moment to enter the hall. As ever, the sight of her took my breath away.

You look like an elf.

I am an elf, silly man.

Instead of her usual hunter's gear, Latera was wearing a deep blue velvet gown decorated with silver embroidery, and her hair was pinned up at the nape of her neck in a trio of elaborate coils. Whenever Latera let Sibeal get her hands on her, she always ended up dressed like elfin royalty. I thought Latera was beautiful in anything, and nothing at all. Especially nothing at all.

"Aren't you a vision," Kemen said when Latera reached us. "Giving up hunting to become a lady of leisure?"

"Never," Latera said. "Sibeal had some books brought up from the archive, and it was dusty work. I had to change into something." Sibeal and I talked.

About Asherah? What did she say?

That if anyone could be a god, it was her.

"Did you find anything?" I asked.

"Not yet." Latera bit her lip. Mar, Caol'non said something upsetting. That's all he's done.

"Kemen, have you ever heard the term heir to the sun?" Latera asked.

"Oh, yes. Many times. When The Deliverer returns she'll wage war against Olluhm and his heirs. His direct descendants are called the heirs to the sun." Kemen's brows lowered. "That would be you, Aeolmar. Maybe your children, too."

I clenched my fist, but refrained from striking the wall. "Caol'non said this to you?"

"He did," Latera replied, then she glanced at Kemen. "There's more."

"I'll leave you to it." Kemen turned to leave us, then paused and said, "If you find anything in those dusty books you'd like me to have a look at, I'd be happy to."

Latera smiled, and I nodded, and Kemen made his way toward the ale-bearing saffira. *"What else?"*

"Sibeal wants to name me as her heir."

"And that's why you're dressed like the Lady of Thurnda," I conclud-ed. "Senan won't be pleased."

"Senan's opinion doesn't matter," she said. "What does matter is that Cerillia quite strongly desires to be the next Lady of Thurnda. I wonder why."

My gaze moved across the hall, and I located Senan and Cerillia, both of them seated in their respective places of honor. "Why, indeed."

"I sent a message to Wren," Latera continued. "I told her all about Caol'non, and Cerillia. I even mentioned that awful necklace Cerillia is always wearing. Maybe Wren can find something."

"What could Wren possibly learn about Cerillia in Teg'urnan?"

Latera shrugged. "Honestly, I've no idea, but Sibeal is at her wits' end." Latera glanced around, then continued speaking in our mind-touch. Apparently, Senan was in one of the northern villages, and that's where he met Cerillia. Sibeal was originally very happy for her son, but she's come to distrust her.

I watched as Cerillia's hair was braided and wound about her head. What was the name of this village?

Dremmsvard.

"Dremmsvard?" I repeated, loudly enough for people to glance our way. That's so far north it's past Grelk's forge. In fact, I believe it's in Tingu. Why was Senan there in the first place?

"I don't know," Latera replied as she rubbed her temple; speaking mind to mind was convenient, but it tended to give her a headache. "But there he was, and now, this." She gestured toward Cerillia. "It's all very odd."

I thought about Caol'non, and Asherah, and the fact that Cerillia's mating feast was the event that had drawn all of us to Thurnda in the first place. "Yes, it is."

Chapter Eighteen

Throughout the entire evening, no matter where he was standing or who he was speaking to, Leran watched Ember. She was always surrounded by others, which didn't surprise him. Who wouldn't want to be near such a beauty, listen to her witty conversation, hear her sweet laughter? Surely Ember wouldn't be bored or alone while in Thurnda, not for a moment.

Surely she had better things to do than spend time with a dour, surly man like him.

Leran looked down at his hands, rough and battle scarred. For all of his confidence with a sword, he had little when it came to finding a partner, and he worried he wouldn't be able to hold Ember's interest for more than a moment. Finally, she was alone, and Leran approached her.

"I thought you agreed to find me afterward," he said without preamble.

"And afterward is now?" she countered, arching her brow. "Forgive me. Time must have slipped away."

"Did you enjoy the ritual?" he asked.

"I thought it was the most foolish thing I've ever witnessed," Ember replied. "Are we really to assume Senan's never bedded that one? She doesn't seem good for much else, except perhaps tatting lace and mending stockings."

Leran laughed aloud at this. "She doesn't, indeed." He tucked a stray curl behind her ear, and let his fingers travel to her nape. "May I ask, how is your needlework?"

"Atrocious," she replied. "I thought, in the matter of long and pointy things, the Lord of Tingu would care more for swords than needles."

"I do," he said, no longer attempting to hide his grin, for he was certain that she was flirting with him. Leran glanced about the hall, ensuring that no one was paying too much attention to the Lord of Tingu and the deva'shi's daughter, and leaned close to her ear. "When will you depart?"

"From Thurnda? Certainly not before the feast's conclusion, but Sibeal has invited us to stay until the next moon," Ember replied. "She's quite excited to have Mother here. I daresay she would host us for the rest of the season."

"I meant when will you depart tonight, for your room," he clarified, slightly annoyed because he felt she knew what he had been after all along.

"And why would you want to know that?" she asked, gazing up at him through her lashes in a way that made his blood hot. He had half a mind to invite her to his own room and leave off this banter. Instead, he led her toward an alcove partially hidden from view by a heavy tapestry, and trapped her between the wall and his arms.

"You know why," he said softly. "Did I misunderstand you, little flame?" Ember did not answer his question, or look him in the eye, but instead touched his forearm; her refusals to answer him directly only made his blood burn hotter.

"Is this the Sala?" she asked.

"Yes," he replied. Her slender fingers touched each of the stones of the Sala in turn, coming to rest upon the heartstone.

"My lord, your stone is pink," she said, with barely contained mirth.

"What?" He looked down and yes, there was an unmistakable pink tinge to the stone. After his father's death, the heartstone had remained a rich, deep red, testament to his love for his mate, until Asherah returned the Sala to Leran. Since Leran loved no one, as soon as the Sala touched his skin, the stone reverted to white. In all the winters he had worn the Sala, the stark hue had never wavered, no matter what he did, or whom he did it with.

And now the heartstone was a pale pink, seeming to pulsate in its intensity as if it had its own heartbeat. The apparent cause of the change was standing before him, gazing at him with her crystal blue eyes.

"No," he whispered.

"What? Is it so wrong to have such emotions toward a half-elf?"

Leran looked up at her teasing voice. *She thinks it changes merely because I desire her.* "The reasons for its change are not so straightforward," he said carefully, since he did not fully understand them himself.

"Then why don't you explain them to me," she said, her voice pitched low. Leran moved to take her in his arms, to get them out of this crowded hall and to the closest patch of solitude he could find, when Ember's back straightened. He glanced over his shoulder and saw her sister approach them.

"My lord," Mara said to Leran with a demure bow of her head, then she beckoned Ember to her side.

She certainly looks the part of a Virgin Queen, Leran remarked to himself as he took in Mara's appearance. Her gown was of a stiff, dark blue fabric, and boasted a high neck with little embellishment. The only aspect of her that reminded him she was a maiden were her auburn waves that swirled across her shoulders and down her back. Leran much preferred Ember's gown, and found himself staring at her arms. As he gazed at her delicate forearm, Leran realized that the Sala was too large for her, and she'd have to wear it closer to her shoulder...

Leran blinked, amazed and more than a bit unsettled by the thoughts that now coursed through his mind, then latched on to Mara's words to lead himself back to reality.

"I'm going to retire now," she was saying. "I thought you would want to accompany me." Ember glanced at Leran, and he realized that the sisters must share a room. He nearly invited Ember to come to his room instead, but remembered that her father was easily as foul tempered as he. No, if he was to get to know the lovely woman before him, he wanted it to be out of the sight of the nosy fae, and he decided to seek her company another time.

"I bid you both a good evening," he said with a slight bow, his gaze not leaving Ember's. The sisters curtseyed to the Lord of Tingu, and Leran turned to reenter the hall. He paused when he felt a hand upon his elbow.

"We will not leave until some days after the feast," Ember whispered in his ear. "Asherah wishes to wait for the full moon's light to travel."

"May I call upon you tomorrow?" he asked, ignoring how his heart leapt.

"If you wish it," she replied, again gazing at him through her lashes.

"Stop looking at me that way," he said as he placed his hand on her neck and drew her face toward his. "You may get more than you're after."

"What if I do?" she asked. She licked her lips, and Leran was struck by how young she looked. Young and fresh, like a newly fallen petal. He stroked her hair, and then caressed her cheek.

"Go," he murmured, "before I say something I regret." Ember nodded, and turned to follow her sister to their room. She only looked back once, and smiled when she saw Leran watching her.

Chapter Nineteen

Ember Speaks

"Really, what were you thinking?" Mara asked me, yet again. She had been prattling away during the entire walk to our chamber, which was on the far side of the palace from the great hall. Apparently, it was quite unseemly to be seen standing so closely to the Lord of Tingu while in a corridor. Who knew?

"I thought he was the most handsome man here, and I would like to get to know him," I replied.

Mara rolled her eyes. "Only you would decide to flirt with the most powerful man in the elflands."

"It's not like I meant to," I said, and that was the truth. I had been so looking forward to this journey to Thurnda, where I could meet people who, hopefully, weren't terrified of my parents. Few men would dare approach me in Teg'urnan for fear of losing their hides to my father—or my mother—and the fact that I looked like a younger version of my mother did not help matters. And those men who had the courage to risk my father's withering glare only wanted to hear tales of his exploits—as if they weren't already well documented!—and were woefully uninterested in me.

Therefore, when we were invited to Thurnda for Senan's mating, I was overjoyed to finally emerge from the shadow of the First Hunter and the deva'shi*. I had spent days with dressmakers, and in the end they had fashioned me many lovely gowns, so many that Mother remarked I could open a dress shop of my own. Perhaps, someday, I will. I certainly don't want to spend my life hunting demons.*

When we reached Thurnda's palace, I noticed Leran almost instantly. By virtue of where he was standing, I knew him to be nobility, the sort of nobility that had been born to his station and was therefore accustomed to the glare of responsibility. But he seemed different, as if his high station did not matter to him, and that he saw himself as nothing more than a warrior sworn to defend his home. Then he was announced, and I learned he was Leran, the Lord of Tingu—the Lord of Tingu!—and I understood my fascination somewhat more.

Having learned his identity, I still could not look away from him. Leran's father, Lormac, was said to have not been a very handsome man, but possessed an innate charisma that drew others toward him; it was well known that Asherah mourned him for many, many winters after his death. Lormac's son boasted the same ability to draw another's eye, but he was as handsome as any man I'd ever seen, with gray eyes that reminded me of pebbles worn smooth by a river, and rich brown hair that hung to his shoulders. In Teg'urnan, men sheared their hair to the nape of their necks in order to mimic the style of the king, who had yet to give up his desert preference for close-cropped hair. That custom did not seem to extend to the north. I couldn't help but imagine my fingers sinking into Leran's hair.

During the welcome feast, I tried not to stare at Leran, but I found it difficult to tear my gaze from him. In his very manner, Leran proved himself to be a kind, courteous man, for while Tingu no longer ruled over all the elfin lands, Leran was still considered their king, in title if nothing more. Eventually I caught his eye, and he smiled as he raised his goblet in my direction, though I realized a moment later he was smiling at Mother. My heart thumped so loudly I was sure that others must hear it, and only through great force of will did I still my hands enough to not draw attention. Then we formally met on the balcony, and in speaking to him, I confirmed what I had suspected but really already knew, that I wanted to get to know Leran.

Of course, naught but a foolish girl would assume that the Lord of Tingu wanted to learn anything further of her, but he again demonstrated his good, kind nature when he rescued Tor from his inevitable humiliation on the practice field. Then when I thanked him, he acted as if it was nothing, and that he'd hardly noticed the bout because he'd been staring at my hair. My hair! Why anyone would look at this tangled mess was beyond me. Perhaps I'll let one of Senan's mate's ladies help me arrange it into something more presentable. I wondered if Leran would like that. From the way he behaved in the corridor, I assumed he desired to know me a bit better, as well. Perhaps we could get to know each other a lot better.

I did my best to ignore my well-meaning sister's admonitions and warnings, and we both settled into our respective beds almost immediately after we got to our chamber. It felt as if I had been asleep for the barest moment before one of the saffira *gently shook me awake.*

"Is it second dawn?" I mumbled. I opened one eye halfway, saw that it was still dark, and plunged further beneath my blanket.

"My lady, the Lord of Tingu wishes to speak with you," she whispered in my ear.

My eyes flew open and I nearly leapt from the bed, demanding that the saffira *tell me what he was doing in my chamber so early, to which she only replied that she didn't know. After all, a* saffira *does not question the Lord of Tingu about his wants, she merely helps him to obtain them. I wrapped a shawl about my shoulders and ran my fingers through my hair, then composed myself as best I could and walked out to receive the Lord of Tingu.*

Leran stood in the center of the front chamber, his commanding presence making the room his domain. He looked quite awake, and I hoped he would overlook my bleary eyes.

"Little flame," he said by way of greeting, and the smile that went with it almost made me forget the early hour. "I trust you slept well?"

"I've hardly slept at all," I murmured as he took my hand, turned it over, and kissed my inner wrist. I liked that. "Why are you up and about so early?"

"I like to walk in the morning, before the child sun rises. I hoped you would want to accompany me."

Again, my heart thumped away so loudly I was astounded he didn't hear it. I was amazed that he had asked me to walk with him, that he wanted my company again so soon, that I was standing there staring at him in my nightdress.

"A moment, my lord," I murmured, and after I had hastily dressed myself, Leran took my arm and escorted me through the palace, then we stepped through one of the tower doors and walked along the battlements. The air was clear and cold, and the towers were so tall I felt we were halfway to the clouds.

"Why do you choose to walk now?" I asked.

"I enjoy the time between sunrises," he said, breathing deeply of the crisp morning air. "It's calm and quiet, like we've been transported to another world without the cares that plague us in this one. Are you

cold?" he asked, eyeing my thin dress and shawl. By contrast, Leran was dressed appropriately for a northern morning, replete with woolen leggings and a thick cloak. If I hadn't been aware of his high station, I would have thought him no more than a woodsman.

"I am, but I don't mind." He looked at me quizzically, so I elaborated. "It never gets cold in Teg'urnan, not really. Even our winters are warm. I like how the cold air makes my skin tingle. It makes me feel—"

"Alive," he finished, when I couldn't find the right word.

"Yes," I murmured, "alive." We stopped at a corner on the battlement that overlooked a large training field, far larger than the one Papa and Tor had sparred in the day prior. "Is this where my father taught elves to fight like the fae?" I asked.

"The way I understand things, you mother did her fair share of instruction," he retorted. "And don't think your father didn't learn a thing or two."

"I'm sure he did," I conceded, having caught a glimpse of an elfin warrior trying in vain to remain hidden. A furtive glance at my surroundings revealed three more warriors. "Do you find me dangerous?"

"You? I could lift you with one hand."

"Then why are we surrounded by your guard?" I asked loudly. Leran glared over his shoulder, and after a jerk of his head, the elves melted away. "Don't you think that was a little excessive? You're only the Lord of Tingu, not Olluhm himself."

"They were to ensure we were alone," he explained. "You weren't supposed to see them."

"You want to be alone with me?" I asked. I had expected him to fabricate some sort of excuse, to change the subject and turn away even, but Leran instead closed the space between us and traced my cheek.

"I can't stop thinking about you," he murmured.

"You've only just met me," I said, trying to downplay his intense gaze.

"I know," he said, and something in his voice told me that he also found it odd. "A few days ago, I didn't know there was a woman as sweet and fiery as you in the world, and now I can think of nothing but. And, that I missed my chance to kiss you goodnight."

"So kiss me good morning," I said, placing my arms around his neck. His eyes searched my face for a moment, then he pressed his lips to mine. Then his arms were around me, and he was kissing me so hard *he took my breath away. I wound my fingers into his hair as if to anchor myself; as I said before, in my limited experiences with men, they all kept their hair sheared as short as possible. If they only knew how inviting it was to thrust your fingers deep into your lover's hair. Not that Leran was my lover. Not that I didn't want him to be.*

Eventually, we parted, and Leran cradled me against his chest while I caught my breath. My pulse raced, my head pounded, and my hands trembled, all from the incredible effect this man had upon me. It was as if he had thrown a rope about my heart and was pulling me into his soul. I wanted to talk to him, to learn if he felt the same, but I worried he would think I was a foolish girl and want nothing more to do with me, so I rested in his arms and remained silent. I certainly wasn't cold any longer.

"I find myself drawn to you," he said at length, echoing my own thoughts. "Do you feel it, too?"

"I do." I fought a shudder as I burrowed further into his arms. I didn't want to acknowledge my shivering, for fear that Leran would send me inside, alone. More, I was not shivering from the cold.

"I need to return to my chambers," he murmured as we watched the child sun rise. "There are many matters for me to attend to before I leave Thurnda." I nodded against his chest, but didn't move to free myself from his arms. I knew that, eventually, he would leave, as would I, and then he would be in Tingu and I in Teg'urnan, which may as well be separate worlds. The likelihood of us seeing each other again was next to nothing. Leran must have been arriving at the same conclusion, for he tightened his arms about me and made no move to release me.

You've kissed him once, *I admonished myself.* One kiss and you've practically decided to become his mate. *I was acting like Mara, who fervently believed that her one true mate would suddenly appear before her, profess his undying love and carry her away. Well, she was still waiting for him to arrive, and in truth, no one but Mara thought he existed. I was not going to behave like her—I refused to behave like her—but as soon as I resolved to take my leave of Leran, he spoke, thus undoing my planned retreat.*

"You will attend the feast tonight?" he asked.

"Of course," I replied.

"Will you dance with me?"

"As my lord wishes."

"I look forward to it," he murmured as he kissed me again. While I was still in the dazed afterglow of our kiss, he removed his cloak and placed it about my shoulders. "I don't want to see you without a proper cloak again."

"As my lord wishes," I repeated, and he grinned. I got the impression he liked it when I said that. Leran kissed the inside of my wrist, and after I refused an escort of his warriors, he sent me on my way.

As I made my way back to my chambers, I felt as if the warmth of Leran's presence surrounded me, and my feet hardly touched the floor, so light was my heart. My near-ecstatic state was apparent to Mara the moment I entered, and she immediately demanded that I tell her everything. I did so quickly, since there wasn't very much to tell, and we began to fantasize about my impending life as Lady of Tingu. They were nothing more than girlish fantasies, of that I was aware, but I could not deny the happiness I felt when he was near, how my heart quickened at the mere mention of his name.

"You see," said Mara, after we'd named, and then renamed, all of my and Leran's future children, "everyone has a soulmate, you just need to be patient until you find him." As I clutched a cushion to my breast and imagined it was Leran holding me, I had to admit that Mara was right. Love finds all of us, eventually.

Chapter Twenty

"May I speak with you?"

Asherah looked up from the heaps of scrolls and maps spread across the table before her, and Leran was momentarily taken back to his youth. His father had loved maps—Leran was taught to read maps before his letters—and he had impressed this love upon his mate. He remembered the two of them, not sleeping as they plotted strategy long into the night, consulting this map and then another, his father leaning across the table to steal a kiss from her...

"Of course," Asherah replied, gesturing with a wave of her hand that he should sit across from her. Leran glanced about at the queen's many attendants, and she understood his meaning. "Leave us," she ordered, and they filed out of the room.

"What's all this?" Leran asked, poking at the maps.

"I'm searching for something Caol'non should know, so I can find out if he does indeed know it and thus prove it's really him," Asherah replied.

"I thought you were confident he is who he claims to be."

"Yes, well. Something isn't right about this, and I need to figure it out."

Leran didn't disagree. "Are you sure he isn't Caol'nir?"

Asherah shook her head. "According to Aeolmar, his father died when he was young. Whoever this man is, he is not Caol'nir."

"And Aeolmar is certain his father's dead?"

"Yes, along with his mother. Aeolmar saw both of their bodies." Leran hadn't realized Aeolmar had also lost his parents at an early age. In fact, he'd never expected to have anything in common with the First Hunter.

"But you didn't come here to ask me about Caol'non," Asherah said. "What can I help you with?"

"What did my father tell you about the Sala?" he blurted out. Asherah's brow wrinkled, her confusion plain on her face. Leran had never spoken with her about anything of a personal nature, and she had clearly thought this impromptu conversation was regarding a matter of state. "You... you are the only one who remembers him wearing it," Leran continued. "Well, I'm sure Aldo remembers, as well as Balthus and Belenos, but I doubt my father confided in them as he did to you."

"Lormac told me many things about it," she said. "He showed me how it helped him wield power over the earth, and how he could convince stones to do his bidding. Once, he used it to heal me."

"He did?" Leran asked, to which Asherah nodded. He'd never realized the Sala could heal. "Did he ever tell you... Do you know how the stones upon the Sala work?"

"Each corresponds to an aspect of the king. An aspect of you." Asherah regarded him for a moment. "Is there something specific you want to know? Otherwise, we could—"

"When did the heartstone change?" Leran interrupted.

"I don't really know," she replied. "He said he heard the Sala speaking to him long before he realized what he felt for me. He tried to ignore it, assuming it would go away."

"But it didn't."

"No, it didn't. Then, whenever I was near him, the heartstone would change color; by the time he worked up the nerve to put the Sala on me, it was bright orange." Asherah laughed softly. "That was the day I met you."

"The day you came to The Seat?" Leran asked.

"If you hadn't approved, he would not have asked me to be his mate," she said, and it was Leran's turn to laugh.

"The moment he returned to The Seat, he told me he had chosen a mate. The next morning, I met you."

"I never knew that," Asherah murmured. She took advantage of Leran's relaxed demeanor, and touched his forearm. "How long has the heartstone been pink?"

"Since yesterday. She noticed it before I did." He glanced up, and marveled that while he would not call her his mother, her black eyes could still draw words from him. "Ember."

"Aeolmar's daughter," Asherah murmured. "She's a lovely girl. If..." she paused, choosing her words with care. "If I had a son who took Ember as his mate, I would be very pleased."

Leran nodded, then he shuffled through the maps on the table. "You and your maps," he mumbled, "just like Da." He was silent for another moment. "Why am I your heir?"

"Oh, Leran, you know why," Asherah replied.

"Shouldn't your heir be your son?" he pressed. "Hells, shouldn't he be the one you wish upon Ember?"

"Finn can choose who he wishes for a mate," Asherah said. "He was born the same day as Ember, and since they've had their whole lives to choose each other, and haven't, I imagine that they will remain apart. As to why you remain my heir, I believe that you, being Lord of Tingu, would well and truly defend Parthalan in the event of my death." Leran said nothing, choosing instead to stare at the Sala. "If you want, I will remove you," she offered, but Leran didn't hear her.

"Is the Sala ever wrong?"

"Not according to your father."

Leran was silent for a moment, contemplating the Sala. "When did you know that you loved Da? Was it when you first saw him?"

Asherah smiled at the memory. "The first time I saw Lormac, I was an escaped slave wearing gear that I'd stolen along the way to Tingu. He was sitting upon that wooden throne he kept at the Keep, his legs too long for the small chair and his knees bent up past his waist." Asherah paused, and added, "He looked ridiculous."

Leran smiled. "We still have that wooden throne."

"That monstrosity would be better used as kindling. But that was how I met him. After we pled our cause, he stood, and he offered to help us, and I thought he was the kindest, most amazing man I had ever met. I don't know if I loved him on that day, but I certainly admired him."

Leran looked her in the eye, and finally asked something he'd wanted to know for quite a while. "And your king?"

"We met during a battle. It was in Finlay's home village, on the edge of the desert. There were demons everywhere, and hunters and villagers alike were fighting for their lives, but I saw Finlay and I ran to him. I couldn't bear the thought of him hurt, even when I had yet to meet him." She watched Leran for a moment as he stroked the heartstone. "Is that how you feel about Ember? That you desire her safety above all else?"

"I... I don't know. Yes, I want her safe, and happy, and..." He stopped short of sharing how he had been imagining Ember nestled in his bed. "I can't stop thinking about her."

"Is it speaking to you?"

The question startled him, but only for a moment. Of course, she would know that. The Sala had never spoken to him, not even once. Leran didn't know why he was denied this aspect, but suspected it had to do with his impure blood.

"No, it is not," he replied. Asherah nodded, unaware that she was the only one privy to the fact that the Sala no longer spoke to the Lord of Tingu.

"Then go to her. Spend time with her. See what comes of it." Leran nodded absently. "Leran, you are a good man, just as Lormac was. I'm certain that Ember can see that about you." Leran smiled tightly at Asherah, then asked her something he'd wondered almost as long as he could remember.

"Do you still miss him? I know you have your king, but do you still feel anything for Da?" It seemed to Leran that if love was the force others made it out to be, Asherah never would have taken another mate.

Asherah rose and circled the table. "Every day, I wish he were here with me. One of the two worst days of my life was when he died."

"And the other?"

"When I told you he was gone." Asherah smoothed Leran's hair from his brow; to Leran's surprise, he let her. "Leran, please believe me that I loved your father more than my life, and I love him still."

"How does your king feel about that?" Leran asked with a smirk.

"He understands," Asherah replied in a tone that made him wonder how the King of Parthalan truly felt. "Now go. Seek out your maiden."

With that, Leran rose, and Asherah escorted him to the door of her chamber. He paused for a moment, then turned his attention back to the only mother he had ever known.

"Thank you," he said. "I appreciate your counsel."

"Of course," Asherah said. "I'm always here for you."

Leran nodded, acutely aware that his pride had been the sole force standing between him and the only parent he had left to him. Not for the first time he felt a tremendous surge of guilt, and wanted nothing more than to lay his head in Asherah's lap, share his thoughts and fears with her, and let her tell him that all would be well. Instead, he smiled tightly at the one who still bore the title Lady of Tingu, and he and his pride left.

Chapter Twenty-One

Latera speaks

I'd spent the morning in the archive, which was where I'd spent most of the prior day, as well. Even though a large amount of books and scrolls had been delivered to Sibeal's chambers, none had the information I sought, and I'd nearly driven the keeper mad with my requests. First, I requested anything with information about the old gods, then Ysr, and finally I'd asked for maps of Thurnda's trade routes. The keepers of the archive had grumbled, but fulfilled every one of my requests.

As a result, I'd assembled more information than I could conceivably review and understand during the short time we'd be in Thurnda. Therefore, I was compiling everything of note and sending it to the smartest person I'd ever met: my sister, Wren. With Sibeal's approval, of course.

Despite the hard work, and more difficult subject matter, I was enjoying myself. I'd always enjoyed research, and a day spent in the archive was a good day, in my opinion. I suppose books were to me as maps were to our erstwhile goddess, Asherah.

The keeper admitted someone, then footsteps approached my table. I looked up from my parchment and saw Asherah herself.

"Hello, Asherah," I greeted.

"Hello, yourself. Sibeal said I'd find you here." Asherah sat across from me, and surveyed the stacks of information I'd amassed. "What are you looking for?"

"What aren't I looking for?" I countered. "Information on Caol'non, maps of Ysr, the old gods... "

"The old gods? Why are you researching them?"

Of course, those were the two words she latched on to. I took a calming breath, and replied, "Caol'non claims they're still worshipped on Ysr." She frowned at my admittedly vague response. "Asherah, strange things are happening, and it's not just Caol'non. Why are so many odd events converging?"

"You mean Cerillia?" she asked, and I nodded. "It is passing strange that she wants to be Lady of Thurnda. There is absolutely no way that could happen, since the title is passed from mother to daughter. As Thurndians, both Senan and Cerillia should be quite aware of the fact that whomever the next Lady will be, it won't be her."

"About that." I folded my hands on the table. "Sibeal wants to name me, and therefore Mara and Ember, as her heirs."

Asherah blinked. "That is... That is interesting. What do you and the girls think about that?"

"I haven't told the girls," I admitted. "As for me, I agreed, but I hope I'm never called upon to act as the Lady."

Asherah nodded. "You've heard that those of Thurnda and Tingu like to keep close, yes?"

"Yes. You said it yourself, back at Teg'urnan."

"So I did. If your daughters became the heirs to Thurnda, and then one went on to become the Lady of Tingu..." Asherah paused, which was unfortunate because I had no idea what she was getting at.

"How would Mara become the Lady of Tingu?" I asked at length.

"Not Mara. Ember."

"But for that to happen—" The pieces fell into place. "Leran and Ember?"

"He came to me for advice. He's quite smitten with Ember."

And who wouldn't be? Ember was intelligent, and vibrant, and a joy to be around... And she had a big, loving, fragile heart. I remembered the last time her heart was broken, and how long it had taken her to put the pieces back together. I didn't want to see her hurt again.

However, she was grown now, and didn't need her mother's protection.

"Ember hasn't mentioned anything, but that's not surprising," I demurred. "It's only been a few days. Let's see how things go before we start planning the coronation feast." I sorted a few of my papers. "How is Finn doing?"

"He seems well," Asherah replied. "I believe he was hoping for a warmer reception from Leran."

"Perhaps he can challenge Tor to a match and attempt to win a troll sword from Leran."

"No," Asherah said, making a cutting motion with her hand. "Absolutely not."

I smiled; no one protected their child with the fierceness of the Faerie Queen, though I did wish she would let Finn live a little. "Come now. Finn's quite good with a sword."

Asherah glared at me. "Enough of that. You're as bad as Aeolmar."

"That's awful! Take that back."

Chapter Twenty-Two

That evening's celebration was much like the one before; long, loud, and full of joy, but Leran wanted it to end as soon as he entered. Cerillia had organized the event down to the tiniest detail, and Ember was seated so far away from him she may as well have been in Teg'urnan. He knew that if he moved his seat, it would upset Cerillia, and it wouldn't do to agitate a lady at her own mating feast. So Leran remained where he was, and regretted the good manners his father had instilled in him.

Leran leaned back in his chair, and watched Ember over the rim of his goblet as he considered Asherah's advice. She told Leran to get to know Ember, but he felt that he already knew everything that mattered: she was the daughter of the *deva'shi* and First Hunter, and once these Thurndian festivities ended, she would return to Teg'urnan while he went back to his life of battle and bloodshed. Pursing her would be a wasted effort, since soon enough they'd be separated by both land and politics. Then Ember's laugh floated across the hall toward him, the bright notes wrapping themselves around his heart the way he had wrapped his arms around her that morning on the battlement. Perhaps he could divine a way to extend his time with Ember, but for how long?

As the remains of the meal were carried away, and goblets were refilled, musicians came forth and the guests began to dance. Senan and Cerillia were the first to rise, followed by Sibeal and a young warrior Leran assumed was her latest lover. He looked down the long table toward Ember, and saw that she and her sister were both pestering Aeolmar to dance with them. He claimed to hate the act and denied having ever danced, when Latera quietly reminded him that he had danced with her in this very hall. Thus admonished, Aeolmar accepted Mara's outstretched hand and led his elder daughter to the center of the floor, closely followed by Latera and their son, Tor. Ember laughed as she watched the four of them bumble about, for apparently there was no dancing in Teg'urnan, when a young elf stepped forward and asked Ember to dance.

Leran fought the urge to leap to his feet and order the man away from her, but Ember graciously took his hand with nary a glance in the Lord of Tingu's direction. She laughed and flirted as she spun and twirled about the dance floor, exchanging her first partner for another, and then another, all while Leran's blood quietly simmered away. When one of Leran's own warriors approached Ember, he had had enough and strode directly to her side.

"May I?" Leran asked, all but ignoring the warrior as he backed away, stammering an apology.

"Chasing men from me now?" she asked with that coy smile of hers.

"It was my turn." Leran drew her against him as his feet followed the steps of their own accord; the tune was common enough, and he had heard and danced to it many times.

"You don't dress like an elf," Leran murmured as he glided his hand down her back. Instead of the stiff, many-layered gowns favored by elfin women, Ember was clad in filmy blue silk that loosely enveloped her form, and his hands told him that she likely avoided elfin chemises and corsets as well.

"I don't," she agreed. "Do you like my dress?" They had reached to a point in the dance where the woman twirled away from her partner, only to have the man sweep her back into his arms. As Ember gracefully completed the maneuver, her thin dress flowing like water over the soft curves of her body, Leran realized how much he appreciated the fae style of dress.

"You're a vision," he replied as he gathered her against him. "The loveliest woman here, by far." Her cheeks darkened, and she hid her face against his chest.

"My lord jests," she said, her words muffled by his tunic. The song ended, and partners were exchanged as the musicians began the next tune. No man approached Ember, so Leran took up the next dance with her.

"No one attempts to cut in on the Lord of Tingu," Ember observed. "You have me all to yourself."

"Good," he replied, and they completed that dance, and the next, after which the musicians laid down their instruments. Ember curtsied low to Leran, and he kissed her cheek, as was customary for a dance partner to do.

"Wait a moment, then follow me," Ember whispered, then she walked briskly toward the rear of the hall. Leran was intrigued, but did as he was told. He strode back to the table and emptied his goblet, then, having decided that he had waited long enough, set off in search of Ember. He couldn't image she had gotten far. As he passed one of the wide pillars at the back of the hall he heard a familiar giggle, and turned to find Ember hiding behind it.

"Why such secrecy?" Leran murmured as he captured her in his arms.

"I wondered if you would chase me," Ember replied.

"Now that I've caught you, what is to be my prize?"

Ember stood on her toes and laced her fingers behind his neck. "Whatever you'd like."

Leran traced her lower lip with his thumb; her lips were soft, softer than anything he had ever touched. Then he felt her fingers weave through his hair and he could hold himself back no longer. He bent to kiss her, so eager she yelped. Then the yelp became a moan, and then she was silent as she kissed him back. Leran lifted her up to make them more of a height, trapping her against the pillar. One hand went to the nape of her neck while the other caressed her thigh, his hips bracing her against the hard stone.

I could claim her right here. Leran nuzzled her neck, both of his hands now gripping her hips. The rest of the revelers lingered at the far end of the hall, and the width of the pillar effectively hid Leran and Ember from view.

Of course, he wouldn't claim her in the back of a hall. She deserved to be laid upon a bed of the finest silks, or spring flowers; as Leran traced the hollow of Ember's throat with his tongue, he imagined her nestled among soft, white furs. Yes, he would lay her on a bed of white fur, then he would lose himself in her, lose himself deeply and never let her go...

"My lord."

Leran ignored the words; if whoever was speaking couldn't see that he was busy, they were clearly blind as well as stupid.

"My lord, I must speak with you."

Leran now recognized the voice as belonging to Balthus, who was neither blind nor stupid, but very annoying. He waved his commander away without taking his mouth from Ember's soft lips.

"My lord!"

"What!" Leran snapped as he spun to face Balthus, keeping Ember in his arms as he did so.

"Forgive me, my lord," Balthus apologized, "but a northern matter needs your attention."

Leran sighed in frustration. The only northern matter that came to mind was the endless encroaching of the mountain trolls, which was something Leran should deal with at once. However, that did not mean he had to enjoy the intrusion. He nodded to his commander, then turned to Ember.

"Little flame, will you forgive me for leaving you?" he murmured as he caressed her cheek with his thumb. "I am assuming that the situation must be very, very dire," he added, glaring at Balthus.

"I will," she replied, "but only this once." Leran smiled as he kissed her wrist, a smile that quickly faded as she disappeared toward the guest's quarters.

"Well? What's so important?" Leran demanded once she had turned a corner. "Has the *mordeth-gall* risen from his grave?"

"The mountain trolls have regrouped, and once again move toward Tingu's borders," Balthus stated.

"How many?"

"At least a hundred, possibly two. They're on foot, and will reach the northern border within a moon."

"The garrison at the border can ably handle that number," Leran stated, annoyed that he had cut short his time with Ember for such mundane news. Even if the garrison couldn't handle the trolls, Thurnda was only a three-day ride from The Seat. Disgusted, Leran walked back toward the revelers; perhaps he could filch a bottle of wine and meet Ember in her chamber.

"My lord, they are joined by orcs."

Leran halted, and turned to face Balthus, he who had ably led Tingu's warriors since his father's reign. The wizened commander looked haggard and a shade paler than normal, something only the threat of orcs could accomplish. "Orcs?"

"Yes. There are at least one thousand, maybe more. They approach from the north, and from the east." Balthus placed his hands on Leran's shoulders. "We need to return to The Seat at once."

Leran nodded; one thousand orcs was the stuff of nightmares. He wished it was only a *mordeth-gall* that threatened his home. "Not until after the feast in four nights' time."

"Leran, we cannot wait!" Balthus hissed. He continued in a softer tone, "Forgive me, my lord, but time is of the essence."

"If we leave prior to that, it will look suspicious, and Asherah may learn of the orcs. I'll not have the Faerie Queen meddling in Tingu's affairs." Balthus frowned, but did not dispute.

"Very well. I'll make the arrangements."

And so it was Balthus that walked with Leran to his chamber; the Lord of Tingu would have no leisurely evening spent with Ember before a warm fire. As Balthus settled before the makeshift map table, Leran rummaged for a flagon of rum, then sat heavily before the fire as he quaffed the fiery liquid straight from the bottle. He made a face as it burned his throat, and passed the bottle to Balthus.

Orcs. It would have to be orcs. Such terrible monsters encroaching on Tingu's borders made him feel that he was an incompetent ruler, unable to keep his homeland safe, and a poor heir to his father's legacy. He thought of all these things as he stared into the flames, but realized that what bothered him most of all was that he was leaving Ember behind.

***

Latera, dancing with her son, watched as her younger daughter danced with the Lord of Tingu, all the while remarking that she had never seen Leran smile so freely. Of course, he hadn't been smiling a few moments ago, when Ember had been in someone else's arms. And the way Leran had stalked up to the pair, glowering at the young elf as if he had committed some terrible affront.

Then the song changed, and Aeolmar cut in on Tor much as Leran had cut in on Ember's prior partner. Tor frowned but said nothing; after all, what boy wants to dance with his mother all night? As she settled into her mate's arms, Latera noted that Leran and Ember remained a couple. Before she could fully contemplate the implications of their closeness, Aeolmar spoke.

"Remember when we spent two seasons here?" he murmured against her hair.

"Those were wonderful days," Latera said wistfully, resting her cheek against his chest. "No demons, no surprise relations popping up…"

"No Teg'urnan," Aeolmar added. He led her about to the music for a time before he spoke again. "Would you like to remain in Thurnda?"

"That again? I thought we'd agreed to stay in the palace. For Asherah."

"We did, but…" Aeolmar closed his eyes, and rested his forehead against the top of Latera's head. "Forgive me, beloved. I only wish to live a quiet life with you, far from anything that could do you harm."

Latera smiled, and kissed the bottom of his chin. "We couldn't come to Thurnda, not with Sibeal planning to name me her heir. Senan would have a fit."

"Senan's a fool," Aeolmar grumbled. Latera thumped his chest; one really shouldn't speak ill of a man at his mating feast. "We don't have to live here, in the palace. I'll build you a home anywhere you'd like." Latera shut her eyes, and imagined a cozy home full of her mate and children.

"Ember seems to like it here well enough, and I think Mara would be happy anywhere," Latera replied. "Has Tor mentioned anything?"

"Since he won a troll sword, he thinks he's an elfin hero." Latera stifled a laugh. "And the girls are giving him quite a bit of attention."

"Quite." Aeolmar jerked his head to the side, and Latera located her son. He was standing near the tables, and he was indeed surrounded by many unattached elfin maidens. Close by him was Mara, doing her best to remain invisible. It pained Latera to see Mara hold herself away from others, but she understood her reticence. She had certainly never put herself in a man's path, not even during the many winters she had been separated from Aeolmar.

Then Finn approached Mara, and the two struck up a conversation. As much as she'd like Mara to find a companion of her own, at least she had her friendship with Finn.

Latera's motherly gaze continued about of the room, and found that Ember still danced with Leran. She remembered what Asherah's told her about Leran's attraction to Ember, and smiled. Perhaps a move north would suit her children in many ways.

"Have you spoken to Asherah about this?" Latera asked.

"No," Aeolmar replied. "I don't know how to begin that conversation."

Latera nodded; the music ended, and she watched Leran tenderly kiss Ember's cheek. Ember whispered in Leran's ear, then she exited the hall; a few moments later, Leran followed. "Difficult it may be, but you should speak to her soon," Latera murmured. "Things seem to be happening."

"Yes, they do." Latera followed Aeolmar's gaze, and saw Balthus enter the hall, his face grim and determined. He watched Leran follow Ember, and set off after them with a scowl worthy of the First Hunter. A few moments later, Balthus and Leran reentered the hall, with Ember nowhere in sight.

"What do you think that's all about?" asked Aeolmar. He and Latera had returned to their seats, and were waiting for the *saffira* to refill their goblets.

"I do not know," Latera murmured, "but I imagine nothing pleasant." Aeolmar nodded in assent, and said that he would speak with Leran. Latera hardly heard him, her mind swirling with the images of the past evening, one question overriding all others: *Why does Balthus dislike my daughter?*

***

Mara watched her parents dance together, how they smiled and teased each other as their movements flowed effortlessly. They were a perfect match, her mother and father were, and Mara had grown up believing she would easily find a partner that loved her as much as her parents loved one another. Her reality had been somewhat different.

The group next to her gasped aloud; her brother, Tor, was relaying how he'd bested their father and won a troll sword. Only, the way Mara had heard the story, it had been a draw. Before she could say as much, Finn sat beside her.

"Tor's in his element, eh?" Finn noticed that Mara's cup was empty, and signaled a *saffira*. "He always was a showman."

"If by showman, you mean someone relating a completely different version of events than what actually happened, then yes, he is." The *saffira* refilled their cups, and Mara murmured her thanks. "Really, the way Tor's going on, soon he'll have saved Thurnda from a host of dragons."

Finn snorted. "Believe me, anyone who's ever seen Aeolmar fight understands that Tor's embellishing things a bit."

"More than a bit," Mara grumbled. "Will you challenge him next?"

"Ah, no. For one thing, Mother wouldn't be pleased."

"And, what's the other thing?"

"I fear I'm not as good with a sword as I'd like to be. If Tor actually beat me, I'd never hear the end of it."

More gasps distracted Mara. Tor had risen from his seat and was miming a great, arching blow, the sort of blow Aeolmar frequently used against his adversaries. Suddenly, Tor lowered his arms, and smiled.

"And that's when Leran declared me the winner," Tor said, as the rest applauded. Mara rolled her eyes.

"Ember said Leran stopped the fight because Mother asked him to," Mara whispered to Finn. "Apparently Leran declared Finn the winner to spare his pride. That, and Papa already has two troll swords."

Finn nodded toward something across the hall. Mara followed his gaze, and saw Leran dancing with Ember. "Perhaps he did it for Ember," Finn suggested.

"Perhaps." Mara watched the two dance, then part. Ember left the hall, and after a moment Leran set out after her. Mara wondered if they thought they'd fooled anyone with that ruse.

"Everyone pairs off so easily," she murmured. "Everyone, but me."

"Did you come to Thurnda looking to, um, pair off?" Finn asked.

She glanced at him, saw that the tips of his ears had pinked. "No, not in the slightest. I've already accepted I'll be alone for a long, long time. Perhaps forever."

"We can be alone together," Finn offered, then he frowned. "Although, if we're alone together, we won't really be alone."

Hesitantly, Mara set her hand atop Finn's. After a moment, he turned his hand palm up and laced his fingers with hers.

"Alone together, to the end," she said.

Finn squeezed her hand. "To the end."

Chapter Twenty-Three

Leran hurried through the corridors, his mind reeling from a meeting with yet another messenger, the third that night alone; true to their position, every scout stationed near the northern border had sent word to Leran at the slightest hint of danger. If Leran never saw another messenger, drenched with sweat and fear, it would be too soon.

The latest messenger had arrived in the small hours of the night. A boy barely large enough to ride a horse had stood panting and wheezing as he gave his grim news: the mountain trolls showed no sign of retreating. Worse, the estimation of the orcs' numbers had more than doubled.

Foul, foul beasts, orcs were. The result of a troll magically breeding with a demon, orcs were the vilest creature Leran had ever encountered. Their hides were tougher than a troll's, and instead of blood or sweat, they constantly oozed—or spurted, or sprayed—ichor, a grayish-green, caustic liquid. Unlike mountain trolls, orcs appeared incapable of higher thought and served as little more than the mountain trolls' cannon fodder.

Leran's grandsire, L'hirre, had smashed the cauldron in which orcs were created, then he'd pushed the mountain trolls back beyond the Northern Waste, but had stopped short eradicating the race. He believed that all creatures, even terrible ones, deserved life, just far from his land, and once the mountain trolls were bereft of their monstrous army, they weren't as much of a threat. His father had felt the same way and had concentrated on keeping Tingu's northern border strong. While both his father and grandsire were still revered as great leaders, neither had foreseen that shortly after Lormac's death a dark sorcerer would unlock Nibika'al's secret of how to cross the mountain trolls with demons, and create a force of slavering, mindless orcs roaming across the frozen landscape.

What's more, these orcs seemed to have been organized by the mountain trolls, and were preparing to launch an offensive against Tingu. While mountain trolls had proven to be cunning adversaries many times over, Leran wondered whose handiwork this really was. He began to list his enemies... and stopped, for the list was long and disheartening, even to him.

Leaving off contemplation of his enemies, for now, Leran concentrated on the facts he knew to be true: he needed to return to The Seat, but he wanted to bide his time and wait for the conclusion of Senan and Cerillia's mating rites. He did not want to risk alerting Asherah to the invasion of orcs, and his long struggles against the mountain trolls that he had so carefully kept hidden from her all these winters.

His imminent departure also meant that he would be leaving Ember behind. He wasn't certain that he wanted to leave her at all, and after the talk he had with Asherah two days ago, he was considering asking Ember to accompany him back to Tingu. If what Asherah had said was true, that the heartstone of the Sala was only a reflection of the king's heart, then he didn't want Ember out of his sight, much less half a world away.

Leran absently touched the Sala, felt the heartstone's warmth. What he wanted was Ember by his side, permanently, and he was prepared to do anything to make that happen.

However, first he needed to learn how Ember felt about the matter. To that end, Leran rushed through the palace, which was empty and dark since the elder sun hadn't even thought about rising. Ember had been pleased to walk with him two days ago, and he hoped to please her somewhat more today. When he reached her door, he knocked softly, wary of waking her sister.

"Enter," came Ember's voice through the heavy wood. He did, and found her seated in the center of the room, facing the door. She was wearing a crimson dress, and her white cloak was neatly draped across her lap. "I've been waiting for you."

"How did you know I would come?" he asked.

"I didn't, but I hoped you might," she replied. "I thought it best to be ready." Leran closed the distance between them and took both of her hands in his. He kissed her knuckles, then turned her hands over and kissed her wrists; he wondered if she knew that elfin men only greeted their lovers in such a manner.

"Walk with me, my sweet little flame?" he asked. Ember smiled as she rose, and allowed Leran to settle her cloak about her shoulders. Then he extended his arm, and they moved through the sleeping castle, upward to the battlements.

"Have you brought your guard?" she asked.

"I let them sleep." Leran opened the door to the battlement, and they were met by a cold, gray rain; being that Ember's chamber was in the center of the palace, neither had been aware that the skies had opened up.

"No matter, we can walk in the rain," Ember said, but Leran was not about to let her suffer a drenching. He wrapped an arm about her waist, resting his chin on her shoulder as he pushed the door shut.

"Why don't we go to my chamber, instead?" he murmured, his lips against her ear.

"Why don't we walk indoors?" she countered, freeing herself from his embrace. She moved to retrace their steps down the corridor, but he caught her elbow.

"We won't be alone," he promised. "Aldo will be there, and other *saffira* as well. If you'd like, you can go and wake Mara." He caressed her cheek, tucking a stray curl behind her ear. "If we do end up the sole occupants of my chamber, you needn't fear me. I don't go where I'm not invited."

"Oh?" Ember asked, arching a delicate brow. "What of the many tales of elfin virility? All falsehoods?"

"All true," he corrected. Leran enjoyed her taunts, more so when he turned them around on her. Instead of taking offense she laughed, so Leran silenced her by claiming her lips in the dark corridor. She wound her fingers into his hair, so tightly so she nearly pulled it from his scalp. He didn't care if she rendered him bald, not so long as he was kissing her.

After a time they parted, breathless and clutching each other, and Ember asked, "Is that how you mean to kiss me in your chamber?"

"Only if you'll allow it." After a journey through the palace that was short in distance but endless for its silence, Leran ushered Ember inside his chamber. Aldo was busy laying out the morning meal, and once he saw Ember he set about procuring her a plate.

"Wait here a moment." Leran disappeared into the chamber beyond, then emerged with a few quiet instructions for Aldo. Ember obediently waited by the entrance, her peaked brows betraying that Leran's behavior intrigued her.

"This way, little flame," he called, and Ember entered the rear chamber to find that Leran had drawn back the heavy curtains and brought the cushioned benches that normally sat before the hearth around to face the windows. The windows were spectacular in that there were no mullions, but rather uninterrupted panes of glass that went from the floor to the arched ceiling.

"The room faces east, so if the clouds break, we'll be able to see the suns," Leran explained.

"This apartment is amazing," Ember said, looking about the room. The front chamber was as large as the entire suite she shared with her sister, and Leran had not only the front room and this private sitting area, but also a sprawling bedchamber as well as a separate room for Aldo. "Sibeal's chambers must encompass half the palace."

"Hers are not as large as these." Ember turned her questioning gaze to him, so he elaborated, "These rooms are solely used by the Lord of Tingu. I may not be king of all the elfin lands as my father was, but the title still brings me a measure of respect."

"More than a measure," Ember said. She sat next to him on the couch, then Aldo set a table before them and proceeded to lay out enough food to feed half of Thurnda.

"Just let him," Leran whispered when she protested that he was overfilling her plate. "He's very set in his ways."

"How old is he?" she asked, not as discretely as she should have, but then Aldo was more than a little deaf.

"No one knows," Leran replied. "Some say he cared for Nexa's children."

"I could believe it," Ember murmured. She settled back against the deep cushions, and watched the wizened man pile her plate high with grilled meats and fruit, along with almost an entire loaf of bread. Once Aldo was satisfied that she wouldn't go hungry, he turned his attention to Leran, heaping twice again as much on his lord's plate. "Would you like to know something? I'm not even hungry," Ember murmured.

"Neither am I," Leran whispered back, then turned to his chamberlain. "Thank you, Aldo," he said with genuine sincerity. The ancient elf bowed and departed; as soon as he was gone, Leran stood and grabbed a plain earthenware pitcher, out of place among the gold and jeweled plates. Carefully, he poured a steaming liquid into a bowl, then offered it to Ember.

"What is this?" she asked as she accepted the vessel.

"Selka. It's like tea, but stronger," he replied. "It will chase the chill from your bones." He watched as she hesitantly sipped, then wrinkled her nose. "It takes some getting used to," he admitted. "I can add honey, if it's too strong."

"It's good," she murmured as she set the bowl on the table. "Bitter, but good." She raised her head, gazing wistfully at the rain lashing the windows. "I wish it was snowing."

"Do you?" Leran asked. "Most wish to see the sun."

"I've never seen falling snow," she said. Ember described the sloppy, wet winters that regularly visited Teg'urnan, but Leran hardly heard her. The mention of snow brought his thoughts back to his homeland, and that he would soon leave Thurnda.

"I must tell you, little flame, I need to return to Tingu," Leran said.

"Today?" she asked.

"Not today, but soon," he replied. "I'll attend the Child's Feast this evening, but preparations are already underway for our departure. We will probably leave directly after the celebration's conclusion in four nights."

"Oh." Ember stared at her hands, and fidgeted with a ring. "I knew you would leave. Tingu needs its Lord there, not away in Thurnda, not..." Ember's voice trailed off as her head dipped forward, her fiery curls obscuring her face.

"As you say, Tingu needs me." *I need you.* Leran reached out to stroke her cheek, moving aside the weight of her tresses so he could see her eyes. He liked that she didn't wear her hair in the elaborate elfin coifs that were fashionable in Thurnda, and that she found the ornate hairstyles as foolish as he did. It was but one of the many aspects of Ember that drew him toward her, like a moth to a flame. "Come with me."

Ember gasped as her head snapped upright. Her face betrayed that she assumed he was joking, as if he wasn't as serious as he had ever been. "I couldn't."

"Why not?" he asked as he drew her into his arms. "I don't want to be apart from you just yet." Ember's eyes traveled down the length of his body, eventually settling on the Sala.

"It's gone the color of my hair," she murmured as she touched the heartstone. "Why does it keep getting darker?"

"You are the reason," Leran proclaimed. "The more time I spend with you, the darker it gets."

"Me? Why me?"

"When I spoke with Asherah, she said—" he began

"You spoke to the queen?" Ember interrupted. "Did you tell her that the stone changes for me?"

"I did," he confirmed. "She's one of the few who remembers my father when he—"

"Fool!" Ember erupted from Leran's arms as she got to her feet. "Do you know who the queen's closest, dearest companion is? My father!" She walked to the windows, staring at the gray rain with her arms wrapped about her waist.

"Ember, you're a woman grown," Leran murmured as he moved to stand behind her. When she wouldn't turn around, he placed his hands on her shoulders, and she leaned into the warmth of him. "He cannot forbid you to be with me."

"He won't forbid me. He'll kill you for touching me. " At last, she faced him. "Mara once had a suitor—once. My father hated him, and now she lives her chaste life as cloistered as any priestess. Why do you think I glance at you over my shoulder, try to get you to follow me away from the others?"

"I didn't care why the chase happened, not so long as I caught you," Leran said as he wrapped his arms around her. "Ember, I'm not afraid of your father. You yourself said that he's not nearly as bad as he pretends to be."

"That was when I was trying to get you to show interest in me," she mumbled into his chest.

"You were?" he asked.

"You knew I was." Ember let him pull her back to the couch and arranged herself in the crook of his arm.

"Let me show you my home," Leran murmured against her hair. "Bring Aeolmar. Bring your whole family, if you'd like. They're all welcome."

"But then what?" she asked quietly. "I live in Teg'urnan. Eventually, I'll have to go home."

He stared at her, for she spoke the truth he was trying to ignore. The faerie palace was far from The Seat; it took eighteen days to reach Teg'urnan on horseback, and that was only if the weather cooperated. Leran also knew that he loved her, no matter that he hadn't known her a full sennight, and he couldn't let her go.

"You could stay," he said. "Make Tingu your home."

"Leran, why would I..." She pursed her lips, then asked carefully, "Why would I do that?"

"You could be my mate. My Lady," he said, the words falling from his lips before his mind understood what he was saying. He did not retract them, nor did he wish to. "Yes, stay and be my mate."

"Leran, you've known me *four days*," Ember said. "Five, if you count this morning!"

"Tell me how many days I must know you, then, to know that you're meant to be mine?" he asked. "Ten? Twenty? One hundred? Then, on the hundred and first, I'll ask you again." Ember stared at him, her delicate brows nearly touching.

"You're serious," she murmured. Leran tried to continue, but she held up her hand. "Please give me a moment to contemplate that the Lord of Tingu has just asked me to become his mate."

Leran watched as Ember moved out of his arms. Then she took the bowl of selka from the table and settled back to sip it. He wondered if she wished for a cup of something stronger.

"Leran," she began, "it's not that I don't want to go to The Seat. Or be with you, for that matter. It's just an awfully big decision to make, knowing one for so short a time." She took a rather large gulp of the selka. "We haven't even lain together." Leran raised an eyebrow, and cocked his head toward the open door of his bedchamber. "That wasn't what I meant!"

"Then, what?" he asked. Ember looked away when she replied.

"All those stories," she murmured, "all those women... What if you haul me off to Tingu, and I disappoint you?"

"All what women?" Leran asked. "What sort of stories do you fae tell about me?"

"There aren't any about you, not like that, but everyone knows about Madoc'na," she replied, referencing the celebration of life that was held on the eve of battle. "And the stories we do tell are all about your many battles. Many, many battles."

Her voice trailed off, and Leran tilted her youthful face toward him, wondering how inexperienced she was. One as lovely as she, with her unusual fire-colored hair and fine features, surely couldn't be bereft of suitors, but the fae did value chastity. It was something Leran had never quite understood; why deny oneself pleasure so easily gotten?

The occasional woman was Leran's only indulgence, and virginity had never mattered to him one way or the other; in fact, he preferred a bedmate that knew her way around a man. More, he wasn't fond of breaking maidens, though as king he was occasionally called upon for the task. But then he hadn't cared for any of those other women, not as deeply as he cared for Ember. As he gazed into her crystal blue eyes, he hoped he would be her next and last lover.

"Worry not about the past," he said. "Of course, if the prospect of my disappointment concerns you so, go lay with a few of my men. Then we'll be on more even footing."

"You'd let your warriors at me?"

"Truly?" He caressed her cheek, drawing her face close to his. "I'd kill anyone who touched you." Her eyes widened, but her playful tone remained.

"Then, since your most generous suggestion is out of the question, I see no solution to our problem," she said lightly.

"The solution is for you to say yes," Leran said. Ember broke his gaze and stared into the selka; she didn't drink it, but rather clutched the bowl like a shield. Leran got to his feet and moved a few paces away. "I don't mean to be so forceful," he said at length.

"Well, you are." Ember set the bowl upon the table and faced him, arms crossed under her breasts, and he saw a bit of the *deva'shi's* fire in her eyes. "Is this how you've gotten your mates in the past? Ordering them into your bed?"

He ran a hand through his hair and turned away; he didn't know how to tell her he'd never had a mate, not even a lovemate. There was no shortage of women for him to choose from, and he had his favorites, but they didn't love him, and the affection he felt for them was nothing, not compared to the woman who now glowered at him. Leran crouched in front of Ember, and took her hands.

"Ember, I'm not ordering you into my bed," Leran said emphatically. "I want to know you, learn everything about you, and tell you everything about me. I want to show you my home. I want a life with you." He kissed her wrists, one after the other, his gaze locked with hers. "Come to Tingu with me. Please."

"So, you don't want me in your bed?" she asked, and he'd finally had enough.

"Perhaps I want you on the floor." She squealed as he snatched her from the couch and into his arms, but he was careful with her. He kissed her until she stopped resisting. Then, since she was so agreeable to it, he kissed her a bit longer.

"Having your way with me under the breakfast dishes," Ember admonished once they parted. "At last, your great plan comes to light."

"Not so," he murmured. "There is no plan. I only wish to sway your heart." Her cheeks darkened, and she ducked her head.

"You've already done that," she whispered against his neck.

"Have I?" Leran asked, slowly stroking her back. "My lady, your words gladden me." She laughed, and he asked her what was so funny.

"Your speech. You're so formal, even while we're rolling around under a table." She gave him a queer look, then burst out laughing once more. "Leran, you're positively grinning!"

"Am I?" he asked, his gray eyes glinting. "Tell me you'll come to Tingu, and I'll grin every day. So much so that those around me will think I've lost my mind, when really I've only lost my heart."

"Will there be seven days of feasting?" she asked. Leran moved to lean against the table leg and arranged Ember in his arms.

"Only if you want," he replied. "No one in Tingu has undergone these rites since before—" He swallowed the sudden lump in his throat. "Since my Da died."

Ember turned over his hand, lightly tracing patterns on his palm. "You called him Da?" Leran made a soft sound of affirmation. "Did he and Asherah have seven days of feasting?"

"They only had one," Leran replied. "Even so, it was more a war council than anything else. Da had no time for rituals and tradition. He always said he was too busy leading. Some say it's why he died."

A rather unladylike snort issued forth from Ember. "That is the most ridiculous notion I've ever heard. As if a few bits of food eaten on a few special plates could change the order of things."

"You don't hold to traditions?"

"Not the foolish ones." Due to her position, Ember couldn't see Leran's face, so she had no idea that he was again grinning like a fool. Her disdain for the dusty old rites was yet another reason why he felt she was meant to be his. "Is there anything else to know about these mating rites, or will you just toss me into bed?"

"Careful," he murmured, "you'll give me ideas. Most will first petition a girl's father, and if her father accepts the man, a payment will be given to her family."

"You buy her?" Ember asked incredulously, now turning to face him.

"More of a gift," he clarified. "For the gift of their daughter, the man will make an offering." He wondered what Senan had offered for Cerillia. Leran assessed her worth as two goats, nothing more. Perhaps a sheep, too.

"Too bad you don't get along with my father," Ember murmured. "If you tried to buy me, he'd likely strike you."

"I would not be buying you," Leran stated again. Understanding that path would take him nowhere, he continued his explanation. "There's also the binding of your hair."

"I don't like my hair bound," Ember said. Leran drew the length of her hair between his fingers; no, he wouldn't like it bound either.

"Then don't bind it. Leave it loose every day for all I care. Those rituals mean nothing to me." He gathered up a great handful of her hair, pressing it to his lips. "You are what matters." Leran laid his arm across her lap and aligned her wrist with his. "Once I place the Sala on you, it will be done. All will know that you're mine."

"Elves do everything so publicly," Ember said. "We fae are much more private, especially in matters of mates."

"How so?"

"Well, there is no public display," Ember began. "There was a feast when Finlay was crowned king, but he and Asherah had been mated long before that." Leran's brow furrowed; he thought Asherah had taken her new mate just before the *mordeth-gall* fell. "It was kept secret," Ember explained, sensing his confusion. "Asherah worried that Finlay would become a target for her enemies."

What sort of man hides behind his woman? Surely Asherah could have made a better choice. Leran left it for now; truly, faeries were more of a mystery than he could sort out in one morning. "If there is no feast, no anything, how does anyone know when a mating has occurred?"

"No one does. It's private, between a man and a woman." She shifted to lean her cheek against his chest, and stroked his palm. "A woman chooses her mate, then the man claims her. It's no more than that. Even if you go to the temple wishing to be bound, there is no audience, save for the High Priestess and Olluhm."

"So if I claim you now, you're mine? I grow to like these faerie ways." Ember laughed, and remained relaxed in his arms.

"Only if I choose you first," she replied. "Otherwise, it's just a bit of pleasure."

"So choose me." He kissed her brow, her nose, her lips. "Say yes," he implored. "I need you to be mine."

"Leran, it's not that I want to deny you," Ember said. "It's just an unusual situation, being that we've known one another for so short a time."

"It is strange, and sudden," he conceded, "but can it not be good, as well?"

Before she could answer, there was the sound of footsteps; Aldo, returning to clear away their uneaten food. Ember moved to rise, but Leran held her fast. "Hush," he breathed in her ear while Aldo assembled the unused plates and bowls. "He'll never know we're here."

Ember giggled at the sheer absurdity of hiding under a table with the Lord of Tingu, but Leran muffled her lips with his own. Her softness welcomed him, and neither noticed when Aldo had stopped his rattling.

"Will there be anything further, my lord?" Aldo asked, so loudly that a startled Leran banged his head on the underside of the table. "Do you require a cold compress?"

"No thank you, Aldo," Leran said ruefully. "You may go." The elder elf bowed stiffly and left. The door was hardly shut before Leran and Ember burst out laughing.

"He won't know," Ember said breathlessly. "How many times has he happened upon you as you lay on the floor?"

"A few times, though I was much smaller then," Leran replied as he wiped her cheeks with his thumb; she'd laughed so hard she cried. "Will you give me an answer today, little flame?" he asked. "Or must I wait one hundred cold nights, then ask you again?"

"An answer to which?" she asked, gazing up through her thick lashes. "Going with you to Tingu, or the other?"

"The questions are one in the same," he clarified, "but if you consent come with me to The Seat, I will wait on the other," he said as he nuzzled her neck. "Spend the day with me. It can be the first of my hundred nights."

"Won't I be in the way?"

"Never," he murmured. "I will warn you, the matters I need to deal with are both numerous and tiresome. You will likely be quite bored."

"Then whyever would I want to stay?"

"Because, my sweet, sweet flame, I cannot bring myself to let you leave, and for the good of Tingu, you should remain." He looked very serious when he continued, "The only way I can fathom handling the matters before me is if you stay close, and let me kiss you whenever no one is looking."

Ember opened her mouth to answer, but was interrupted by a yawn. "I didn't sleep last night," she murmured.

"Why not?"

"I waited up for you." Leran rose and scooped her into his arms, then he strode to his bedchamber and gently laid her on the sumptuous bed. "What are you doing?"

"Allowing you a chance to rest," he replied, brushing the hair back from her brow. "I cannot have the future Lady of Tingu falling asleep during matters of the land."

"I can't spend the day with you," Ember said, yawning again. "Senan's mate has our day planned to precision, from our noon meal to where we're seated for the Child's Feast." She went on to detail the many activities Cerillia was subjecting them to, which included the indignity of a traditional velvet gown.

"Pity," he murmured, caressing the thin fabric that covered her forearm. "I like your silk dresses."

"She means to stick me in a corset, as well," Ember grumbled.

"The woman is mad," Leran agreed. He heard the outer door open, followed by Balthus's purposeful stride. "All the more reason for you to rest now." He pulled a blanket over her, and watched as her eyes closed.

"Ember," he murmured, and her eyelids fluttered open. "Will you give me your answer tonight? I give you my word; if you don't want to remain in Tingu, I will send a retinue of my finest warriors to escort you to wherever you wish to go."

"You want to show me your home so badly?" she asked. He bent to kiss her, conveying a wealth of emotion in the soft touch.

"I do," he murmured against her lips. "I do."

"Then I will tell you tonight."

As soon as the words were spoken, Ember's eyes closed. In another moment, she was asleep. Leran smiled as he stood, gazing at the woman who was to be his. He'd had little use for women in his life of politics and battle, and he'd certainly never thought he would have a mate. But here she was, a half-elf like him who filled his heart.

His heart quivered as he gazed at his maiden; there was a real possibility that Ember would decline his offer. Leran forcibly shoved these fears to the side as he left the bedchamber. If she said no, he would simply make plans to visit Teg'urnan. Yes, once this latest incursion was put down, he would travel to Teg'urnan where he could woo Ember at his leisure, then perhaps he would invite her family to The Seat. *Yes, I will invite my kinswoman Latera, surely she will bring along her children...*

So deep he was in his plans for Ember's future, Leran was startled by Balthus's presence. He'd quite forgotten him. "Is there more news?" Leran asked his general.

"Not as of yet." Balthus looked past Leran and frowned. "You've gotten her into bed?" Leran's only reply was to shut the chamber door. "This is foolish, Leran. We've a host of orcs bearing down on us and you're lying with faeries!"

"She's only half fae," Leran defended. "Her mother is Latera."

"All the more reason you should leave her be. This could cause unneeded tension between Tingu and Parthalan."

"When did my bedchamber become your concern?" Leran snapped.

"When the woman in it distracts you from your duty," retorted Balthus. Leran grabbed him by the shoulder and forcibly moved him away from the door.

"Do not wake her," Leran warned, "and do not challenge me. I have given every moment of my life for Tingu. You know that more than anyone."

"My lord," Balthus murmured, dropping his gaze. Leran nodded; he wasn't about to make Balthus utter an actual apology. Leran moved to sit where he'd asked Ember to be his mate only a few moments ago, and poured himself and Balthus bowls of selka.

"The messenger said thousands upon thousands of orcs now roam across the northern wastes," Leran stated, easily shifting into his role as scion of Tingu. "I ask you, who has the power to control so many?"

"There isn't much to control," Balthus stated. "Their minds are little more than tundra rats, scrounging for roots and nuts. Like as not, they've just been breeding."

Leran shoved away the image Balthus's words created. "Perhaps so. Once this latest horde is put down, we should seek out their dens. A good burning should take care of them."

Balthus grunted, and went to retrieve a map of the Northern Waste. Once he was out of sight Leran leaned back and grabbed his bowl, letting the heat seep into his fingers. *I can do this. I've always won in the past. Once I've destroyed the orcs, the trolls will be a small matter. Then, I will rebuild my kingdom.*

He took a long pull of the liquid, scorching his throat but not caring. *With Ember at my side, Tingu will be rebuilt. Once I have a Lady, the elfsong will come to me. I'll yet be the man Da was.*

Chapter Twenty-Four

Ember woke shortly before noon, having dreamt of men shouting. Slowly, she crept out of Leran's bedchamber, wary of who she might find, but the apartment was vacant, save for Aldo snoring in his chair. She very much doubted that he'd been the loud voice in her dreams. After leaving her cloak draped across the bed, Ember left Leran's chamber.

She met Mara in the corridor as she walked to Cerillia's chambers. "Where have you been all morning?" Mara asked. "Any why are you so rumpled?"

"I slept in this," Ember replied. "Leran came for me before the suns rose, and then we ate together. I was so tired afterward he put me to bed."

"Bed?" Mara repeated.

"Not like that," Ember said. "I was the only one in the bed." Before she could continue, they arrived at Cerillia's chambers. Mara knocked, and Cerillia herself flung open the door.

"Ember! Mara," Cerillia said as she beckoned them inside. As ever, she was wearing her ornate golden necklace. Ember was beginning to wonder if it was a piece of jewelry, a mark of ownership, or a shackle. "We've been waiting for you!"

Ember had already suspected that Cerillia was a madwoman, and the fact was confirmed that afternoon. It seemed that she had prepared her whole life to become the mate of an elfin lord, and she was determined to have each night of the celebration be as perfect as possible.

"Her whole life revolves around catching a mate," Ember murmured to Mara. "The poor thing knows nothing except which lace goes with which velvet."

"Aren't we all like that?" Mara asked. "About preparing to be someone's mate, I mean. Isn't that what everyone wants?"

"If that's so, then why are you still ignoring Kemen?" Ember asked. When Mara didn't answer, Ember guided her sister to a stack of fabric far from Cerillia's ladies.

"Mara, I must tell you something you cannot repeat," Ember whispered. "You know where I have spent these past mornings?"

"In the Lord of Tingu's arms?" Mara said. Ember ignored her dry tone and pressed on.

"This morning, Leran asked me to go to The Seat with him," Ember said. Mara's eyes widened, but Ember continued, "He wants me to stay there with him. As his mate." Mara gasped so loudly the others looked over, and Ember pulled her farther away from them.

"Hush," she whispered. "If Papa hears of this, he will be furious!"

"He will not," Mara said. "Papa would be happy you found your mate."

"I think he would be happier if I entered the temple," Ember murmured, though that wasn't likely to happen. Ember could not imagine a worse existence than being cloistered in a few small stone rooms and grinding herbs all day. Even Mara wouldn't enjoy that, and Mara never liked to have any fun. "He wouldn't be pleased if I lived so far away."

"Not so," Mara said, shaking her head. "He wants to leave Teg'urnan."

"He does?"

"I heard him talking about it with Mother."

"Have they asked the queen?"

"Not yet. They're both worried that Asherah won't be able to handle matters without them." Ember nodded; though she'd been young at the time, she remembered well when the Faerie Queen delved into the madness that had cost her the sight in her left eye. Asherah claimed to be healed, both mentally and physically, but she had never been the same.

"I wonder where Papa will take us," Ember mumbled. "Maybe to the westlands, where he was born? That would make Tingu even farther away..."

"Ember." The seriousness of Mara's tone made her leave off her wonderings. "Do you want to go Tingu with Leran?" Ember hadn't really thought about that. She enjoyed Leran's company, of that she was certain, and she knew she would miss him terribly once he was gone. But The Seat was so far from Teg'urnan it may as well be in another realm; Ember knew Leran had only made the journey to Teg'urnan twice, both times before she was born.

All this and more swirled through Ember's mind, and she forgot to answer Mara. "If you don't want to be with him, then you need to tell him no," Mara said. "Otherwise, you're just being cruel."

Not be with him? The mere concept of not being near Leran filled her with sadness; until she'd stopped to consider her life without him, she hadn't considered her life with him. Before Ember could tell Mara that she might want to go to The Seat after all, Cerillia and her flock descended on the sisters.

"And what have you two found?" she chirped. Her voice, ever cheerful, was like a rasp to Ember's ears. She couldn't understand how Senan could stand to be in the same room with her. *Then again, they're probably not talking.*

Mara led Cerillia to a deep blue velvet gown, lovely though very, very chaste. While a few of the women tried to persuade Mara to lower the neckline just a bit, Cerillia cornered Ember. "And you?" she pressed. "What will you be wearing tonight?"

"Oh, likely something in green," Ember replied. Cerillia's chosen gown for the evening was red, so she'd decided that by dressing the rest of the ladies in varied shades of blue and green, she'd stand out all the more. While Ember would never admit to such a petty act, she'd deliberately chosen to wear crimson that morning.

"But which green frock?" Cerillia pressed, gesturing toward the heaps of gowns.

"Oh, I brought two that are green," Ember began, but Cerillia spoke over her.

"No, no, those fae dresses simply won't do," she said. "Well, not tonight anyway. Tonight is The Child's Feast, so you must dress like a proper elfin lady And," Cerillia leaned close, but still spoke loudly enough for the rest to hear, "if you want to catch an elfin king's eye, you must look like an elfin queen."

"I'm not trying to catch anyone's eye," Ember protested.

"That's because you've already caught it," said one of Cerillia's ladies. "We all saw you dance with Leran last night, and watched him chase all the other men from you," she continued in response to Ember's stare. "And, we saw the two of you disappear together."

"Disappear?" Ember murmured, then the rest surrounded her like a pack of starving dogs scrabbling toward the tiniest morsel of gossip. Their questions were so intimate that Ember blushed furiously, and Mara looked like she was about to faint.

"There is nothing between us," Ember said, when she could get a word in. "Gods, you're all babbling away like I'm carrying his babe, but we've only known each other a handful of days!"

"Forgive us," Cerillia apologized. "It's just that no one's ever known Leran to keep company with a woman. Many have tried to soften his heart, and none have succeeded, except you."

"None?" Ember repeated, and they all nodded gravely. "What about Madoc'na?"

"He has to partake in Madoc'na," was the reply from an older elf. "As Lord of Tingu, his prowess is tied to the land."

"Oh." Ember thought on that a moment. "But, what if he took a mate? Then surely he couldn't participate."

"That would be between the king and his mate, now wouldn't it?" the older elf replied, her eyes twinkling. Ember now recalled her name: Gilda. She didn't like her. "They say Leran's father always took a few women to bed, even after he was mated with Asherah."

"Asherah would never allow that," Mara gasped.

"Oh, but she did. At least, that's what my aunt told me. She was at that Madoc'na before they marched on Teg'urnan, and she remembers everything." There was a round of assertions, for apparently one's aunt was as reliable a source one could obtain with regard to the royal bedchamber. Ember tried to turn her attention back to the awful gowns when Cerillia said something else that caught her ear.

"For generations, those in power have sought to unite the royal lines of Tingu and Thurnda," Cerillia was saying. "Perhaps, it has finally come to pass."

Ember grazed her fingertips across a gown; it was dark green, the color of pine boughs, and the bodice was heavily embroidered with gold thread and intricate beadwork. It likely weighed half as much as she did, even without the many layers of undergarments that came with it.

I would never wear anything as heavy and cumbersome as this. Then she recalled Leran's grin, the way she felt when he held her, the warm heartstone of the Sala. She wondered if Leran would like to see her in a traditional elfin gown.

"Perhaps it has," she murmured.

"Not that you need the dress," Gilda smirked. "We all saw him kissing your wrist."

"What does that have to do with anything?" Ember asked.

"Come, my faerie cousin," Cerillia said knowingly as she grabbed the green gown and tugged Ember toward the seamstresses. "I've much to teach you about elfin men."

Chapter Twenty-Five

Leran slid his arms into the coat Aldo held out for him, closing his eyes as the weight settled onto his shoulders. The coat was a fine example of the embroiderer's art, being that the dark azure silk was worked with both gold and silver thread, along with many precious stones. The patterns woven into the cloth told the history of Tingu, from the moment the earth cried out in terror, to Nexa's last victory. More, the coat had belonged to Lormac.

Leran remembered seeing his father wear it, the last time being the Madoc'na before he'd gone off and died at Teg'urnan. Leran had only worn the garment once before, when he came of age and was confirmed as Lord of Tingu; his life of battle and bloodshed left him little use for such frivolities as jeweled coats. However, tonight he would have his answer, and the least he could do was look like a king when he welcomed Ember as his queen.

"Do you know anything about the Sala?" Leran asked Aldo.

"I know that whenever the heartstone darkens, a Lady will soon be named," Aldo replied in his typical rote manner. "I assume the woman in question is the one from the floor?"

"Yes, Aldo," Leran replied, his smile creeping into his voice. "Her name is Ember."

"Lady Ember," Aldo intoned. "She'll be the first with such a name." Aldo paused. "She is Lady Latera's daughter?"

"She is," Leran replied. "Both of her parents are warriors."

Aldo straightened Leran's collar. "A good bloodline for a Lady, then. You have chosen well, just as your father chose well."

Leran's throat tightened. "I am glad you think so."

"The ceremonial robes are in storage at The Seat," Aldo continued. "Shall I have them retrieved upon our return?"

"Yes, Aldo," Leran murmured, "That is an excellent notion."

His duties completed, the chamberlain bowed and left the Lord of Tingu alone with his thoughts. Leran studied his reflection, the gray eyes and brown hair that were so like Lormac's had been, but that was where the similarities ended. He didn't have his father's height, as evidenced by the coat's shortened sleeves, nor his sharp features. Leran's face had been softened by his mother's beauty, the mother he didn't remember. The mother he did remember, he'd rejected.

As he often did, Leran imagined he was speaking with his father, seeking whatever guidance he would share.

"Da, am I right to take a mate?" he asked the mirror. Leran pushed up his sleeve, then twisted the Sala so he could see the red heartstone. He understood that to make Ember his Lady, he would need to place the armband on her, at least ceremonially, though in truth he wouldn't miss its weight. Asherah had kept it for centuries after his father died—being that she remained the Lady of Tingu, it was rightfully hers—so most of his rule had been spent without it. He was once called Leran Bare-Armed in Nugt, but no longer. It's hard to speak after your tongue's been cut out.

Then Asherah sent Latera north to return The Sala, and Leran could hardly look at it. It had sat in its box, power washing out from it in waves, threatening to choke Leran by its very presence. But he put it on, just as he'd done everything else that was expected of him, and waited for the voices of his ancestors to speak to him through the armband's five sacred stones.

They didn't.

At first, Leran thought he'd put it on incorrectly, so he put it on his other forearm. Then each wrist, followed by his ankles. He even slept with it atop his chest, his neck, his belly, but it remained silent. The Sala, which should have been his link to his ancestors' much-needed wisdom, refused to speak to him.

He told no one of this silence. No, it wouldn't do to have others know that the sitting Lord of Tingu, the one who was only half an elf, was bereft of the wise council of those that went before him. He wondered what would happen if others realized his deficiencies; he imagined Balthus reclaiming his regency, and Leran being locked away until a suitable replacement was found. Only, he was Lormac's sole child, and Nexa's last living heir. There was no one else.

So he wore the object, heavy as it was, and if the sight of it inspired confidence in his men, then so be it. Now that he'd met Ember, and the heartstone darkened, Leran felt hopeful, not only that he'd found his mate, but that the Sala had finally deigned to accept him.

With a final nod to his reflection, Leran exited the room and found Balthus waiting for him. He'd been his father's most trusted commander and had served as regent while Leran grew to manhood. He hadn't been a very good regent, being that the land split across seven deep fissures, but he was a full-blooded elf. Leran often wondered how it had felt for Balthus to hand over the land to a half-breed like himself, or if Tingu would be better off with Balthus as its Lord.

"Preparations are going smoothly," Balthus said without preamble. He wasn't the sort for greetings and formality, which Leran appreciated. "If you still wish to leave quietly, we may do so the morning after the final feast."

"Good." Leran felt Balthus' gaze upon him, but assumed it was because of his wearing Lormac's coat. Others often said how similar Leran was to his father, but Leran couldn't see it.

"The faerie girl?" Balthus asked, and Leran realized it wasn't the tunic that held his attention. The coat's sleeve was still pushed up and the Sala's heartstone was still facing outward, red as a ruby.

"Her name is Ember," Leran said, as he covered the armband. "She's coming to Tingu with me," he added with more confidence than he felt.

"A host of orcs is ready to descend upon us, and you're scouting for bedmates?" Balthus asked incredulously. "You're as foolish about women as your father was."

No one, not even Balthus, was granted leave to speak ill of Lormac. "What would you have me do?" he demanded, rounding on his second. "If she is to be my mate, she will live at The Seat. If we are attacked, then our Lady is attacked along with the rest of our people. As it should be."

"Forgive me," Balthus began, "but you're sure this girl can handle such matters?"

"Her mother is the *deva'shi*," Leran replied.

"Her father is First Hunter," Balthus replied, letting the insinuation hang in the air.

"When my father met Asherah, what advice did you offer?" Leran demanded. Being that the current Lady of Tingu was a full-blooded faerie, he imagined that Ember's elf blood would be better received by his people.

"You're assuming that Lormac would have listened to advice concerning Asherah," Balthus replied with a chuckle. "He loved her, fully and completely. No amount of talk could have swayed his heart, not that anyone would have spoken against her. Everyone loved Asherah, elf and troll and faerie alike."

"No one found a faerie an odd choice as the Lord of Tingu's mate?"

"If they did, they wisely kept it to themselves." Balthus smiled to himself, recalling a long-ago occurrence. "She rode to battle beside your father. An elfin woman would never have done that, but Asherah, like Lormac, didn't care for rules and propriety. There was a battle to be fought, and she fought it."

Leran grunted. He had seen Asherah in riding leathers and armor often enough, but Ember wore dresses even when seated upon her horse. What's more, he remembered what Aeolmar said a few nights ago, that neither of his daughters were destined to be warriors.

I don't want her to fight, he decided. *Perhaps I'll teach her some swordplay, but not to the point where she'll be battle ready. Perhaps—*

They entered the feasting hall, and Leran's mind went blank. At the edge of Cerillia's ladies stood Ember, clad in a deep green and gold gown, and looking every bit the elfin lady. Her fiery hair was swept away from her face, held in place with golden pins, and, coupled with the gown's low collar, afforded an excellent view of her elegant neck. Leran strode directly to Ember, pausing only to offer the obligatory greeting to Cerillia.

"May your belly swell like the waxing moon," he murmured. Cerillia blushed as her women chittered, but Leran ignored their babbling. Instead, he approached Ember and kissed the inside of her wrist.

"My lady," he murmured, his lips against her warm flesh. He could feel her pulse quicken beneath her skin. "You look like a queen."

"Do I?" she asked, the teasing lilt already in her voice. "The queen of what, exactly?"

"You know," he replied. He moved to escort her to his table, but she halted him.

"I must sit with the women," Ember said, her annoyance plain. "We're supposed to fawn over her womb, as if something wonderful and fantastic will spring forth at any moment." Leran laughed silently; Ember found these archaic customs as foolish as he did. Although, he would gladly endure a seven-day feast if she wished it.

"Will I have my answer tonight?" he asked. Since all eyes were on Cerillia, he pulled Ember close and stroked her cheek. "Or will you grace me with your reply now?"

"Tonight," she breathed. "After the feast."

Leran held her gaze for another long moment, then kissed her wrist before he released her. He found his place at the table of honor, and was surprised to find himself seated next to Asherah.

"The Lord and Lady of Tingu, together again," Leran said. Asherah smiled tightly, and he hoped he hadn't upset her. "How did you avoid sitting with Cerillia, and spending the evening braiding her hair?"

"As Lady of Tingu, I declared myself exempt from such customs," Asherah replied. "Cerillia didn't put up much of an argument. I suspect she doesn't want a broken woman like myself close to her burgeoning belly," she added, indicating her injured eye.

"Like as not, she's worried that eyes will rest on you rather than her," Leran replied. For all of Asherah's self-depreciating comments, the Faerie Queen was a woman like no other. Faeries all looked somewhat alike, or at least they did to Leran, what with their straight hair in varied shades brown, and green or blue eyes. Asherah, however, bore white hair and black eyes, coloring unique amongst elf and fae alike. Even her clouded left eye did little to detract from her beauty.

Ember had the red curls of her mother, a shade unique to the Thurndian elves. Ember was also the most elflike of Latera's three children, a fact Leran found appropriate. Though, had she been fae through and through, he wouldn't have cared. In Leran's mind, Ember was already his mate. They just needed to complete a few formalities.

"You look at her as though you can barely stand to be separated from her," Asherah observed.

Leran blinked, and refocused his gaze from Ember to Asherah. "You're not wrong."

"Have things progressed?" Asherah asked calmly, leaving it for Leran to interpret if she was asking after the state of Tingu, or the greater matter of him and Ember.

"Have you spoken to Aeolmar about us?" he countered.

"I have not," Asherah replied. "Would you like me to?"

"Ember worries her father won't approve of us being together," Leran explained.

"What did you say to that?" Asherah inquired.

"I told her she was grown, and her choices were her own. Then I asked her to be my mate." Asherah set down her goblet with purpose and waited for Leran to continue. "She said she will give me an answer tonight."

"Tonight," Asherah repeated, then Senan stood to address the hall. He thanked everyone for attending and declared that since he met Cerillia, his life was near perfect.

When was his life not perfect? Leran kept his thoughts to himself, and raised his goblet along with the rest. If Senan found happiness with Cerillia, so be it.

"Sibeal will be pleased," Asherah said. "About you and Ember, that is."

"Why would Sibeal be interested in anything that happens between Ember and me?"

"She's going to name Latera, and therefore Mara and Ember, her heirs," Asherah replied. "At present, they are the last female descendants of Elvasla."

"And I am the scion of Tingu," Leran muttered. Asherah opened her mouth to speak, but Leran continued. "I want you to come to The Seat."

"Oh, Leran," Asherah murmured. He understood she was overwhelmed; if she accepted his invitation, it would be the first time Asherah had been to The Seat since Lormac's death; Asherah had honored Leran's request to never set foot in Tingu unless he invited her. Leran had always wished she would defy him, but the Faerie Queen was not one to break her promises.

"It will be good for you to come," he said quickly. He would have said more, but another lord, someone Leran didn't recognize, chose that moment to offer his own speech about Senan and Cerillia's mating.

Leran changed his mind. If Ember wanted a seven-day feast, he would agree to the event, but he would not enjoy it.

At last, the long-winded lord took his seat. "About going to The Seat," Asherah began.

"Perhaps not now, but maybe for the next season," Leran said, recalling the orcs ranging near his border. "Or, you could arrive in autumn, and winter at The Seat. I remember how you enjoyed the winters with Da."

"Perhaps we shall," Asherah murmured, only to fall silent as the *saffira* began laying out the meal, giving Leran time to consider what she said.

We.

Of course, Asherah would bring her new mate and her son to The Seat. Were anyone to ask him, Leran would have feigned an easy acceptance of such; after all, why should he care who Asherah took to her bed? Why should he care that she'd borne a son to her new mate? It's not like Leran need vie with him for Asherah's attention, and not like she'd borne a child to Lormac...

Finally, a *saffira* came around with food and began filling their plates. He would have thanked the *saffira*, but laughter distracted him. Leran looked toward the women's hearth and saw Ember, amused by something that clearly had not amused Cerillia, if the latter's scowl was an indication. What's more, Ember was taking the gold pins from her hair and allowing her curls to tumble across her shoulders, something else Cerillia disapproved of, but he already knew that Ember wasn't one to cave to the whims of others.

Micon of Rael stood and called for attention. "He's still in power?" Asherah mumbled.

Leran shook his head. "It's not the same Micon. It's his son, though they look uncannily similar." Micon the Younger related a story about Senan and Cerillia that was more suited to a gambling table than a formal hall. Leran noticed that while many laughed at the vulgar tale, some—including Cerillia—sat in silence.

Finally, two good things happened. Micon reclaimed his seat, and a *saffira* offered to refill Leran's goblet. "Please," he said, noting how the girl smiled at him. A sennight ago he'd have had Belenos asking after her name, her station, and the location of her rooms; Leran always preferred sleeping alone. Today, he only asked her to leave the bottle.

"You truly would not mind hosting us?" Asherah asked. When Leran didn't answer, she followed his gaze to a head of red curls. "Perhaps you should also invite the First Hunter," Asherah said, now being careful to maintain a disinterested tone. "As his mate and children are cousins of yours, I imagine they would enjoy a glimpse of their heritage."

"I believe I shall," Leran murmured, smiling appreciatively at the queen. He enjoyed the times he spent with Asherah, despite the fact that he had all but banished her from his life, and for not the first time, he felt a pang of regret. He still remembered the day she returned to The Seat, her and Tingu's legion robed in mourning yellow as she relayed the news of his father's death, and how he'd lashed out at her with a child's anger. He had only known that he hurt, and he had wanted Asherah to hurt as well.

Leran leaned to the side and began to tell Asherah of how he had missed her, of the many times he had wanted to send for her just so he could lay his head in her lap as he once did and have her comfort him, when he saw Ember abruptly rise and leave the hall. Ember did not look back, but then she had no reason to, and Leran faltered in the midst of his long overdue apology. Asherah saw her departure as well, and placed her hand on Leran's arm.

"Go," Asherah said.

Leran looked from the door Ember had departed through to Asherah. "I need to finish what I was saying."

Asherah shook her head. "No, you don't. I understand why you acted the way you did, and I don't fault you for it. I never did."

He stared at her, having assumed that she would hold his many years of indifference and outright hatred of her against him, but she did not. Time rolled backward, and he was again a young boy hiding behind his father's legs as he met Asherah for the first time, and instantly wanted her to be his new mother.

"Thank you, Mama," Leran murmured as he rose and left the table; he heard those around him gasp at his endearment, but he ignored them all as he set off down the corridor. He didn't know if Ember had meant for him to follow her to her chambers, but what he did know was that he needed her. He hoped that she needed him, too.

Chapter Twenty-Six

Ember Speaks

Gods! The feast dragged on and on, each moment longer and more boring than the last. Senan would say something, then someone else would offer a toast, then another, blah blah blah. I felt like the evening would never end and I would be forever trapped in my seat, with Leran just out of my reach.

The few times I'd glanced in his direction, I'd almost immediately caught his eye, his gaze as hungry as I felt. Mara must be right about what it is like when you meet your one true love, for this yearning I had toward him made no sense. No one should want another so strongly after knowing them for only a few days, yet I'd heard Papa tell the story of how he met Mother many times. He claimed he loved her if not the first instant he saw her, then certainly by their first shared sunset. Of course, by that time she had saved him from a demon attack and had caused the death of Mersgoth, the same mordeth *who had tortured and then killed Father's parents and siblings. That sort of event will usually endear someone to you.*

Nothing of the sort had happened between Leran and me; well, unless you count his asking me to accompany him to The Seat, and... Did he really want me to be his mate? More, did I really want him?

And I wouldn't just be his mate. I would be his queen, the Lady of Tingu to his Lord. I had no idea of how to be a queen, or run a land. I barely even gave our saffira *orders, and left those sorts of tasks to Mara. Going from Regular Ember to Lady of Tingu was more than I could comprehend.*

"I just don't know," I murmured to myself.

"What's that?" Mother asked. If I was a rational person, I would have shared my feelings with her. Unlike my father, Mother and Leran had always gotten on well, and any advice she gave me would be devoid of Papa's long distrust of the Lord of Tingu. Of course, Papa

distrusted everyone who lived outside Parthalan's borders, and a fair few within them. It was a wonder he spoke to anyone.

"Nothing. Forgive me," I said, then turned my attention toward the latest well-wisher while I removed those maddening pins from my hair. The speaker called for Thurnda's fields to be as fecund as Senan's mate's womb with such florid eloquence that most didn't realize he was describing, in vivid detail, her mate rogering her in the storeroom behind the kitchens. I wonder if it was a true story. Based on his mate's unamused face, I judged it to be.

The toaster—Micon of Rael—concluded his speech amidst roaring laughter, Senan's included, and as the lord took his seat, I glanced at Leran. He was laughing along with the rest, his handsome face made more so with the addition of his boyish grin. Could I spend my life gazing at that grin?

I think I could.

"I'm going to my room," I said suddenly.

"Are you ill?" Mother asked, her forehead wrinkling in concern.

"I'm just tired," I said hurriedly. "This has been a very exciting journey," I added with a nod to Senan's mate. I must remember to learn her name.

"Then you should certainly rest," Mother said with her gentle smile. By contrast, Mara, who was well aware of what was on my mind, and had surely surmised what I now planned, pursed her lips and glared daggers at me. She had never approved of my flirting in the past—once, she had even called me a philanderer—but she wouldn't stand between two soulmates, which is surely what Leran and I were. Would she? I had a sickening feeling that she would follow me back to our rooms, but then she managed a tight smile.

"I mean to remain," Mara declared. I nodded my thanks as I left the hall without further conversation. I didn't dare turn around to see if Leran saw me, or if he intended to follow. For all I knew, he had reconsidered his offer. Gods, I hope he hadn't.

Once inside the chamber, I leaned back against the door, my heart racing as I hoped Leran would follow me, and not knowing what I would do or say if he did. Since I was still wrapped in the heavy elfin gown that Senan's mate insisted I wear, I decided to change. What I hadn't realized when I'd agreed to wear this gown was how hot velvet can be, especially when it's piled on top of a hundred undergarments.

I twisted about as I tried to extricate myself; not only did the gown weigh nearly as much as I, the buttons that ran up the back of the gown were so tiny I could hardly grasp them. Of course, neither Mara nor I possessed a buttonhook (ridiculous contraption, that) and after much struggling that resulted in only a few buttons undone, I gave up. I spied a pitcher of wine and I rushed to pour two goblets, reasoning that if I couldn't manage better apparel, I could at least offer Leran something to drink. I was wondering if Leran liked wine or if I should send for rum or tea or that dark bitter drink he favored, when it struck me that I was fretting over what a man I hardly knew preferred to drink. Then my door creaked open, and he was there; the wine would have to do.

I spun about, gown half-unbuttoned and goblets in hand, and saw Leran standing in the center of the room. He hadn't knocked, but merely strode into the room as if... Well. As if he was the Lord of Tingu, come to claim his mate.

"Your dress," he murmured. I followed his gaze and saw that my neckline had dipped quite low, and my undergarments were more than a bit exposed.

"I was going to change," I explained, gesturing wildly with the goblets, wine sloshing about, "and offer you wine, but I don't have a buttonhook so I couldn't unfasten all the buttons, and I didn't know if you even liked wine or— "

"I like wine," he said, effectively putting a stop to my babbling tirade. "I hope you don't mind that I didn't knock."

"I don't," I said, and he smiled. Somehow, his smile put me at ease. "I suppose it doesn't matter what I wear. You've already seen me in my nightgown."

"You looked lovely in it," he said. With that, he stepped behind me, and glided his fingertips along the open edges of my gown. "Would you like some assistance?"

Normally, I would have made a joke about him acting as a lady's maid. I didn't. "Please," I murmured.

Leran caressed my neck and shoulders, possibly giving me time to change my mind, then he moved my hair aside and kissed the nape of my neck. Oh, Cydia preserve my honor. Slowly, deliberately, he plucked the buttons free, all the while being careful not to touch what was beneath. His hands were gentle, firm.

I, on the other hand, worried I would faint at any moment. My heart pounded and my hands trembled while I repeated to myself over and over that this really wasn't a significant event. I don't have a buttonhook handy, and Leran was simply helping me. That's all. Even so, underneath this gown I have on a chemise, corset, and what felt like a hundred underskirts. It's not like he's stripping me bare.

"Why did you leave the feast so early?" I asked, my voice having gone husky.

"When I saw you leave the hall, I realized that I simply cannot bear to be apart from you," he replied. He'd reached the last button, and slid the gown forward off one arm, then the other while I juggled the goblets. Leran chuckled, then liberated the goblets from my hands and set them on a side table while I clutched the gown at my waist. "Not tonight, not ever again."

"Truly?"

"Truly," he affirmed. Then Leran was in front of me, his gaze so heavy he pinned me in place. "My lady, will you have me?"

"H-Have you?" I stammered, unsure if he meant in my bed or as my mate. But then, I suppose the questions were one and the same, much like me accompanying him to Tingu and becoming his mate. If I agreed to one, I agreed to both.

I bit my lip and stared into his gray eyes. He was a beautiful man, what with his wide, clear eyes, and his soft brown hair brushed away from his noble face. The gold circlet on his brow and the elaborate clothing he wore seemed to fade into the background; Leran was so much more than what a bit of gold and gems could convey. He was just him, wonderfully him.

I realized I'd been silent a bit too long. Leran must have realized it too, since he unexpectedly dropped to his knees before this half-elf in her undergarments. I remembered my readings of Nexa, and that she hadn't knelt before kings or gods, only deigning to bend her knee before he whom she took as her mate.

Leran took my hands, leaving my gown to fall to the floor as he softly kissed each of my wrists. "Ember, will you be mine?" he asked.

"My lord, I will have you," I murmured, though the last few words were lost as Leran stood and kissed me. Then I was in his arms, cradled as if I were precious to him.

"Which room is yours?" he asked.

I jerked my head toward my door and he lifted me against him, neither of us minding our path as we kissed and stumbled toward the bed. We fell onto the cushions, a mad heap of limbs and mouths as we scrambled to learn each other. I unbuttoned his ornate coat and push it off his shoulders while he dealt with the laces of my corset. I drew a grateful breath as he eased that topmost layer from me, then he stood to remove the rest of his clothing.

I sucked in my breath at the sight of Leran naked, standing over me like a god. He climbed back onto the bed and I reached for him, but he gently grasped my wrists and pinned them over my head. I felt metal against my skin; he'd slid the Sala onto my arm. I really was his.

"Let me pleasure you," Leran murmured, then made good on his words. He stripped away the many underskirts, one by one, then set to work on the final layer of my chemise. Slowly, he bared my skin, taking the time to touch and kiss and taste all that he uncovered. I had never felt such passion, such desire, and while I wavered between laying back and enjoying his attentions and telling him to just get on with it, I realized that I loved him. It must be love, for there was no other explanation for the instant affection I had felt toward him, and I was overcome with the need to tell him. Why I needed to tell him now, before our lovemaking, I cannot say, but I had to say something, if for no other reason than to learn if he loved me as well.

"Leran," I gasped as he acquainted himself with my naval. By now he had unfastened my chemise well past my waist, and only a thin layer of cloth lay between he and I; the many confusing elfin undergarments that had taken me so long to put on proved no match for Leran's deft fingers. How many times has he removed these items? I said his name again, a bit more desperately this time. He looked up, but instead of answering me, his eyes glinted and he dove under the hem of my chemise.

I squealed with laughter as Leran made his way up my body, pushing my chemise upward as he did so. He paused when he reached my thighs, and my laughter faded into lower tones. A few long, blissful moments later, he resumed climbing me like a tree, and worked my chemise up and over my head. I assumed the moment had arrived, but he drew back and gazed at me.

"Like what you see?" I quipped.

"I do." He caressed me, tracing a long line from my shoulder to my hip. Gods, I don't think I've ever been as happy as that moment, naked in bed with Leran. "Do I make you happy?"

Does the Lord of Tingu read minds? "You do," I replied. "You make me very, very happy."

My reward was his smile, sweet and guileless, and my heart nearly burst. Leran must love me, surely he must! Why else would he care so much about my happiness, put my pleasure before his own? If only he hadn't said anything further.

"You're like a little dove, pale and soft and smooth," he murmured as he caressed my breasts. He gathered me against him as I wound my fingers into his hair. "I knew the Sala wasn't wrong."

Sala? What did the Sala have to do with this? "What?"

He drew my arm before me, and showed me the stone that had been orange yesterday, but was now closer to red. "You see how the heartstone becomes darker when you're near? The Sala has chosen you as my mate," he said, his voice muffled as he nibbled my neck. I placed my hands on his chest to halt him. Did he really just tell me that he was here in my bed because of a stone changing color? Not because he loved me?

"Why would it do that?" I asked carefully, hoping he would say that the Sala recognized the deep, true love he had for me and thus confirm he was my soulmate. He didn't.

"You're descended from Elvasla, your mother is the deva'shi,*" he murmured as his lips explored the hollow of my throat. "I expect it saw you as a good match."*

A good match? A good match! I shoved him away from me, but even with the element of surprise, he hardly budged. "Get out of my room!"

"What's the matter?" he demanded.

"You see me as a good match? Because of a few ancestors? I thought you loved me!"

"I do," he insisted. "I said those things in jest!"

"But you're here because of that piece of metal, not because you love me." I nearly choked on the words. I had never felt so hurt, foolish, despondent. "Get out."

"Ember." He said my name so softly it was like a caress. Leran moved to nuzzle my neck, but I turned away. "Ember, please forgive me. I do

love you. I don't understand how I could love you already, but I do. Perhaps one never understands love, only that it is."

His words were like needles raking across my flesh. I wanted to throw my arms around him, declare that I loved him and let him take me, but I couldn't. I would never know if he loved me, or if he just did whatever the Sala told him to do. "I told you to leave."

My wrists were pinned above me again and Leran put and his full weight on top of me. The length of him pressed into my belly, and I hated myself for how I wanted him still. "I am not leaving!"

"You mean to force me?" I spat. He was taken aback by my words, so much so he loosened his grip.

"I would never hurt you," he said. He sat back on his heels, and allowed me to sit up. "And I am not leaving until you hear me out."

"If you won't leave, then I will!" I shouted. "I want nothing to do with you! Not now or ever!" Then, in a fit of rage worthy of my father, I took off the Sala and threw it across the room. Yes, I flung a priceless elfin artifact against the wall, where it hit with a dull thud.

Leran was understandably shocked, so I took advantage of the moment as I leapt from the bed and stormed out of the bedchamber. As I reached the front room, I realized that not only was I naked (I was not going to wear that horrible velvet gown, not ever again), I also did not want to confront others who may be in this end of the palace, and there was really no place private for me to go. Leran must have realized this as well, for he seemed to be patiently waiting for me to reenter the bedchamber.

So I opened the main door and then slammed it with all my might before creeping into Mara's chamber. As I silently burrowed beneath the blankets, I heard Leran call my name twice, the second time sounding so dejected I nearly ran out of the room and into his arms, but my fury kept me hidden. Then he was silent for so long I wondered if he had resolved to wait out my return, or if he had fallen asleep, but then I heard him dress and make his way to the front room. He paused, I imagine looking about the room for me, then I heard the door shut behind him. The gentle creak of the door somehow unhinged my tight hold upon my emotions, and my anger gave way to despair.

By the time Mara returned to her room, I was in the depths of sadness. I hadn't bothered to redress and my sister found me as I'd left him, naked and half drowned in tears; I can only imagine what she thought transpired between us, but she said nothing as she climbed onto the bed and put her arms around me. Mara knew when to speak, and when words would only rub salt into the wounds, and this was the latter.

"Did you ever cry over Kemen?" I asked eventually.

"Many times, little one," she murmured as she wiped my cheeks. "Many times."

Chapter Twenty-Seven

Leran sat at the desk before the hearth with his head in his hands. Maps and documents were spread before him, and he saw none of it. He couldn't stop thinking about Ember's face, and the red spots of fury on her cheeks as she stormed away from him.

I've ruined many things, but nothing so badly as this. He had no idea what to do or how to fix things. Until a tear splashed onto the desk's surface, he didn't even know he was weeping.

Leran didn't stir from his desk until second dawn. Hoping she'd had time to calm down, he returned to Ember's room, but the *saffira* who answered the door told him she'd taken ill, and would see no one. Undaunted, Leran made his way to the kitchens and secured a fresh loaf of bread and a bowl of hot broth, hoping the food would soothe Ember's frayed nerves. The *saffira*, unimpressed with his peace offering, still refused him entry. When Leran had railed that he was Lord of Tingu and could not be refused by anyone, Mara appeared in the doorway.

"Leran," Mara said. "If she hears you shouting, you'll only upset her more."

"I am trying to fix this," he seethed.

Mara glanced at the tray in his hands. "Do you really think a bit of bread and soup can mend a broken heart?"

That comment broke him. Leran flung the tray against the corridor wall, cursing as the bowl shattered and drenched the floor in slippery broth. He watched the *saffira* rush to clean up his mess, then he stalked across the palace to his apartments. When he entered, he saw Aldo and Balthus speaking, ignored them, and returned to his desk. A few moments later, Aldo brought him a bowl of selka.

"Are you willing to speak with Balthus?" Aldo asked.

Leran nodded. Aldo disappeared, and before he realized it, Balthus was standing in front of him.

"Leran, the time for waiting is over." Balthus dropped several scraps of parchment onto Leran's desk. Leran didn't move to read them since he already knew what they were: messages from across Tingu, warning of the imminent invasion of mountain trolls and orcs.

"I couldn't agree more," Leran said.

"Then we can leave today?"

Leran raised his head. "No. My orders have not changed."

Balthus frowned, his gazed moving across Leran's haggard form. "She rejected you?"

"Who told you that?" Leran demanded, rising to his feet.

"Your appearance," he replied. "I know what rejection feels like. What you need is a distraction."

"And fighting orcs is the perfect distraction?" Leran sat heavily, then he crumpled up the messages and tossed them into the fire. "As much as I'd love to run my sword through something right now, we will not leave earlier than planned. Tingu's secrets will remain so, for now." Balthus moved to speak, but Leran cut him off. "On your way out, please tell Aldo I'm not to be disturbed."

Balthus nodded, and left. Leran burned the last message, then he stared at the flames until all traces of orcs and mountain trolls were gone. By then, his selka had gone cold, but Leran didn't ask Aldo for a fresh bowl. Instead, he stared at his reflection in the dark liquid, the hated face of a man who had hurt his beloved, possibly beyond repair. *Only, I can't really call her my beloved, can I? I ruined things before I earned that right.*

Leran blew out a heavy sigh, and tipped some rum into the selka. Maybe if he got drunk and passed out, this would all go away. Maybe he had gotten drunk and passed out, and this was just a nightmare. Yes, that must be it, for even he wasn't so foolish as to destroy the best thing that had ever happened to him.

"My lord," Aldo said, rousing Leran from his contemplation of selka. He glanced toward the windows, and saw the suns dipping low in the sky. He'd been sitting in front of the hearth, alone and morose, for hours. "I know you requested your solitude, but the *deva'shi* is requesting an audience. She is quite insistent."

Leran sighed; he was living his nightmare. "She may have come to kill me."

"Should I fetch your sword?" Aldo asked.

"No. I deserve it."

"I'm sure." With that, Aldo retreated to the outer chamber, then he escorted Latera Demon-killer before Leran's desk. She was dressed like a huntress, complete with leather leggings and gauntlets, but she wasn't wearing her swords. Leran felt he may yet survive the day.

Then he met her eyes, eyes that were cold with fury, eyes that reminded him so much of Ember's. Latera's arms were folded beneath her breasts, her lips pursed and bloodless.

"Please," Leran said, gesturing to the chair across from him, "sit. Would you like Aldo to bring you anything?"

"I want to know what happened."

Leran sighed again. It was useless to deny or stall Latera; being that she was the *deva'shi,* she bowed to no god or ruler. He drank from his bowl, wishing he had added more rum.

"Where would you like me to begin?"

"At the beginning, preferably."

Leran drank again, this time rum straight from the flagon. "I will begin yesterday, at second dawn. I went to Ember's chamber to ask her to walk with me. We'd done so before, and I greatly enjoyed her company. It was raining, so we came here instead."

"You brought my daughter to your chamber," Latera stated.

"It was that, or let her get soaked in the rain." Leran glanced up. "We shared our morning meal. Then, I asked Ember to return to The Seat with me, as my mate."

"Why would you do such a thing?" Latera demanded. "She's hardly more than a child, and you hardly know one another!"

Leran swallowed, then he extended his arm and pushed up his sleeve. Latera's gaze fell upon the Sala, and the blood red heartstone.

"Oh!" Latera gasped, sitting heavily. "Oh."

"She agreed to give me an answer last night, after the Child's Feast," Leran continued. "When she left the hall, I followed her to her chamber. I asked her if she would have me, and she said yes. Then we went to bed."

Leran paused, searching Latera's face. "I didn't love her."

Latera nodded, her gaze fixed on the heartstone. "Ember said as much." She glanced up. "Please continue."

"I... We were happy, so happy that we started jesting with one another. Then I told her that the Sala was not wrong, and..." Leran dropped his head to his hands, tearing at his hair. "Instead of telling her how much I love her, I made a joke. An ill-timed, ill-thought joke, and now she hates me." His shoulders shook, and his voice was ragged. "You are correct. I hardly know her. And I hardly know how I will live without her."

Latera reached across the desk, and touched the heartstone. "It's as red as it was when I returned it to you," she murmured. "Before Aeolmar and I were mates, we fought often, about everything. We would argue about things as petty as the clouds in the sky, or the best way to brush a horse. Once, I was so furious I threw him out of my chamber and told him never to return." Latera laughed. "We were so loud half the palace heard us."

Leran ran his fingers through his hair, and raised his head. "What made you so mad?"

"Oh, Mar was worried, being that I'd returned to Teg'urnan covered in gore and demon blood," she replied. "I misinterpreted his concern as him not trusting me."

"How did he repair things?" Leran asked.

"He didn't. I followed him to the arena, and we got into a shouting match loud enough to wake the dead. Then, he told me he loved me, and... And here we are."

"You're saying that I should lure Ember out to the practice yard and yell at her until she loves me again?"

"No, I'm saying that you shouldn't be so quick to assume she doesn't love you," Latera replied. "I won't try to make this easy on you: she is despondent. I've never seen her so upset. She really believes that you didn't want her out of love, but because of her lineage."

Leran tipped back the flagon, found it empty, set it down and scrubbed his face instead. "And you, *deva'shi*? What do you think?"

"I think it's not my opinion that matters." Latera rose and circled the desk until she was next to Leran, and smoothed the damp hair from his brow. "Ember has sworn me to secrecy, so you needn't worry about idle gossip. You have time to let her anger settle."

"The *saffira*—" Leran began, remembering the broken soup bowl.

"I've ensured their silence," Latera said. "I'm rather good at intimidating people, no matter my stature." Leran nodded, feeling hope for the first time since he'd left Ember's chamber.

"Will she see me?"

"Not today, and probably not tomorrow. But if you love her, isn't she worth waiting for?"

"She is," Leran said. "She's worth everything."

Chapter Twenty-Eight

The next afternoon Latera hurried out of the royal archive with three scrolls clutched against her breast. After she'd spent the prior day comforting Ember, questioning Leran, and then deflecting Aeolmar, she needed the archive's quiet solitude. Her search paid off, and in the darkest, dustiest corner, she found three ancient scrolls that may answer at least some of her questions.

The scrolls were the oldest items she'd yet found, which meant they might be from before Olluhm's time. It also meant that they were written in elfin, a language almost no one spoke any longer. But there could be a clue hidden within these scrolls, and Latera fully meant to exhaust all options available to her. The last thing she wanted was for Asherah to learn of that heir to the sun prophecy, and—

"Asherah!" Latera had nearly bumped into the queen, and the subject of her thoughts. "I'm so sorry, I didn't see you."

"It's all right." Asherah looked over the scrolls Latera carried as if they were precious. "You were in the archive again?"

Latera wrinkled her nose. "I was. I must say, for a land as wealthy as Thurnda the archive is a disorganized mess. Even Sarfek kept better order, and he was evil."

Asherah laughed shortly. "He was quite well organized, as was his brother. What are you looking for?" When Latera bit her lip and cocked her head to the side, Asherah pressed, "What does Aeolmar have to say?"

Latera winced. "Is it that obvious when we touch one another's minds?"

"Yes."

Latera blew out a breath, and began, "Caol'non insists that the Ish h'ra is due to return. I am trying to find out if he's correct."

Asherah looked beyond her friend to the archive's door. "And you think the answer to a god's plans lies in Thurnda's archives?"

"It might." Latera sat on a nearby window ledge. After a moment, Asherah joined her. "I am trying to find something—anything—that dates from the time before Olluhm ascended. Perhaps there will be a clue, or a mention of something we in Parthalan have forgotten. As you know, elves record what happens in the fae lands, but since the fae don't really interest them, all these records end up forgotten."

"And you think you can unearth this forgotten knowledge?"

Latera shrugged. "I unearthed a wealth of Parthalan's secrets while in the mortal realm. I'm sure I can figure out a measly god or two."

"Sometimes I don't know who's more arrogant, you or that mate of yours." Asherah touched the edge of one of the scrolls. "Why did you pick these three?"

"They're the oldest scrolls I've found so far," Latera replied. "But they're written in elfin, which hardly anyone speaks anymore."

"Aldo speaks and reads elfin," Asherah offered. "I'm sure he would help you translate them. There is also an extensive archive in Tingu. From what I recall, it's quite orderly."

"I'm sure it is, if Aldo's the one managing it."

They smiled at each other, then Asherah said, "Leran invited me to The Seat."

"He did? Are you going?"

"I... I don't know. It's been so long, and I don't know if Finlay would be amenable to such a long journey north."

"Finlay would do anything you asked of him," Latera said. "He would build a palace out of snow and ice and shiver in it for all eternity, if he thought it would make you happy."

Asherah smiled. "He would, wouldn't he?" She looked out of the window, and saw Leran walking the battlements, alone. "Leran has made me swear to not ask you about Ember, but if you'd like to talk about it, I'm willing to listen." She faced Latera, and added, "It doesn't seem to be going well."

"It certainly isn't," Latera said. "Has he shown you the heartstone?"

"He has."

Latera shrugged. "Then, I suppose everything rests on Ember." Latera glanced about the corridor, thus ensuring they were alone. "He upset her a great deal, but from what they both say, it was a simple misunderstanding."

"Both? Have you talked to Leran?"

"I demanded he tell me his side of the story," Latera replied. "Would you have done any less?"

"No. I wouldn't have." Asherah dropped her gaze to her hands. "I'm sorry both of my sons trouble Ember so."

Latera squeezed Asherah's forearm. "None of this is your doing, and that business with Finn was a long time ago. They were young, and foolish. Surely you remember what that's like?"

"I'm a fool still," Asherah replied.

"Aren't we all?" Latera bit her lip, and asked, "What do you think about Cerillia?"

"I haven't thought about her very much at all," Asherah replied. "Why?"

"She has a very strong desire to become the Lady of Thurnda," Latera replied. "Which is odd, to say the least. Wouldn't every Thurndian know that the title is passed from mother to daughter?"

"I imagine they would," Asherah said. "More, Senan should know the line of succession better than almost anyone. How did she convince him to go along with her plan?"

"I don't know," Latera said. "But it makes me nervous. People who feel that they're owed power tend to make rash judgements."

A gong sounded. "No," Asherah whispered.

"Just when I thought this would be a quiet trip," Latera said, then she turned toward the window and found Leran. "What direction?" she yelled.

"South," he replied. "Meet me at the lower gate!"

Latera ran back to the archive and gave the scrolls to the keeper to hold for the time being, then she rejoined Asherah. "Leran said to meet at the lower gate," she said. "Let's get out there, and see who's attacking us."

***

Leran rushed through the corridors as he headed toward his chambers. He had no idea who or what sort of attack was bearing down on the palace, and truth be told he didn't care. It was the second day since Ember rejected him, the second day of him living his absolute worst nightmare. In that time she'd neither left her room nor responded to any of his messages, and Leran's hurt and guilt over his actions had coiled themselves around his heart. If he didn't hit something soon, that coil may very well destroy him.

When Leran reached his chambers, Aldo waited outside the door. "Your sword and armor," he said.

"Thank you," Leran said as he put on the swordbelt. "Any word on what's coming?"

"It appears to be mostly mountain trolls, with a demon or two mixed in," Aldo replied, as he moved behind Leran to buckle on his breastplate.

Odd, trolls coming from the south. "At least it's not orcs," Leran muttered, then he spied Finn standing across the corridor from him, without a sword in hand or any other sort of weaponry on his person. Leran beckoned him closer, and asked, "Have you a sword?"

"A sword?" Finn repeated. "What for?"

"For the battle," Leran replied. "Aren't you going out with us?"

"I-I've never been in a battle," Finn replied. "Not a real one. And I'm a better archer."

Leran almost turned away, since he had no use for a grown man who'd yet to be blooded. What he needed were his men, Tingu's well-trained warriors who would put down this incursion quickly... But he remembered when he was young, and how not one of his generals were willing to risk taking the young and untried Lord of Tingu onto the battlefield.

That all changed the day Aldo handed him his father's sword despite the others' caution, and Leran went out and proved himself.

Leran eyed Finn. As much as he'd needed Aldo to believe in him, Finn needed Leran.

"Crossbow or longbow?" Leran asked. "Which do you prefer?"

"A crossbow is deadlier, but a longbow is faster." Finn's eyes widened, and he said, "Mother will not allow me to join the battle!"

"Your mother isn't here to share her opinion. What do you want to do?"

Finn lifted his chin. "I want to fight."

"Then we'll fight together. Aldo, we need a bow and quiver for the prince, along with some armor." Aldo nodded and disappeared through the door. Leran turned back to Finn, and said, "You'll ride with me. Unless you'd rather join the Parthian forces?"

Finn paled, but his back was straight and his chin high. "I'll ride with Tingu."

Aldo emerged with a longbow and full quiver, and Leran's spare breastplate and bracers. Finn had barely had time to accept the weapons when Leran began moving down the corridor. "Quickly, Finn. Our foes won't allow us a respite, not until they're dead."

Leran led Finn down to the organized chaos of the stables. They buckled on the rest of their armor and checked their weapons, and soon enough they emerged on horseback with the rest of the warriors.

"You've had training?" Leran asked, and Finn affirmed that he had. "How much?"

"Not enough, I'm afraid." Finn looked toward the south, where the trolls had been sighted. "Do we know how many demons are with them?"

Leran shrugged. "Does it matter?"

"It might. If there are more demons than trolls, we should send the horses back," Finn replied. "Horses are their favorite food. The larger ones will lure the horses into a trap, then the lesser demons will crawl underneath and rip out the horses' bellies with their teeth."

"I take it Latera handled the bulk of your training," Leran said, and Finn laughed shortly.

"She did. She's the one who encouraged me to take up the bow."

"Elfin women are brilliant. Always listen to them," Leran said, then he relayed what Finn had shared to Balthus. They conferred for a moment, then Leran and the rest of Tingu's warriors dismounted. Finn moved to dismount as well, but Leran halted him.

"You need the advantage of height," Leran said, jerking his chin toward Finn's bow. "You shoot, and we'll protect your horse."

"How will you keep up?"

Leran grinned. "Worry not, Finn. We'll keep up."

***

The battle proved to be a short one, and despite Finn's warnings, there were few demons to worry about. Leran's blood sang as he fought, but despite the thrill of battle, he kept close to Finn's horse. He'd promised to defend Finn's horse against any demon that might approach it, and he had no intention of reneging on his word. That, and Finn's bow easily felled as many foes as Leran's sword, maybe more.

Afterward, Leran and Finn walked back to the palace together, leading the brave but winded horse behind them.

"You did well," Leran said. "Asherah will be proud."

"Gods, I hope so." Finn glanced at Leran, then looked away. "I don't want you to think I hide behind her. I don't, but she worries. Actually, she's terrified one of her enemies might target me, or Father. It's why she's always charging off ahead of us." Finn smiled. "She wants to protect us, not baby us."

"She's always been a protector," Leran said. "It took a long time for her to accept that I don't need her protection, but despite all that if I called on her, she'd stand between me and any foe."

"She would," Finn agreed. "Then she'd lecture you about it for the next two days."

Leran threw back his head and laughed. "That she would."

They reached the plain before the palace, and the men cheered at the sight of the women lined up along the rampart above the main gate, waiting for their return. Standing in the center of the rampart, in the place of honor, was Sibeal. Leran caught her eye, and she nodded her approval. He didn't see Cerillia or Senan on the rampart, which he found odd. Then again, he found many things odd about that couple.

Finn tapped Leran's arm, and said, "Look, it's Mara and Ember."

Leran followed Finn's gaze, and he saw Ember watching him. It was the first time he'd seen her since she'd stormed away from him after the Child's Feast, and Leran dared to hope that she'd been watching for his return. He raised his hand, and imagined being greeted by his mate upon his homecoming; she would rush into his arms, happy and proud and so relieved he was home safe. Instead of smiling or calling out his name, Ember looked him over, then she turned and went inside.

"Why did she do that?" Leran muttered.

"You're covered in blood," Finn said. "You probably scared her. Although Ember's not one to get scared."

"Then why would she be scared now?"

"Finn!"

Asherah pushed her way through the returning warriors and stopped short when she reached Leran and Finn. It was plain that she wanted to take her son aside and check him for wounds, and possibly reprimand him for entering the battle in the first place, but she restrained herself. "I didn't realize you went out with the rest."

"Leran encouraged me," Finn said. "I shot from horseback while he fought on foot."

"We worked well together," Leran said. "You should be proud."

Asherah smiled. "I am, as is Finlay."

"We all are," Latera said, as she joined them astride her golden mare. "Finn's arrows were much needed."

"Wait, why didn't you send your horse back?" Leran demanded. "I thought the demons ate them."

"If you think I'll let a demon get close enough to my horse to bite it, you're mad," Latera said, then she fell silent as Mara emerged from the lower gate and pushed her way through the crowd.

"Who's she looking for?" Leran wondered. What with Latera being one of the few on horseback, she was easy to spot. Then he watched as Mara ran toward one of the returning hunters.

"I didn't realize Mara was spoken for," Leran said.

Latera swung down from her horse and said, "That's Kemen. He and Mara are, shall we say, complicated."

Leran's gaze slid toward his cousin. "Is anything easy with your family?"

"Evidently not." One of the Parthians hailed Latera, and she led her horse away from them. Leran glanced up at the balcony, saw the Ember hadn't returned. He looked toward Finn, who was frowning at the ground.

"Why the long face?" he asked. "Victory deserves celebration."

Finn visibly shook off whatever troubled him, and said, "You're right. All victories should be celebrated! Who knows what ills tomorrow may hold? We need to live in the moment, not for what might be."

"My thoughts exactly." Leran clapped Finn's shoulder. "Perhaps you're right, and we were meant to be brothers all along."

Chapter Twenty-Nine

Ember Speaks

When the alarm had sounded, notifying us of the mountain trolls amassing outside the gates, I hardly cared. We were inside this stone fortified castle, so weren't we safe? I hadn't left my room for two days, and had no intention of doing so for something as trite as a battle I wouldn't even fight in.

Then Mara told me there were demons among the attackers, which meant the hunters were going out as well. Since we now had a stake in the fight, Mara and I followed the rest of the women to the ramparts above the gates and watched the soldiers assemble. It was a grand tradition to watch the warriors ride out to battle, we were told. As we observed the elves milling about below, I learned that all of Thurnda's warriors were men.

"Where are the hunters?" I asked.

"There," Mara said, pointing to a small group on the left of the assemblage. Present were our parents, and Tor, along with Asherah and Finlay. "Where's Kemen?"

No sooner had Mara said the words than Kemen appeared below us. "Keep the ale cold for me," he called up to Mara, smiling.

"I shall," she replied, waving as he joined the others in their formations. Everyone seemed to be accounted for, but all the warriors remained rooted in place.

"What are they waiting for?" I asked. The whole of Thurnda's soldiers were assembled, along with the Parthian hunters, the trolls were moving toward us, and yet they stood there immobile. Shouldn't they get moving toward these foes? Even Sibeal, from her vantage point at the far end of the balcony, held herself.

"Look," Mara said, and Leran himself strode out of the palace stables, with Tingu's warriors following him. "Finn's beside him."

"Odd." I didn't think Finn had ever been in a battle, but I deliberately didn't pay attention to his antics. Thurnda's men cheered at the sight of Leran, as did the hunters. As for Leran, he uttered a great war cry and led the mass toward the incoming trolls and demons.

"Why was everyone waiting for Leran?" I wondered.

"The Lord of Tingu is our war chief," Sibeal said, as she came to stand beside me. "With Leran in resident not a single elf would go to battle without his consent."

"He has every elf's respect, regardless of whom he rules," I said, and Sibeal nodded.

"Much like his father before him, Leran leads with a just hand, and a sharp sword." Sibeal patted my hand, then she went to a chair set in the center of the balcony.

"Are we supposed to wait for them to return?" I asked.

"Could you really bring yourself to look away?" Mara countered. I had nothing to say to that, but she was right. As I watched Leran move farther and farther away from the palace, I realized I would be the one rooted in place until his safe return. And if he didn't return...

The fighting was out of sight of the palace, though we could hear it, and it seemed like it took days for the warriors to return. In reality, it wasn't so long, perhaps an hour or two, but by the time a runner appeared waving the red flag of victory I'd been clutching the balcony's railing for so long my hands were white and cramped. The others cheered at the sight of the flag, but I didn't. Victory was all well and good, but I needed to know who was coming home.

The warriors trickled in, and the first familiar face I saw was my mother astride Enna. Close to her was Papa, and I spotted Tor bragging about his latest exploits among a few very patient elves. While I was grateful for their safe return, they weren't who I was searching for.

"Where's Kemen?" Mara asked, her voice a bit panicked. "Do you see him?"

"Not yet," I replied, then Leran came into view. He was walking among the masses as if he was a common foot soldier and not the king of all of them, laughing and telling jokes as if he'd been at a party instead of fighting for his life.

"I see Kemen," Mara said, then she raced down the balcony's steps to greet him. I should have followed her—to greet my parents, my *brother, anyone—but then Leran looked up and his gaze met mine, and I couldn't move. He raised his hand and grinned, and my relief at his return threatened to overwhelm me. I did the only thing I could do, and retreated from the balcony before I started bawling in front of the whole of Thurnda.*

I found a quiet corner and laid my head against the cool stone wall, and forced myself to take slow, even breaths. Why was I reacting this way? I'd been furious at Leran ever since I learned he only wanted me because of the Sala's stupid color changing stones, and had already resolved to have nothing more to do with him. If he'd gone and met his end at the end of a troll's spear, it would have made things easier for me.

I'd no sooner formed the thought than big, wracking sobs overtook me. Gods below, a single errant thought about Leran's demise had reduced me to a simpering fool. I needed to lie down, or have something to eat, or leave Thurnda and never think about elves again.

Yes. What I need to do is go home. I pictured Teg'urnan in my mind's eye, and willed myself to calm down. After a few more deep breaths, I wiped my eyes and stepped into the main corridor.

And directly into Leran's path.

"Wait," he said when I turned away. "I was looking for you."

I gritted my teeth, then I faced him. Up close, I saw the mud and blood spattered across his boots and armor, the small cut on his neck. "You need a bath," I said.

He looked down at himself. "I expect I do." He stepped closer to me. "Have you been crying?"

I didn't want to answer that. "Is there something you wanted to ask me?"

"There's to be a celebration, for the victory," he replied. "Will you be there?"

"I've nothing to celebrate," I snapped. I spun on my heel, intending to return to my room, when he stepped in front of me.

"Ember," he said. "I'm sorry."

"If you're so sorry, then get out of my way." I sidestepped him, and continued on my way.

"I'm sorry for what I said," he continued, raising his voice as I moved farther away from him. "I was wrong. Ember, please talk to me!"

"I am not having a discussion with a bloody warrior in a corridor," I yelled over my shoulder.

"Very well. I'll have that bath, and then we'll talk."

I didn't turn around or otherwise acknowledge him. When I reached my room, I went inside and slammed the door, then I slid to the floor in a sobbing heap.

I had to get out of Thurnda.

Chapter Thirty

Leran's day had gone from bad, to good, to confusing.

The guilt and despair he'd woken with had been all but eradicated by the thrill of battle; again, the elfsong flowed within him. And when he returned from battle, and saw Ember on the ramparts waiting for him, he dared to hope that everything between them was repaired.

Then Leran raised his hand in greeting, and Ember fled from the rampart.

Leran immediately went after Ember, and found her red-eyed and furious. He didn't know why she'd been crying, and wondered if him wanting her to have wept over him made him a bad person. Ember refused to reply to his question or even talk to him, citing his bloody armor as the main reason.

Stupid reason. Regardless, Leran returned to his chambers intent on cleaning up; he had every intention of celebrating the day's victory, with or without Ember. As Finn said, all victories should be celebrated. When he entered his chambers, he was met by a frowning Aldo.

"What is it?" Leran asked.

"Balthus sent you a gift," Aldo replied. "However, I'm not certain it's wanted."

"Where?" Leran asked, and Aldo nodded toward the bedchamber. Leran sighed, then he opened the chamber door and found four men and women lying on his bed in varying stages of undress.

"You're all lovely, but you need to go," he said. When no one moved, he pointed at the door. "Now."

The individuals pouted as they got up from his bed, but Leran wasn't interested in them or any other courtesan in Thurnda. After he'd removed his filthy gear, and bathed and dressed for the celebration, he found Balthus waiting in the antechamber.

"Really? You didn't like any of them?" Balthus asked when Leran emerged.

"No." Leran sat across from him. Aldo poured wine for both of them, and left them alone. "Were the trolls after us?"

"No idea," Balthus replied. "They've attacked Thurnda a few times over the past few winters, but this is the first time they approached the castle. It's also the first demon attack Thurnda's seen since before the last *mordeth-gall* fell."

"There's still no new demon king?"

"Not that we're aware of."

Leran rubbed his eyes, then he drank the rest of his wine. "Is there more news from the north?"

"The situation remains unchanged." Balthus leaned back and regarded his king. "Are we still waiting until after this blasted mating celebration is over before we leave?"

"Yes." Leran stood, and set his empty cup on the mantle. "Now, we've another celebration to attend."

"You need to take your mind off of her," Balthus said. "Find a distraction, at least for tonight. This longing will drive you mad."

"Who's to say I wasn't already mad?"

With that, Leran left his chamber and made his way toward the greater hall. As he walked, he thought about the battle. The force of trolls had been small, and badly trained. The demons had been the bigger threat, but the fae hunters had put them down quickly enough. He wondered if whomever had sent the demons hadn't realized the hunters were in residence. He also wondered if the attack was meant to keep him in Thurnda, and far from the trolls massing north of The Seat. Leran was so deep in thought that he rounded a corner and nearly flattened Ember.

"Forgive me." Leran reached for her, only to let his hand fall. "I didn't see you."

"It's fine," Ember murmured, dropping her gaze to the floor.

"I'm glad you decided to come to the hall tonight."

Ember frowned. "I was told it was mandatory."

Leran wondered who told her that. "May I speak to you?"

"You are speaking to me now," she answered, keeping her gaze on the floor.

"Alone," he clarified.

"I don't think there's anything either of us has to say that can't be said in a room full of people."

If that is how she wants to play, I will play. "I don't mind if all of Thurnda knows that the most beautiful sight I've ever beheld is you naked beneath me," he said, his voice rising toward the end.

"Leran!" she hissed. "What is the matter with you?" Her gaze darted about the hall, and Leran took advantage of her distraction to move closer to her.

"Come to my chamber," he implored. "I need to talk to you."

"I-I don't think that would be wise," Ember said as she moved away. Leran grabbed her elbow; she looked pointedly at it, but did not pull away. He knew she wouldn't create a scene in the hall if it could be helped.

"Then come out to the balcony," Leran said by way of compromise. "Please." Ember nodded, and he guided her to the very spot where they met only a sennight ago. He kept his hand on her elbow, as if she would run away if given half a chance.

Once they were on the balcony, she pulled away from him and went to stand at the railing. Leran closed the doors and breathed deeply of the cold air. "When I saw you waiting on the rampart with the others, I hoped you were waiting for me," he began. When Ember remained silent, he added, "No one's ever watched for my return."

She glanced at him, then resumed gazing at the mountains in the distance. "I find that hard to believe. No one in Tingu cares if the king survives his campaigns?"

"They care more about me as a king, than me as a man." When her response was again silence, he said, "Regardless if you were there for me or not, the sight of you on the rampart made me very, very happy."

"Good," she said, and offered no more.

"That night, after you left me," he began carefully, "where did you go?"

"Mara's room," she said at length.

"Mara's room," he repeated. He hadn't looked for her there, not wanting to disturb her sister.

"Afraid I was wandering about the palace bare as an egg?" she asked with a raised brow.

"I was afraid my foolish tongue caused you to hate me," he said, ignoring her attempt at levity. "Then I didn't see you at all in the morning..." He closed the distance between them, startling Ember with his sudden movements. "I can't bear the thought of you sad. Please, let me make it up to you."

"Just leave me be," she mumbled as she stepped back from him, crossing her arms over her breast.

"I can't," he said. "I won't." Her gaze darted away, but he reached out to her cheek and gently turned her face to his. "You're cold," he observed.

"I'm fine," she protested as she backed further away from him.

"Ember, what can I do?" he implored. "I told you that those words were said in jest. Please." He reached for her, and she let him take her hands in his. "I thought you wanted to be with me."

"I do, but..."

"But what?"

"I don't think you want me in the same way I want you," she murmured.

"How do you want me?" he asked. When she didn't answer, he continued, "Be my mate. Be mine, let me love you forever." He thought these were the words Ember needed to hear, what would soften her heart and let her be with him. He couldn't have been more wrong.

"Oh, that's rich!" Ember yanked her hands from his and stepped back. "You want to keep me as your brood mare? Mixing your bloodline with Elvasla's?"

"What? No!" Leran stepped forward and grabbed her shoulders. "Ember, I love you! I don't care who your ancestors were!" She winced at his voice, so he softened his tone when he continued. "Can you honestly say you don't love me?"

"Can you honestly say you wouldn't have pursued me if your Sala hadn't told you to?" she countered. Leran pursed his lips and said nothing; he refused to lie to her. "That's the problem, Leran. I'll never know why you want me. What if I agree to our mating, and someday your Sala tells you to go off and pursue another?"

"I would never forsake you," he said as he caressed her cheek. "Never, not for anything." Ember closed her eyes and turned her face toward his open palm. Leran pulled her into the circle of his arms, and buried his face in her hair. "Don't pull away," he murmured into her hair. "I've missed you." Ember nodded against his chest, and Leran wondered if she understood how much he needed her. He hadn't slept these past nights without her, but had lain awake wondering if she was thinking about him, and if she would ever forgive him. "If I hadn't said those things about your bloodline, if I had only told you I loved you and asked you to be my mate, what would you have said?"

"I would have accepted," she said into his chest. "Nothing would have made me happier." Leran tilted her chin up to his and searched her pale crystal eyes, heartened by her affirmation.

"Nothing is different," he said, holding her face close to his. "I love you, Ember. Be mine, now and always." He kissed her, tentatively at first, but grew bolder when she didn't push him away. Her hands found their way into his hair, and she coiled it around her fingers as she accepted him. Or so he thought.

"Everything is different," she murmured when they parted. "I would have learned eventually why you took me as a mate; the only difference is being heartbroken then, or now." Her voice was sad, and Leran believed she was heartbroken. He certainly was.

"You're being unreasonable," he snapped, his temper getting the better of him. "I won't keep explaining myself! Accept me, and be done with these games!"

Ember stared at him for a length of time; he could plainly see her inner turmoil as she wrestled with her emotions. Then her face softened, and Leran thought she would finally agree to be his, but she backed further away.

"My answer is no," she whispered as a tear rolled down her cheek. "I'm sorry, Leran, but I can't live my life wondering if you love me." She turned away, but Leran caught her wrist.

"Don't wonder," he murmured against her neck, "know." She leaned back against his chest, and he felt her tremble. "Don't cry, little flame, just let me prove myself to you. Tell me, what can I do?"

"I don't think there's anything to be done." She shook her wrist free of his grasp and moved to reenter the hall.

"Ember," he called.

"Leran, just leave me be."

Chapter Thirty-One

Ember Speaks

Gods, leaving Leran alone on the balcony was the hardest thing I have ever done. My heart felt as if it was torn from my breast, and my eyes and throat burned with tears I refused to shed while in the public space of the palace. I wanted nothing more than to return to my chamber and bawl with my head in Mara's lap, but I was expected at tonight's celebration. The lack of my presence a few days past had been noticed, and I had to be seen about the palace lest others wonder what had happened to me.

The morning after I'd learned that only Leran's armband loved me, Mara had managed to shoo away all of the saffira, *and Senan's mate, but when I hadn't been seen at the midday meal the one person to whom we could not refuse admittance appeared in the doorway. Our mother, the First Huntress, Latera Demon-killer.*

You'd never know just by looking at her that she was the feared and legendary deva'shi, *the elfin girl who killed the* mordeth-gall *with a single strike to the heart. She was small, her arms so slender they looked like they would splinter under the weight of a sword, with the fiery red curls and pale blue eyes that I had inherited. Indeed, many remarked that I was a replica of my mother, and I took it as the highest compliment.*

Mother deftly stepped past Mara, not believing her excuses for my absence for a moment, and managed to keep her composure when she saw me. I knew my eyes were swollen and red, my cheeks and neck also flushed from the many tears I'd shed. I hadn't budged from Mara's bed, and I was wearing the rumpled chemise that Leran had divested me of the prior evening.

"Would you like to tell me about it?" Mother asked as she sat beside me.

"No," I replied. *"I'd like to pretend that none of it ever happened."* She was silent for a time, and I laid my head on her shoulder. Mara sat on the other side of me and took my hand.

"Was it a man?" she asked.

"Yes," I replied.

"Did he hurt you?" she asked, an edge to her voice that few ever heard. Most mistakenly believed that my father was the more dangerous of my parents, being that he was the First Hunter of Parthalan. Why, when Mother stood next to him, she hardly reached his shoulder; she would often say that she was naught but a pebble against the great mountain of her mate. But they were all wrong, for when her mate or children were threatened, my mother was the deadliest force in all the nine realms.

I was silent too long, and Mother began questioning Mara. *"Has she told you what happened?"* Mother demanded. *"Is she hurt?"*

"No, no," I said. *"He would never hurt me."* That much was true; Leran would die before he let anything harm me. I knew that as surely as I knew my own name. *"He... I thought I loved him, and he me, but he only wanted to mix his blood with mine."*

Mother's brows knit together. *"He only wanted to get you with child?"* she murmured, and I nodded. *"Who in Thurnda would dare to suggest that?"*

"Only the Lord of Tingu," Mara muttered. I shot her a withering glare, but too late.

"Leran?" Mother asked.

"Yes." I snuffled, and Mara handed me a handkerchief. *"Leran."*

"That was why he left the feast directly after you. He was supposed to say something about Senan's mating, but he just got up and left."

"He did?" I asked, but of course I already knew that he'd left. I didn't know that he'd walked out before delivering his assigned speech. Senan's mate must have turned purple at the affront.

"Why do you think he doesn't love you?" Mother asked.

"His armband," I replied. *"He said that the Sala picked me as his mate. I asked him why, and he said I was a good match because of Elvasla. Because of you."* I nearly choked on the last words, and I fell into Mother's arms as I sobbed hysterically. *"I couldn't be with him once he said that. I just couldn't,"* I sobbed into her shoulder.

At length, my tears stopped, if only for a moment, and Mara fetched cold water to wash my face. It felt refreshing on my swollen eyelids, but did little to numb my pain. Mother bustled about, getting me a fresh dress and asking the saffira *to fetch me some broth and watered wine.*

"Drink this," she said as she presented me with a bowl of tea. Mother and her tea. "Love, I hate to ask you this, but do you need a healer?"

"We didn't lie together," I said, since that what was what she really wanted to know. I decided against telling her how close we came to completing the act.

Mother didn't say anything, but sat beside me as I dutifully drank my tea. When I put down the bowl, she began brushing my hair, like she had done when I was a little girl. "You won't tell Papa, will you?" I asked.

"I don't think that would be wise. Unless you'd like him to beat Leran to a bloody pulp?" I laughed shortly; indeed, Leran would be lucky to escape Father's wrath with his legs intact. "If he asks me, I will tell him," she warned.

"I know." I hadn't expected her to lie to him. I just didn't want it brought up. "When may we leave for Teg'urnan?"

"Perhaps in a few days we will be able to escape this rampant hospitality," she said. "Are you up to facing the court, or shall I say you have taken ill?"

"Maybe this evening," I said, but I stayed put until my lack of presence could be explained away no longer. It had taken me all morning gather the nerve to venture forth from my chamber, and as luck would have it that was when a band of mountain trolls chose to attack. Now we were to celebrate Thurnda's victory, and Mother had told me in no uncertain terms that I needed to make an appearance.

Of course, Leran found me as I made my way to the hall. I wouldn't have been surprised if he'd had men stationed outside my chamber alerting him to my every move. Then he'd tried to embarrass me by saying he found my naked form beautiful, but in truth the words made my heart glad.

I'm not a beautiful girl; pretty maybe, but not beautiful. I'm shorter than both faeries and elves tend to be, my skin is so pale it's nearly white, made all the paler thanks to my fire-bright hair. Coupled with my round cheeks and big eyes, I am certainly no beauty. Mara, on the other hand, is beautiful, with her long auburn hair and slender form. Men flocked to her, and hardly noticed me in her shadow.

Leran thought I was beautiful.

Then he asked me to be his mate—gods, he asked me to be his mate!—and I did what I had to do. I said no.

As I made my way through the hall, my head held high and throat burning with unshed tears, I looked to the elfin women of Thurnda. Elfin men saw themselves as the superior gender and kept their women at a smaller hearth in the rear of the hall; more, the men did nothing but train for battle and run off to war, leaving all matters of the home to their mates. Worse, while the women performed their labors, they were expected to wear the heavy velvet gowns with the many confounding undergarments I had grown to abhor.

As I walked past them in my light fae dress, my hair loose and uncoiffed, I realized I did not want to live like an elfin woman. No, I wanted to live like a fae, free and able to choose my mate and my own path in life. Leran had done me a favor by telling me the truth, and spared me from a life that would never satisfy me.

I was almost smiling when I reached at the smaller hearth, but my mood dissipated when I saw Mara's slumped shoulders and downcast eyes. I sat next to her, and asked her what was wrong.

"Nothing," she muttered. "Absolutely nothing."

"I'm surprised you're here at all," I said. "After the way you ran into Kemen's arms, I thought you'd be with him."

"That's part of the nothing." She raised her head and looked at a point across the hall. I followed her gaze, and saw Kemen drinking with Leran's second general, Belenos. "I ran out there like a fool, and he smiled, said he was fine, and continued on with the rest of the warriors." Mara faced me. "It was like he forgot who I was."

"Well, you have been pushing him away for years," I said. "Maybe he finally gave up."

Mara frowned and looked at her hands, then Leran entered the hall. He looked toward me, his brows pinched together, then went to speak with Asherah. Father and Sibeal were also there; I imagined they were making plans for our departure. I couldn't wait to see the gray spires of Teg'urnan again, and the statues of the stag and doe as they leapt toward each other across the gates.

Senan's mate and her ladies whispered among themselves, looked pointedly at me, and laughed.

"Did I do something amusing?" I demanded.

"Oh, no, no cousin," she replied. I did not know why that woman kept referring to me as her cousin, but Mother had assured me we were not related. Thank all the gods for that bit of fortune. "We were just discussing how you seem to have lost Leran's favor."

I raised an eyebrow. "Have I?"

"If the amount of women coming and going from his bedchamber is any indication, you certainly have." They laughed again, while my blood boiled. Who Leran associated with was none of my concern. That didn't mean I wanted to hear about it, especially not from this lot. "It looks like we won't be Ladies together, after all!"

I blinked, since her comment made no sense. "What are you to be the Lady of?" I asked.

"The Lady of Thurnda," she replied. "And if you let Leran rut like a—"

"The Lord of Tingu's and my affairs are none of your business, and I'll thank you to keep your nose out of it," I said, rising to my feet. "Surely you must know that you'll never be Lady of Thurnda."

She stood up and stamped her foot. I hadn't done anything that childish since before Tor was born. "I most certainly will!"

"Have you put Senan under a spell?" I demanded, and they all gasped. "I can think of no other reason why he'd keep you around, foolish sheep that you are."

I spun on my heel and walked away from that clutch of fools, Mara close behind, while they all complained about my audacity. Well, I was audacious, and intelligent enough to understand that Thurnda's line of succession did not include her. It was unfortunate that Senan had tied himself to such a fool, but that was his problem, not mine.

"That's going to make our time here considerably more awkward," Mara said. I peeked over my shoulder, and saw Senan's mate glaring daggers at me. I smiled. She frowned and slammed her hands onto the table, and upended her wine cup into her lap. Perhaps the gods were kind, after all.

"It was already awkward," I replied. "Perhaps we can find a map and a set of horses, and leave for Teg'urnan before anyone realizes we're gone." I found Mother seated near the greater hearth; she'd grown *tired of all these mating ceremonies days ago, and had resumed sitting with the hunters. Mara and I joined her.*

"What happened over there?" Mother asked, jerking her chin toward the women's hearth.

"Looks like some wine was spilled," I replied. A saffira *set full wine cups in front of Mara and me, and whispered that the Lord of Tingu was about to speak. Then Leran rose, and all eyes turned toward him.*

"I would like to thank Sibeal for her most generous hospitality," Leran said to the assemblage. "Truly, she has been a wonderful host. I wish Senan and his mate many, many winters of happiness." There were low murmurs of approval, and Leran waited a moment for them to subside.

"I regret to say that the time has come for our most gracious queen to depart from Thurnda's soil," he continued. "But I have invited Asherah, Lady of Tingu and mother of my heart, to accompany me to The Seat of Tingu, and she has graciously accepted. She and all of her companions will depart with me in three days' time."

What? All of her companions? I looked to my mother, but her wide eyes told me that she'd known nothing of Leran's plan. She leaned to the side murmured something in Papa's ear; I heard him say that it was an honor for us to be invited to The Seat as Leran's guests, and Asherah had been greatly pleased by the invitation.

Well, that was it then. If we didn't go, we would be refusing the Lord of Tingu and thus cause what could be an irreparable rift between him and Asherah. If I asked to return to Teg'urnan alone, both Papa and the queen would demand to know why, and my humiliation would be made public.

"It seems we're going to Tingu," I murmured to Mara as she squeezed my hand. Sibeal rose from her seat, and the hall quieted once again.

"Thank you, Leran, for your kind words," Sibeal began. "I too wish to congratulate my son on a life well lived, and a mate well chosen. Please, everyone, drink to their long and happy lives!"

The hall erupted in cheers, and Senan crossed the room to join his mate. I raised my cup and drank with the rest, the wine like vinegar on my tongue.

"As many of you know, Senan is my only living child," Sibeal continued. "That puts the House of Thurnda in a particular quandary, since rulership of this great land is passed from mother to daughter...

But a solution has arisen, one which has been approved by the Lord of Tingu himself."

Sibeal searched the crowd. When she found Mother, she said, "Latera Demon-Killer is not only the deva'shi, *she is descended from my own sister, Elvasla, the greatest Lady of Thurnda we have ever known!"*

At the far end of the room, Senan stood, his face a mask of fury. His mate pulled him back to his seat and whispered something in his ear. Whatever she said, it didn't calm him.

"Latera, do you consent to you, and your daughters and their daughters, being my heirs?" Sibeal asked.

"I do," Mother said. "I am honored. We are honored, Lady Sibeal."

"We're Sibeal's heirs?" I whispered, my heart racing. Deep down, I'd hoped I was wrong about Leran wanting me because of my ancestors, but Sibeal had proven me wrong. "I-I don't know how to feel about this."

Mara squeezed my hand again. "Neither do I."

Once the meal ended, and most were milling about as they discussed the coming trek to The Seat, I waited impatiently for Leran to be alone. It took some time, being that he was engaged in a rather heated discussion with Balthus; at least someone other than myself thought Leran's behavior was rash and foolish.

At length Leran saw me watching him, and sent an angry Balthus on his way. "Little flame," he greeted as he approached me.

"My lord," I said loudly, so no one would think we were on intimate terms with each other. We weren't, not any longer. "When did you learn Sibeal was going to make Mother her heir?"

"I knew she was considering it, but I didn't know she'd made a decision until just before she made the announcement," he replied. "I don't think Senan is pleased with her."

"Is that why you invited us to Tingu?"

"No. I wasn't intending to do that until we were on the balcony, and you walked away from me." He moved to touch my cheek, but I pulled away as I indicated the others with my eyes. Leran drew me toward an alcove that mostly obscured us from view, the very same alcove where he had first put his arms around me.

"What do you mean to accomplish with this trip?" I asked wearily. "I've already told you my answer." I would have said more, but he placed his fingers upon my lips.

"I know well what you said. You may as well have carved it upon my heart with a dagger." His voice cracked at the end; until that moment, I hadn't thought he hurt like me. I would have done anything to keep him from hurting.

"Then, what?" I asked, for I simply could not fathom what dragging me to Tingu would accomplish, aside from saddle sores.

"I refuse to give up on you," he replied. "If you leave now, I'll likely not see you again for many winters, if ever. If you come to The Seat, I have a chance to prove myself."

"Is that what you've been doing with all those women?" I demanded. "Proving yourself?"

"What women?"

"The ones coming and going from your chamber at all hours."

"Ah." Leran's head drooped. "Balthus keeps sending me courtesans. I sent them all away." He met my gaze, and added, "I didn't touch any of them. Not a one."

"I believe you," I said, and his face relaxed. "Why is Balthus sending them to you in the first place?"

"He thinks I need a distraction, from this." Leran extended his arm, and I glanced at the Sala. The heartstone was a hot, pulsating red.

"Does the color only change when I'm near?"

"No," he replied. "It began to darken when I met you, and has grown steadily darker since. Before I met you, it was white as snow."

"White as snow," I repeated. "There is snow in Tingu?"

"So much you can lose your horse in it," he said. "You'll enjoy winters at The Seat, I'm sure of it."

I didn't know what to say to that. Winters at The Seat meant that I wouldn't be home in Teg'urnan, another of the many reasons why we could not be together. Leran gazed at me, hopeful and a little annoyed at my silence, but my loss for words was no longer an issue when my mother suddenly appeared at my elbow.

"Lady Latera," Leran said with a respectful bow of his head. At times like this, I greatly enjoyed her status as a living legend.

"Leran," she said; being that she was the deva'shi, she needn't address him by his title. Somehow, she was outside the false ranks of *nobility. "Come. We need to prepare for our trek to Tingu," she said to me, placing a hand on my elbow as she guided me away from Leran.*

"My lady!" I turned and saw that Leran had grabbed Mother's shoulder to halt her, not a good decision on her best days. "May I have a word with you?"

"You may," Mother replied. I stood my ground, but Leran didn't seem to mind.

"I love Ember," Leran said emphatically.

"As do I," Mother said coolly.

"I only want Ember's happiness."

Unexpectedly, Mother's eyes softened. "As do I."

With that, Mother and I turned and left the Lord of Tingu standing there, and made ready for our journey to The Seat.

Chapter Thirty-Two

"These celebrations usually last all night," Latera said as she and Ember walked toward the guests' wing. "If you want to return for a bit, I'm sure we can avoid Leran. If you want to avoid him, that is."

"I think I'd rather stay in my room," Ember replied. "Maybe I'll start packing. We've another journey to make, now."

"We do." They reached Ember's door, and Latera took her hands. "Please, promise me you will eat something, and get some rest, and please, if you need me, come find me. I'm always here for you, no matter what."

"I know you are," Ember replied. "And don't worry about Leran. Soon enough, we'll be home, and he'll remain in Tingu, where he belongs."

Latera cupped her daughter's cheek. "Are you sure you don't want to be with him?"

"I don't know," Ember admitted. "Not if his idea of fun is dragging me from one land to the next."

Latera smiled. "I'll check on you and Mara in the morning," she said, then she left Ember and began walking toward the public areas of the palace. Normally, Latera would have persuaded Ember to return to the celebration, and take her mind off things, but not that night. Latera understood that much had happened between Ember and Leran, and her becoming Sibeal's heir, and now they were to make an extra trip to Tingu. Latera needed time to think, too.

Besides, she's grown. I can't hold her hand as I once did.

So the First Huntress left her daughter to begin packing for their second journey to an elfin land in as many moons, and hurried through the corridors in search of Sibeal. While she'd agreed to be named Thurnda's heir, she hadn't realized Sibeal meant to make a public announcement in the main hall. She wondered if it Sibeal had been aiming to take a bit of wind from Cerillia's sails, and divert the court's attention away from her. If that had been her intent, Sibeal had certainly triumphed. As she often did when she felt uneasy, Latera reached out to her mate.

Mar?

Beloved.

Ember's taken to her room—

Again?

She wants to be alone with her thoughts.

The entire palace is celebrating, and Ember is by herself, thinking? Latera couldn't see Aeolmar, but she could feel him frowning. *When are you going to tell me what's really going on?*

It should come from her.

She felt him grumbling, then he said, *Fine. But if her answers are inadequate, you and I will speak.*

All right. For now, I'm going to speak to Sibeal.

Want me to join you?

Perhaps. I will let you know.

Be safe, my nalla.

Latera smiled when he called her *nalla*, which meant beloved in the old language. Aeolmar didn't use the endearment often, but whenever he did, it warmed her to her very soul. She was still smiling when she approached Sibeal's rooms, and heard shouting coming from within. Latera pushed open the door, and found Sibeal glaring at Senan.

"You could have warned me," Senan yelled. Since the door was behind him, he hadn't seen Latera enter, but Sibeal had. "Am I not worth at least that?"

"When did any of this become about your worth?" Sibeal retorted. "The rule of succession is clear."

"And to name Latera as your heir," Senan spat. "How do we know she's truly one of us?"

"I'd rather not be in the same lot as you," Latera said, moving to stand beside Sibeal. "Do you have a problem with me, Senan? If so, please state it." When Senan remained silent but fuming, she continued, "What, you were full of bluster a moment ago. Do I not get to be shouted at, too?"

"Who are you?" Senan bellowed, red-faced with spittle flying. "When you first turned up on our doorstep, we thought you were fae! Then you're an elf, and now you're to rule us all?"

Latera laughed. "Sibeal, is he drunk?"

"Oh, I hope so," Sibeal replied. "It's the only explanation for his behavior."

"I am not drunk," Senan yelled. Latera crossed the room and grabbed the front of his tunic.

"Good," she began. "I want you to remember every word I say." She paused, waiting for him to protest. He didn't, unless you counted the veins bulging in his forehead. "You know exactly who I am. Don't pretend otherwise. As for me ruling you, you had best pray that does not come to pass."

"Why is that?" he snapped.

"I don't take kindly to men who upset their mothers." Latera released his tunic and stepped back. "Leave, and get hold of yourself. Take the entire night. I expect you to make full apologies in the morning."

Senan scoffed. "You can't order me to leave a room."

"Can't I? Shall I call on my mate for assistance, or Leran?" Latera arched an eyebrow. "Shall I make good on my word and remove you myself?"

Senan paled, then he spun on his heel and left the room. Latera blew out a breath, and faced Sibeal.

"What in the nine realms just happened?" Latera asked.

Sibeal shook her head. "I have no idea. My sweet, gentle boy is gone. Only Cerillia's mate remains."

"Should I send for guards?" Latera asked, but Sibeal shook her head.

"Senan's sole weapons are words," she replied. "He abhors violence in all forms."

Latera thought words were just as harmful as a sword, but kept her opinion to herself. "I'm glad you'll be safe."

"From Senan, yes. We all are." Sibeal approached a side table, and poured two goblets of wine. She handed one to Latera, and said, "I'm sure you didn't come here to discuss my difficult child."

"All children are difficult, at times," Latera said, as she accepted the goblet. "I've been thinking about me being your heir."

"You have already agreed," Sibeal began, but Latera held up her hand.

"I have, and I am honored. Truly. But it seems that the person who should be named your heir is Elvasla's daughter, not me. If Priya returns, and has an interest in Thurnda, I'll not stand in her way."

Sibeal sighed. "Yes, well, you are correct. And it is good of you to step aside for Priya, should she decide to return." She drained her goblet, and moved to refill it. "I wish I knew where she was. I once suspected she returned to the mortal realm."

"Really? Do you know where she would have gone?"

"Her father, Tarac, built an estate for himself and their children. I image that's where she would be."

"Tarac," Latera repeated. She knew the name and the land well, since her mother had lived in Tarac before she became the Queen of Gannera. "Perhaps, when I next visit the mortal realm, I will visit Tarac's estate myself."

Sibeal leaned forward. "Have you been there?"

"I haven't, but I know a few who have."

Chapter Thirty-Three

Asherah Speaks

I woke the next morning in our temporary bed, with the welcome warmth of my mate pressed against my back. Finlay had an arm wound around my torso and a leg thrown over my hip, and I couldn't have moved if I'd wanted to. Not that I wanted to. I could have remained in his arms forever.

I listened to his slow, regular breaths, and thought about the night before. I don't know what had been more amazing, Leran inviting me to The Seat, or Sibeal publicly naming Latera as her heir. Both announcements had caused an uproar, Leran's because he had invited a whole swath of Parthians to the elves' ancestral home. However, I thought Sibeal's announcement was the event that would end up affecting us all, and I didn't think it would be all good, either.

I rolled over and faced Finlay, and my none too gentle movements woke him. When he opened his eyes, he smiled.

"Beloved," he said, then he kissed me.

I kissed him back, and asked, "Why is Sibeal so concerned with an heir now?"

"Why are you always thinking about other people when we're in bed?"

Thus admonished, I nestled closer and toyed with the curls over his heart. "I'm thinking about you, too. How can I not, with you laying all over me?"

He slid his other arm underneath my side, then rolled onto his back as he dragged me on top of him. "There. Now you're laying all over me."

"I do like it here." I felt his cock pressing against me, so I sat up and took him in hand. I almost continued our banter, then I thought the better of it and slid myself onto him. Finlay's eyes widened, and he laughed, surprised and delighted and gods, how I adored this man. He

pulled me close and kissed me, and I proved he was always first in my thoughts.

Afterward, I dozed with my cheek pressed against his chest. "Why were you thinking about Sibeal?"

I raised my head. "Now who's bringing others into our bed?"

"Don't make me distract you again."

"Wasn't I the one distracting you?" Despite my question, I moved to the side and propped myself up on an elbow. "You don't find it odd that she needs an heir now?"

"I suppose I don't," he replied. "It seems that she doesn't trust Cerillia, and wants to keep her far from the throne. She probably assumes that having a named heir will ensure that." Finlay paused, then said, "Apparently, Senan was heard shouting at his mother last night, after her announcement."

I shook my head. "Nothing good is going to come of this. Not for us, or Latera and her girls, and definitely not for Sibeal."

"Do you think Senan would try to harm her?"

"I don't know if Senan could harm her. From what I understand, he's never picked up a sword in his life."

"Unusual, for an elf."

"Very."

Finlay trailed his fingertips along my forearm. "Speaking of elves, Lady of Tingu—"

"I know you don't like hearing me called that."

"I don't mind." He traced patterns around my knuckles. "How do you feel about finally returning to The Seat?"

I flopped onto my back and stared at the bed canopy. "I... I don't really know. Long ago, I made peace with never seeing my old home ever again, and now... Now, it hardly seems real. I don't know if I'll believe it's happening until I see it with my own eyes."

"Do you think being there will help you remember?"

"I don't know the answer to that, either." I faced him again, saw the worry in his summer blue eyes. "How do you feel about going to The Seat? Did you ever think you'd be this far north, away from your warm desert?"

"While I do not like the cold, I am interested in the lands, and the people," he replied. "Do you think any trolls will be in residence at The Seat?"

Most didn't know that Parthalan's king was descended from trolls; it seemed that long ago a troll smith fell in love with a fae woman who hated the cold, so he brought her to the desert where they lived happily and had an abundance of children. Eventually, more trolls migrated south, and they founded Finlay's home village of Cadogan. Many, many years later, Finlay and I met, and he left his warm climate for me, and I am so glad he did.

"Perhaps, but even if they aren't we can always send for Grelk," I replied. "Or we could pay a visit to his forge. Grelk loves meeting new people, and he's a character unlike anyone else I've ever encountered."

"Then I'd say we're both looking forward to visiting Tingu."

"Yes. I'd say we are."

***

All too soon, we got out of bed and ventured out into the palace proper. The overall mood was tense, to say the least.

"Why is everyone so unhappy?" I muttered. Everyone we came across, from saffira *to warriors, appeared harried and anxious.*

"Last evening's announcements must have been more significant than we realized," Finlay replied. We entered the hall and saw Balthus near the greater hearth, clutching a handful of parchments.

"Balthus," I called. He quickly pocketed the parchments and approached us.

"Queen Asherah, King Finlay," he greeted. "What can I do for you?"

"You can explain why everyone in Thurnda is so morose," I replied. When he only frowned, I asked, "Is it because of Sibeal's announcement?"

"I don't know if the news of the deva'shi *possibly ruling Thurnda is what's bothering people," Balthus replied. "From all accounts, Latera is well loved."*

"But you do know," Finlay prompted. "Don't you?"

"I do, but these aren't things I've been given leave to speak of," Balthus replied.

"I'm still Lady of Tingu," I reminded him. "Come, now, you used to tell me everything, whether Lormac approved it or not."

He frowned. "Yes, my lady. As for how some are behaving... Leran can be most difficult, at times."

I laughed. "Yes, I know. Remember when he refused to wear clothes for an entire moon?"

The corner of Balthus's mouth twitched. "I do."

"Well, then, as long as he's not bare arsed in the snow, I'd say things aren't so bad."

I looked expectantly at Balthus, lest he thought I would let him get away with a blatant non answer. "His sudden decision to bring you all to The Seat is causing us a great deal of effort, which I don't think Leran anticipated. Not that we don't want you to visit," he added. "It's been too long."

"Thank you," I said; despite my calm demeanor, I was a wreck inside. I really was going home, after all these many winters. "Is there anything we can do to help with the preparations? We don't want to be a burden."

"You, my lady, are never a burden, nor are your people," he replied. "As for how you may help, keep your people vigilant and your swords sharp. By your leave?"

I nodded, and Balthus bowed once and left the hall. After he was gone, Finlay said, "This is about more than a few announcements. Elkin was right. Something is happening in the north, and Leran is the force standing between it and Parthalan. What's more, I suspect he's ordered his people's silence."

I considered Leran, my caring, intelligent boy who'd once run to me for all things, and how we'd finally begun reconnecting after a lifetime spent on opposite sides. Had we been separated by more than distance and grief? I didn't know, and I didn't know how I could find out.

"But, what is he holding back?" I wondered. "What's on the other side of this wall?"

"Should we ask more of his people?"

I shook my head. "Leran's people are loyal to him unto death. I'm surprised Balthus said as much as he did. He wouldn't have, had I not once been his queen."

"You're his queen still," Finlay said. "Do you think this has anything to do with the old gods, and Caol'non's return?"

"I wish I knew."

Chapter Thirty-Four

Aeolmar took the long way from the guest quarters out to the training yard by crossing the palace square. It was cold and damp outside, but Latera had told him, in detail, of her encounter with Senan the prior evening. Senan had shouted at Latera, which meant that Aeolmar needed to avoid Senan, at least for the time being. Aeolmar had the utmost respect for Sibeal, and therefore would rather endure the coldest, wettest walk in history than beat her son to a pulp in her own house.

Nevertheless, he did enjoy imagining a confrontation with Senan, and telling the Thurndian lord exactly what he thought of him. He was on his third such scenario when he rounded the corner past the stables and saw Finn.

Finn was alone in the yard, sword in hand, and was going through the motions of a practice routine. Aeolmar knew the motions well, since it was the exact routine his father had taught him, and the one he taught to his own children; since Finn was the same age as Ember, he'd trained with her and Tor, as well. Then Finn and Ember had their falling out, and Finn had put down the sword and taken up the bow. He was an excellent archer, as he'd proven in the battle against the demons and trolls a few days past.

Aeolmar wondered if Finn stopped coming to him for lessons because he'd been frightened of him. While Aeolmar had a reputation of being a gruff and unyielding man—a reputation he'd carefully cultivated over the years—he understood Finn and Ember were children at the time, and that sometimes children have arguments, and do foolish things. Hells, Aeolmar still did foolish things often. And he would never take out his anger on a child, his own or someone else's. It galled him that he may have unintentionally pushed Finn away, and Aeolmar strode onto the grass, intending to make whatever reparations he could.

"I'm surprised you remember that routine," Aeolmar called. "We haven't practiced that one in ages."

Finn lowered his sword and smiled. "I've a good memory, both in my head and in my arms."

"I can see that." Aeolmar drew his own sword. "Care for a partner?"

"You have time for a match, my lord?"

Aeolmar snorted at the Finn's use of the title. "Finn, I'm fairly certain you outrank me. Sword up!"

Finn blocked Aeolmar's initial strike, but only just. Aeolmar went hard, and while he didn't use the same amount of force he'd used sparring with Tor, nor did he go easy on Finn. In the end, he was proud of how well Finn did, but not surprised. He had been his first teacher, after all.

Afterward, they retreated to the guard's tower. During his first trip to Thurnda, Aeolmar had learned about the small room behind the sentry's post that was kept stocked with food and ale. Sibeal understood that happy and well-fed soldiers led to a well-guarded palace. The guards were only too pleased to accommodate Aeolmar and Finn, and soon enough, they both had full mugs and a platter of food between them.

"I'm impressed, Finn," Aeolmar said. "I'm also a bit disappointed you took up archery, instead."

"There's something about a bow," Finn replied. "It's a different sort of concentration than the sword. When I'm setting myself up, aiming my bolt, it's almost peaceful. There's nothing peaceful about sword fighting, especially when you're teaching it."

"No, I suppose there isn't."

"Aeolmar, can I talk to you about something?"

"Of course," he replied, assuming Finn wanted to discuss something else about swords, or another form of combat.

"My mother," Finn began. "You've known her for some time, correct? Longer than Father's known her?"

"Yes. I came to Teg'urnan some years before they met."

"Did she ever talk about gods then?"

Aeolmar paused with his mug halfway to his mouth. "To be honest, the only time I've heard Asherah speak of gods is when she's cursing them." He set down his mug, and asked, "Is she cursing them now?"

"No, but she's always talking about them," Finn replied. "I hear her and father going on about the one she's named after, Ish h'ra."

Aeolmar blinked. "She claimed she's named after Ish h'ra?"

"Not specifically, but isn't she?" Finn pressed. "That's her name's form in the old language."

Aeolmar grunted, feeling foolish as he wondered what other clues he'd overlooked. This one had been staring him in the face for so long he might as well be blind. "That was a name she took on after she burned the *dojas*. I don't know what she was called before that time."

"Well, however she got the name it's all she talks about now. And she keeps picking up little things that to relate to the Ish h'ra, things like memories, and locations, and..." Finn frowned. "Remember when Sarelle put a spell on her, and she lost herself? I don't want that to happen again."

"No one does," Aeolmar said. "Have you spoken to your parents about this?"

"What would I say? Hello, Mother, are your wits about you today?" Finn shook his head. "I was young when it happened, but I remember how she forgot me. And how she forgot father. You were away at the time, but it was terrifying to watch her lost inside her own mind."

Aeolmar also remembered that as a bad time, but not because of Asherah's madness. He'd been away from Teg'urnan on a quest to rescue Mara, and he almost hadn't found her in time. Kidnapping and torturing Mara had been another facet of Sarelle's plan to destroy Asherah, and somehow regain Olluhm's favor. In the end, Latera had executed Sarelle, which all agreed was a just end to the former priestess.

"I will say this," Aeolmar began. "It is my duty to protect the queen, and if anyone tries to bespell or otherwise harm Asherah, I will eliminate them. Assuming your father or my mate don't do away with the threat first," he added.

Finn nodded. "That's good to know."

"But also, Asherah has always been curious about her past," Aeolmar continued. "Perhaps these memories are only that. Would you like me to talk to her?"

"No, no. I know she worries that some think she's still mad. And she's not. She's better," Finn insisted with such conviction Aeolmar wondered who he was trying to convince. "Perhaps I can find a way to talk to her, without it seeming like I'm spying on her."

"You're not. You love her, and you want her to be well and happy. She'll appreciate that."

"She will, won't she?" Finn grinned. "Thank you, Aeolmar. You've put my mind at ease, and made my sword arm sore. All in all, this was a pleasant time."

Aeolmar returned his smile. "When we're at The Seat we'll see about getting you a troll sword of your own. I'm sure Grelk will craft something amazing for you."

Finn's smile widened, and Aeolmar was reminded of a merchant he'd met in Cadogan long ago. "You really think he will?"

"Finn, I'm sure he'll be delighted."

Chapter Thirty-Five

Ember Speaks

We were told the journey from Thurnda's palace to The Seat of Tingu would take eight days. I've been made to understand that one can manage the journey in three, but our large numbers meant that the travel was slow going to begin with. Balthus, Leran's second, stated this fact loudly and often, lest any of us forget how much he'd like to leave us Parthians behind.

The traveling arrangements alone took two days to sort out. While I'd done all I could to avoid Leran during that first day, it is nearly impossible to completely evade one within the confines of a palace, even a palace as grand as Thurnda's. However, I must admit that Leran was nothing if not courteous to me, as he asked how I was, and if I needed anything for the coming journey. I'd worried that he would try to corner me again, like he'd done on the balcony, but Leran seemed to have accepted my choice. For now.

Gods, if only he had been a cad about the whole matter, I could have hated him and been done with it. But no, Leran proved time and again that he was a good and noble man, with good and noble intentions, and I had to struggle to remember why I couldn't be with him.

His well-meaning nature was apparent the morning of our departure. We were set to leave at noon, and Mara and I were packing up the last of our belongings, she much more efficiently than I, when there was a knock at our door. I opened it to find Aldo, Leran's personal saffira, *standing in the corridor. His arms were laden with wool and leather.*

"Hello, Aldo," I greeted. "What brings you here?"

"The Lord of Tingu wished to send this traveling gear to you and your sister," he replied. Upon further inspection, Aldo's burden comprised footed stockings, and fur-lined leather leggings meant to be

worn over them. The stockings were a thin yet dense weave that felt as soft as silk, yet were as sturdy as wool.

"What sort of fabric is this?" Mara asked, as she rubbed the stockings between her thumb and forefinger. "I've never seen the like."

"It is called casimhirre," Aldo replied. "The goats that scrabble about the northern reaches of the World's Spine tend toward a long, silky fur. Our weavers make good use of it."

"This must be costly," I said, and Aldo affirmed that this casimhirre had a comparable value to cloth-of-gold. There were four sets of hose and leggings for me and four again for Mara, value enough to fund another seven days of feasting. "Why did Leran send us all of this?" I asked, since Leran had sent us two sets of boots yesterday, and woolen cloaks the day before.

"I receive woefully few explanations regarding his intentions," Aldo replied. "However, he did state, several times, that your riding dresses are unsuitable for Tingu's cold. I imagine he'd rather not like it if you were chilled." Mara and I were both stunned by Leran's kind gesture. Then, Aldo asked me to return Leran's cloak.

"His cloak?" I repeated.

"Yes, my lady," Aldo said. "My lord informed me that he lent it to you some days past. He will need it for the coming journey."

"Of course," I murmured, then bade him wait a moment while I retrieved it. I knew exactly where Leran's cloak was, folded neatly on the far side of my bed. It had been there since I returned from our walk on the battlement, save for a few evenings past when I'd used it as a blanket. My mother once told me a story of how, when she was separated from Father during her time at the Eastern Border, she would wrap herself in the cloak he'd given her, imagining that she lay in his arms. Well, I had been feeling desperately lonely after my second refusal of Leran, but of course I couldn't go to him for comfort. Not after rejecting him not once, but twice.

So I wrapped myself in Leran's cloak, trying to get the feel of what it would be like to lie in bed with him; I'd imagined that I would feel safe. Warm. Complete. Exactly the way I felt when he did hold me, even that last time on the balcony. Instead, I was only reminded of the fact that I was alone, and heartbroken, and about to be dragged far to the east of Thurnda, all so Leran could assuage his wounded pride. That, and the clasp kept sticking me in places I'd rather not be stuck, and it smelled strongly of wood smoke.

Still, I kept it next to me as I slept, almost like a talisman. I liked being able to reach out and touch it, a tangible reminder of what might have been. I picked it up and shook out the length of it, and sighed. After holding his cloak one last time, I carefully refolded it, arranging it so the clasp was once again visible, I returned to where Aldo and Mara waited.

"Here you are," I said, grateful my words were steady. "Please, tell Leran that his gifts are much appreciated."

"I shall, my lady." With that, Aldo unceremoniously dropped the heap of leggings in the doorway, took Leran's cloak, and left. While I thought this was further proof of his senility, the hose was indeed warm, and neither Mara nor I shivered while wearing it.

Of course, now I had to face Leran bound from foot to waist in a gift of his, but again, he was gracious. He asked if the fit was good (it was perfect, as if they'd been made for me), and if I approved of the colors he'd chosen (a mossy green and pale blue, and both shades were lovely), and after I affirmed both he did not mention it again. Gods, he was infuriating.

This sojourn to Tingu couldn't be over quickly enough.

Chapter Thirty-Six

Aeolmar stood on the landing above the palace's main steps, over-seeing the rest as they organized baggage, provisions, and the like for their trek to The Seat. While no one had directly discussed the situation with him, he understood that Leran's motivations behind inviting the Parthians to Tingu weren't only to mend his relationship with Asherah. The fact that both Leran and Ember had been avoiding him strengthened his theory. When he repeated his question to his mate about what was happening, Latera had told him to ask Ember directly.

"I can't," Aeolmar had replied. "She's hiding from me."

"She'll talk when she's ready," Latera said, and that was the last bit of information she'd offered on the subject. No matter. Aeolmar was a patient hunter.

For Leran to go through all this trouble, he must be quite taken with Ember. Indeed, Leran had offered to finance the entire party's journey out of Thurnda, and he spared no expense. Tingu was known to be the wealthiest of the elf lands, with The Seat's treasury supposedly filled with more gold and gems than a thousand kings could spend. Aeolmar had never put much stock in rumors, but the largess before him told him that at least some of the stories were true.

Senan joined Aeolmar on the landing, and scoffed at the prepara-tions below them. "Leran's showing off," Senan grumbled.

"Perhaps he is," Aeolmar conceded, though he did wonder who exactly Leran was trying to impress. "Thank you again for hosting us. I hope you and Cerillia will be happy together."

"Yes, well. I suppose that's up to Mother."

Aeolmar, unsure if Senan was about to complain about Latera being named Sibeal's heir or Sibeal herself, remained quiet. Either way, he didn't have the time or desire to listen to Senan's family drama. He scanned the crowd, and saw his daughters near one of the baggage carts.

"A moment," Aeolmar said, then he remembered how Senan had shouted at Latera; while his mate didn't need or request his protection, it was still his duty to defend her. "Before I go, know this. Speak rudely to my mate again and I'll tear out your tongue."

"You dare," Senan began.

"I dare, and I will," Aeolmar replied. "Don't test me."

Aeolmar walked away from Senan's spluttering apology, and toward his daughters. He caught Mara's eye first, and jerked his chin toward Ember. Mara shook her head, then she stepped away to check their horses. When Ember looked up, she was alone with her father.

"You look like an elf," he said, indicating the many layers of outerwear she'd received from Leran.

Ember gathered her new, thicker cloak about her. "I suppose I do."

"What's wrong?" Aeolmar asked.

"What makes you think anything's wrong?" she countered. When he remained silent, she demanded, "What did Mother tell you?"

"She said that I should ask you what's been happening," he replied. Ember frowned and wrung her hands. "Is there anything you'd like to tell me?"

"Yes. I regret promising that I'd never lie to you." They stared at each other for a moment, then she said, "I don't need you fighting my battles for me."

"I am well aware of that." Aeolmar sat on a stack of trunks. After a moment, Ember sat beside him. "I only want you to be happy."

"I know."

"Based on your new cloak, and boots, I assume Leran is behind your mood?" Ember nodded. "Do you not feel the same about him?"

"No. Yes. I-I..." She dashed her hand across her eyes. "It's complicated."

"I know it is."

Ember glanced up at him. "How could you possibly know that?"

"I remember how it felt wondering if someone loved me back."

"Did they? Love you back?"

"Your existence is proof she did." When Ember nodded but otherwise didn't reply, he asked, "Unless that's not the case? Are his attentions unwanted?"

"Well, I told him to leave me alone, and he refused," she began. "I kept away from him for a few days, then he retaliated by inviting all of us to The Seat. So now, instead of returning to Teg'urnan and forgetting about him, I get to be dragged across the elflands while he acts like a maddeningly polite man."

Aeolmar snorted. "I've used many words to describe Leran, but I've never once called him polite." They laughed together. "If he's bothering you, I can kill him."

"Papa! You can't!"

"Of course I can," Aeolmar said. "I'm sure it wouldn't be much of a fight."

"I know you're capable of killing him," Ember said, "but doing away with the Lord of Tingu is a bad idea. The queen would be devastated."

"If you're more concerned with Asherah's reaction than your own, perhaps he isn't the one for you."

Ember leaned against his shoulder. He put his arm around her. "You really think he's not?"

"What I think doesn't matter," Aeolmar replied. "Only you know if he'll make you happy."

"I know." Ember fidgeted with the edge of her cloak. "There's something else, about us."

Aeolmar's gut twisted as a thousand horrible ideas formed in his mind. "Something good, or not so good?"

"You know about Leran's armband? The stupid Sala?"

"You mean the armband Nexa herself created, Tingu's most valued possession?" he countered.

Ember looked up at him, wide eyed. "Is it really that old? Well, I didn't know that when I threw it at him."

Aeolmar stared at his daughter, mouth agape. "You threw it at him?"

She sighed. "I did. The heartstone." Ember bit her lip, and continued, "It turned red."

Then Leran does love her. "And that didn't please you?"

"It did, then it didn't, and now..." Ember gestured at the assembled carts and horses, waiting to set out for Tingu. "And now here we are."

"Indeed." Aeolmar smoothed back Ember's wild curls that were so like her mother's, all the while struggling to remember everything he'd ever heard about the Sala. Namely, he wondered if the heartstone meant that both parties were in love, or just the wearer. Then Ember sighed, and Aeolmar's heart ached for her. No matter what the heart-stone's color meant, his duty was to his daughter.

"If you don't want to go to The Seat, say the words and I'll take you home."

"You would?"

"Of course I would."

"Thank you, Papa." Ember smiled, and Aeolmar wondered how many more times he would be able to comfort his little girl. He suspected that day might be the last.

"Well? Are we headed north, or south?"

"I think north, for now," she replied. "I know how rare it is for outsiders to be invited to The Seat. This may be a once in a lifetime opportunity. We shouldn't waste it."

"Agreed. North it is, then." Aeolmar stood, then he helped Ember to her feet. "Meanwhile, I will keep a map on me at all times, in case we suddenly need to travel south." He leaned closer, and added, "An emergency could arise at Teg'urnan, you know."

Ember smiled. "I suppose anything could happen."

"I'll also keep a close eye on Leran, learn his habits. Just in case you change your mind, and decide you'd like me to kill him."

"Papa!"

***

Mara knelt in front of her trunks as she watched her father and sister, and almost wished she was the one being comforted. Aeolmar had a way of making those he cared about feel safe, no matter their circumstances. After Mara had been abducted by Sarelle, and subsequently rescued by her father and the hunters, she'd become Aeolmar's shadow, and had constantly followed him around Teg'urnan and even on a few of his patrols. Aeolmar never complained, or tried sending her away. Instead, he made room for her wherever he was, and in time Mara felt strong enough to go about her day without him. Mara had never been as grateful for anything as her father's quiet patience.

"Need help with those?"

Mara glanced upward and saw Kemen standing over her. "I was just checking the clasps," she said.

"And they're good?"

"They are." Mara stood and dusted off her hands. "Are you also going to The Seat, rather than home to Teg'urnan?"

"I am," he replied. "Asherah believes it's best if we remain together. I have to say, I do agree with our queen. Things happen in the north."

"What sort of things?"

"The sort of things even bards won't sing about." Kemen surveyed the waiting horses and carriages. "You'll be on horseback the whole way?"

"Yes, of course. Why?"

"If it gets too cold, a carriage might be more comfortable," Kemen said. "If you need one, let me know. One's been set aside for you and Ember. Tor and Finn could ride along with you, I suppose."

"That's very kind, but you don't need to go out of your way for me."

"I'm not. The Lord of Tingu himself requested it." Kemen leaned closer, and said, "Seems he has a thing for redheads. That, I also agree with."

Mara smiled, surprising both herself and Kemen. "Do you, now?"

"Everything good here?" Caol'non asked, startling Mara. She hadn't even seen him approach them.

"Yes, of course," Mara replied. It unnerved her how much Caol'non resembled her brother. Caol'non gave her a curt nod, then he turned toward Kemen.

"Your father is Krylle," he stated. "The priest."

"That he is," Kemen replied. "I understand your father was once Prelate. Amazing, the things our families have gotten up to. Well, Mara, if you're set, let's be off."

Kemen took Mara's hand and guided her through the stacks of luggage, and away from Caol'non. "Where are we going?" Mara asked.

"Wherever he isn't," Kemen replied. "He bothers you."

"He does, but it's not his fault," Mara replied. "It's all very strange, him reappearing after all these years."

"Until everyone—and by everyone, I mean the queen and your father—are certain he's not a threat, I don't want you to be alone with him." When Mara's fingers tensed against Kemen's, he continued, "I know I don't have the right to tell you who you can and can't associate with, but I would rather anger you than see you hurt."

"So I'm to be a mad, safe woman?"

Kemen glanced at her face, and relaxed when he saw her smile. "Or a safe madwoman. The choice is yours."

Mara's smile widened. "Thank you, Kemen. I appreciate your concern. I'm just surprised you're interested."

"Why is that?"

"After the battle, you..." Mara bit her lip and turned away, and wished she hadn't brought it up. "I felt like you were ignoring me."

"Forgive me. I thought you wanted more space between us. I now see I was wrong." Kemen bowed over her hand and kissed her knuckles. "If you'd like, I'll ride with you today."

"That... that would be nice." When Kemen's smile became a grin, she said, "I've never seen you smile so much."

"You like it?"

"Yes. I do."

"Then I'll keep it up."

***

Having seen to Ember, Aeolmar stood and searched the crowd for his eldest child. He saw Mara speaking with Kemen, and frowned. He wasn't pleased by Kemen's continued pursuit of Mara, but she was an intelligent woman who could make her own decisions. Besides, he'd just promised Ember he would kill the Lord of Tingu if she wished it. He couldn't go around threatening all of his daughters' suitors, at least not on the same day.

Then Caol'non approached Mara and Kemen. Aeolmar couldn't hear what was said, but Kemen quickly led Mara away from Caol'non. Having had enough of this stranger with his father's face, Aeolmar approached him.

"Stay away from my family," Aeolmar said.

"I am your family," Caol'non shot back. "That man—"

"That man has been one of my hunters for decades," Aeolmar said. "I've only known you a handful of days. Whose opinion do you think I should trust?"

"Does blood mean nothing to you?"

"If it means so much to you, where were you?" Aeolmar demanded. "Where were you when your supposedly much-loved brother was murdered?"

Caol'non paused. "The fire was deliberate?"

"I set the fire," Aeolmar said. "The day before I burned my home to the ground, Mersgoth killed my family."

"The one who marked Alluria," Caol'non said. "I didn't know."

"No. You didn't. And you don't know anything about us now."

Aeolmar stalked away from Caol'non, intent on finding his mate. He found Finlay instead.

"Is it wise to have this Caol'non accompany us to The Seat?" Aeolmar demanded without preamble.

"Probably not, but I think it's best to keep him with us, if for no other reason to keep an eye on him," Finlay replied. "Has he done something?"

"He's existing," Aeolmar said. "That's enough."

"Do you believe his story about the old gods?" Finlay asked. "Asherah does."

"I... I don't know what to believe." Aeolmar rubbed his eyes. "Leran sent two of his men to Ysr. When they return, and give us their report on the state of the island, we'll be able to discern if anything he's said is true."

Finlay nodded. "Until then, I'll assign a few soldiers to watch Caol'non. If he does anything odd—well, odder—we'll know."

Aeolmar grunted. "I wish I knew if I could believe him."

Finlay clapped Aeolmar's shoulder. "Patience, friend. Soon enough, all will be revealed."

Aeolmar recalled his conversation with Finn the day prior, and said, "How is Finn taking all of this?"

"Like this is a grand adventure, which is how he sees everything," Finlay replied. "He's even taken to walks with Asherah every evening before supper."

"That's wonderful," Aeolmar said, and decided to keep his conversation with Finn to himself. He scanned the gathering below, and spotted each of his children, and Finn, in turn. They all appeared to be doing well. "As long as the children are happy, we're doing something right."

Chapter Thirty-Seven

Ember speaks

By the end of the third day of our journey, Leran's genial nature began to wear down my defenses. He'd located a secluded vale for us to spend the evening, and at our nightly meal, he went out of his way to be a wonderful host. I went so far as to laugh at one of his jokes, only to quiet myself when I saw my father's watchful eye upon us. He hadn't let the Lord of Tingu out of his sight since he'd offered to forgo a trip to The Seat and take me home, and I daresay he was waiting for the perfect opportunity to tell Leran exactly what he thought of him. Leran's good behavior was driving Papa crazy.

That evening I fell asleep easier than I had in days. The mountain air helped to clear the cobwebs from my mind, and I hoped I was coming to terms with my feelings for Leran. I loved him, true, and my heart ached to be so close to him, but it was only temporary. Soon enough we would leave Tingu and its lord behind, and I would be able to forget him, just as he would be able to forget the tiny half-elf who'd aggravated him so. Imagine my surprise when I woke in the small hours of the night to find Leran crouching above my bedroll.

"Is something wrong?" I asked, too startled to be offended by his intrusion. I glanced about the tent, and saw that both Mara and Tor were sound asleep.

"I want to show you something," he whispered.

"What is it?"

"Get up, and I'll show you." He rose and extended his hand, and I let him help me up. He had an oiled hide and a fur blanket thrown over one shoulder, and my cloak in his hands.

"Where are we going?" I asked.

"If it's all right with you, I'd like it to be a surprise." I must have regarded him dubiously, since he asked, "Do you trust me?"

I nodded, because I do trust him. I'd trust him with my life. He settled the cloak about my shoulders and I looked for my boots, but he murmured that I wouldn't need them and swept me into his arms. I protested quietly, so as not to wake my siblings, but he ignored me as he carried me toward the tent flap.

"Now, close your eyes," he murmured as he tugged the hood over my face. I grumbled something rather impolite but did as I was told, and wound my arms around his neck while I wondered where he was taking me.

Eventually he stopped walking, then I heard him throw the hide onto the ground before he settled us on top of it, and the fur on top of us. "You may look now," he whispered, his lips against my ear, and I opened my eyes to the most beautiful sight I had ever seen.

It was snowing.

Leran had settled us beneath a pine tree, and the wide spread of its branches sheltered us from the falling snow. But it was so beautiful, so magical and pristine and white. I crawled forward from his lap to let the flakes land on my upturned face. They were so cold they tickled, and I laughed at the tiny frigid bursts against my skin.

"It's beautiful," I breathed. "Did you know it would snow?"

"I did not. When it began falling, my first thought was to wake you. Now come back here before you're chilled." I crawled back to him, my gaze never leaving the accumulating whiteness before me, and let Leran wrap me in the fur he had so thoughtfully brought. I was cold, but Leran's chest was warm, and strong, and solid, and as he shared his warmth with me, I could hardly remember why I'd refused him.

"Thank you," I murmured.

"You are very welcome, love." He cradled me in the cocoon of his body as he did everything in his power to keep me from the cold ground. As he stroked my hair, I suddenly understood something he'd said.

"You were awake when the snow began?" I asked. He sighed before he answered me.

"I find it difficult to sleep more than a few moments," he replied. "There is strife in the lands north of Tingu, and I think often of the matters I dealt with in Thurnda... and there is a woman who occupies my thoughts."

"Maybe you should find another woman," I suggested.

"No," he said firmly, and fell silent. I stole a glance at his face, and he did have dark smudges beneath his eyes, along with fine lines bracketing his mouth that hadn't been there a few days ago.

"If this woman you think so highly of told you to sleep, would you do so?" I asked.

"Perhaps," he admitted, "but what about tomorrow night?"

It was my turn to fall silent, for in truth I had no answer. I didn't know what was going to happen tomorrow, or when we reached The Seat. Hells, I didn't know what would happen when next I spoke.

"Sleep here, now," I said suddenly. "I'll wake you before first dawn."

"You refuse to admit you love me, yet you'll sleep with me beneath a tree during a snowstorm?"

"I never said I don't love you," I corrected, "and if you don't sleep, you'll get so exhausted that you'll fall off your horse and injure yourself, thus making our journey days longer than it needs to be."

"I love you, too," he murmured as he kissed my temple. I pursed my lips; he had tricked me into saying it, but it was said nonetheless. "Since you're in a mood to talk with me, I'd rather spend the night hearing about how much you love me."

"Let me think about it," I said as I burrowed further into his arms. I felt around his body for a moment, then pulled his forearm before me. I touched each stone of the Sala in turn, leaving the heartstone for last. "Does each stone have a meaning?" I asked.

"They do," he replied. He removed the armband and showed me the first stone I'd touched. "This represents elfin strength— "

"You are very strong?"

"Strong enough," he replied with a grin. "This one is for courage— "

"And you are either very brave, or very foolish," I pointed out.

"Do you want to learn about the Sala or not?" he asked. "Behave."

"Forgive me," I said, trying to sound sufficiently contrite. "Please. I want to know."

"The next is what gives me power over the earth and stone. It's charged with the blood of Nexa." I traced the outer edge of the stone; it was a mottled gray and green, like an emerald shot through with silver.

"You have power over the earth?" I asked, and he nodded. I had no idea he could wield such forces. "Show me?"

Leran leaned forward and brushed the fallen snow and pine needles from the ground, then placed his palm flat upon it. I felt the gentle shimmer of magic, and a ruby the size of my palm emerged from the cold dirt.

"How did you do that?" I asked, as he handed me the gem.

"I wanted to find you a red gem, for your hair," he explained. "I called it to me."

"It's priceless," I murmured, turning it over in my palm. "Nir si'lan." A puff of flame was born in my palm, and even in its rough state, the ruby was a thing of beauty. Leran raised an eyebrow at the flames that danced upon my skin, but he had known my parents too long to think I was without magic of my own.

I murmured the words to extinguish the flames and pushed the ruby toward Leran. "It's yours," he insisted.

"But you found it."

"We can spend the night arguing over a rock that's mine to give, or I can resume teaching you about the Sala." Thus admonished, I settled back against his chest and touched the fourth stone of the armband.

"This is a portion of Nexa's bower in The Seat," he explained.

"Nexa's bower? What's that?"

"I'll show you, once we reach The Seat," he promised. "See how it's a clear green? That means that I'm of her bloodline, otherwise it would be clouded and opaque."

I nodded, and then placed my fingers on the fifth stone. The heart-stone, by now a bloody red. "And this one?"

"It reflects the heart of the king," Leran said softly. "The darker the stone, the stronger I feel."

"It was always white before? Even with all those women you've been with, it didn't change?" I teased, but he didn't rise to the bait.

"Never. Not a one," he replied. "After my father died, it stayed a deep red until I put it on. He loved Asherah very, very much." Leran was silent again, and I could almost see the memories of his youth flitting behind his eyes. I didn't intrude upon them, and waited for him to continue. "When she sent the Sala back to me, it reverted to white the moment I placed it against my skin. It stayed that way until I stepped onto a balcony in Thurnda, and found you." I nodded as I traced the stone, which pulsated warmth.

"The heart of the king," I murmured.

"My heart," he emphasized. "Ember, I need you to understand. The Sala doesn't think for itself, it doesn't decide who should be my mate. It only reacts to how I feel."

"Then why did it change in the first place?" I asked. "You didn't even know who I was when you walked out to the balcony." No, that wasn't quite right—he'd thought I was Mara, the only living woman with a bloodline similar to mine.

Leran was speaking, but I was so deep within my thoughts I hardly heard him. He must have asked me something that I ignored, because he turned my chin up to face him. "What are you thinking?" he asked. I sighed; he wasn't going to like the conclusion I'd come to, but I wouldn't lie to him. He wouldn't lie to me.

"I think I understand how you want me," I said. "You're the last of Nexa's line, aren't you? And Sibeal made Mama her heir." He immediately understood what I was getting at and I was right, he wasn't pleased.

"You think I want you for an heir of my own?" he asked incredulously. "You overestimate the value of Elvasla's blood, love."

"Not just Elvasla's," I said. "Mother is also of the royal line of Gannera, and Father is twice-born of gods."

Leran asked what I meant about that last bit, and I told him that while Caol'nir was descended from Solon, Papa's mother, Alluria, was Olluhm's daughter.

"My father knew Caol'nir well," said Leran, "as did Balthus. They both thought quite highly of him." He was silent for a time, mulling over what he had learned. "And Latera... So you think my blood is so tainted by my mother that I need a woman of a strong elfin line to strengthen my heir's claim to Tingu?"

"I don't think you're tainted!" I rose up on my knees and faced him. "You are many, many things, Leran, but all your mother did was give you life. I just thought... I thought that since you had no heirs, you were looking to get one," I said in a small voice. When I said it aloud, I realized how ridiculous the notion was.

"Would you rather I'd spilled my seed into the first wanton who would have it, and been burdened with a mistake as my father was?" he asked bitterly. Wonderful. In my quest to share my inner feelings with Leran, I'd managed to drag up the painful emotions he struggled to keep buried.

"You are not a mistake." I placed my palms on either side of his face and forced him to look at me; his gray eyes were wracked with pain. "You are not tainted, and not a mistake. You are strong, and kind, and courageous, and Tingu is your birthright, no one else's. Anyone who says otherwise is a fool." I slid my fingers into his hair, and pulled his face forward so his forehead rested against mine. "You're a good, good man."

"Careful, love. If anyone overheard you, they'd suspect you cared about me." Well, if he was teasing me, he obviously didn't feel all that bad.

"They'd be right," I said before I knew what my mouth was saying. Leran took advantage of my mouth's confused state and kissed me. It was soft, and tender, and cracked the tough shell I'd built around my heart over the last few days.

"Get back here," he said when it ended. "You'll freeze, otherwise." He enfolded me in his arms and wrapped the fur about me, covering me up to my ears. Now that he mentioned it I was cold, and I figured he was cold as well, so I burrowed beneath his cloak. After a moment's hesitation, I unfastened his tunic below his neck and put my cheek against his bare skin. He tucked my head under his chin, and we sat huddled together while the snow fell around us.

"What if I promise never to get you with child?" he asked at length. "Then would you believe that I love all of you, not just a child you may someday bear?"

"Leran, you can't make that promise," I wearily replied. "Aren't you the last of Nexa's line?"

"Then I'll give you a hundred children," he murmured, his lips against my skin. "Whatever you want, love. Just tell me what you need and I will make it happen."

"It's not just children," I said. "I cannot live like an elf."

"Are we so distasteful to the fae?"

"There's nothing wrong with elves, but I have grown up fae," I said. "Faerie women are free to do as they will— "

"As are elfin women— "

"Whom you keep at a smaller hearth and treat as less than men!" He chuckled, the laughter rumbling deep in his chest. How I loved his laugh.

"Is that really what you think?" he asked. "We revere our women. Any elfin man would give his life for a woman he'd never met, so precious are they. That's why we don't understand why faeries send their women out to battle. We would never put our mates in harm's way."

"Then why the smaller hearth?" I pressed.

"They have a separate hearth so they need not be bored by talk of battle and the like from the men. As to why the hearths tend to be smaller, I don't know the exact reason. I believe it's because there are far fewer women." Leran shrank down in the cloaks and furs and poked me with his cold nose. "As my mate, you will be the most important woman in Tingu."

"I would be your equal?"

"No. You would be my superior."

"So I could order you around?" I asked, and his face stretched into a grin.

"If you'd like," he replied. "I'm afraid you do that now."

"What if..." I paused, trying to imagine the proper torment. "What if I ordered you to dance naked in the snow?" His hands immediately went to his belt, but I stayed him. "Leran, I was joking! I certainly don't want you to get frostbite. Not there!"

"Neither do I." He took my hands from his belt and moved them under his shirt to the warm, smooth skin of his abdomen. I loved the feel of my skin against his, so much so I hardly knew what I was doing as I glided my fingers across the corded muscles, then around his sides to his back. Leran maneuvered me so my belly was against his, my legs on either side of his waist.

"Ember," he murmured as he bent to nuzzle my neck, "my little flame. I love you. Let me make you mine." He shifted, and I felt him against me, as hard as he had been that night in my chamber. Whenever I was in his arms, the man's root swelled to the size of a tree trunk, and I can't say I wasn't flattered.

"I haven't chosen you," I said. I didn't know if the Lord of Tingu ascribed to fae customs, but I was half fae. I supposed I should. "Claiming me won't make me your mate unless I choose you first."

"You said you would have me," he gently pointed out. Hmm. I'd forgotten that.

"I changed my mind," I retorted.

"Then change it back." His mouth continued to wend its way down my neck and across my breast, until my silence became oppressive. "Do you still doubt that I love you? That I will care for you, put your needs above mine?" I wouldn't meet his eyes for a moment. "Do you not love me?"

"Leran, you know what I feel for you." There. That was all I was willing to admit in the dark of night.

"Then why you are still refusing me?"

"You would want me to live in Tingu, wouldn't you?"

"Of course. You would live with me at The Seat."

"I've lived my entire life in Teg'urnan. My whole family is there." I raised my eyes to his. "If I stayed with you, I would be leaving behind everything. Everyone." A tear rolled down my cheek and splashed onto the skin I'd bared beneath his neck as I told him my fears, that I would be all alone at The Seat. No overbearing father or prudish sister, no annoying younger brother... just me.

"Enough!"

I don't know if he meant to, but Leran had imbued the word with the authority of the Lord of Tingu, effectively ending my rambling. I don't think I could have spoken if my life depended on it.

"No matter what I say, you devise a reason to refuse me," he all but growled. "Excuses, followed by more excuses."

I had already told him no. Rather than say that directly, I tried to reason with him. It was like reasoning with a rabid elephant. "I don't think it's a good idea for me to stay in Tingu," I said softly.

"Why?" he demanded.

"I don't think I'm meant to be your mate." The anger bled from Leran's gray eyes, leaving behind pain and despair and, oddly, love. I no longer doubted that he loved me; in fact, I knew he would lay down his life for me. But what I'd said was true, all the reasons I'd given him good ones.

"Thank you, for waking me to see the snowfall," I said as I got to my feet. I had to leave then and there, because if I stayed a moment longer I was liable to do or say something I'd regret, but I'd forgotten my lack of boots and yelped when I stepped into the cold snow. Without a word, Leran lifted me into his arms and carried me back toward the tents. I bit back my protests as I wound my arms about his neck, sinking my fingers into his hair.

"I love it when you do that," he murmured.

"What? This?" I tugged at his hair, and was rewarded with his boyish grin.

"Yes, that." I tugged a bit harder, only to remember that I wouldn't be doing that ever again. I pressed my face against his neck; his skin was warm and soft, and he smelled like... like Leran. Of the earth, and stone, but really just like him.

"I'm sorry," I whispered. "I just— "

"Stop." We reached my tent, and he used his boot to clear the snow from a patch of ground. "I don't want to hear it again." He set me on my feet, and smoothed the hair back from my brow.

"Take me to your tent," I said suddenly. Leran cocked an eyebrow at my suggestion. "You said you can't sleep. Maybe I can help."

"You refuse to become my mate, but you'll lie with me so I can sleep?"

"Just sleeping," I said hurriedly. "Nothing more."

"Mmm. So I'm allowed to hold the woman I love, and nothing more." When he said it that way, it did seem unbearably cruel.

"Leran, that's not how I meant it," I began, but he waved away my apology. All I was ever doing was apologizing to this amazing man who had offered me his entire kingdom. More, he offered me his heart.

"Thank you for the offer, but no. If I can't have all of you, I want none of you."

Those words stung me like the venom of a thousand bees. "Leran," I said, "please don't be angry with me."

"I'm not." He wrapped his arms around me and kissed my forehead. I got the distinct impression that he was saying goodbye not only to me, but to the prospect of being mated to me. It hurt. I know, I had refused him, but it still hurt.

"I wish things were different."

"So do I." He kissed me again, and then I watched the man I love walk off in the newly fallen snow.

Chapter Thirty-Eight

The next morning, Leran woke alone. He smiled as he remembered sitting with Ember as they watched the snow, how interested she'd been to learn about the Sala... and frowned when he remembered her offer to sleep with him. Of course, the offer had been for only sleep, and he'd refused. Now, he wondered if he'd acted rashly, and should have accepted.

I keep making demands, and they scare her. I must find a way to meet her in the middle. Leran rose and dressed, and had no sooner pulled on his boots than Balthus drew the tent flap aside.

"We've news," Balthus announced, and he ushered a scout inside.

"What sort of news?" Leran asked, and the scout relayed that the mountain trolls had burned many of the bridges that spanned the Dan'ai River. Burned was an understatement; the trolls had thoroughly soaked the wooden edifice in pitch before setting it alight, thus ensuring that it smoldered away even as the snow fell the prior evening. When the scouts had reached it earlier that morning, it was still smoking.

The lack of the bridge by no means left them stranded, since there was another bridge made of stone further down the river. However, it would extend their journey by a day, maybe more, and Leran didn't know how much longer he could keep the truth from Asherah and the rest of her people.

A string of curses that would have done his father proud exited Leran's mouth, then he clenched his fist. "Let's find something to eat," he said as he left the tent and stalked toward the cooking fires. "You're certain it's impassable?"

"The m—" Leran's icy stare reminded the boy that he was not under any circumstances to speak of the mountain trolls. He had managed to keep Asherah unaware of the mountain trolls' advances for many winters, and he didn't mean for her to learn of them now. "The bridge has been completely washed out," the scout said decisively, pleased by his quick thinking.

"Please advise the queen that our progress has been somewhat delayed," Leran said to the boy as calmly as he could manage. "After we break our fast, we will continue on to the stone bridge. We should arrive at The Seat shortly after noon tomorrow." Leran dismissed the messenger, who looked more than a little relieved, and turned to Balthus. "They have never been so brazen."

"The addition of the orcs seems to have strengthened their resolve," Balthus quietly commented. Never in Leran's reign had the mountain trolls ventured so far into elfin territory, and while they were still in the northern reaches of Tingu, they were far too close to The Seat for comfort. "Perhaps we should speak with the Parthians."

"No." Leran did not expand on his statement, and Balthus knew better than to press the issue. Leran glanced about at the party; no one took the news of a washed out bridge too harshly, which was one less concern. He found his horse, and led it toward the river. Suddenly, Ember was standing in his path.

"Watch where you're going," she gasped, startled by his abrupt movement. *She must have approached me,* he realized, for why else would she be standing so close to him? *But why would she do that?*

"Forgive me," he mumbled, "my mind was someplace else." He moved to lead the horse around her, but she halted him with a hand on his arm.

"Leran," Ember said, her voice washing over him like a caress. "Is something the matter?" As she looked up at him with her crystal blue eyes, he wanted to say that yes, something was very much the matter, then sweep her into his arms and tell her everything about the mountain trolls and the orcs. She would be scared, yes, but he would be there, and he'd assure her that he wouldn't let any harm come to her.

And how will that end? Me, alone again. Her latest refusal still stung, more so because he so clearly remembered the sensation of her skin against his. Without speaking, Leran shoved past Ember and led his horse to water, and then sat heavily on the river bank, heedless of the snow and frozen mud. He let his head droop against his chest, trying unsuccessfully to purge his mind of Ember's lovely voice, her eyes filled with concern, only to have her image replaced with that of trolls and orcs overrunning The Seat.

After a time, Leran heard footsteps approach, and saw Latera's son leading three horses.

"My lord," Tor said with a respectful bow of his head. "By your leave?" Tor asked, gesturing toward a somewhat dry patch of ground. Leran nodded, and Tor sat beside him. They watched the horses drink for a time before Tor spoke again.

"Why are you determined to make my sister miserable?"

"I've done nothing but grant her every request," Leran retorted.

"I find that unlikely."

"What has she told you?" Leran demanded.

"Nothing," Tor replied, flinging small stones into the river. "Ember confides in Mara and no one else. Not even Mother."

"Then why do you assume I am the cause of her misery?"

"Last night, I woke to find the Lord of Tingu carrying my sister out into the darkness. In time, Ember entered the tent alone, crawled into her bedroll, and cried until dawn." Tor turned to face Leran. "You wouldn't know anything of that, would you?"

"She was crying?" Leran ran his hand through his hair, then scrubbed his face as if rubbing his own cheeks would wipe away Ember's tears. "I... I didn't know she was so sad."

"Unless I am mistaken, and I don't think I am, you're the one who made her sad." Leran did not miss the hard edge to Tor's words, but before he could remind the boy of his place he continued, "I'll warn you, king or no I'll not have you harming my sister."

"And what will you do? Tell one of your parents?"

"I dealt with the last myself. I'll deal with you myself, as well."

If any other man had so blatantly threatened the Lord of Tingu, he would have been dead before he was finished speaking, but Leran could care less about the insult. "The last? Has someone hurt her?" Leran demanded. Tor pursed his lips, perhaps realizing that he shared something he shouldn't have, but Leran would not be put off.

"I will tell you exactly what transpired between your sister and me, so you understand I'm not some sort of brute," Leran hissed. "I asked her to be my mate, and she said no. She came up with a litany of reasons as to why she won't accept me, and they're all rubbish, but still, she refused me. *She* refused *me*. So I brought her back to the tent and left her there, alone, as she wished." Leran leapt to his feet and flung a rock toward the river; he missed the water entirely and watched the rock bounce off a tree with such force it gouged the bark. "Hells, I love her so much I can think of nothing but her, but what else was I to do? She said no."

"You didn't try to claim her?" Tor asked, surprised.

"No. She is untouched."

"By you," Tor mumbled. Leran spun about to face him, looming over the seated faerie.

"What happened to her? Why do you feel the need to defend her?" When Tor remained silent, Leran crouched down and grabbed his tunic. "I can order you to tell me. Or learn it in other ways." Leran made the Sala's stones glow; it was nothing but a harmless trick, but Tor didn't know that. Tor seemed to weigh his options for a moment, then he took a deep breath and spoke.

"Ember chases men all over Teg'urnan. She's quite a flirt, mostly because no one would dare touch her. I mean, if Mama didn't kill the man, then Father surely would."

"Go on," Leran prompted.

"It was a game with her, batting her eyelashes at men and running off. But there was one man, probably the only man who isn't scared of our parents, and Ember let herself fall for him. He told her he loved her, that she would be a wonderful mate... he even said he would bind himself to her."

Leran grunted at this revelation. Amongst elves, a mating was considered complete when the man claimed his woman under mutual consent, but the fae went so far as to have their gods entwine the couple's very essence together. Leran couldn't imagine the sensation of a part of him living in another body, but admitted that he would welcome sharing such closeness with Ember.

"She's not a bound woman," Leran pointed out. "Did he leave her?"

"No. He lied to her." Tor stood, and it was his turn to loom over Leran. "He told her that he never loved her like a mate. Still, he tried to claim her."

"I had no idea," Leran said as he shook his head. "Did the bastard force her?"

"Ember won't tell me. She's afraid I'll kill him. I nearly did." Tor looked the Lord of Tingu in the eye, and revealed his last bit of information. "And he's no bastard. He's Asherah's son."

***

Ember fidgeted restlessly while she stood with her sister and father, trying to pay attention to their conversation but unable to get Leran out of her mind. She had been so confident in her refusal of Leran, first because she doubted his love for her, then for her reticence to live like an elf, and finally that she couldn't bear to live so far away from her family. All good, sound reasons, and each of them reason enough to say no.

But she couldn't forget that he brought her out to see the falling snow. In Thurnda, she had told Leran how she wanted to see it snow, and he'd remembered. And the snow had been lovely, far lovelier than she imagined. As Leran held her beneath that tree, keeping her warm amidst the sparkling white powder, she felt happy. Safe. Complete.

If only he hadn't asked her to be his mate again, the night would have been perfect. It hurt her to say no to him, but again she had known deep, deep in her soul that it was the right thing to do... until he returned her to her tent and walked away from her. Ember felt her heart tearing itself free of her breast, protesting his leaving. Then he had all but ignored her earlier, pushing past her as if they had never met, and the stone in her chest swelled to a boulder. If this was the weight of a broken heart, Ember wasn't sure she could bear it.

"Here's Tor," Aeolmar said, and she turned to see her brother clamber up the bank leading their horses. *Gods, he's as clumsy as an ox.* Leran followed him, which Ember found unusual; she hadn't seen her brother speak with Leran once since they'd left Thurnda. Then Tor took the reins of Leran's mount as Leran searched the assembled fae and elves, his eyes coming to rest on a head of blond curls that was all too well-known to Ember. With his face set as if he were about to enter a battle, Leran strode toward Finn.

In a burst of comprehension, Ember raced after Leran, pausing to glare at her brother. "Fool!" she hissed as she raced past Tor and flung herself in front of Leran. "What are you doing?" she demanded.

"I'm going to speak with the Faerie King and his son," Leran said icily as he stared at Finn.

"What did Tor tell you?" Leran slowly turned to regard her. She flinched under the weight of his gaze.

"Is it true?" he asked.

"You don't know what's true!" she said. "Tor doesn't even know what happened! You cannot confront someone over a rumor!"

"Then tell me what's true." Ember pursed her lips and held her tongue. "Either you tell me now, or I ask him myself. What will it be, little flame?"

"I thought you wanted nothing to do with me," Ember countered, unable to keep the pain from her voice.

"This is different," he hissed. "If that fool has harmed you, I'll punish him myself."

"He hasn't—"

"Tell me what he hasn't done." Leran's gaze was firm, his back straight as an arrow. Ember sighed; clearly, she'd lost this battle.

"Not here. I'll tell you tomorrow, after we arrive at The Seat."

Leran shook his head. "Today, while we're riding."

Ember nodded, unwilling to keep arguing, then she turned to rejoin her family. She would have preferred to speak of such matters in a room with a closed door, but she knew that Leran would not be swayed. Actually, she would have preferred to never speak of the incident in question again, but that seemed to be a luxury she was not allowed.

"Mind your own affairs," Ember all but growled when she reclaimed her reins from Tor. "I don't need all of elfdom knowing my private matters."

Tor mumbled something about her needing someone to look out for her, but Ember hardly heard him. All she knew was that she had gotten quite good at forgetting that that day with Finn had ever happened, and now she was being forced to relive it.

Once the party was moving again, Leran and Ember managed to get themselves to the rear of the procession. Leran issued a few commands to his guard, and the warriors gave the pair a wide berth. The two rode in silence for a time as Ember struggled to find words.

"It was nothing, really," Ember said at length.

"Your brother doesn't think it was nothing."

Ember sighed, and stared at her horse's ears as she continued. "Finn and I were born on the same day; him in the royal bedchamber, me on the edge of a battlefield. We grew up together, spent every day together... We would always play in the queen's garden. From the time we could walk, that was where we could be found. One day, we played a little too much." She closed her eyes as she remembered that day, the dappled sun on Finn's bare chest, the heady scent of flowers around them. Finn had suggested that they take a swim to combat the heat of the day, and Ember had readily agreed. They swam together often, only this time as Finn stripped naked she realized that her playmate had gone and become a man. Ember, suddenly modest, changed her mind about the swim, but Finn plied her with sweet words until she disrobed as well.

And so they swam, and it was the same as it had always been, just her and Finn. Then they crawled upon the bank to let the suns dry them and Finn had gazed at her hungrily, then he touched her...

"What happened on the bank?" Leran asked softly.

"He... We were at an age where we were curious. About one another. He told me things he thought I wanted to hear." She laughed shortly. "I did want to hear them. But he didn't mean any of it."

"He told you he loved you?"

Ember nodded. "That, and other things." Leran reached over and grasped her hand; she smiled when he squeezed her fingers, but it didn't reach her eyes.

"Love, did he... What did he do to you?"

"Nothing I didn't agree to." She felt the muscles in his hand go rigid. "You don't need to defend my honor. Mother—and therefore my father—know exactly what happened, and Finn managed to keep his head." Leran exhaled in a great sigh; it touched Ember that he was so concerned about an incident that had occurred long before he'd met her.

"Does Asherah know?" Leran asked.

"Yes." She fell silent again, losing herself in her memories of all those days spent in the garden, how she had always enjoyed Finn's easy manner, his warm smile, how she would go along with his schemes; really, she would have done anything he asked. Her easy acquiescence was because as far back as she could recall, Finn had promised to take her as his mate once they came of age.

The matter hadn't even been in question, not even among their parents; all just assumed that Ember and Finn would be together forever. Then the day came where he got her out of her clothes and on her back, and Ember thought the day had come at last. She still remembered the confusion in his eyes when she asked when they should be bound.

"Bound?" Finn had questioned. She had tried to ignore the note of surprise in his voice, as if they hadn't discussed their mating a thousand times before.

"Our mating won't be official otherwise," she said.

"Mate?" he murmured as he nuzzled her breasts.

His question had shocked Ember, so much so that she lay there silent, no longer feeling his body against hers. "I thought... I thought you wanted me as a mate. You said you loved me."

Finn sat up, his brows close together. "Ember, those things we said to each other. We were children."

"And now? What are we now?"

She remembered how he shoved a hand through his hair and looked away. "Now that we're older, I understand more of what love is, and... And I love someone else."

Ember, shocked and furious, had struck Finn with all her might before she grabbed her clothing and left the one-day king lying in a pool of his own blood. When Tor had found her, crying and spattered with blood, he'd assumed the worst and gone after the Prince of Parthalan. The whole incident had put Teg'urnan in a mild uproar that Ember hated being the center of. Only her insistence that Finn had not harmed her physically kept the situation from spiraling further out of proportion.

"When he said those things to me, I was so mad I hit him. I broke his nose," Ember told Leran. "I was so worried that I would be punished. Then Tor ran off and had him at the end of his sword. I believe Finn was more embarrassed than I was."

"I can still punish him," Leran offered. "We take such offenses against women quite seriously here in the north. If such a thing had happened to my daughter, I'd have the bastard castrated."

"Castration is a trifle harsh." She gave Leran a sidelong glance. "What exactly did Tor say to you?"

"When I returned you to your tent, Tor assumed I tried to claim you. He made it seem as if you had once been forced." Ember laughed shortly.

"My dear brother needn't worry so," she said, "and neither should you. Finn left my virtue well intact." Ember noted the lopsided grin that bloomed across Leran's face.

"I'm glad," Leran said.

"Are you now?" she asked, arching her brow at him. "I'd heard that the Lord of Tingu liked his women with experience."

"Actually, I prefer redheaded maidens," Leran said, and Ember laughed again. Not the tight, mirthless laughter from before, but a deep, rich laugh that reverberated from her core. She had never told anyone the full extent of how badly Finn had hurt her, but she found that she no longer needed to. As she rode next to Leran, she realized that Finn's callous words didn't matter, not any longer. She was happier without him.

"Leran, why are you so concerned?" Ember asked. "This happened many winters ago."

"I worry because I don't want you hurt by anyone or anything." He squeezed her fingers. "You may not be my mate, but you'll always be my Ember." She smiled, then dropped her gaze to her hand in his. She wondered if her refusals of Leran had aught to do with Finn; it had never occurred to her that harsh words spoken so long ago would make her reticent to take a mate, even someone she loved. She ran down her list of excuses in her mind, and realized that Leran was right: she had been grasping at straws, and saying anything she could think of to avoid committing to him.

More, he was here with her now. Her brother had told Leran the barest shred of a rumor and he had immediately come to her defense, when she knew her refusals must have hurt him deeply. Finn had eventually apologized to her, but only because the king and queen forced him to do so. They were not friends, not any longer, and she couldn't imagine Finn coming to her defense, over an imagined assault, or anything.

She couldn't imagine her life without Leran's hand in hers.

Ember sidled her horse closer to Leran's, now determined to tell him what she felt. She did not expect him to ask her to be his mate again; no, she had wounded him too badly. But she loved him, amazingly more now than she already had, more than she thought her heart had the capacity for. She stroked his long fingers, gathering her courage to recant the terrible way she'd treated him, but before she could work up the nerve, he spoke.

"You were born on a battlefield?" Leran asked.

"I was."

"Tell me about it?"

And she did.

Chapter Thirty-Nine

Asherah Speaks

I peeked over my shoulder, and smiled when I saw Leran and Ember riding close together. They were talking and laughing, and I hoped that whatever bad event that stymied their courtship was far behind them. "It seems they're repairing whatever went wrong between them," I said to Finlay.

He turned to regard the pair. "Good. It's always best to clear the air, the sooner the better." Finlay reached out and grasped my hand. "I know you're happy for them."

"I am," I said, then I noticed Finn riding alongside Mara. He seemed to be telling her a story complete with wild gestures, and Mara couldn't stop laughing. "Both of my sons are doing well. It makes my heart full." Finlay squeezed my hand and said something, but I was distracted by a snowy crag in the distance.

"What is it?" Finlay asked.

"That crag," I replied, jerking my chin toward it. "There's a trail that runs up the mountain, and on the far side is a valley. It's warmer than the surrounding area, and the locals used to have much success farming there."

"What did they grow?" When I didn't reply, Finlay asked, "Was it grain?"

"I… I don't know." I faced him, and said, "I also don't know how I know about that valley. I've never been there."

"Perhaps you saw it on a map," Finlay suggested. "Or, perhaps you once stopped there when you lived in Tingu."

I shook my head. "I've never been on this road before. And, when I lived at The Seat we never once went to Thurnda. Never. Sibeal always traveled to us."

Finlay's brows pinched, then he asked one of our escorts to hand over their map. He did, and after a bit of fumbling, Finlay had it unrolled and properly oriented.

"You're correct about the valley," Finlay said, then he passed the map to me. According to the symbols, grain was still grown there. "Not that I doubted you. But you doubted yourself, yes?"

"Yes." I rolled up the map, and cast another glance toward the crag. "This has been happening more and more."

"What has? You remembering things?"

"I'm remembering things I shouldn't know," I replied. "All of these facts and stories are bubbling up, and for the life of me, I can't imagine how they got there. I can feel these memories, pushing toward the surface of my mind, clawing for purchase. It's like they're in a race to see which ones I'll notice first." I faced Finlay, and said, "I think they might be from before."

"From before you were queen? And before that?"

My gentle, loving mate didn't mention my time as a prisoner, and I appreciated that. "Yes. Before."

He nodded. "We always thought you were from the south, but maybe that was due to my prejudice, and wanting you and me to hail from the same area. I must say, no southern women look anything like you."

I remembered the women in his village, and how all of them had dark hair and brown skin like his. "But my shrine was in the desert."

"The Ish h'ra had shrines all across Parthalan," Finlay began, then he realized what I'd said. "Your shrine?"

"Yes. I think it might have been mine, once."

He reached toward me. "Hand over that map."

I did, and he spent a few minutes examining it. "Here," he said at last, pointing to an area near the road we were currently on. "This is supposed to be one of the Ish h'ra's ruined shrines. We can go have a look around, and see what comes of it."

"What comes of it?" I repeated. "What if we learn... What could we learn there?"

Finlay shrugged. "Maybe something, maybe nothing." He paused, and asked, "Do you want to go? We don't have to."

I took the map from him, and looked over the area where this shrine supposedly was. It wasn't very far from our current route. With any luck, Finlay and I could be there and back before most realized we were gone. "Yes. Now that I know it's there, I have to see it."

***

I spoke with Balthus, and he agreed that there was a ruined shrine a short ride east of the road we were on. What he did not agree with was Finlay and me leaving the main party to have a look at it.

"Asherah, it is not safe," Balthus said.

"Balthus, I can take care of myself," I said. "How many times have you fought beside me?"

"Things are different now," he growled.

"Different how?" I countered. Balthus frowned, and looked toward the same crag that had sparked my memory.

"It's a different land, now," he said. "The dangers out there are many. The trolls—"

"What of the trolls?" Finlay demanded.

"Forgive me, my lord, but have you ever dealt with a troll in the flesh?"

Finlay threw back his head and laughed. "I've been dealing with trolls all my life. The worst was an aunt of mine, Agnietza. She made the worst slop you've ever smelled, and claimed it was dinner. Of course, being that we were under her watch, we had to eat it. I couldn't wait to be old enough to cook my own food."

Balthus's face went from that of quiet exasperation to the peculiar pallor of a man who'd swallowed a bug. And now we knew that Balthus had had no idea my mate was descended from trolls.

"At least take a guard with you," Balthus said. "I can spare six men."

"We'll take two," I countered. "And Balthus, please don't tell Leran. Don't interfere in his time with Ember, either," I added.

Balthus's frown became a smile. "I do miss the days of you running things up here."

"Remember that, the next time I tell you my plans and you decide to disagree with me."

Balthus dipped his chin. "I will, my lady."

Soon enough, Finlay, the two warriors, and I were riding eastward. Once we were out of sight of the rest, I sent the two warriors back. They protested, but since I was their queen, there was little they could do but obey.

"The elves defer to you the same way they defer to Leran," Finlay observed.

"And why wouldn't they?" I asked. "I'm still their queen, for now."

"You really think something will come of Leran and Ember?"

"I'm not sure," I admitted. "Whatever does come of it, I hope it makes both of them happy."

The map we were using wasn't very detailed, but that hardly mattered. Once we left the main road, I felt the shrine all but pulling me toward it, as if a rope had been thrown around my soul and was dragging me home.

Home.

"Maybe I am from the north," I said.

Finlay's gaze slid toward me, his only reaction. He'd long ago grown used to my random and disjointed ramblings. "Does this area seem familiar? Like the crag did?"

"I feel like I'm going home."

Before either of us could say anything further, the shrine came into view. It was little more than a ruin, but the massive white marble pillars were still standing, three of the walls were visible, and the roof was present but listing to the side. Despite all of the evidence of time's passage, the shrine was mostly intact, which was a miracle in and of itself.

"Look," I said, pointing toward the ruin. "The roof remains. As long as the roofs survive, we have a chance."

"A chance at what?"

"Victory."

I slid off my horse and approached the shrine. It was much larger than the one we'd visited in the desert, and larger yet than the repurposed one at Iruna's former home. This shrine was large enough to house priests, and acolytes, and scores of worshippers. I went around to the back, and saw an amphitheater ringed with seats carved from the living rock. I remembered speaking here, to my people. I remembered rallying them, and asking them to be strong for just a little longer.

"Be strong for what?" I muttered, then I called, "Finlay? Where are you?"

"Inside."

I followed his voice, and found him standing in what remained of a large central chamber. "Look there," he said, indicating a stairwell. "There's more, underground."

"It's where we hid." I approached the doorway, but Finlay touched my arm.

"Sher, that doesn't look safe," he said. "We'll have to excavate most of the ground floor before we're able to venture below."

I glanced at him. "We will?"

"If you want to know what's down there, it's the best course of action," he replied, and I could see his merchant's mind calculating time and figures. "At the very least, we'll need to haul away the loose stone, and shore up the roof."

"We?" I repeated.

"Yes. We." He faced me. "It's important to you, so it's important to me."

I went into his arms, and let him comfort me the way only he could. "You have no idea what this means to me."

He pushed back my hair, and rested his forehead against mine. "I have an idea. There's something else I want to see. Come outside."

We separated, and walked out of the shrine hand in hand. Finlay led me around to the side, where we could see the flat plane of the roof. It was perched at a precarious angle and was covered in a thick layer of gold.

"That is a lot of gold," Finlay said, and I agreed. "How is it that this gold has laid here undefended for centuries, yet no one has claimed it?"

"It's the Ish h'ra's gold. To take it would risk her wrath." I approached the roof, standing on my toes to get a better look at the symbols carved into the precious metal. "Although, only the northern shrines got the gold roofs. We did it to irritate Olluhm, so the reflected light would blind him when he was overhead driving that chariot he'd stolen. I remember looking down at the roof, and seeing—"

"Sher."

I blinked, and refocused from the roof to my mate. "What?"

"You looked down at the roof?" he said. He glanced around the clearing. The shrine was the tallest structure around. "How?"

"I... I am not sure." I shook my head. "I don't remember that part. Not yet." I felt my hands tremble, so sure and unsure of what I was seeing. What I was feeling. But it was too much, too soon, and my mind couldn't make sense of it.

"Too soon?" Finlay said, and I realized I'd been speaking out loud. "You've been searching for answers for how long? If anything, this hasn't come soon enough."

My trembling became rampant shaking. "I don't know if I can do this."

"Of course you can. You're Asherah the Ruthless. You can do anything." Finlay embraced me, and I let myself cry against his neck. They weren't tears of sadness, or anger, or humiliation. They were my tears of joy, and contentment, and they helped me wash away more of the layers so my memories were a bit closer to the surface.

Along with my memories, my true self was being uncovered, just a bit more.

Finlay could feel my true self emerging, too. I could tell by the way he tightened his arms about me, the strong yet gentle way he kept me safe while I emerged from this cocoon. He was my man from the desert, my stalwart constant.

"What do we do next?" Finlay asked, once my tears had ceased. If there was one thing I'd learned, it was to carefully uncover my memories only a few at a time, lest they overwhelm me.

"For now, we must return to the others," I said. "There's a massive archive at The Seat, and Latera said she wanted to have a look 'round. I think I'll have a look with her."

"What's Latera searching for?"

I dug my fingers into Finlay's jerkin. "The old gods."

He nodded. "Then you and Latera will walk this path together."

"And you?"

"I will be right beside you."

Chapter Forty

Ember speaks

That last day's journey to The Seat stretched into four; first, there was the delay regarding the bridge, then Asherah and Finlay withdrew from the rest of us, and to top it off we came across odd signs of battle that were enough to divert my father's attention from me and my persistent suitor to the possibility of attack. Demons were rare this far north, yes, but Father told many stories of the time he spent expunging the filth from Grelk's lands, and there had been demons involved in the attack on Thurnda. So while the threat of a demon attack was slight, it still remained a possibility.

Leran, as one could guess, was thoroughly distracted from me by the notion of demons in Tingu. At first I found his preoccupation a welcome reprieve, but by the second evening I missed him, and when I went to bed on the third evening, I lay awake nearly half the night hoping he would appear in my tent, ready to show me a snowfall or an interesting rock or anything at all, so long as he came for me. But, not surprisingly, he didn't.

I had no right or reason to expect his attentions, not after the many ways I'd refused him. Leran was no fool, and he wouldn't keep asking me the same question, only to get the same reply. But after we'd talked about what had happened between Finn and me all those winters ago, my heart softened toward Leran. Had it softened enough for me to remain in Tingu with him? I didn't know, but I wanted to find out.

So there I was, laying in my bedroll listening to Tor snore and Mara mutter away in her sleep (she's done that for as long as I can remember, and it's more than a little annoying) with my mind racing so fast I couldn't hope to fall asleep. Gods, I just wanted Leran to hold me.

Taking total leave of my senses, I plunged into the night clad only in my thin sleeping dress, and found Leran's tent. I crept inside, grateful that he was the sole occupant, and slipped into the bedroll beside him.

I had this foolish notion that I would lie against his back for a time before returning to my own tent, and he'd be none the wiser. Instead, Leran immediately rolled over and threw an arm around me.

"Ember?" he asked as he opened his eyes, thus confirming I wasn't a dream. I wondered if he dreamed of me. "Is something wrong?"

"No, nothing," I murmured. "I just... I waited for you these past few nights, but you didn't come for me. Not that you had to, or that you'd even want to, but I missed you so much, and I didn't know what else to do."

"Hush," he murmured in response to my babbling. "You're here now." I burrowed into the circle of his arms. I'd half thought he would send me away, but he didn't. I was so, so glad he didn't.

"You're naked," I scandalized, feeling his smooth expanse of skin from back to hip.

"It's my bed, and I'll be in it however I like," he retorted.

"Aren't you cold?"

"I have my little flame to keep me warm." I touched his face, tracing a line from his forehead, down his temple and to his cheekbone, my fingertips at last coming to rest on his lips.

"You don't mind if I stay?"

"Stay forever," he whispered, then he kissed my forehead. Reassured, I tucked my face against his neck, warm and content for the first time in more than a sennight.

I was understandably confused when I woke in my own tent shortly before first dawn. I sat bolt upright, assuming that I was still in Leran's bed and that he had already risen; but no, I was alone in my bedroll. And there was Tor, snoring away as if it were his life's mission.

Well, if that was a dream, it was certainly a pleasant one. *I readied myself for one more day of this journey, hoping it would truly be the last, and wondered if last night really had been a dream. If it hadn't, that would mean that Leran had carried me back to my tent while I slept. That would be unlike him, but who knows? Maybe I wasn't as welcome in Leran's bed as I'd hoped.*

I really did miss him. I wish I had gone to him last night, just to talk if nothing more. Of course, I easily could have gone to him... Could have, if I hadn't already refused him, only to realize (too late) that I was refusing another man, and a man who shouldn't be affecting me any longer, at that.

"Leran, they were just words," I'd said that day after I explained to Leran what had happened between me and Finn. After hearing the boring tale of my birth, Leran had resumed his interrogation into my past lovers. He seemed worried that Finn had indeed forced me, and that I was trying to alter the facts to save Finn's hide. Little did Leran know, I would have been the first to skin him, queen's son or no. "I swear to you, he did not hurt me."

Leran dropped my hand, and caressed my cheek. "I only used words, and look how much I hurt you," he said softly.

"You didn't," I mumbled. "I was angry, and I acted rashly, and—"

And then the tears were falling, and my breath came in ragged gasps. In a feat of dexterity that only the Lord of Tingu could have managed, Leran grasped me about my waist and hauled me into his arms, wrapping me in his cloak while he signaled one of his warriors to take my horse's reins. I worked my fingers into the laces of his jerkin, holding on to him as if it meant my life.

"I'm so sorry," I began.

"Hush," he murmured, smoothing back my hair. "I hold the blame. I should have waited until we reached The Seat to ask you about such things." He tilted up my chin, his gray eyes looking deeply into mine. "Forgive me, love?"

At that moment, I just wanted to kiss him. No, I wanted to throw my arms around his neck, beg him to forgive me for acting like the foolish girl I was, and remain in his arms until the end of time. Instead of any of that happening, Belenos approached us with the warning that my mother was looking for me. In another moment, I was back on my horse and riding away from Leran, leaving all I had wished to say unsaid.

Well, the midst of a journey is not a good place to recant one's words, anyway, so I resigned myself to waiting until we reached our destination. At noon we were assured that The Seat was less than a quarter day's ride away, and stopped for refreshment. Most headed inside the hastily erected tent for a quick meal, but I found a quiet spot near a gnarled old tree and spread a small rug before it. I still had many thoughts to sort out, and I couldn't do so while the rest of our party chattered away around me. I hadn't made the least bit of headway when the man at the center of these thoughts strode up to join me. He carried a bottle of wine, and two goblets tucked under his arm.

"It occurs to me," Leran began as he sat beside me on the rug and poured the wine, "that we never had our wine." We never had what was to come after, either. I kept my quips to myself as I accepted the proffered goblet; the wine was cool and sweet, and was made from the white grapes that only grew in the east of Parthalan.

"You don't prefer elfin brandy?" I asked.

"I try to avoid the stuff," he replied. "My father enjoyed it, but I'd rather not feel like my gullet is on fire."

"I agree," I murmured.

"We half-elves must be made of softer stock," he said, and I smiled.

"I suppose so." I sipped my wine, enjoying it and his company.

"Was last night a dream?" I asked suddenly. Leran raised an eyebrow at my inquiry, which was answer enough for me. "Never mind," I mumbled.

"Did my little flame dream of me?" he asked.

"Never mind."

"Oh." He leaned back, grinning smugly. "So, it was that sort of a dream."

"What sort?" I asked, and that smug face of his got even smuggier. "It was nothing like that!"

"Your red cheeks tell me otherwise." My hands flew to my now-warm face, and I glared at him. "At least tell me about it."

I sighed; there really was no point in denying him. "I missed you, so I went to your tent," I said, leaving off how I'd been lying awake and hoping he would come to me.

"I wish you had," he said.

"In the dead of night? If your men saw me skulking about your tent, they would have likely attacked me as an intruder."

"Not so," he said. "Every one of my warriors has been instructed to allow you full access to me."

"Do they grant all visiting maidens entry?" I asked dryly.

"No. Even Balthus isn't afforded such access." My brows knit together, and Leran leaned forward to explain further. "I couldn't risk you being turned away. What if you decided to choose me?" He smiled, and I saw the hope in his eyes. Oh, how he made things difficult for me.

The others began to exit the tent, thus ending our bit of privacy. Leran helped me to my feet; while his form hid me from the rest, *he caressed my cheek. "I'm glad you've come to see my home," he murmured.*

"You didn't give me much of a choice," I pointed out.

I expected his latest smug grin, but not the kiss he pressed to my forehead. "You're right. I didn't."

The soft press of his mouth took me back to the prior evening, during what I now knew to be the most pleasant dream I'd ever experienced. Leran had held me close, so very close, and asked, "Little flame, what are you so afraid of?"

Afraid of? Oh, so many things. My parents riding off to do battle with some monster or another and never returning. Tor challenging the wrong person to a duel and ending up maimed or dead or maybe just horribly humiliated and me having to deal with him. Mara taking a mate and leaving me all alone. Asherah going insane. Again. Teg'urnan crumbling to dust.

Giving Leran my heart, and him not loving me back.

The memory hit me in a rush, along with all my fears and hopes. I decided to concentrate on hope. "Perhaps," I began, then thought the better of it. No, I must say it. I swallowed the knot in my throat and continued, "Perhaps, once we reach The Seat, we can talk."

"About?" he asked. Damn him, he knew about what, he was just tormenting me.

"About whatever you'd like," I said.

"I like talking about you," he murmured, then he kissed my wrist. Gods, whenever he pressed his lips to the thin skin over my pulse, I felt ice slide down my back; it was too much, yet not enough. "I haven't given up on you, little flame."

He hadn't? Then there was hope, after all! Before we could say any more, Balthus appeared and he and Leran spoke in those quiet tones they shared whenever they thought they were being secretive. It seemed that no one had ever told them that two grown men, hunched over and whispering, attracts a great deal of attention.

We mounted up, and it wasn't long before we were cresting the last hill before The Seat. The sight was beautiful to behold, with The Seat itself being a mountain of shimmering amethyst and emerald clusters that erupted from the ground at sharp angles. The palace that sat before it was carved of the same green and purple stone. It was half again as large as Teg'urnan, and while the smooth gray stone of my home was beautiful, it paled in comparison to this tribute to elfin royalty.

We paused before the Gate, and Leran performed the opening ceremony. My position afforded me an excellent view of Asherah, whose eyes shone with unshed tears. I remembered that The Seat was once her home, and that this was the first time she had seen it since shortly after her mate, Leran's father, perished all those winters ago. I couldn't imagine the mass of emotions tumbling about inside of her, she who still bore the title Lady of Tingu.

"My lady."

The soft words jolted me from my contemplation of the queen, and I focused on Leran standing next to me with his hand outstretched. "It's customary to dismount, and walk to The Seat." A quick glance told me that all eyes were upon us, with reactions ranging from the thinly veiled amusement on Asherah's face, to Balthus's scowl, to Papa's smile.

"Shouldn't you walk with the Lady of Tingu?" I asked once he had helped me from the saddle.

"Yes," he replied, then tucked my hand in the crook of his arm. I don't know what I had expected, certainly not for the others to fall into step behind us, but they did, and followed Leran and me as we led them up the winding path. "Do you know how my father asked Asherah to be his mate?"

"Why don't you tell me?" I countered, though I knew the story well.

"He presented her with the Sala before the whole of elfin nobility," he replied.

"Mmm. Publicly, so she couldn't refuse him?" I asked with a raised brow. "You are your father's son."

"That I am," he agreed. We traversed one of the looping bends, and I was becoming more aware of the press of others behind us. What must they be thinking of Leran choosing me to accompany him on this path? It was obviously some sort of a tradition, and if I'd learned nothing else during my time in the north, it was that elves took their traditions quite seriously.

"Where did your father accomplish this romantic feat?" I asked.

"In the main hall," he replied. "I was sitting on Da's shoulders as he walked among the lords, giving his great speech about how fae and elf should fight as one."

"You must have been quite small, if you fit on his shoulders," I observed, imagining a younger version of Leran clinging to his proud and noble father.

"I was," he confirmed. "He rallied everyone to his cause, and one by one the lords pledged their loyalty to Da. Then everyone in the hall gave a great war cry, and in the midst of it all he turned to Asherah. She was standing next to his throne, and she cheered loudest of all."

"And then?" I prompted.

"He strode through the crowd as if the hall was empty, dropped to his knees and declared her his mate."

"And she accepted?"

"Most do," he said sardonically, but I didn't mind the gentle barb. I'd earned it. "I'd never seen him so happy as when Asherah said yes." Leran reached across my torso to take my free hand with his, and gently squeezed my fingers. "Come to the hall with me?"

So he could repeat what his father did? No, no, no. I didn't want any more trickery or public displays. I just wanted to talk to him, quietly, privately, and sort out my muddled emotions. Why did everything have to be done before the whole of the land? Why can't these elves just do their business behind a closed door?

Then I saw his eyes, gray and full of love, and I couldn't voice the least of my concerns. I couldn't hurt him again.

I don't want to be afraid any longer.

"It's lovely here, before the entrance," I said, and it was. Huge amethyst pillars jutted from the ground, and the steps were carved from the purest citrine. Engravings depicting battles and gods and who knows what else wrapped around the pillars and arched over the doorways, which on first glance appeared to be oak, but I later learned were silver blackened with the blood of Nexa's enemies. At the apex of the steps and centered before the doors was a statue of Nexa, her skin carved from translucent crystal, her hair a rich gold, and emeralds for her eyes.

Leran turned to me, at first irritated that I didn't want to go to the hall, but my hopeful face made my meaning clear. He opened his mouth, but before he could speak, a steward rushed out of the great doors and began shouting about demons and mountain trolls, and those behind us rushed forward as news of an imminent attack spread *amongst us. This time I squeezed Leran's hand, and we did make our way to the great hall, but for a very different reason.*

Chapter Forty-One

Leran stood in center of his hall, his arm fast about Ember's shoulders. He ignored the others that crashed around him, remaining still as stone amid the crush of bodies. Those left behind at The Seat had flowed into the hall, all of them grateful and relieved that their king had returned. The reports of the mountain trolls slow but steady movement toward Tingu's northern border had terrified most, for they remembered well the many battles fought against them. Each elf clamored to be heard, wanting to know when they would march, what weapons to take, what to do if the trolls made good on their threats and laid siege to The Seat. Throughout it all, Leran gazed only at Ember's face, and let her serve as his anchor amidst the tumult.

"What do you mean, another war?" he heard Asherah's shrill voice demanding. Leran's steward, recognizing the Lady of Tingu and hoping she had brought her legion as aid, had rushed forth and told her everything. She demanded details and the steward readily provided them, and why wouldn't he? Asherah was the Lady of Tingu, just as much their ruler as he was.

Perhaps, she's more of a ruler.

Leran squeezed his eyes shut, and heard his world crumble around him.

"Leran, what's happening?" Ember asked. He opened his eyes and found her staring at him, her delicate brows knit together in concern. "Leran, please talk to me." He moved his free hand to the nape of her neck, and stroked her jaw with his thumb as he replied.

"There is a large force of trolls moving to attack my border," he said quietly. He had no desire to raise his voice; the words were for her alone.

"Trolls?" she repeated, confusion added to her concern. "But, they just attacked in Thurnda. I thought you did away with them."

"Mountain trolls have been harrying my northern border for almost as long as I can remember." The blood drained from Ember's face. Leran gathered her close and said, "Don't worry, little flame. We've fought them before, and we'll beat them back once more. They won't prevail."

"I know." She pulled back and regarded him, and while she was still pale, he could see courage in her eyes. "I believe in you." Leran wondered if she knew how much those words meant to him. If only he could believe in himself. Then he heard Asherah shouting, and realized that she was filling the role of leader while he stood off to the side.

"Whatever happens, today and from now on, know that I love you," he said.

"And I love you," she admitted. *Better late than never,* he mused, but kept his wry comment to himself. Leran kissed her wrist before he turned to face his father's mate, and reclaimed The Seat as his own.

"That border has been quiet for centuries," Asherah was saying to Balthus. "Why are they rising against you now?" Balthus cast a concerned glance toward Leran, but he waved his commander on. They were long past the point of denying Asherah knowledge.

"My lady, we have been in constant conflict with the mountain trolls ever since Lormac's death," Balthus gravely informed her. Asherah turned from the elfin general to Leran, her fury barely contained.

"Why have you never told me of this?" she demanded.

"Elves take care of elves," he said. "We held our border."

"Why did you even invite me here if you were in the midst of this secret... secret..." Asherah glanced around, then approached him and lowered her voice. "What did you mean to accomplish by bringing us here? To help you fight?"

"No," Leran began, then he wondered—had he really wanted Asherah's help? He was smitten with Ember, that much was true, but he wasn't so far gone that he forgot his duties to Tingu. Perhaps his heart had led him to a place his mind was too stubborn to reach.

Leran looked Asherah in the eye, and told her the truth. "I never wanted to need your help."

"Whether you need it or not, you have it," she said. "I will forgive you for not informing me of these threats in the past, but from this day forward you will advise me *at once* of any risks against any of my borders. I am still Lady of Tingu, as well as Queen of Parthalan." Leran nodded, and Asherah again addressed the entire room.

"Since we are here, warriors of Parthalan will once again fight alongside Tingu's brave men," she declared. "Leran, you shall have full command of my legion, and we will accompany you." Leran realized that by 'we', Asherah meant not only the Parthian legion but also herself, her mate, and Aeolmar and Latera.

"You cannot ride to battle with me," Leran hissed. "I cannot spare men to guard you!"

"You don't need to," Finlay stated. "I assure you, Asherah the Ruthless is more than a match for any troll."

"As is my mate," Aeolmar said as he stepped forward. "Beloved, have you your swords?"

"I do, and they're sharp as ever," Latera confirmed. Leran watched the First Hunter and his mate, and how Aeolmar was overjoyed to have a woman who rode to battle beside him. His eyes traveled about the room in search of Ember; while he was speaking to Asherah, she'd moved to the rear of the hall and stood between Tor and Mara. He remembered Aeolmar lamenting that neither of his daughters had taken to the sword and Leran's heart fell, as much for the knowledge that Ember would never be a warrior queen, and that despite all of his careful planning, he would be leaving her behind.

"They remain here," Leran declared as he pointed at the sisters. "I'll not have my legion slowed by women." Too late, he remembered that the queen and Latera were riding with him. Thankfully, no one alerted him to the obvious, and he turned to bark unnecessary orders at Balthus.

"We can march by noon tomorrow," Asherah stated.

"We leave at second dawn," Leran declared. Asherah opened her mouth, but he didn't give her time to speak. "If your fae need additional rest, feel free to catch up."

Leran glowered at the assembled faeries, daring any of them to challenge him. He didn't like having his authority called into question; it put him in mind of when he approached his manhood and reclaimed his regency from Balthus. While Balthus had never doubted him, knowing that Lormac's blood flowed strong in Leran's veins, Leran had heard the whispers that he was too young, too untried, and that perhaps a message should be sent to Teg'urnan for aid. He'd found the source of the whispers and had them removed, for he, like his father before him, would not accept anything less than the full support of his warriors. Once those who had spoken against him were gone, The Seat rumbled with a new set of whispers that compared Leran to Asherah the Ruthless, this time in a favorable light.

"As you have proclaimed," stated Asherah. "I, and my legion, am under your full command." While she was the queen of both elves and faeries, she would not speak against Leran in his own hall. No, Asherah would wait until they were alone to regale him with her opinion of how he had botched the entire situation. Leran understood quite well that the addition of Parthalan's legion would have quelled the northern insurgence quite some time ago, but he'd wished to handle matters on his own, as his father always had.

Asherah's words did give the rest of the fae over to Leran's command, so they moved to the rear of the chamber and began plotting their campaign. Leran moved to grab a map of the World's Spine—his father had always begun his campaigns by carefully consulting his maps, and Leran did the same—but when he turned to place it on the table he caught sight of Ember. She was standing rigid as a statue, clutching Mara's hand in a white-knuckled grip.

Had he really been about to declare her his mate when this mess fell upon him? He recalled Ember's words the night of the snowfall and wondered if she was right, that the two of them weren't meant to be mated. The fae gods themselves seemed intent upon keeping them apart.

Still, he couldn't bear to be so close to her and plan a battle, so he chose retreat. "Map out the route we took last time," he said as he dropped the map in front of Belenos. "I must see to something in the armory."

Only Belenos and Balthus realized that this was unusual for Leran, since he had always planned their routes himself and would as soon strike someone down as let them touch one of his precious maps. But Asherah and her Parthians did not know that, and Leran's trusted commanders remained silent as he escaped to the solitude of the armory. He had known it would be empty, being that detailed inventories were kept so each warrior could be armed at a moment's notice. Nevertheless, Leran began counting out spears and assembling them into piles in a feeble attempt to quiet his mind.

The armory was eerily still, with the lamplight reflecting a multitude of patterns from the polished weapons and shields. Many found the room disconcerting, but Leran had always enjoyed the final preparations for battle. *No, it is a war; we have been warring with them for so long I hardly remember what that border's like when it's quiet.* He scowled when he remembered Asherah's admonishment, but knew she had a point. Tingu was a part of Parthalan, and the aid of her legion might have ended the mountain troll menace long ago. *If only my pride wasn't stronger than my sword arm, I'd have put an end to these threats long ago.*

Leran worked methodically and quickly, and had soon assembled three heaps of spears and was counting out the fourth when he felt Ember behind him. She made no sound, and he tried ignoring her, but the weight of her presence necessitated that he face her. When he did, the sight of her nearly caused him to stumble.

Ember's face was pale with fear, her lower lip quivering while she wrung her hands. The daughter of the *deva'shi* was someone who should fear nothing, but she was awash in terror, all over him.

"I don't want you to go," she said, breaking the silence at last.

"I have no choice," he said, then resumed counting spears. "I must lead my men."

"Let Balthus lead them," she pressed. "Hells, let Asherah! But don't go!"

"Ember, I cannot send my warriors off without me against a horde of trolls and orcs—"

"Orcs?" Leran had meant an off-handed comment, but at the mention of orcs she closed the distance between them. "You said nothing of orcs!"

Leran ran a hand through his hair; she was right, no one in Parthalan knew of the orcs. Asherah may yet have his hide. "Whether I did or not, still I must lead. My warriors cannot follow another." Her brows knit together, and Leran explained before she could ask. "When a warrior recites the elfin oath of fealty, he gives me command of his body." He took her hand and pressed her fingers to her palm, then brought her fist to her opposite shoulder. "'My honor and my blood to you' is the oath."

Ember stepped closer, and placed her free hand upon his chest. "But, if there are orcs, there will be demons as well."

"Good thing we're bringing along your mother," he said with a smirk.

"Leran! This is not a joke," Ember snapped.

"I am not treating it as one," he bellowed. "I am Lord of Tingu, and I will lead my men!"

Ember stared up at him, her wet eyes shining, and touched her fingertips to his jaw. "But what if you don't return?"

"My return matters to you?"

"Of course you matter! You know you matter."

"Then why won't you become my mate?"

"I may as well be," she retorted. "You've been marking me all along."

"What in the nine realms are you talking about?"

"Kissing my wrist," she shrieked, now thrusting the appendage before his face. "Senan's mate's aunt told me what that means! You were marking me as yours all over Thurnda!"

Leran chuckled; for her to bring up such a trivial matter now, when they were so far removed from Thurnda in both time and space, she must be genuinely concerned for him. "This was Cerillia's kinswoman, Gilda? Her wagging tongue caused her to be banished from The Seat."

"Cerillia?" Ember repeated. "Who is that?"

"Cerillia is Senan's mate," Leran replied. "You didn't know her name?"

"I had other things on my mind than that fool," she murmured. "So? What does it mean?"

Leran brought her wrist to his lips, first kissing the outer portion. "This is a respectful greeting, like one would offer a kinswoman. And this," he murmured, turning her wrist over to kiss the softer, more delicate inner skin, "is meant to greet one's lover."

"So she was right," Ember said triumphantly. "You told everyone but me that I belong to you."

"I seem to recall many, many conversations trying to garner your agreement," he argued. *Is she here merely to fight with me?*

"If everyone thinks I'm yours anyway, let me ride to battle alongside you," Ember said. "Like Asherah and your father, and my parents."

"No!" Leran's outburst startled Ember, more so when he dropped to his knees and took her hands. "No. Not only will I not allow you to march in the frozen north, I cannot spare men to protect you."

"I can protect myself."

"Aeolmar said—"

Ember laughed shortly. "I can imagine what he said. I cannot fight as well as him, or my mother, but I wield a sword with some skill. I didn't shy away from his lessons like Mara did." Leran pulled her closer, a smile tugging at his mouth as he imagined his sweet flame riding at his side.

"Did Aeolmar ever slap you with the flat of his sword?"

"Only when I wasn't paying attention. You'll let me?"

"The answer is still no. I won't have you going anywhere you could be harmed."

"But if I'm not there, who will protect you?" Ember returned her hand to his face, dragging her fingers along his cheekbone before sinking them into his hair.

"You worry so much about me?" he asked. Ember said nothing, and instead wound his hair around her fingers. Leran loved it when she did that, the way she tugged at his hair until it nearly hurt. "I like that you worry," he said as he arched his neck. Ember withdrew her hand and tried to step back, but he held on to her.

"If I really was your mate, I could forbid you from going," she replied without meeting his eyes, or answering his question.

Leran moved to lean his back against the wall; after a moment, Ember settled beside him. "And I would defy you by going anyway." He wrapped his arm around her, and she rested her head on his shoulder. "You must understand, love, my grandsire not only made all of the elfin lands subservient to him, he expunged the mountain trolls and sent them back to the north. My father held our borders, strong and true, and quelled every uprising. Then he died, and our borders shattered. I've worked my whole life to repair them."

"Why didn't you ask Asherah for help?" Ember asked. "Surely she would have aided you." Leran sighed; if only it had been that easy.

"I wanted to. More than anything, I wanted to, but I couldn't. I was desperately trying to prove myself," he began. "Da had always made his kingship seem effortless. None of the elfin lords dared rise against him, and the trolls and orcs cowered behind their mountains. Then, Da was gone. In his wake, a boy rose to power, and all saw their opportunity." He fell silent for a moment as he threaded his fingers into Ember's curls. "The trolls attacked first. I was too young and untried, so Balthus led my warriors. While they were gone, an envoy from Nugt came and petitioned for independence. I was furious that their leader, Ais'nn, would do such a thing, and signed the proclamation casting them from Tingu."

"You could have denied him," Ember said quietly. "Then, he'd have been forced to war."

"Mmm." Leran was impressed; she must listen closely in Teg'urnan's court. "I did him one better. I added that Nugt was to accept no aid from Tingu or anyone associated with Tingu, and to do so would make them subservient to me for my lifetime, plus three generations." Ember wrinkled her brow, so he explained, "Nugt is an infertile land of rocks and ore. They have the finest stonemasons in the realm, but can't grow a morsel of food."

"And no one would trade with them," Ember surmised. "Devious. But why didn't they appeal to Parthalan?"

"Because, my little flame, your queen is Lady of Tingu. To request her aid would have violated the treaty." Ember gazed at him approvingly. "Nugt was the first to return to Tingu."

"Did they beg?" she asked.

"Somewhat." His tone changed back to serious. "You see, those who had pledged loyalty to my father were reneging on their claims, and I had to make a choice: fight with them or fight the trolls. I chose to fight the trolls, but I needed to do so alone. None of my lands would have returned to me if I'd accepted Asherah's help." He laughed soundlessly. "If she only knew of the many, many times I wanted to send for her... but I couldn't. The Lord of Tingu needs to be strong."

"When I was small, I wished the queen was my mother," Ember confided. "She was always so beautiful, with her white hair and perfect gowns, nothing like my mother with her leather gear and swords. Our chambers were always full of horsehair and blood, no matter how much the *saffira* scrubbed."

"I remember when I met Asherah," Leran began. "I thought she was the most beautiful woman in all the realm, and that I was the luckiest boy to have her as my new mother." He fell silent, remembering those portions of his youth he usually kept locked away. "I'm sorry."

"For what?"

"For letting this happen. I should have..." He balled his hands into fists, and tipped his head back against the wall. "I don't know what I should have done."

"It's all right." Ember gently touched his hand. "You said the trolls have been defeated before. Tingu will prevail." He smiled at her confidence in him.

"I shouldn't have tricked you into coming here," he said. "I should have let you return to Teg'urnan. You would have been safe there."

"Safer, maybe." She was silent for a moment, concentrating on her fingers as they twined with his. "What... what if you don't return?"

"I always have in the past."

"Promise me you'll come back." He tilted his head and regarded her pretty face.

"I swear it. I will come back to you," he said.

"The fae," she began, then fell silent. After a moment she continued, "Faeries, when we make an oath to another, we kiss to seal the vow."

"Do you? I'm not a faerie."

"Oh, Leran, why must you be so difficult?" To that, he kissed her fingertips, enjoying the anger that simmered in her blue eyes. Before he could taunt her further, she grabbed handfuls of his tunic and kissed him so hard he fell sideways against the carefully arranged piles of spears. He braced his back against the wall while keeping Ember in his arms, then he settled her so she faced him on his lap. It was the position they had been in while they watched the snow fall, and in his rooms in Thurnda; Ember had laughed, and likened it to climbing a tree. Then, she had tried to divert his attention with her taunts, pretending that their courtship was a game.

Now, she kissed him as if she would cease to exist without his touch. Her fingers moved to loosen the rawhide cords of his jerkin, then she pushed the heavy leather from his shoulders. By the time it fell to the floor, she was struggling with his tunic.

"What are you doing?" Leran asked when she left his tunic to worry his belt.

"I want you," Ember replied as she kissed his throat. Leran placed a palm on each side of her face, and gazed deeply into her eyes.

"I meant what I said," he said softly. "If I can't have all of you, I want none of you." Ember looked at him for a long moment, and Leran worried that he had just lost his only chance to be with her. Then she smiled, the loveliest smile he had ever seen, and asked a question he never hoped to hear.

"Then, you'll have all of me?" Leran blinked, and Ember continued, "Leran, my love, my mate. I choose you."

Leran crushed her against him. "You make me so happy," he murmured against her neck, then he claimed her lips with such fervor he rendered the both of them breathless.

The armory door flung open and a group of men clamored inside. "Hush," he whispered, hardly more than a breath in her ear, as he tried to flatten himself between the wall and spears. Finally he heard the armory door clang shut, and Leran and his almost-mate got to their feet.

"What are you doing?" Ember asked as Leran laced up his tunic.

"There will be people in and out as we make preparations to march," he said hurriedly. "Will you wait for me in my chamber?"

"What about Madoc'na?" she asked, for the feast's preparations were already underway.

Leran paused, his jerkin in hand. "You want it to be public?"

Ember's eyes widened when she realized that he meant their claiming would be public. "No, I... I thought it was required that everyone attend."

"It's not," he said. "We eat, then I ring a bell, and so the rest begins." He stroked his thumb across her cheek. "I realize we elves are, as you say, all about tradition, but I'd rather not share you. Not tonight."

"Nor I, you," she said. "I don't know where your chamber is."

"Ask Aldo to escort you," Leran replied.

"Your chamberlain walks women to your bedchamber?" she asked, arching her brow.

"He's the only one I trust with you," he said as he caught her in his arms. Her hair was mussed, her clothing rumpled, and Leran loved the disheveled look of her, because he was the cause of it. "You'll wait for me?" he asked as he traced a line from her throat down her breastbone.

"I will."

Chapter Forty-Two

"You've been to one of these before, haven't you?" Finlay asked.

Asherah glanced at her mate. They were standing at the entrance of Tingu's great hall, which was in the final stage of preparations for that evening's Madoc'na. "I have."

"And, ah." Finlay cleared his throat. "Did you enjoy it?"

Asherah laughed. "Actually, I left before the bell was rung."

"There's a bell? Whatever for?"

She took Finlay's hand and led him deeper into the hall. "You see the table on the platform? That's where the Lord of Tingu and his honored guests will sit. When the king steps down from the platform and onto the main floor, he rings that bell." She pointed toward an ancient bronze bell set in an alcove next to the platform's steps. "After the bell is rung, the food is cleared away, and the rest begins."

"You mean to tell me you skipped the most infamous celebration in all the elflands?"

"I didn't skip it. I attended the feast." Asherah gazed about the hall, her eyes shining. "The last time I was in this room, Lormac was alive. Torim was alive." She brought Finlay's hand to her breast, just above her heart. "I'm glad you're here with me."

He stepped closer to her, and tucked a length of hair behind her left ear. "I'm glad I'm here with you, too." He looked beyond Asherah and frowned. "How do you think Finn is doing?"

Asherah turned around and located their son. Finn stood on the platform behind the seat that had been reserved for him, frowning. "We should talk to him. Let him know he doesn't have to be here if he's not comfortable."

"But if he leaves, then what?" Finlay asked. "Some might take him leaving early as a sign of weakness."

"Finn is not weak," Asherah said. "Anyone who says otherwise will need to deal with me."

"Sher, you cannot fight his battles for him. Not any longer. He's a man grown. He can, and should, make his own mistakes."

Asherah leaned against Finlay's shoulder. "Why are you always the wiser of us? It's not fair."

Finlay's arm snaked around her waist. "I had to learn wisdom, to be worthy of you." Movement at the side of the hall caught his eye. "They're setting out the feast."

"Let's take our places," Asherah said as she drew him toward the platform. "This will be the first time the King and Queen of Parthalan have attended a Madoc'na. If the fates are kind, it won't be the last."

***

"It's an orgy," Aeolmar declared.

"It's not just an orgy," Latera said. "It's a celebration of life."

Aeolmar snorted. "And how does life begin?"

Latera smiled. "You're so literal."

Tor looked up and down the length of the table. It was so heavily laden with platters and pitchers it was a wonder it wasn't bowed. "The food doesn't get in the way of... all that beginning?"

Latera swallowed her laughter. It was a wonder she didn't choke. "Mar, have you any advice for your son?"

"Yes." Aeolmar grabbed a pitcher of wine and refilled Latera's goblet. "Be respectful."

"Why wouldn't I be respectful?" Tor shot back.

"I didn't say you wouldn't be," Aeolmar replied. "But Madoc'na is an ancient tradition, and anyone who takes part must appreciate the seriousness of the event. If you run around without having thought things through—"

"Or not having thought at all," Latera interjected.

"You'll end up in the dungeon, or worse," Aeolmar finished.

"What could be worse than the dungeon?" Tor asked.

"You don't want to know." Aeolmar looked toward the steps that led to the platform, and smiled. "Ah. Here's Mara now."

Mara greeted Asherah and Finlay, pausing to squeeze Finn's shoulder on the way, then she sat next to Aeolmar. "Is Tor asking about orgies yet?" she asked.

"I was not!"

Latera laughed again, and noticed how Finn's eyes tracked Mara's every movement. Her gaze then fell on the empty chair next to Mara. "Will Ember be along soon?"

"She's getting ready," Mara said quickly. Latera wondered what that really meant, but before she could ask anything further, Leran ascended to the platform. He located Latera and strode to her side.

"Cousin," Leran greeted as he approached her. "Spare a moment for me?"

"Of course." Latera rose and followed him to the far end of the platform. "Can I help you with something?"

"The scribes are already calling this a momentous event," he began. "What with the *deva'shi* being present." Latera nodded, and waited for him to say what was really on his mind. "The feast will be rather short. I wanted to let you know, in case you wanted to leave before the celebration begins."

"Thank you. Why will the feast be ending early?"

"Ember." Leran moved closer, and added, "She chose me. She's, ah, waiting for me."

Latera surprised him first by smiling, then by embracing him. "That's wonderful. I'm very happy for you. Both of you."

"Do you mean that?" he asked. "Aeolmar won't be along to murder me in my bed?"

"He may, but only if Ember requests it." She drew back, still smiling. "Well, let's get this event underway. You've a mate to return to."

Chapter Forty-Three

Leran stood behind his chair in the middle of the platform, happy and anxious and wondering if he could skip the feast altogether. He had never missed a Madoc'na, not the feast nor what came afterward, not once since he became king. Leran had left early many times, usually to finalize preparations to march to whatever battle awaited him, and occasionally to take a partner to a more private location. Now, he wished he could send someone else to handle his duties for him.

But, there's only me.

Soon, there wouldn't be only him. He'd have his mate, his Lady, his Ember, and he would never be alone again.

His gaze moved from one end of the platform to the other, taking in all those in attendance. His chair was in the center of the table, while Asherah, Lady of Tingu, sat on his right. Leran smiled, since this was the last day Asherah would claim that title. Next to Asherah was her mate, King Finlay, and next to him was Finn.

Leran had come to like Finn, for all that he momentarily wanted to murder him. But Ember had convinced him that everything that happened between her and Finn was nothing more than the result of the two of them getting carried away when they were young, and he believed her. What's more, as he'd observed the Faerie Prince over the rest of the journey, he realized that Ember wasn't trying to spare Finn from his wrath. Neither Latera nor Aeolmar held any animosity toward Finn, and Mara was his frequent companion. Leran therefore concluded that Ember was right on two counts: a simple misunderstanding had been blown out of proportion, and Tor was an overprotective sibling. Besides, if Finn had actually harmed Ember, Latera would have gutted him long ago, no matter who his parents were.

And, Leran liked the idea of having a brother. When Finn first mentioned that he'd considered them brothers of a sort, Leran had thought him foolish. Then he got to know the younger man, and by the time they'd fought beside each other in Thurnda Leran had decided that yes, Finn was his brother in all but blood, just as much as Asherah was the mother of his heart.

Leran's smile widened. A moon ago, he'd been an orphan fighting for his life in the Northern Wastes. Now, he was going to eat with his family, and then join his mate.

My life is good.

He looked to the left side of the platform, where the *deva'shi* sat with her family, and noticed Ember's empty chair. When he'd asked her to wait for him, he hadn't considered that she would be missing the chance to eat, and wondered if she would be along shortly. Frowning, he approached Mara.

"She's getting ready," Mara said before he asked. "She was worried if she sat with you now, it would detract from the rest of the celebration."

"Thank you," Leran murmured, then he beckoned a *saffira* and asked them to bring food to Ember's room. He appreciated her respect for Madoc'na, but he wouldn't have her starving while she waited for him. Once the *saffira* set about putting a meal together for Ember, Leran grabbed her chair and set it next to his own.

"Finn," Leran called. "Sit beside me, brother?"

Finn looked up and grinned. "I'd love to."

***

"Look at how happy he is," Latera said to Aeolmar, indicating Leran with her gaze. "I've never seen Leran laugh so freely."

"Feeling like you belong can change everything about a man," Aeolmar said. "And being surrounded by family goes a long way toward that belonging. I know that firsthand," he added, as he squeezed Latera's knee beneath the table.

"Does that mean you're going to make more of an effort with Caol'non?"

Aeolmar looked over the hall, searching for the stranger with his father's face. "I want to," he admitted. "But before I do that, I need to know if I can trust him."

"And if you can't?"

Aeolmar grabbed his wine cup. "Then, I don't know what I'll do."

***

Leran had never felt so impatient in his life.

All around him, his guests laughed and enjoyed themselves, which was how it should be. The evening's purpose was one last celebration, in case anyone didn't survive the coming battle. Leran wasn't concerned about his survival; hells, if the mountain trolls hadn't killed him by now, they likely never would. Still, all he could think about was Ember, alone and waiting for him.

"Why do people eat so slowly?" he muttered.

"Are you that eager for the battle?" Finn asked.

"No. Not the battle."

"Ah. Then you're eager to reunite with Ember."

Leran regarded Finn. "What makes you say that?"

"It's rather obvious," Finn replied. "Firstly, you two have been chasing each other since the day we arrived in Thurnda. Do you really think no one noticed?"

"I... I hadn't really thought about it," Leran admitted.

"And she's the only person absent tonight. Waiting for you somewhere private, I assume?"

Leran scowled at his plate. He hoped she was waiting for him, but was secretly afraid she'd gotten bored, or changed her mind, or decided she would be better off without him. "I hope so."

"If she said she'd wait, she will," Finn said. "Ember is one of the best people I've ever met. She would never break her word, not to you or anyone."

"You think so highly of her, yet you rejected her?"

It was Finn's turn to frown. "I take it you know what happened when we were younger." When Leran nodded, Finn continued, "Ember was my first friend. Sometimes, she was my only friend, but that's just it—we were friends, not lovers. Don't get me wrong, she would have been a fine mate, and a wonderful queen. But, I don't love her. Ember deserves someone who adores her, and I didn't." Finn glanced toward his parents, and added, "Everyone deserves to be loved."

"Do you love someone?"

"Yes, but... I'm working on it." Finn grinned at Leran. "Well, what are you waiting for? Go to her."

"I..." Leran was about to list the many traditions associated with Madoc'na, and why he should wait to ring the bell for at least a little longer, and shut his mouth. What was the point of him being a king in his own hall if he couldn't indulge himself?

What was the point of being Lord of Tingu, without his Lady?

"Finn, you're brilliant," Leran said as he shoved back his chair. "Easily the best brother I've ever had."

With that, Leran stepped down from the platform and rang the bell, and the true celebration began.

Chapter Forty-Four

Mara stood in the corridor, toying with the laces of her bodice. Inside the hall, the elfin festival of Madoc'na was well underway; when her brother had questioned the celebration's purpose, her mother had explained that it was held on the eve of battle, and affirmed life in the face of death. Her father had snorted, and called it an orgy. Latera hadn't disagreed.

"Gods, please let Papa be right," Mara mumbled. After the preparations for the coming battle against the mountain trolls had begun, Mara was led to the room she would share with Ember, but once she was inside, she learned that she'd be staying there alone. Ember had forgiven Leran, and chosen him as her mate.

Mara was happy for her sister, and helped Ember prepare herself for her evening with Leran. Only when Ember left to be with the man she loved did Mara crumple to the floor, sobbing for the life she'd almost had. The life she would have had, if she hadn't been kidnapped and then tortured by Sarelle in an attempt to regain Olluhm's favor. Her father had rescued her, and the wounds on her body had healed in time, but her spirit was still fragile, so fragile that she worried she would never be able to be with anyone, never mind whomever she chose as her mate. What she wouldn't give to be fearless again.

I can't be fearless if I stay hidden in my room, crying alone.

Mara got herself up off the floor, and after washing her face and combing out her long auburn hair, she resolved to first enjoy the feast, and then join Madoc'na. Mara hadn't so much looked at a man since that time with Kemen on The Swan's rooftop, and even that had ended up with her abducted and tortured in unspeakable ways. None of the bad things that had happened to her were Kemen's fault, and Mara had never blamed him. But still, they happened.

She tried convincing herself that her torture had made her reluctant to enter into a relationship, but that wasn't the whole of it. The problem was that she couldn't move past what had happened to her, while also not knowing what she might have had with Kemen.

That problem had led Mara to a single, desperate solution: if she got the courage to lie with someone, then she could get over Kemen. By doing it anonymously at Madoc'na, Mara hoped she could save herself a measure of embarrassment, but she hesitated before she joined the rest; she'd left the hall with her parents earlier, hoping they wouldn't suspect what she had planned. Now she stood near the hall's entrance, her feet rooted to the floor. What if one of the Parthian soldiers were inside, and recognized her? What if Tor was there? Or her parents?

And there was the fact that by doing this, she'd never go to her future mate as a virgin. The thought pained Mara, but she could see no other way. Besides, her father had always told her that if a man loved her, he'd care nothing about her past experiences. Again, she hoped he was right.

"What do you think you're doing?"

Mara jumped, and turned to face Kemen. His gaze alighted on the loose stays of her bodice. "Mara, you don't want to go in there."

"Don't I?" she countered. "When did you become so well-versed in what I do and do not want?"

"I know you want to go to your mate a virgin," he said. "I also know that the man who wants you to choose him is not in that hall."

"How do you know?"

"Because I'm standing right here."

Mara bowed her head. "That... that was a long time ago. Things have changed."

"I know." Kemen slid his hand along the back of Mara's neck, then down her body until coming to rest on her elbow. "Come."

"Kemen—"

"There is a balcony where you may watch what happens in the hall unseen," he said. "If, after learning exactly what goes on during this event you still want to take part, I'll walk you there myself."

Mara nodded, and let Kemen lead her to a set of stairs. Truth be told, she was relieved that he'd stopped her from going into the hall, but she was still curious.

Mara stepped onto the balcony. The space above the railing was covered with stone latticework, which let those on the balcony remain anonymous. She peeked through the carvings, and saw that she could indeed watch what was happening below. Then she gasped.

"They're nearly naked," she whispered, staring at the writhing mass of bodies. "All of them. And they're... they're..." Her gaze darted around the hall, pausing on a man with white blond curls. "Gods, Finn is down there."

Kemen glanced at the Prince of Parthalan. "So he is."

"Asherah will skin him for this," Mara muttered.

"Do you know how it begins?" Kemen asked, coming to stand behind Mara. She shook her head. "When it's between a man and a woman, the woman initiates each and every assignation."

"She... they do?"

"Yes." He moved closer, and placed his hands on her hips. "When the lady sees a man she's interested in, she loosens her dress and offers him a glimpse of her breast." Kemen tugged at the laces of Mara's bodice, drawing the fabric downward. He leaned forward and murmured, "Not going to stop me?"

"You've seen my breasts before," she replied.

"That I have." Kemen kissed a path from Mara's neck to her shoulder. She leaned back against him, closing her eyes.

"After... after she has the man's attention," Mara began. "Then what?"

"If the man is also interested, he nods. Then the woman fully bares her breasts." Kemen pushed Mara's dress lower, her breasts rounding into his hands. He stroked his thumbs across the tips and she moaned, steadying herself by reaching back and grabbing his shoulder.

"And then they make love?" Mara asked.

"Not yet," he said, his mouth hot against her skin. "First, the woman needs to approve of the man." He returned to kissing her neck, while Mara watched what happened below.

"How does she approve?" she asked at length.

"He shows her his cock."

"He just takes it right out?" Mara squeaked. Kemen chuckled, then he touched her chin and tilted her head toward the lattice.

"Look, in the far corner by the hearth," Kemen said. Mara looked, and saw two who must have recently joined the ritual. The woman's breasts were bare, and right before Mara's eyes, the man unfastened his breeches and showed her his cock. The woman stepped forward and grabbed it. After a few strokes she nodded. A moment later, the man was inside her.

Mara gasped and moved back from the lattice, feeling Kemen's cock press against her buttocks. She closed her eyes for a moment, then made her decision and turned around.

"Show me your cock," she said.

Kemen's green eyes widened, then he smiled. "You've seen my cock before."

She wouldn't let him tease her, not when something so important was happening. "I need to approve of you. It's what happens next."

Without taking his gaze from hers Kemen reached down and unlaced his clothes. Mara took his member in her hand, stroking her fingertips down the length of it. It was hot and hard, wrapped in the softest skin she'd ever felt.

"All right," Mara said, then she was in Kemen's arms. He kissed her deeply, lifting her up under her thighs and pressing himself against her center, making stars explode behind her eyes. "Now?" she asked against his mouth.

"Not like this," Kemen said. "I don't want a night with you, Mara. I want a life. Choose me."

"I-I don't know if I can," Mara said, a tear slipping down her cheek. "I want to, but..."

"Hush, *nalla*," Kemen said. "Let me love you tonight, love you properly in a bed, and prove to you how I care for you." When she opened her mouth to protest, he kissed her again. "I won't take your virginity if you don't want me to."

Mara shifted her hips against his. "I want you to. I want you, Kemen."

Kemen set her on her feet, and tugged her bodice up over her breasts. "Come, *nalla*," he said after he'd fixed his clothing. "The night grows short, and there are many ways I need to love you."

Chapter Forty-Five

Leran stood outside his chamber door, hesitating. His tasks that had been waiting for him before he entered the hall earlier that evening had taken much longer than he had anticipated, even though the brunt of it fell to Balthus since Leran's mind wasn't centered on the coming march north. Even so, when Leran rang the great bell, the one that had been rung all too often during Leran's reign, that signaled the commencement of Madoc'na, and the Lord of Tingu hastily left the others to it. Even his curiosity about how the faeries would react to the elfin celebration of life and death could not keep him from this last, most important act.

Yet, he found he lacked the strength to enter his chamber. Every fiber of his being wanted to shove the door open, and find Ember where she waited for him; he imagined her lying in his bed, so small amidst the cushions and furs. He could still feel her skin on his, the sensation at once a cold rush and spreading warmth.

Here was a man who regularly faced down orcs and trolls, one who would keep fighting with naught but a stick, if he had to, yet Leran was afraid that if he opened the door, Ember wouldn't be there.

He shook his head in a vain attempt to center his thoughts; he truly didn't know what he would do if she decided it was too much for her to be mated to the Lord of Tingu and returned to Teg'urnan with her family. Leran leaned his head against the doorframe, knowing he would be utterly bereft without her, hoping for the sake of the foes he was to engage that she was in his chamber, for their deaths would not be as swift if he slaughtered them while mourning her departure.

At last, he pushed the door open. Leran crossed the antechamber and looked immediately toward his bed through the open doorway, then his heart fell; it was empty. He halted and shut his eyes, wondering if he had approached Ember in a different way, said or done something else, if she would have stayed. *Nothing could have made her remain against her will.* He laughed at the thought, realizing that he had managed to fall in love with the one person in the realm who was as stubborn as him.

Leran resigned himself to a night alone, but as his eyes adjusted to the dim light, he caught a glimpse of green fabric draped across a chair in the antechamber. He approached it and saw that Ember had indeed waited for him, but had fallen asleep before the hearth. He sat heavily before her, relieved and excited and so incredibly happy that she was there.

She had taken off her shoes, and her little feet were tucked underneath her while her head rested on her arms. Ember wasn't wearing the same dress she had traveled in, but the green gown she had been wearing when they met. Then he noticed how her curls tumbled around her face and down her back as if they hadn't been restrained in a braid earlier in the day, and the string of pearls woven into her hair, and realized that she had taken the time to bathe and present herself as his mate. He looked down to his own clothes, and while he wasn't filthy, he was still wearing what he had journeyed in from Thurnda, and decided that he should take a moment to bathe while she slept. As he moved to rise, Ember opened her eyes and smiled.

"You're here," she said, as she straightened herself.

"I've found an ember before my hearth," Leran teased, then he captured her feet and gently drew them onto his lap.

"As if I haven't heard that all my life," she said dryly.

"I like your dress," he said as he stroked her foot.

"I thought you might," she said. "You certainly liked it the last time I wore it."

"Seductress," he said. Ember shook her head and let her curls tumble around her shoulders, red and rich and seeming to be living fire. "I worried you wouldn't be here."

"You know I couldn't let you leave," she began, "not without..." Her voice trailed off, and once again, Leran finished her thought.

"Becoming mine?" She didn't speak, but looked at him so intensely he thought she must surely be looking at his soul. He rose to his full height, then extended his hand to help her up, noting how her fingers trembled against his.

"If we do this, it's not lovemaking. It will be a claiming." Leran did not know why he felt the need to differentiate between the two. As far as he knew, the acts were one and the same, yet he suspected it would be different with Ember. No, he knew it would be different, and as much as he wanted her, he would not force her into something she could not be happy with.

"Do you love me?" she asked.

"I do. More than I can describe." Once the words were spoken, her fingers ceased their trembling, and tightened about his.

"Then I'm yours."

Chapter Forty-Six

Ember Speaks

Leran insisted upon bathing.

Apparently, my efforts to please him had not gone unappreciated. I knew well how he liked that green dress, and Mara was kind enough to lend me her string of black pearls and helped me weave them into my hair. Of course, this was done after I had bathed, scented and oiled my skin, and coaxed my hair from its normal appearance of mad chaos into something resembling artful disarray. It had taken me nearly half the night to prepare myself for Leran, and to think I worried he wouldn't notice.

So I helped him out of his gear, and sat by him as he washed away the grime of the day. The bathing chamber was certainly worthy of a king, with the walls and floor tiled in a creamy marble streaked with gray, and an enormous sunken tub that appeared to be carved from one massive gray boulder. Hot water replenished the tub via unseen plumbing, and rich and heady incense perfumed the air. The ceiling was covered with the same glowing crystals that covered the bed-chamber's ceiling, and they emitted a soft, warm light that illuminated Leran as he stretched out in all his glory.

"Get in here with me," he said as he leaned against the far side of the tub.

"I will not!" I said indignantly. He pushed off the wall of the tub and came toward me, resting his elbows on the ledge.

"It's nice and warm in here," he murmured, wiggling his eyebrows.

"It's nice and warm out here, as well," I pointed out. If he thought that after all the effort I had put into making my hair presentable, I was going to submerge myself in that tub, he was a fool.

"Out, before your feet wrinkle," I ordered before he could proposition me again. As he stepped out of the water, I grabbed a length of soft linen and began drying his back.

"Have you spent time as a bath attendant, love?" I ignored his innuendo, but explained a few things to him, anyway.

"As you know, my father is a proud man." I also ignored Leran's snort. "He also hates it when Mother worries. When Tor and I were small, she couldn't go hunting with him, and as a result, he wouldn't tell her if he had any injuries." I urged Leran's arms away from his sides to better dry him.

"So she began insisting he get in the bath as soon as he returned. She told him that he needed to rest and let the hot water unwind the knots from his back and legs, and then while she dried him she would find all the injuries he'd otherwise ignore." I smiled, remembering a time shortly after Tor started walking when Papa had hidden a terrible gash to his leg for nearly a sennight. I've never heard her scream so much, before or since.

As I remembered my mother dragging Papa to the healer's ward, my hands came across a bit of skin as slick as ice. It was a small scar, half moon in shape, above Leran's flank. I traced it for a moment; I imagined it was an old puncture wound, likely a very deep one.

"Is this from an orc?" I asked softly. Leran twisted about to see which scar I meant.

"It's from a troll's spear," he said quietly. He took my hand, and pressed my fingers just below his left hip bone. "This is from an orc."

I stood in front of him as my fingers traced the scars; three perfectly symmetrical marks that marred his skin. "They have three fingers?"

"Some have three. Others have four, or five." I grazed my fingertips across his skin, warm and wet from the bath. There were a multitude of small scars across his abdomen and chest, as one would expect of a warrior. My warrior.

My hands trembled against his skin, my throat burning with unshed tears. Leran was a warrior. Every time he ventured forth from The Seat there was a strong likelihood that he wouldn't return to me. Gods. I didn't know if I could survive the loss of him.

I pressed my forehead against his chest and willed myself to be calm. The last thing I wanted to do was share my fears with Leran, lest he think I was just reaching for another excuse to avoid him, which couldn't be farther from the truth. I wanted him so badly I ached.

But Leran knew my temperament better than I; just as he had known I loved him when I said no, and he had known that all my reasons for refusing him were nothing more than half-hearted excuses, he understood my worry over his safety.

"Hush," he murmured as he wrapped his arms around me. "I'll be fine."

"But what if you're not?" I whispered. "What if you're hurt?"

"Then I'll heal." He turned my face up to his, and I beheld a loving pair of pebble gray eyes. "If I get hurt, I'll heal, but whether I'm injured or not, I'm coming back to you. I promise. Don't cry, little flame," he murmured as he wiped my cheek.

"I'm not. Your hair is dripping on me." We laughed, and he flicked his hair back over his shoulder while I dabbed at his chest with the linen. "I wish you weren't going. I feel like I've found you only to lose you."

"If there's one thing I've learned, it's that life is more often than not unfair. One needs to take whatever happiness life sees fit to give us." He pushed back my hair, and took the linen from my hands. "I'll gladly take the happiness that I've been given with you," Leran murmured as he bent to kiss me.

I wound my arms around his neck, twining my fingers into his wet hair and wringing stray droplets down his back. I felt his hands glide across my shoulders, searching for the fastenings to my dress. He couldn't have been more wrong, since it was secured by jeweled buttons that ran down my bodice. I plucked them free and let him slide the green silk from my body. Leran kissed my shoulders, pleased that I had worn nothing else.

He slid his hands down to my hips. "Wrap your legs around me." Leran lifted me as I twined my legs around his waist, then he brought me to bed.

I have never in my life beheld a sight such as the Lord of Tingu's bed. It was large—no, enormous—and was ornately carved from dark, dark wood. The whole of it was wrapped in heavy velvet drapes of such a deep purple they were nearly black. The glowing crystals across the ceiling illuminated the silk cushions scattered across the bed, and I wondered how many people could fit there at once. Leran laid me amidst the cushions and closed the drapes, effectively shutting out the rest of the world.

Then, there was nothing but Leran.

Unlike our encounter in my chamber in Thurnda, Leran didn't pin my wrists over my head and strive to pleasure me as if it was his mission. Oh, pleasure me he did, but he let me touch him as well, and my hands and mouth roamed across his skin. Our desires were much more languid than before, as if we had finally accepted that neither of us were going anywhere, and there was no place we would rather be than with each other.

Leran paused, his body held rigid above mine. "Can I tell you something?"

"You can tell me anything."

"I..." He took a breath, and began again. "I've never brought anyone to bed before."

I drew back, momentarily questioning everything I thought I knew about the man pressed against me. "You're a virgin?"

"No," he replied, with a soft laugh. "I mean, I've never brought anyone to this bed. My bed. It always seemed too intimate, like they didn't belong here... Or maybe, I didn't belong with them. But now you're here, and I can't imagine ever letting go of you." He kissed me between my breasts. "Thank you for seeing past the brutish warrior I've become. Thank you for seeing the real me."

I caressed the top of his head, pressing my cheek against his damp hair. "Thank you for being patient with a foolish girl from the south. Thank you for waiting for me to understand how much I need you."

Leran kissed me again, then he drew back and removed the Sala from his arm. He moved to place it on me, then he paused. "If I put this on you, you need to promise not to throw it at me."

I shrank down amid the cushions. "I promise. Sorry about that."

Leran slid the armband on me. "There. You're mine now, privately, just like you wanted."

"Almost," I said, then I drew him back to me. Leran knelt between my knees, then his eyes locked with mine as if to ask permission; I nodded and he pushed forward, his gaze never breaking mine, and finally gave me what I wanted so dearly. Himself.

It was sharp and hot, so much so I gasped and grabbed at Leran's arms; I hadn't expected such a stab, but he was a big man. I don't think he had either, and he slowed himself to a gentle rock as he cradled me in his arms. Then the hot stab faded to a gentle heat, which was itself replaced by more sensations than I have names for, building and building until I felt my skin was too small for my soul. I cried out at the end, and Leran answered me with a cry of his own.

He was mine now. My mate.

Chapter Forty-Seven

The morning after Madoc'na dawned bright and clear. Leran stepped outside The Seat, breathed deeply of the cold, crisp air, and smiled. *Yes, this is a good day to ride to battle. A good day, indeed.*

Leran walked beside his horse to the front of the assembled warriors, as was custom for the Lord of Tingu to do. By walking while the rest were mounted, he showed his warriors that he was no more or less a man than they, and their blood as worthy as his. It was a necessary act to remind his warriors that while he was their king both by strength and by birthright, first and foremost he was an elf.

He reached Balthus, and they exchanged a few words; his general had done an excellent job of assembling the warriors, not that Leran had expected less of him. Balthus had commanded the legion many times, and he'd always done admirably well. However, it was the first time since Leran had become a man that he relinquished command to his general, but Balthus had quelled his concerns, claiming that a true warrior never forgets how to lead his army.

Leran had been glad of Balthus' quick affirmation the night before, and while his general had either stayed awake or rose before first dawn to prepare for the coming battles, Leran held Ember in his arms as he told her over and over again how he cherished her. Then the elder sun rose, and the lovers reluctantly followed suit. Ember helped him into his gear before quietly slipping away to her sister's chamber; since they hadn't been seen together, hardly anyone knew that the Lord of Tingu had at long last taken a mate. He wondered how his warriors would react, especially since Leran had sworn many times to never tie himself to a single woman. Then again, those oaths had been sworn long before he'd met his little flame.

Some had already greeted Leran with a few comments regarding his absence at last evening's Madoc'na. The jeers were well meaning, since most assumed that he'd brought a woman or two some place private. Little did they know that he'd been in his own bed, with his own mate, and there would be no more wild nights of Madoc'na for him.

The concept struck him as he stood before the assembled warriors of Tingu and residents of The Seat: most had no idea that Tingu's scion would soon have an heir. *Soon enough, at least.* Leran's mouth quirked into a smile; of course, it was too soon to know if he'd gotten her with child last night, but he intended to take every opportunity to work toward that goal.

His men cheered again at the lopsided grin he wore, wrongly assuming that it was due to his eagerness to engage the enemy in battle. *Let them think what they like*, he mused as he surveyed his warriors, all clad in fine armor and bearing swords, spears, and shields. Parthalan's warriors were off to the side, led by Asherah. The foolish faeries, fancying themselves hunters rather than warriors, carried no shields and wore no metal plate but light leather gear, better suited for riding than battle. He understood that it was their practice to engage demons in this fashion as a way of insulting the enemy, the lack of armor or shield meaning that they needed no such protection against their foe's weak attacks. While that tactic may work well for demons, he doubted it was a sound tactic against a mountain trolls or orcs, and he did not relish the thought of Parthian royalty getting mortally injured on his lands. He hoped Balthus had packed a few extra shields.

As Leran called for the shields to be brought forth, his gaze settled upon his brother in all but blood: Finn.

Leran recalled fighting at Finn's side in Thurnda, and realized he was looking forward to a second campaign with him. Facing the enemy alongside his family was a new feeling for Leran, and one he enjoyed. As Leran approached Finn, he noticed how stiffly he sat atop his horse, both man and mount fidgeting. Leran realized he was staring at something, and followed the Prince of Parthalan's gaze. When Leran realized what Finn was gazing at so intently, he halted.

Finn was staring at Mara.

Leran looked closely at Finn, and noticed his arrow-straight back, his white-knuckled grip on the reins. At Madoc'na, Finn had told Leran that he loved someone, but the situation seemed complicated. Now Finn was terrified, and not for himself.

"Finn," Leran called. "Dismount, please."

"May I ask why?" Finn inquired.

"Yes, Leran, why?" Asherah demanded.

"I need some to remain behind, and protect those who will remain at The Seat," Leran continued. "Belenos will lead an honor guard, but I would like a fae representative, as well."

Finn swallowed hard. "You think I'm the right man for that?"

"Yes. I do."

Finn's gaze flicked toward Mara, then he dismounted. "I accept. Thank you, my lord."

"Leran," he said, and Finn smiled. "I am no lord to you, brother."

Leran turned toward Asherah and Finlay. "By your leave, will you allow your son to remain at The Seat as a member of the honor guard?"

"If Finn agrees, so do I," Finlay said. "Thank you, Leran."

"Yes, Leran." Asherah leaned down and placed her palm against his cheek. "Thank you."

Leran nodded at the queen, then returned his attention to Finn. "You've met Belenos?" Leran asked, and Finn nodded. "He will give you your assignments, and a new sword. My guard only uses the finest troll-forged weapons."

"I'm better with a bow," Finn said. "Crossbow, if you have a spare."

Leran nodded. "I remember. Belenos will get you a crossbow. We're all counting on you, Finn."

"I won't let you down." With that, Finn left the assembled soldiers and wended his way toward the honor guard already stationed at the Gate. Leran waited until Finn reached Belenos, then he walked his horse to the front of the assemblage. The warriors were waiting in orderly formations outside the Gate, and all Leran had to do was ceremonially close it and the march to battle would begin.

Leran looked up, and felt his heart beat faster. Atop the Gate, standing in the place of honor, was his lovely mate. *Aldo must have told her where to stand*, Leran mused, for Ember had no way of knowing that the Lady of Tingu was meant to watch her mate depart, and wait for his return, from that vantage point. He raised his hand in greeting; after she'd left that morning, Leran had found the strand of pearls from her hair amidst the bedclothes and wound it around his wrist as a token. Ember smiled at the sight of the pearls, and nodded as if pleased by his action.

She's beautiful, and brave. Fearless. Everything a warrior's mate should be. He knew she was frightened for him but stood strong, her jaw set and chin lifted, with her long hair streaming behind her in the wind. It struck him again that his people didn't know what a fine queen they had been given, and for the second time, Leran altered his path.

The murmurs that arose from the ranks quickly grew to a dull roar, but Leran ignored them all as he strode to the Gate, then mounted the narrow steps to where Ember stood. She didn't ask why he was there, but stood stoically in the face of his approach. Then, she laughed.

"What's so funny?" he asked. Ember touched the pearls he'd wound around his wrist.

"These are Mara's," she said.

"Oh. Do you want me to take them off?"

"No. They suit you."

Leran smiled, then he pushed up her sleeve and touched the Sala. "You must do something for me."

"Anything."

"Once you can no longer see me on the horizon, you must seal the Gate," he said quickly. He wished he had more time to teach her of the Sala, but that would have to wait until his return. "Use this stone. It will be similar to when I found you the ruby, remember?" She nodded as he touched the stone made from Nexa's bower, and instructed her how to use it.

"The Gate will remain sealed until either you or I reopen it," he continued. "As the Lady of Tingu, it falls to you to defend The Seat in my absence."

"I thought no foe had ever breached The Seat," she said.

"None ever have."

She nodded. "Won't you need this for the battle?"

"I need you safe, nothing more." He pulled her to him and caressed her cheek. "I need only know that you're here, waiting for my return."

Then he kissed her so passionately no one doubted that Ember was now the Lady of Tingu. He held her as tightly as he dared, not wanting to injure her with the armor he wore, and for only that moment, he allowed himself to worry that she wouldn't be there when he returned. Ember felt his fear and murmured that she would wait for him, and kissed him again to seal her vow.

When they parted, Leran turned to his assembled warriors. He grasped Ember's hand and raised her arm over her head, displaying the Sala as his men let out a great whooping cheer, for there had not been a Lady at The Seat in far too long. Even Ember's parents cheered, though he suspected that Latera would have a few words for him. He welcomed them, as he would now welcome words from Aeolmar or even Tor. They were his family.

Leran caught Ember in his arms and kissed her again. "I love you, little flame."

"And I love you, my mate." He kissed her once more to an even louder cheer, then descended from the Gate and mounted his horse.

"Let's kill our foes quickly," he yelled to his men. "I've a mate to return to!"

Chapter Forty-Eight

Normally it was a three-day march to the northern border from The Seat, but the size of the elfin and fae force meant travel was slower. However, while it was assumed the mountain trolls had already crossed the border, no one knew how far they'd infiltrated Tingu, or their current path. They could meet their enemy today, tomorrow, or in a sennight's time.

"Olluhm's Balls," Aeolmar grumbled. He hated not knowing where his enemy was holed up, and the cold, and almost everything else about this campaign. He couldn't wait to stab something.

"What was that?" Caol'non asked. Aeolmar bristled; he'd been successfully avoiding Caol'non since they'd departed from Thurnda, and now he'd somehow maneuvered his horse alongside him.

"Nothing," he said. "Just thinking out loud."

"I didn't notice you and your mate, or the king and queen, at Madoc'na," Caol'non said.

Aeolmar's gaze slid toward Caol'non, then he faced forward again. "Was that your first Madoc'na?"

"Yes," he replied, "but I'm familiar with the custom. My father—your grandsire—was a great friend of the elves. He attended many Madoc'nas."

"Mmm. Is that how he got you?"

"No. My mother's name was Iseault, and she was from the west," Caol'non replied. "She once lived near your home, in Savey. Surely you knew that?"

"How would I? My father never once spoke of her."

Caol'non grunted. "Her memory had always pained him. She died while we were young, and Caol'nir took it very hard. Fiornacht, too."

"Fiornacht, who died in the temple," Aeolmar said.

"Yes."

"Why weren't you in the temple with him?"

"My assignment that day was to guard the king."

Aeolmar snorted. "The traitor."

"Yes. He was a traitor, though I didn't believe it at the time. Caol'nir realized what was happening before any of us, but no one would listen to him."

"Imagine the lives you would have saved if you'd paid attention."

"I think about that every day." Caol'non paused. "You can hate me if you like, but nothing could make me hate you."

"I don't hate you," Aeolmar admitted. "I just don't understand the secrecy, the hiding... It makes no sense to me."

They rode in silence for a time. "We fought, Caol'nir and I."

"Did you fight often?"

"No. Once we were men, we hardly ever disagreed about anything. That's the thing about being a twin; no matter what happens, you always have someone who believes in you. Someone who's on your side." Caol'non studied the reins in his hands.

"We fought because your father was being an ass," Caol'non continued. "Your mother was marked by the oldest, meanest demon in Parthalan, and their great plan was to hide. Only they couldn't hide, because that mark called to Mersgoth like a beacon."

"You thought they should find Mersgoth, instead," Aeolmar said, and Caol'non nodded.

"We could have tracked him. Laid a trap for him. Hells, between myself, my father, and my brother we could have killed the demon... But Alluria said no." Caol'non glanced at Aeolmar, and continued, "My brother was hotheaded, but Alluria was the most stubborn woman to ever draw breath."

Aeolmar suppressed a smile. "I remember. Why didn't she want you to go after Mersgoth?"

"Honestly, I think she was scared," he replied. "When the *mordeths* attacked the temple, she was locked inside with them. Sarelle, the High Priestess, laid a trap for the priestesses, Alluria included." Caol'non paused, and added, "We never did find out what happened to Sarelle."

"My mate killed her," Aeolmar replied. "I'll tell you the story later, when Latera's with us."

Caol'non nodded. "Latera did well to end Sarelle. Getting back to me and your father, Alluria wanted to hide, and Caol'nir did whatever

Alluria wanted. We fought, and fought again, and after their son was born, I set out on my own. I couldn't bear to watch them sit back and wait for death... Now, I wish I'd stayed with them."

Aeolmar cleared his throat. "When I learned that they fled from the demon, instead of bringing the fight to him, I also thought they were wrong."

"I would give anything to have been there the day Mersgoth found them," Caol'non said. "I might have died as well, but maybe I could have saved your parents. Maybe I could have saved your siblings. I'm sorry I wasn't there."

"I... understand," Aeolmar said, and he did. He hadn't been present when Mersgoth attacked his family, either. "Why did you decide to leave Ysr now?"

"I told you, the Ish h'ra is due to return," Caol'non said. "I am here to protect what's left of my family."

"Where's Tor?"

"Your son?"

"No. Your father."

"I don't know."

Aeolmar glanced at Caol'non again. "When this business with the orcs is through, we need to find him. If we're targets, he could be, as well."

Again, Caol'non grunted, and Aeolmar at last understood why Latera hated it when he responded to her in the same manner. "Know this, he will only be found if he wishes it."

"One of my huntresses can find anyone, no matter where they hide." Before Aeolmar could continue, the younger Tor brought his horse alongside Caol'non.

"I've got my troll sword," Tor declared, holding up the sheathed blade. "Leran just gave it to me!"

"There is no way Grelk completed a sword in a day," Aeolmar said.

"He didn't," Leran said, as he approached Aeolmar's other side. "I gave Tor one of my own swords, for now. Whenever Grelk completes the special blade, Tor will have two troll swords."

Aeolmar dipped his chin. "That's very kind of you."

"It's nothing. Besides, we both know Grelk doesn't hurry to finish his projects." They rode in silence for a moment, both watching as Tor showed off his new weapon to Caol'non. Finally, Leran said, "I will be good to her."

"If I thought otherwise, I'd have long since brought Ember back to Teg'urnan," Aeolmar said. "But, Ember loves you. She's like her mother in that she loves deeply, and without regret."

"I am honored she chose me."

"You should be." Aeolmar glanced at Leran, then faced forward again. "I have told her I'll kill you if she's mistreated."

"Please don't take offense, but I'm far warier of Latera than you."

Aeolmar smiled. "Wise words."

"I'm not surprised your daughter is the new Lady of Tingu," Caol'non said. "Being that you have so much of the gods' blood, others are drawn to you, and your children."

Aeolmar remembered the steady stream of visitors they'd had at his family's cottage in Savey. "Is it the same with you? I recall my father always having a small army of admirers."

"That's how it was while he was in Tingu," Leran said. "Mention Caol'nir's name to Balthus, and you'll hear a tale of how our warriors started looking to Caol'nir, and his father, for leadership. Balthus was not pleased," he added.

Caol'non laughed. "My brother was the most amenable of us. Children and adults flocked to him, looking for a bit of advice or a kind word, and they always got it. He was an excellent teacher, though his benevolent heart made him an awful soldier."

"What did he teach?" Tor asked.

"Swordplay, mostly, but he would help anyone in need," Caol'non replied. "Caol'nir was the best of men, as is your father, and now you."

Tor grinned, then he and Caol'non moved ahead as Tor asked many questions about the grandsire he'd never met.

"Do we still think Caol'non may be threat?" Leran asked.

Aeolmar watched Caol'non and his son as he replied. "I am not sure what to think."

CHAPTER FORTY-NINE

The next day, the elfin war party pushed further into the Northern Waste. The frigid land lived up to its reputation as a place of frozen earth and cruel winds that found their way into the many layers of furs and wool all were wrapped in. Leran had worried how the delicate fae would react to such a harsh environment, but none complained, at least not within his hearing. If only he could convince them to wear armor and carry shields, he might be able to make something of this motley legion.

Suddenly, Ember's mother reined in her horse. *Latera,* Leran admonished himself, *I must keep referring to her as Latera.* He moved abreast of her, and saw that his cousin was staring eastward.

"What do you sense?" he asked.

"Demons," she replied, "a fair amount of them. They're just beyond the ridge."

Leran saw nothing, and heard even less thanks to the biting wind. Still, he knew better than to question the *deva'shi* when it came to demons. "I'll have the archers assemble along the crest."

"You don't need archers," Latera said matter-of-factly. "You have me."

Leran watched as Latera dismounted, then passed off her horse's reins to one of the handlers. Heedless of the frigid wind, she removed her cloak, overtunic and gloves.

"What do you think you're doing?" Leran demanded. Latera had stripped down to her light leather riding gear, her arms and neck bare. "This isn't some warm meadow in Parthalan! The cold will kill you before the demons have a chance!" Instead of reacting to his anger, she winked at him.

"I wonder if you'd be so concerned if I wasn't your mate's mother?" she mused. Before Leran could reply, Latera ran toward the ridge and was quickly out of sight.

"You're just going to let you mate run toward certain death?" Leran demanded of Aeolmar.

"You of all people should know better than to underestimate the *deva'shi*," Aeolmar replied as he swung down from the saddle. "Latera will have rendered the bulk of them limb from limb before your archers have time to notch their arrows." Aeolmar similarly shed his cloak, then drew his sword with a wicked grin. "Still, I'd hate to let her have all the fun."

"Faeries," Leran muttered as the First Hunter ran to join his mate.

"We are an unruly lot," Asherah murmured, startling Leran. He hadn't noticed that she'd moved up beside him. "Leave the demons to Aeolmar and Latera. We've some orcs and trolls to deal with."

Leran glanced toward the ridge, then he instructed a company to remain, as much to lend aid to Latera and Aeolmar, should they need it, as to help them catch up to the rest when they were through with the demons. Once that was done, he and Asherah resumed traveling northward toward the border.

"I'm happy for you, Leran," Asherah said.

"I'm happy for myself," Leran said. "You know something? I cannot remember the last time I was happy for myself. For Tingu and my people, yes, but not myself."

Asherah frowned at her hands. "I'm sorry for that."

"Don't be. You were never the cause of my dissatisfaction. If any-thing, by bringing your court along with you to Thurnda you have improved my life a hundredfold."

"Careful. I am not above taking full credit for your happiness. Al-though, I suppose Ember does deserve a measure."

Leran smiled. "More than a measure."

Asherah glanced at the now-empty spot on Leran's forearm. "I assume the Sala approved of her?"

"I have no idea what the Sala thinks, or if it even does," Leran replied, amazed at how easily the words fell from his lips. He'd sworn to never tell anyone that the Sala was silent to him in all things, and was prepared to take the secret to his grave. Now that Ember had accepted him, the Sala's relentless quiet wasn't the sore spot it once was. "It's never spoken to me, not even once. I suppose it only converses with full-blooded elves."

"Really?" Asherah asked. "Even after you performed the ceremony in The Seat, it remained silent?"

Leran pulled his horse to a halt and regarded Asherah. "Ceremony?"

"Yes. Lormac explained the ritual to me many times," she replied, stopping as well. "You enter the crystal cave and place the Sala on Nexa's bower, then you sprinkle a drop or two of your blood upon the armband's fourth stone. It's how the ancestors know to speak to you." Her brow pinched. "I thought Balthus, or Aldo, would have told you."

"If they knew about this ceremony, they kept it to themselves," Leran said. "What you're saying is that the Sala doesn't speak to me because I haven't properly introduced myself to the ancestors? Not because they've rejected me?"

Asherah reached over and placed her palm against his cheek. "How could anyone reject you? You're the most perfect elf ever to draw breath. Lormac and I both thought so."

Leran exhaled, and let go of his deepest, most private shame. "I always assumed I was unworthy."

Asherah shook her head. "Only you are worthy. Tingu is your birthright, no one else's. I'm sorry you didn't know about the ritual. I should have made sure someone told you."

"It's not your fault. Besides, I might not have listened." He covered her hand with his own. "Thank you. For many things, not just this."

Asherah dipped her chin. "You're very welcome."

He flicked the reins, and they resumed following the rest of the party. "Let's go kill a few orcs together, shall we?"

"I'd love to."

Chapter Fifty

Ember speaks

Here I was, Lady of Tingu and an actual queen in my castle, and I was bored out of my mind.

Leran and the others in the war party had been gone for three days, and I'd long since run out of ways to amuse myself. The Seat's saffira didn't want me to exert myself by doing more than lifting a bowl of tea, never mind attempt anything more strenuous, like going for a short jaunt on horseback or otherwise explore the palace grounds. It was as if Leran had specifically instructed his staff to keep me from any and all injury, no matter how small, accidental or otherwise.

Hmmph. That is probably exactly what he did.

If Mara noticed these restrictions, she either didn't mention them or didn't care. She'd finally been with Kemen, and since that night she'd been as content as I'd ever seen her. I suppose it was fitting that two sisters found their mates on the same night, and I for one couldn't wait to officially start my life with Leran. Now, if only I could find some way to occupy myself until he returned.

What I really needed was a distraction, so I could leave off my constant worries over his safety. But both Aldo and Belenos had as-sured me, and re-assured me, that this was little more than a standard campaign, and the addition of Parthalan's legion made it all the safer for my mate. I believed they were telling me the truth rather than offering a few platitudes to appease me, and while I appreciated both of them, it hardly helped. The only thing that would help was Leran, safe and home and in my arms.

Soon, Aldo had assured me. Leran would be home soon.

And until then, at least I had my sister to keep me company. Mara and I walked down the main corridor of The Seat while on our way to our noon meal, which had become part of our daily routine. When we rounded the corner, I saw Finn standing at attention before the throne room's doors, and rolled my eyes.

"Why did Leran pick Finn for the honor guard, of all people," I grumbled.

"Probably as a favor to Asherah," Mara said. Finn noticed us, and waved.

"I don't need an honor guard," I said.

"Your mate thinks otherwise, Lady of Tingu," Mara said, and I laughed. Everything between Leran and me had happened so fast, and I could hardly believe any of it was real.

"Perhaps you'll have a mate of your own soon," I said.

Mara blushed crimson. "Perhaps, but it won't be Kemen."

I glanced at my sister. "I thought you'd been so happy these past few days because you'd finally had your moment with him."

"That's true, but it's not all of it," she said. "Kemen and I were never meant for each other, not really. I see that now, and I can move on. It's freeing, to leave the past behind."

"It truly is." Mara's happiness coupled with my own meant I didn't mind Finn's presence so much. "Finn," I called, as we entered the hall. "Come out to the balcony with us. The view is amazing."

Finn hesitated, and with good reason. I hadn't spoken to him on purpose in years, and he was smart to be wary of me. But I was now a woman grown, and a mated woman at that, and as Mara said, leaving the past behind was a liberating experience. Besides, if Finn bothered me, I could have him thrown into a dungeon. Being the Lady of Tingu had its advantages.

The three of us stepped out onto the balcony, and were greeted by the awesome majesty of the World's Spine. The mountains jutted out of the ground at steep angles, and some of the peaks were higher than the clouds. According to Belenos, the World's Spine was what kept Tingu safe from its northern enemies, and I believed it.

"I always wanted a sister," Finn said, out of the blue. "And now look at us. We're all siblings."

"Are we, now?" I murmured. I supposed that since Leran considered Asherah his mother, Finn was by default his brother. "I hadn't thought of that."

Finn grimaced, and stared at his feet. "I didn't mean anything by it. Just that... just that, it's nice to be friends again."

I set my hand on Finn's. He looked up at me, and smiled. "It is nice. I have to say, I always wanted a brother, too."

"What about Tor?"

"A less annoying brother," I clarified.

"You think I'm less annoying than Tor?" Finn asked, and I laughed. "That's the nicest thing you've ever said to me."

"Well, don't tell Tor I mentioned him at all. If you do, neither of us will ever hear the end of it." An unusual movement near the base of the mountains caught my eye.

"Belenos," I called over my shoulder. He was at my side in an instant. "Is there a town of some size to the northeast?"

"There is not," he replied. He followed my gaze and saw what prompted my question: a great plume of dark smoke.

"Is that the battle, then?" I asked, my voice cracking as I imagined Leran fighting his way through a mass of trolls and orcs. No need to worry, though. He would be fine, he had survived many such battles. He would be back in a few days, well and hale and—

"No." The word turned my blood to ice. "They went in the opposite direction." Slowly I turned to regard Belenos, but his gaze remained fixed upon the smoke.

"Then, what can it be?"

It was then we saw the rider on the horizon, both man and horse sweat-soaked and terrified. The rider spotted us and held up a green flag, some sort of signal I couldn't decipher. Before I could ask, Belenos spoke again.

"It's a signal from the second watchtower," Belenos said. "Green signifies orcs."

"Orcs," I repeated. "How long do we have?"

"A day, if we're lucky," Aldo said, as he joined us on the balcony. "I fear we won't be."

"All right." I silently asked my father for guidance, and continued, "We'll need to assemble a company and meet the orcs as far beyond the Gate as we can. How many horses do we have ready?"

"My lady, horses aren't the issue," Belenos replied. "Most who stayed behind did so because they weren't fit for battle. If we meet the orcs on open ground, they will likely overwhelm us."

"Then we make our stand here," I said. "We'll barricade the doors, send archers up to the battlements. Have we any siege engines?"

"We do, but—"

"Then let's roll them out and assemble some missiles," I said. "Stones, hunks of metal, rotting cabbages. Let's move them!"

"We will," Belenos said, "but you cannot be a part of the battle. My lady, please take your sister and retreat to the inner sanctum," he said gravely, referring to the crystal cavern in the heart of The Seat that held Nexa's bower. He moved to leave the balcony, but my hand on his arm stayed him.

"I can't retreat. Without Leran, I need to lead." Belenos frowned. "With Leran gone, it falls to the Lady of Tingu to defend The Seat."

Belenos pursed his lips. "I was tasked with keeping you safe."

"And I am tasked with defending The Seat."

"She's right," Aldo said. "With our Lord away, our Lady becomes our war chief. A moment, Lady Ember, and I will fetch you a sword."

"And some armor," I called after Aldo. I turned to Mara and Finn. "We only need to hold them off until Leran returns. We can do this."

They both nodded. After a moment, Belenos did as well. "Very well," Belenos said. "Let us make those beasts regret the day they set their sights on our home."

Chapter Fifty-One

Leran rode near Asherah for the rest of the day. He enjoyed spending time with her, even if it was time leading up to battle. Near noon, when the suns were directly overhead, he directed her attention to a hill in the distance.

"According to the scouts, the orcs should be in the next valley." Leran pointed toward the hill. "Just beyond that rise."

Asherah followed Leran's gaze. "Odd, that they would congregate in a spot that makes them easier to kill. It makes me wonder if this is a trap."

Leran scoffed. "Of course, this is a trap, just as the attack in Thurnda was a distraction. Everything this far north is a trap, as I'm sure the demons were earlier."

Asherah looked westward, and smiled. "Speaking of demons, they're no longer anything. Here come Latera and Aeolmar now."

Leran followed her gaze, and saw the First Hunter and Huntress returning to the main party, both of them wearing wide grins. "That was fast."

"That's Latera." Asherah raised her hand to greet her hunters, then Finlay approached her.

"Do you have the map?" Finlay asked. "I need to check something."

Asherah passed him her map. He scanned it, then he showed her a symbol east of where they currently stood. "What is it?" Asherah asked.

"This is one of Markham's old estates," Finlay replied. "I remember coming across it in the archive. It's the only one we haven't been able to verify in person, on account of where it's located."

"Markham had an estate in Tingu?" Asherah glanced at Leran. "What does your map say?"

Leran glanced at his map, and quickly found the area in question. "I remember this," Leran said. "My grandsire's grandsire gave the land to

Parthalan. He and the fae king had a bet as to whether or not grapes could be grown this far north." Leran held up the parchment, and pointed at the area in question. "The estate is marked with a grape leaf, and... and I don't know what sort of flower that is."

"It's a melon blossom," Finlay said. "Iruna was fond of decorating with them."

"Who is Iruna?" Leran asked.

Asherah faced him, and held her hair back from the left side of her face. "She's responsible for my eye, and these scars. But," she turned back to her mate, "she can't really be here. Can she?"

"I don't know," Finlay said. "What I do know is that no one has seen her or Avinor since they left Teg'urnan after they were stripped of their titles, and that this is the one place the legion hasn't checked."

"This Iruna has resources?" Leran asked, and Asherah and Finlay both affirmed that she was once the wealthiest woman in Parthalan. "For decades, we've wondered who could be behind the orcs, and who's been supporting the mountain trolls. But, why would Parthian royalty come here?"

"Because this is the one place we wouldn't look for her," Asherah replied. "She knew I would keep my promise to you, and I did, possibly to all of our detriment."

Leran frowned. "Mistakes were made on both sides, but we can still stop her. This estate is five days east of here. After the orcs are dealt with, we'll plan a visit."

Asherah nodded. "Then, we'll know what she's been up to."

Latera and Aeolmar reached them, both out of breath but otherwise unharmed. "Hello, everyone. What happened while we were gone?" Latera asked.

"We learned that Iruna has an estate in Tingu." Asherah passed her map to Aeolmar. He looked it over, then showed it to Latera.

"Look," Aeolmar said. "The estate is near Dremmsvard."

"What is Dremmsvard?" Finlay asked.

"It's the village where Senan met Cerillia," Latera replied. "And look, Iruna's estate is marked with a grape leaf and melon blossom. Every time I saw Cerillia she was wearing that collar of golden vines and flowers."

The five of them sat in silence, contemplating the information. "When—why—was Senan in Tingu?" Leran asked.

"You didn't know he was there?" Asherah asked.

"No. For him to have traveled that far into Tingu without sending word to The Seat is a violation of my treaty with Thurnda." Leran looked at Latera, and said, "I swear to you, I won't hold his actions against Sibeal."

Latera nodded. "I appreciate that." She looked toward the rise. "One thing at a time. We'll deal with the trolls and their pet orcs, then regroup at The Seat so we can learn about this estate of Iruna's, and the rest of Dremmsvard."

"The scouts from Ysr should be back soon, too," Finlay said. "Perhaps the Ysrian trade route ran all the way to Dremmsvard."

"You can't think all these instances are related?" Latera asked, as she and Finlay urged their horses toward the rise.

Finlay shrugged. "Anything's possible, and as they say, strange things happen in the north."

Leran watched as Latera and Finlay planned out their investigations into Ysr, Dremmsvard, and this awful-sounding Iruna. "Why are we even here?" he muttered. "Those two could effectively run the entire realm."

Asherah smiled. "They certainly could. We're lucky to have them on our side."

"We're lucky to have each other," Leran said, then he flicked his reins. "Let's move."

Chapter Fifty-Two

The Seat was in an uproar as everyone scrambled for weapons. The honor guard had armed themselves quickly enough, but the sad reality was that Belenos was right. Most of those who were currently at The Seat had been left behind because for one reason or another, be it lack of training or lack of strength or stamina, they were unfit for battle. With a host of orcs bearing down on them, they would have to fight, regardless.

Mara hated fighting. She suspected she'd hate dying even more, which was why she was running from the royal armory, which held mostly swords and spears, to the footman's armory near the main gate. While she could execute a few maneuvers with a sword, she was a much better fighter with a knife. She had her own knife strapped to her thigh, but wanted a few extras in case she lost hers in battle. More protection rather than less, her father always said, to which her mother said always out-think your enemy.

"Do orcs even think," Mara muttered, as she shoved open the armory door. Once inside, she learned that along with knives, the footman's armory also stocked bows and arrows. She knew this because Finn had slung his crossbow across his back and was stuffing every bolt he could find into a massive sack.

"Finn?" Mara asked. "What are you doing?"

"What does it look like I'm doing?" he countered. "I'm going to kill the orcs."

"You can't kill all of them," Mara said. "Hells, you can't even kill most of them. What are you going to do, run out there shooting wildly?"

"I'm not going out," he said. "I'm going up."

"Up?"

"There's a precipice over the palace doors," he said, hefting the sack of bolts onto his back as he left the armory. "With the advantage of height, I can take out dozens, or even a hundred of them."

"Finn, don't do this," Mara shouted, running after him. "You'll get yourself killed!"

"We'll all probably die anyway," Finn said. "But I can hold them off for a time, maybe long enough for Leran to return. I can give the rest of you a chance."

They reached the doors. Finn pushed it open, and beyond the Gate they saw the dust being kicked up by the advancing orcs and trolls.

"Finn," Mara said, "Please, I don't want you hurt."

Finn grasped Mara's hand. "Believe me, I don't want to do this either." Finn slid his other hand along the back of Mara's neck. "Do something for me?"

Mara nodded. "Anything."

"Tell my parents I love them. Tell Ember I'm glad we're friends again. Tell Tor..." Finn grimaced. "He probably wouldn't want any last words from me."

"Don't say that," Mara said. "No last words. We will speak again, Finlay Torim."

The corner of Finn's mouth curled up. "Now that's a name I haven't head in a while."

"Stay alive and you'll hear it again, you cocky bastard," Mara said, then Finn pulled her close and kissed her. At first, Mara was shocked, then she wound her arms around his neck and kissed him back.

"What was that for?" she asked when they parted.

"Just me, being a bastard," he replied, then he kissed her nose. "And cocky, can't forget that." They laughed, then Finn became serious again. "Be safe, dearest Mara."

With that, Finn continued down the corridor and stepped out of the palace doors. Mara went out after him, and watched as he scaled the front of The Seat. A moment later, Mara ran inside and told Belenos what Finn had done.

"A brave act," Belenos said. "Let's fight hard, to ensure he didn't go up for nothing."

Mara clutched her knife. "We'll fight hard. For Finn."

Chapter Fifty-Three

Latera and Finlay were still in the lead when they crested the rise, and got their first glimpse of the orc infested valley below. Along with the sight, the rank orcish stench reached them as well.

"Gods," Finlay said, as he covered his mouth and nose. "Is that how they fight? By stinking so badly they make their opponents retch?"

"It's worse once they start oozing," Leran said, as he joined them.

"Oozing?" Finlay repeated.

"You can't really call it bleeding," Leran said. "They don't have blood, not like we do, but more of a caustic ichor."

"Wool guards against ichor's burn," Aeolmar offered. "If the weave's tight enough, you won't feel a thing."

"Our armor's treated against ichor's bite." Leran glanced at the Parthian's flimsy leather gear. "Don't get too close to them."

"We should have brought Finn," Asherah said. "With his bow, he could have picked them off from a distance."

Leran nodded, but didn't regret his choice to leave Finn behind at The Seat. He also realized that no one else was aware that Finn's heart belonged to Mara, and he decided to keep his brother's secret.

"My archers are more than capable," he said instead, then he signaled to Balthus, who called for the arches to assemble on the ridge. "We'll launch a few volleys to thin them out, before we descend into the thick of it."

"My lord," Balthus called, as he approached them. "Do you see it?"

"See what?" Leran countered.

"Not only are there easily a thousand orcs and trolls below us," Balthus said. "All of the orcs seem to be female."

"Interesting." Leran raised his left arm, his hand clenched in a fist. Balthus nodded at the signal, called for the archers to notch their arrows. They did, and when Leran lowered his arm, the archers loosed their first volley.

"Hardly thinned them," Finlay muttered.

"Fear not, we have many more arrows," Leran said, grinning. "But not too many. It would be a shame to let the archers have all the fun."

Chapter Fifty-Four

Soon after the orcs appeared in the distance, they destroyed The Seat's perimeter defenses, and the front hall was transformed into a makeshift infirmary. While Ember fought in the thick of it, Mara ended up in the center of the hall's chaos, shouting orders, assessing wounds, and directing the healers. They had a system: those not likely to survive their wounds were on the left side of the hall, while those with only superficial wounds were on the other. Far too many lay on the left.

"Make way," Belenos bellowed, his voice cutting through the din. "Make way for the wounded!"

Mara spun around and saw Belenos and Ember supporting an individual between them, a man so battered and bloody she wondered if he was already dead. Then she recognized the crossbow strapped across his chest, and her heart fell.

"Finn," Mara cried, rushing forward. "Is he dead? What happened?"

"Still alive," Ember said. "The orcs knocked him loose." They reached an empty cot, and laid Finn across it. "Stay with him?"

Mara nodded, and Ember and Belenos returned to the battle. Mara shouted for water and bandages, and took stock of Finn's injuries. There was a wound above his eye that looked like someone had smashed a rock against his head; she wondered if an orc had struck him. He was covered in dust and debris and the orcs' stinking ooze, and Mara set about removing his clothes and washing the ichor off of him. Once she got to his lower half, she realized his leg was broken.

"Bonesetter," she shouted. "I need a bonesetter!" Mara tore open Finn's leggings, gasping when she saw the open wound on his thigh. "And a needle and thread!"

The bonesetter and the stitcher came, both of them amazed that the wounds hadn't already killed Finn; indeed, the bonesetter thought he'd be dead before morning. After Mara threatened to throw him out with the orcs, the healer relented and set the shattered bones, then the stitcher mended Finn's torn skin as best she could, and no one else questioned the treatments she ordered for Finn.

Throughout the rest of the day and night, Mara stayed at Finn's side, intermittently fussing over him, talking to him, and tending his many injuries. The orcish army was driven back during the night, but Mara hardly noticed. She feared leaving Finn's side for even a moment, lest he be alone when he woke. As it happened, when he finally stirred his head was resting in Mara's lap, she having dozed off against the wall.

"Mara," Finn rasped, so softly that at first it didn't wake her. "Mara?"

Mara blinked herself awake, and saw Finn frowning at her. "Finn," she murmured, smoothing back his hair. "Finn, your open eyes are the most beautiful thing I've ever seen."

"Are you all right?" he asked.

"Yes," Mara replied. "We all are, because of you." Finn moved his arm, only to wince in pain. "Don't try moving. Let us take care of you."

"Did it all for you," Finn mumbled, as his eyes slipped closed. "All for you."

"All of what?" Mara asked. Finn mumbled something, but Mara couldn't understand him. Mara gently moved until her face was close to Finn's. "Tell me again."

"I went up there for you, Mara," he breathed. "I... I couldn't let them harm you. Not before I got the courage to tell you."

"Tell me what?" she asked. Finn's head lolled to the side, then he forced his eyes open.

"Gods, you're beautiful," he murmured. "If the last thing I see is you, I'll die a happy man."

"You will not die," Mara said. "I won't allow it. Stay with me, Finn."

He smiled, and shut his eyes. "Is it any wonder I love you so?"

Mara gasped, then Finn slipped from consciousness

Chapter Fifty-Five

Asherah Speaks

I slogged through the battle, striking orc after orc and honestly not seeing the end of them. Where were all these beasts coming from? And where were the trolls? The way I understood things, orcs needed their trolls much as livestock needed handlers. Without the trolls to organize the orcs, they were as likely to wander off the side of a cliff as attack us or anyone. But these orcs appeared to be managing themselves.

None of this is right. *I stopped walking, though my feet kept sliding on the frozen mud. The only creatures I could see in front of me were orcs.*

I glanced to either side. Orcs. I dared not turn my back on these beasts, but I feared orcs were behind me, as well.

Hells.

Where was everyone else? How could I have been so careless as to let myself get separated from every single faerie and elfin warrior? I could imagine the tales the bards would sing about my demise: Asherah, once called The Ruthless, died of her own stupidity.

Not stupid. Enticing.

That thought was not my own; or perhaps it was a thought I hadn't remembered. So many memories had been returning to me as of late, though this one seemed as useless as all the rest. No one cared if I was enticing, not one bit.

The orcs advanced. Apparently, they thought I was quite enticing. I stepped back. Sounds of snorting and hooves scraping against the ice came from behind me. I was indeed surrounded.

I adjusted my grip on my sword, then I lowered my stance. If today was to be my end, it would be a warrior's death. Asherah the Ruthless ended up dead from her own stupidity, but she died bravely.

No death. Not today.

That voice… I gasped, nearly losing my grip on my sword. The voice in my head was Torim! After all this time, my Torim, my first love, had come back to me.

Don't remember me as Torim. Remember me as Nyshanti.

"*Nyshanti?" I said aloud. "Torim, I never once called you Nyshanti.*" Didn't you?

Gods. Did I? I thought about the word nyshanti. *It was from the old language, and it meant dawn. Torim had always reminded me of a golden dawn, what with her thick golden hair and smooth, dark skin. I was pale and cold like the stars, but she was warm and loving like the sun. My Torim.*

My Nyshanti.

All at once I remembered: a woman bathed in golden light, an army of beasts just beyond the gate. They were coming for her, but I wouldn't let them take her. Nyshanti was mine! I reached into her golden light and—

"*Asherah!*"

My eyes snapped open, then I squeezed them shut. The plain was choked with fetid, greasy smoke. I clapped my hand over my mouth and nose and looked for the voice's source.

"*Asherah," Kemen repeated, striding toward me through the smoke. "You did this?*"

"*Did what?" I asked, then I realized the source of the smoke. The orcs were all dead and burnt, every last one of them.*

"*H-How did this happen?" I asked.*

"*You happened," Kemen said. "I was fighting my way toward you when you started screaming in the old language. You summoned dawn's light, and burned the orcs to cinders." Kemen paused. "The Deliverer decimated her foes in much the same way. It's why Olluhm feared her. I'm told he fears you still, Ish h'ra.*"

"*You can't possibly think I'm her," I said. "It's ludicrous.*"

"*Is it?" Kemen reached inside his tunic and withdrew an amulet. "My father believes it to be true, and he's not the only one. Sarelle thought you were The Deliverer. Said it herself. She wanted to give you to Olluhm, in order to regain his favor.*"

I took a step back. "Kemen. Listen to yourself. You know I am not a god."

"Perhaps not any longer." Kemen reached for something in his belt. Not trusting him, I adjusted my hands on my sword, and moved to block.

A dagger sailed through the air and landed in Kemen's throat.

Kemen dropped to the ground, dead. I spun around and saw Caol'non approaching us.

"You murdered him!"

"I saved you from him." Caol'non strode past me and reclaimed his knife from Kemen's throat. "He was going to kill you."

Caol'non rolled Kemen's corpse over, revealing his hand resting on a dagger's hilt. "You don't know that," I said.

"I know enough." Caol'non pulled the amulet from Kemen's neck, then he quickly searched his person. When he stood, he said, "On Ysr, we learned that the vanquished ones have two types of followers. One group seeks to restore you, the other to release you in death. Kemen belonged to the latter."

I stared from Caol'non, to Kemen, to the scores of burnt orcs that littered the field. "Give me the amulet," I said, and he handed it over. "We will speak of this again, but until I tell you otherwise, this incident stays between us. Understood?"

"Understood, my lady."

I sheathed my sword, and scanned the horizon for the others. "What else do those on Ysr say about me?"

"That they can't wait for you to return, and set things right."

Chapter Fifty-Six

Leran fought alone, as was his preference. Orcs, while numerous, were rather easy to dispatch once you got past the smell. What Leran couldn't understand was why all of these orcs appeared to be female.

He had never noticed any sort of gender with regard to the orcs, and, being that they were created, rather than born, he'd assumed they were all neutral. Now, as he hacked his way through crowds of obviously female opponents, he recalled Balthus's recent suggestion.

Perhaps the orcs are breeding.

Leran shuddered at the thought, and barely parried an orc's strike in time. Beyond this newfound gender, these orcs were more organized than they'd ever been before. The reason the mountain trolls used orcs in place of their own soldiers was because what they lacked in intelligence was made up in ferocity, but these orcs were different. He noticed orcish commanders issuing orders, and a hierarchy that didn't involve trolls.

That was when he realized that the mountain trolls were no longer in the battle.

"Balthus," Leran bellowed. All of the scouts had reported trolls and demons advancing alongside the orcs, and while the demons had already been dealt with, that didn't explain what had happened to the trolls.

"Leran!"

Leran twisted around mid-strike, and saw Balthus advancing toward him. "Where are the trolls?"

Balthus, having the advantage of being on horseback, scanned the valley. "There aren't any!"

Leran spun around, checking the ridge that bordered the valley on three sides. His stomach dropped as he envisioned the trolls waiting behind the rise until his warriors were winded, then swooping in and trapping them between their advance and the orcs. Leran was about to call for a retreat, when a blinding light flashed across the valley.

When the light dissipated, scorched orcish forms littered one side of the valley.

"What in the nine realms was that?" Leran demanded.

"Whatever it was, it didn't kill all of them." Balthus pointed with his sword, and Leran saw a clutch of screaming, slavering orcs. Leading the pack was one bigger, louder, and—Leran assumed—smellier than the rest.

Leran adjusted his shield. "I'm taking the big one," he said to Balthus, then he ran to meet the enemy.

***

After the battle was done, Balthus found Leran as he picked his way among the corpses. "This was the strangest battle I've ever fought," Balthus said.

"Agreed." Leran sidestepped a pool of ichor, and poked a body with his sword. When it didn't move, he continued, "How did the orcs gain intelligence?"

"How did they gain breasts?" Balthus dismounted, and crouched to examine the largest orc. "Have there always been women? Did the men keep them home, the way we keep our women at home?"

"I've no idea. I've never thought about orcs this much, ever. I'd rather not be thinking about them even now." Leran joined Balthus, and scowled at the corpse. "This one was definitely in charge. I heard her yelling orders."

Balthus grunted. "Their queen, perhaps."

"If there's a queen, there's also a king." Leran looked up from the body. "We just need to find him."

Chapter Fifty-Seven

Latera Speaks

For all their numbers, the battle was over quickly enough. While the orcs did spurt a burning ichor, it was no worse than demon blood. Despite Leran's worries, we Parthians handled the beasts quite well.

Well, we were handling them, until a light brighter than a thousand angry suns flashed across the valley and decimated the orcs. While I was grateful for the light, in my experience, natural phenomena did not help me win battles. No, someone or something had sent that light, and I needed to know more about it.

I needed to find Aeolmar. We could speak mind to mind, yes, but I needed to see him. To touch him, talk to him, know that he was safe. As I made my way across the valley toward where the rest were setting up camp, Asherah crossed my path.

"Kemen," Asherah began. "He did not make it."

I nodded, my heart heavy. Even though Mara claimed she'd moved on from Kemen, I knew she would mourn him. Truth be told, I would mourn him, too. "Thank you, for telling me. I'll make sure we bring him home."

Asherah nodded, then she was moving again. I thought her actions strange, but we had just bested a host of orcs. Perhaps the battle had affected her more than she realized. I'd just decided to check in with Finlay when Leran approached me.

"We were lucky we had the deva'shi *with us, on this victorious day," he declared, and every elf within earshot let out a great whooping cry.*

"I'm sure all of you had nothing to do with our triumph," I said to the crowd at large. They laughed, and a few chanted my name. At least they appreciated me.

"Where is that mate of yours?" Leran asked.

"This way." I resumed walking toward Aeolmar, Leran beside me. "Why do you need him? Lessons in swordplay?"

Leran laughed. He'd been laughing more freely these past few days, and I was fairly certain I knew why. "Ember told me you were the better teacher."

"Oh? Did she give a reason?"

"Yes. She said that instead of trying to defeat your opponent through brute force, you out-think them."

My face warmed unexpectedly. I'd never realized she paid such close attention to my ramblings.

We came upon Aeolmar, and Leran asked both of us to follow him a short way from the camp. He stopped before a low, pillared building that looked like, of all things, a bathhouse.

"What's this?" Aeolmar asked. "A house in the middle of nowhere?"

"Actually, it's a hot spring," Leran replied. "There are hundreds of places like these scattered across Tingu, where the water bubbles up from the earth's hot core. Some are tucked away in caves and next to mountains, but many, like this one, are looked after."

"It is a lovely building," I said.

"Yes. Well." Leran cleared his throat. "In Tingu, it's customary for a man to give his mate's parents a gift. When I mentioned this to Ember, she compared it to me buying her. She said such a thing wouldn't please you."

"She was right," Aeolmar said, as he crossed his arms over his chest. "Ember's heart is hers alone to give."

"You're right, but she is still half an elf, as I am, and I wish to honor our ways. Therefore, I give you this." He extended his arm toward the bathhouse.

"You're giving us a bathhouse?" I asked.

"Not quite. Well, I suppose you can have it if you'd like. There's another, larger covered hot spring on the far side of the field. I've instructed my men to avoid this house, and direct everyone toward the other. What I'm giving you is an afternoon alone with each other."

Aeolmar's face didn't change, but I felt his happiness through our bond. "Thank you, Leran," Aeolmar said at length. "This is a most wonderful gift."

"Yes, Leran," I added. "Thank you."

Leran returned my smile, and with a curt nod he was off. I looked up at my still-scowling mate and laughed.

"Come inside," I said, grabbing his hand and tugging him along. *"Maybe a hot bath can unwind that frown of yours."*

Chapter Fifty-Eight

Asherah speaks

I stood in the main area of Tingu's camp, craning my neck from side to side as I searched the throng for Finlay. He was nowhere to be found, and for a few heart-stopping moments, I feared the worst. Then I felt a hand on my arm, and there he was; he'd been searching for me, too.

"Beloved." I threw my arms around his neck, then I whispered, "We need someplace private."

He nodded. "I have a place."

Finlay took my hand, and led me through the maze of tents to a smaller one far from the rest. The interior held a cot, a small table set with a wineskin and a loaf of bread, a washbasin, and a brazier some wonderful person had thought to light.

"This is one of the private tents," Finlay said, as he pulled the flap closed behind us. "How did it happen?"

"How did what happen?"

"The orcs," he said. "Reports are coming in of an entire field of orcs burnt to death."

I sighed; I supposed that left far too big a mess to hide. I unbuckled my sword belt, then sat to remove my boots. "Let's get out of our gear," I said. "We may as well be comfortable."

As we stripped out of our battle gear and washed up, I told Finlay what had happened. The cot was so small that when we sat on it and faced each other, our knees bumped together, which made it especially awkward to relate how my former lover had lent me her power over dawn's light to destroy the orcs.

"Nyshanti," Finlay said, once my story was complete. "I've never once heard you say that word."

"I can't remember having ever said it," I said. "But, I think I used to say it. Before."

"Before?"

"Before I lost my memory."

He gazed at me thoughtfully, my man from the desert. Finlay was one of the most intelligent people I'd ever met, and his mind saw patterns and made connections others couldn't dream of making. "And what of Caol'non's claims, that some seek to restore the old gods, while others want to release them? You believe him?"

"I think I do." I took his hand, and laced my fingers with his. "I think I must."

Finlay pushed a lock of hair behind my ear. "Remember when I took you to Ish h'ra's shrine in the desert? You were so happy. You looked... you looked like you had come home."

I placed my hand over his. "Most of that happiness was because you were with me."

"Be that as it may, you had the same look about you when we visited the other shrine a few days ago."

I thought of that larger shrine, and the massive gold roof. "Perhaps our presence at the shrine is what alerted Torim."

He smiled tightly. "And now that your Torim's back, what?"

"What about her?" I repeated, but his pained expression revealed his thoughts. "You're my mate, not Torim, or Nyshanti, or whatever she's calling herself these days. She and I were lovers once, but we've moved on." I took a breath. "I have moved on. This new mystery is something for you and me to figure out on our own. We lead Parthalan together."

"Together, always," he said, then he kissed me to seal the vow. "There's something else."

I rested my forehead against his. "Isn't there always?"

"Iruna's estate," Finlay began. "Do you find it odd that these intelligent, well-organized orcs appeared so close to the one estate of hers we haven't checked?"

I leaned back and stared at the tent's ceiling. "That is intriguing, but how could she be influencing orcs?"

"I don't know," Finlay admitted. "It's another mystery to solve."

Chapter Fifty-Nine

The three days is took for Leran's party to return to The Seat were some of the best days he'd ever had.

His elfin warriors had been victorious, Tingu and Parthalan alike had suffered minimal casualties, and he'd fought surrounded by family. If Leran had been asked if this was the best campaign he'd ever led, he would have responded with a resounding yes. He'd found his Lady, the elfsong flowed throughout him, and he was finally the king he'd always wanted to be. For the first time in a long time, Leran thought his life was good.

Then, they crested the last rise, and saw The Seat.

Or rather, what was left of it.

The Gate has been leveled. The flat area in front of The Seat was littered with corpses; bodies of elves and trolls were much in evidence, but most of the corpses were orcish. All at once, he realized why there hadn't been any trolls among the orcs they fought.

The trolls had lured him away from The Seat, and attacked his home.

The home where his mate had been waiting for him.

Leran screamed Ember's name and galloped to The Seat, riding his horse up the main stairs and past the massive silver doors, now hanging off their hinges.

He saw the corpse of the largest orc he'd ever seen, run through and splayed out on The Seat's grand steps.

If there's an orc queen, there must be a king.

"Ember," Leran bellowed. "Ember!" His heart pounded, his gut twisted, and his mind raced from one horrible scenario after another. She had wanted to come with him, and he'd left her behind.

He'd left her behind, and then she was attacked.

No foe has ever breached The Seat. Those were the very words he had spoken to Ember, how he had reassured her that she would be safe while he was gone, and now he repeated them over and over to himself. His horse's hooves clattered down the corridor, evidence of battle throughout.

At last, he reached the great hall, which was now filled with Tingu's fallen. Leran launched himself from the saddle and ran amongst the wounded and dying, searching for a clear blue eye or a flash of bright hair. His mate wasn't in the front of the hall, nor did she lie in one of the sick beds off to the side, and his gaze settled on the heap of hastily shrouded corpses. His heart in his throat, he took a step toward them, when a feminine hand touched his arm.

"Leran," she said, and when he saw her red hair he pulled her into his arms. But the hair was too dark, the form too tall, and Leran drew back to regard Mara.

"Is she... Where is she?" he asked. Mara smiled, her eyes indicating a point behind him. He turned to see Ember, Lady of Tingu, clad in battered, bloodied armor (*Where did she find armor small enough to fit her?*), seeing to the wounded along with the healers; the armor had made his mate unrecognizable to him. She was unaware of his presence, and Leran watched as she swabbed a wound with the detached gentleness of one who has cleaned many, many such gashes.

She's here. She's here, and she's alive. At length, Ember felt his gaze upon her, and dropped the damp rag as she ran to her mate and flung herself into his arms.

"I hoped you weren't dead," she murmured as Leran crushed her against him. He didn't know how long they stood there, holding each other amidst the wounded, nor did he care. His mate was alive. That was all that mattered.

"By Nexa, what happened?" Leran demanded.

"Orcs happened," Ember replied. "You could have warned me about the smell."

"And what would you have done?" Leran asked. "Burned herbs?"

"Perhaps," she replied, leaning back so he could see her sparkling eyes. He kissed her then, she who had defended The Seat in his absence, but ended it sooner than he'd wanted due to the cheers from those around them.

"I thought you lot were wounded?" he called out, glowering good naturedly about the room. He kissed Ember's fiery hair, bound in a messy braid, and they endured a few more cheers.

"Gods, speaking of stenches, what is that?" Ember asked, as she poked at the cloth sack dangling from his belt.

"It's the orc queen's head," Leran explained. "I took it as a trophy for you."

"Toss that stinking thing out onto the orc king's corpse," Ember said. "They can rot together."

Leran handed off his grisly trophy, then he returned his attention to Ember. "Tell me what happened?" he said, smoothing her hair.

"We were attacked by a host of trolls and orcs," Ember replied simply. She limped toward the wounded, and Leran noticed her uneven gait.

"You're hurt," he said, but fell silent when she squeezed his forearm.

"Not here," she said, and he nodded his understanding. She had led these warriors through the only attack The Seat had ever known, and could not appear weak. He had felt that way many times, hoping not to pass out from blood loss while he rallied those around him.

"You will show me," he said, his tone letting her know that it was not a request. He would know what wounds his mate sustained, and be damned if he let a healer touch her. It was his place to care for her.

"As you wish, my lord," she said, then she swayed on her feet.

"When did you last rest?" he asked.

"I expect when you did," she replied, but he shook his head.

"We camped last night, unaware of this attack," he said, then swept his arm about the room to show her the rest of the party filing in. "You have done enough, Lady of Tingu. Let us take over." Ember protested, listing the many things she needed to see to, when Leran cupped her face with his hands. "What good will it do if you collapse from exhaustion?" he asked. "Let the healers do their work. When you are rested, you can resume your duties."

Ember nodded, but instead of walking toward their chamber she mumbled that there was one more wounded she needed to check on. Leran grumbled as he followed her, only to fall silent when he saw Finn's unconscious form, his head and shoulder thick with bandages. Ember knelt at his side, and grasped his uninjured hand.

"Finn's amazing with a crossbow," she murmured. "He climbed up above the main doors, and held off the orcs while we scrambled for weapons." Leran crouched on the other side of Finn.

"He's responsible for those bodies near the Gate?" Leran asked, and Ember nodded. "How was he injured?"

"Orcs, stupid though they are, determined from where the bolts were fired, and threw things at him until he fell into the midst of them. I hope he doesn't die," she sobbed.

"He won't," Leran said. "I promise." He stood and called for healers, then sent for Asherah.

The Queen of Parthalan lost her austere mask at the sight of her son, clinging to life by the thinnest of threads. She sank to her knees and drew Finn's hand onto her lap. Ember launched into an explanation of Finn's injuries, offering the queen much more detail than she had to Leran. She described how he scaled the front of The Seat bare-handed, with a crossbow strapped to his back along with a sack of bolts that weighed nearly as much as he did. While the rest of those left at The Seat, mostly *saffira* and those too young or infirm to be a part of the legion, searched through the weapons the warriors had left behind, Finn held the charging beasts at bay.

"Then the orcs saw him, and knocked him free with a rock to the head. Then he fell into the mass of them," Ember concluded. "It took so long to get to him. I thought he'd been trampled to death." Indeed, he looked to have been trampled; the long bone of his leg was certainly broken, blood darkened the bandages across his torso, and his shoulder was at an unnatural angle and was likely dislocated. That, coupled with one of the worst head wounds Leran had ever seen, did not bode well for the faerie prince.

"Who retrieved him?" Asherah asked, her voice hardly more than a whisper.

"I did," Ember replied. A single tear slipped down her cheek, splashing onto Finn's bruised chest. Mara, who'd been sitting on the other side of Finn, wiped his brow with a damp cloth. "Even if he was already dead, I couldn't leave him with them." Asherah nodded, then looked from her son's battered face to Ember.

"As he wouldn't have left you," Asherah said. "Thank you, for bringing him back."

"Anything you need is yours," Leran said. "All my healers, my mages, everything is at your disposal. We will make him well." When Asherah merely nodded, Leran turned her face toward him. "Mama, he will not die!"

Leran hadn't realized what he said, but Asherah did. "I will have both my sons well and whole," she murmured as she stroked his cheek. Leran nodded, then moved aside since King Finlay had arrived alongside a score of healers. Ember rose as well, only to sway in exhaustion. Leran caught her, and ignored her protests while he carried her to their chamber.

"You've had the leg guard on for too long," he said as he deposited her on a bench inside their chamber door. "It's why you're limping."

"How can you tell?" she asked.

"Many ways," he replied as he knelt to unbuckle the armor. "Firstly, I recognize this armor as what I wore when I was a boy."

"It was all we could find that would fit me," she replied sheepishly.

"And you wear it better than I ever did," Leran complimented, flashing her a quick grin. "But I remember well how the fastenings for this guard chafed me behind the knee. Also, since it's been gathering dust since I grew out of it, the leather's become a good deal stiffer." He tugged at the strap, earning a small yelp from Ember. At last the guard was free, and Leran saw the true reason for his mate's limping: in addition to the raw abrasion behind her knee, the fine woolen breeches she wore under the armor were caked with dried blood.

"This will need to be soaked off," he said, for the fabric was well embedded in the wound. He scooped her up and strode to the bathing chamber.

"Leran, no," she protested. "Just fetch a basin. I don't want to foul the bathwater."

"Bathwater, being that its purpose is for bathing, is meant to be fouled," he said. He set her on the edge of the tub, then crouched behind her as he unbuckled the rest of the armor. When Ember was clad in naught but the woolen under things, he stripped naked and got in the tub in front of her, then gently worked the wool free of her leg.

"Most of it's not blood," Ember said. "Those orcs are... soggy."

"Yes, they are quite disgusting," Leran agreed, concentrating on the wound so he wouldn't imagine his mate set upon by a horde of the slavering beasts. Losing his patience he tore the breeches around the wound, and set about gently sponging Ember's raw skin. "I'm glad you chose to wear wool."

"I already knew that it guards against ichor." Leran raised an eyebrow, so she explained her odd bit of knowledge. "You were off with my father for what, six days? How many times did he tell you about his great victory against the orcs?"

Leran smiled as he loosened the fabric. "A few."

"Mmm. Imagine how many times you would have heard it if you'd grown up with him," she said, then sucked in her breath as Leran finally worked the breeches free of her flesh. He saw that while the wool had offered her some protection, the ichor had tinted her skin a sickly green.

"Take that off," he ordered, indicating her tunic with his eyes. "If we don't wash away the ichor, it will poison your blood," he explained as Ember shed the ruined garment. Leran tried to be gentle as he washed her, but the ichor had long since dried to the consistency of leather.

"How long were you besieged?" he asked, as he peeled a large piece of dried ichor from her shoulder. He flung it to the far side of the chamber, and hoped to never look at it again.

"They came three days after you left," she replied. "We routed the last of them yesterday."

"Two days, then," Leran murmured, reading a map of Tingu with his mind's eye. "They must have split their force at the mouth of the river, which explains why we encountered so few trolls," he mused, knowing the length of that route. "With me away, they expected to find The Seat an easy target, but they didn't know the Lady of Tingu was guarding her home."

"Fat lot of good I did," she grumbled, then she grabbed a comb and set to work on her tangled hair. "If you had been here—"

"If I had been here, we would have been attacked just the same," Leran spoke over her. "The Seat is still standing, and we live while our foes are dead. I couldn't have done any better."

She paused. "Do you really mean that?"

"You think I tell lies to my mate?" Leran countered. "What sort of stories do you fae tell about me?"

"Only ones in which the Lord of Tingu is handsome, and strong, and takes very, very good care of those he loves." Ember leaned against his chest. "I hated being apart from you. From now on, I go to battle with you."

"Absolutely not," he said, sliding his arms around her shoulders. "At least, not until you've had some training."

"I've had plenty of training. Who do you think killed the orc king?"

Leran blinked. "Really?"

"Really." Ember slid out from under his arms, and dunked her newly combed hair in the bathwater. When Ember surfaced, she was facing him, her hair once again lustrous now that the dust of the siege was rinsed away, her pale eyes sparkling.

"Nexa save me," he murmured, "are you really mine?"

"Yes, beloved," she replied, "just as you're mine."

***

A short while later, Leran untangled himself from Ember's arms. "Come," he said. "There's something I must do."

"You aren't going to get dressed first?" Ember asked. He pulled a tunic over his head, then he picked up Ember's nightgown from the foot of the bed and handed it to her. After she put it on, she asked, "I take it I'm to perform this great task with you?"

"Come, love." He pulled her up, and tugged her toward the rear of their bedchamber. "We're going to the True Seat."

"We're not in The Seat now?"

"We are, but we're headed to its core." He led her to the rear of the chamber, and into the tunnel that led to the crystal cave. "Up here is the True Seat, with crystal stones that represent each and every one of my ancestors from Nexa all the way to my father. And, there's one for me."

The tunnel inclined upward, and at the end of the passage Leran led Ember into the crystal cave that was the true home of the elves. A multitude of white crystals, identical to the ones that made up the roof of the bedchamber, were also present in the cave, and their soft light illuminated the interior. The centerpiece of the cave was Nexa's bower, a deep green crystal that was the size of a grown man. The bower had several niches and shelves in it, and a multitude of items rested in them.

"Leran, it's beautiful," Ember said. "Where is your stone?"

He showed her a gray crystal that glowed with its own light. "It's the color of your eyes," she said, stroking the top of it. "Will I ever have a crystal?"

"I... I don't know," he replied. "We can ask Asherah. She's the one who told me I'd never triggered the Sala properly." He touched the sacred armband she wore. "May I?"

"Of course." Ember slid the armband off and handed it to Leran. "How do we trigger it? And, why do we need to?"

Leran held the Sala with both hands and blew out a breath. "There are many aspects to the Sala, and I promise I will teach you all of them. One of the most important aspects is that it allows me to speak to my ancestors."

Ember spun around the room, taking in the myriad crystals. "You can speak to all of them?"

"I suppose."

Ember glanced at him over her shoulder. "You're not certain?"

"See, that's the thing. They've never once spoken to me, not when I was a boy, not when my father died, and not when I was named king. I used to blame their silence on the Sala. I spent the beginning of my rule without it, being that Asherah had held on to it. It was hers, by rights. Then she sent it back to me—sent it with your mother, of all people, though we hadn't known we were cousins, then—and I thought once I put it on and the ancestors would finally speak to me."

When he paused, Ember said, "But they didn't."

"No. They didn't." He met her gaze. "You are the second person I've ever told about this."

Ember went into his arms. "Who was the first?"

"Asherah. I told her only a few days ago, when we were riding northward. It felt so good to finally let go of my old humiliation, to accept that while I wasn't enough for my ancestors, I was still good enough to lead Tingu... But I was wrong."

"Of course you were wrong. Who cares if a bunch of dead elves think you're good enough, what do they—"

Leran placed his finger on her lips. "There is a ritual to introduce myself to my ancestors, so to speak. I never knew, not until Asherah told me."

"Oh. So they weren't being mean to you?"

He smiled at his mate's ready defense of him. "No. They weren't."

She glanced at the crystals. "That's good. Did she explain this ritual?"

"Yes. She did."

Ember held him for another moment, then she stepped back. "All right. What do we do?"

Leran's gaze moved about the chamber, alighting on a sharpened length of stone that rested on one of the niches. "According to Asherah, I need to set the Sala on Nexa's bower. Then, I'm to draw my blood with the bower's knife, and rub some into this stone." He indicated the clear green stone on the Sala. "That's how they'll recognize me."

Frowning, Ember picked up the knife. "This knife? It doesn't look like it's been sharpened in an age."

"It probably hasn't been." Leran set the Sala on Nexa's bower. "Since I have a mate, you need to do the bloodletting."

"Oh!" Ember tested the edge on her thumb, and found it was sharper than it looked. "Where would you like me to cut you?"

"So eager to wound me?"

She ducked her head. "This is important to you, so it's important to me. Your thumb, maybe?"

"All right." Leran extended his hand. Ember grasped it, then paused.

"Shouldn't you be wearing a bit more clothing when you meet these glorious ancestors?"

Leran threw back his head and laughed. "You think my bare legs might offend them? It hardly matters. Da brought me here right after I was born, naked and squalling. They didn't mind then, and I don't think they'll mind now."

"As long as you're sure." Ember held his thumb steady, then she slashed the knife across the pad of flesh. The blood welled up immediately. "I'm so sorry!"

"Don't be. I asked it of you." He pressed his bloody thumb to the Sala. "There. It's done."

"Now what happens?"

"Truly, love, I've no idea."

No sooner had Leran spoken than the light increased in the cave. He glanced at the ceiling, at first assuming the increased illumination was due to the small white crystals, but Ember grasped his arms.

"Leran, the cave," she said, while staring at the larger crystals toward the rear of the chamber. One by one, the crystals started to glow as if they were lit from within. "Is this a good thing?"

"Yes." He turned in a slow circle, watching as the stones of his ancestors illuminated one by one. "They're here. Ember, I can hear them." He squeezed his eyes shut, listening to the many voices wash over and through him. He'd once wondered if having so many voices in one's head would drive a person mad. Now, he knew the truth. They were a comfort like none other.

"Ember, they see you, too." He laughed. "They love you. Every last one of them thinks you're a wonderful Lady. They say The Seat is lucky you were here. The way you defended—"

Leran paused, his head cocked to the side. Then he smiled. "My father's here. I can hear him. He..." Leran pulled Ember into his arms and kissed her hair. "He's going on about how blessed I am that you chose me."

"I'm blessed, too." She drew back, and wiped the wetness from his cheeks. "Which stone is his?"

Leran led her to a crystal that was larger than his own, but the same shade of gray. Ember placed her hands on the top of the stone. "Lormac, I am so happy to meet you. I've heard so much about you."

"I told him you're descended from Caol'nir, and the *deva'shi*," Leran said. "He says you're a born warrior." Leran paused, then snorted. "He says you'd have to be, to put up with me."

"Your son is a born warrior, too," Ember said. "Remember, he also needs to put up with me." She stepped back so she could view both Lormac's crystal and Leran. "I see a lot of you in your son. Thank you, for making him into such a wonderful man." When Leran covered his face with his hands, she asked, "What did he say?"

Leran pulled his mate into his arms, and in between his tears of joy, he relayed every word the ancestors told him.

Chapter Sixty

Asherah speaks

We spent the night surrounding Finn, with me sitting on one side of his cot, Mara on the other, and Finlay pacing near his feet. I would have paced, too, if not for the exhaustion that held me down like a waterlogged cloak. Fear was what kept my eyes open, staring at Finn's sleeping face. I was terrified that if I shut my eyes, when they again opened, he would be gone.

"By all the living gods, I will not lose my son," I muttered.

"Kemen used to say that," Mara said, her voice hardly more than a whisper. "About living gods, that is. He had all these notions about gods. Dead ones, living ones. I don't know how he kept them all straight."

I reached across my son's form and touched Mara's hand where it grasped Finn's. Mara put her free hand on top of mine.

"You cared for Kemen a great deal, didn't you?" I asked.

"There was a time when I thought of nothing but him, but then we were attacked, and Finn was hurt..." She shook her head. "Now I don't feel anything at all."

I squeezed her hand, understanding all too well the cold emptiness that inevitably followed not only battle, but a lover's death. I remembered Kemen's amulet, and withdrew it from my pouch. I hadn't taken the time to examine the amulet when I confiscated it from Caol'non, so I did now. It was a beaten gold disc on a leather thong. Etched onto the face of the disc was a sun shot through with a spear.

Exactly what—or who—did that represent?

"Here." I thrust the amulet toward Mara. "Kemen was wearing this. I'm sure he'd want you to have something to remember him by."

Mara turned the amulet over in her hand, her face blank. "You were with him when he died?"

"I saw it, yes." My heart beat too fast, the lump in my throat threatening to choke me. I hadn't lied, but I also had no idea what I would say if she questioned me further. Then, to my utter relief, Aeolmar appeared at the foot of Finn's cot.

"How is he?" Aeolmar asked.

"No worse," I replied. Indeed, Tingu's best healers had been tending to Finn, doing everything in their power to keep him on this side of the veil.

Aeolmar nodded, then he moved to Mara's side. "How are you?"

"I'm all right." When Aeolmar's frown didn't lessen, she added, "Promise."

Aeolmar squeezed her shoulder. "Asherah, Grelk is here. He's asking for you."

I didn't want to leave Finn's side, but the ruler in me understood that I could do more good by speaking with Grelk than by sitting uselessly in the sick ward. The mother in me thought I was heartless. I leaned over and kissed Finn's forehead, then I rose so Finlay could claim my seat.

"He will make it," Finlay said, his fingertips grazing the back of my hand as we passed. "Believe in him."

"I do," I said, then I walked with Aeolmar toward Lormac's old war room. "I'm surprised Grelk deigned to leave his forge."

"As am I. Whatever Leran put in his message must have piqued Grelk's interest."

"Who else did Grelk summon?" The King of the Forge was one of the few people who could arrive at The Seat, start barking orders, and expect them to be followed. To my knowledge, the only other person who wielded such influence was Aldo.

"Many people, but he was most interested in you."

A lot of people seem interested in me, lately. *I thought about Caol'non's sudden appearance, Kemen's certainty that I was the Ish h'ra, and Latera's interest in Thurnda's archive. Kemen had said that Sarelle had named me as Ish h'ra, which meant the rest of the hunters knew...*

"Do you think I'm a god?" I asked Aeolmar.

His gaze slid toward me. "I have wondered, on occasion." We reached the war room, but Aeolmar paused with his hand on the door. "Are you a god?"

"I... I am not sure," I replied. "If you learn anything tantalizing, please share it with me."

"I shall."

We entered the room, and saw Grelk and Latera hunched over her swords. He said something that pleased Latera and she threw her arms around the troll's neck. Grelk, who plainly adored Latera, blushed as much as one could under his many layers of soot.

Grelk saw me and stepped back from Latera, his head cocked to one side as he took in my appearance. "You finally remember, eh?"

"Not everything," I replied. I hadn't realized it until that moment, but Grelk had lived among the old gods. He was a contemporary of The Deliverer. Of me. "I still don't remember most things."

"But you have more memory, yes?"

"Yes," I agreed. "More memory."

Before we could speak further, many entered the room at once. Leran and Ember emerged from the back stairs that led to the royal apartments, and Tor entered through the same door Aeolmar and I had. Behind Tor was Caol'non. The sight of them standing together was disconcerting. They looked so much alike it was as if Caol'nir was with us.

I stepped closer to Leran, and glanced at the Sala on Ember's arm. "Did it work?"

"It did," he replied with a grin. "Thank you." Leran turned away from the others, and said, "Da sends his love."

"Oh." I covered my mouth with my hand, swallowing the swell of emotions and so very glad Finlay wasn't here to witness my blubbering. I managed to get myself under control, and only then did I notice the silence in the room. Grelk had approached Caol'non and was staring at him. Not the way he'd looked at me, with open curiosity, but with a confusion I rarely saw on the old troll's face.

"You not Solon-son," Grelk said at last.

"My father's name is Tor," Caol'non replied.

"Solon-son is what Grelk called my father," Aeolmar said, then he said to Grelk, "This is my father's twin brother. His name is Caol'non."

"I mentioned Caol'non in my message," Leran said. "He claims there are armories full of troll weapons on Ysr."

"So?" Grelk countered. "We know where every weapon we make be. Always have."

"*Does that mean you supported the first Parthians against Olluhm?*" Aeolmar asked.

"*All troll against Olluhm,*" Grelk replied. "*Even mountain troll. We ally with elves instead of fae, Olluhm think we no good. We give the resistance weapons, we show him!*"

"*But, trolls have always been friends of Parthalan,*" I said, searching my memory to ensure that was true. "*Haven't they?*"

"*We friends of Parthalan's people, but not Olluhm,*" Grelk replied. "*Olluhm bad, very bad, but his first born was good. First born like mother.*" Grelk winked at Tor. "*Hopefully you like your mama, eh?*"

Tor reddened down to his collar. "*Is that why you call us Solon-son?*" Aeolmar asked. "*Because Solon was a better man than his father?*"

"*Mate's brain wear off on you,*" Grelk said, now winking at Latera. "*Too bad she no share beauty, too.*"

Aeolmar smiled. "*Did Solon tell you to stockpile weapons on a remote island?*"

"*No. We send weapons before he born, with first Parthians. They go there to hide from Olluhm, and wait.*" Grelk fixed me in his gaze, and said, "*When The Deliverer returns, she vanquish this sun and put back old one.*"

"*She can't,*" I said, rather desperately. "*Nyshanti is gone.*"

"*Gone from here,*" Grelk said. "*No gone for good. Nyshanti patient. She will wait till you need her.*"

"*Who is Nyshanti?*" Leran demanded. Before I could answer, Latera spoke.

"*Torim is Nyshanti,*" Latera said. "*Isn't she?*"

"*H-How... Why do you say that?*" I asked.

"*At the temple in the mortal realm, the oracle's room has the word* nyshanti *carved above the door,*" Latera replied. "*Inside that room is where I saw Torim.*"

I gasped, the final piece having fallen into place. "*I am not her,*" I whispered, backing toward the wall. It was one thing for Finlay and me to follow clues and memories, and something else to be confronted with the truth like a slap across the face. "*Perhaps I was once, but not now.*"

"*Who aren't you?*"

We looked toward the door as one. Finlay stood there, my poor mate who'd been sleeping beside a god. Not that I believed I was a god. Not *yet. I was half terrified that if I accepted I was The Deliverer, we would then learn this was all a misunderstanding. The other half of me was just terrified.*

"Has something happened to Finn?" I demanded.

"Yes. He's awake." Finlay looked around the room. "What's happening here?"

"We will talk about it after I see Finn," I said as I left the room and all but ran toward the infirmary. Would they tell Finlay what they—we—had learned? This possible last, final confirmation that I was who I feared to be? I didn't know how I felt about that. I didn't know how I felt about anything. Suddenly I was as numb as Mara, and damn it all, I wanted to stay that way.

Chapter Sixty-One

Latera Speaks

I watched Asherah flee from the room, past Finlay and away from the truth she'd searched for since before she'd been named Queen of Parthalan. At long last, she knew who she really was. We all did. What would happen next was anyone's guess.

Finlay watched his mate disappear down the corridor, then he regarded those of us left in the room. "Explain. Now."

Aeolmar approached Finlay, and drew him toward Grelk. Since Finlay didn't need to be crowded, I went to my daughter.

"My Lady," I began, then both Ember and Leran embraced me. It was wonderful, being held by both my daughter and her mate.

"You're all right?" I held Ember's face in my hands, searching for cuts or bruises or any other sort of wound. "The truth, now."

"I'm all right," she replied. "Well, my leg could be better, but it's just a scrape. How's Finn?"

"Not well, I'm afraid. But Finlay said he woke up, and according to the healers, that was the sign we were all waiting for." I shuddered; head wounds were a nasty business, and Finn had suffered a horrible one. "They say if he makes it through the next few days, his chances are good."

Leran jerked his chin toward the knot of people conferring with Finlay. "What upset Asherah?"

I followed his gaze. Finlay stood in the center of the room, stone faced, while Grelk and Aeolmar spoke to him in low tones. "Apparently your father fell in love with a god."

Leran's head swung toward me. "Exactly what does that mean?"

"Asherah, our sweet, loving Asherah, is Ish h'ra, The Deliverer." I glanced at Leran. "According to the stories, Olluhm couldn't kill her, because the people's love for her was too strong. Gods draw strength from their worshippers," I added.

"When he couldn't destroy her, he took her memory," Leran concluded, and I nodded.

"It seems that Asherah's companion, Torim, was also a god," I said. "She was called Nyshanti then, and she may be the key to all of this."

"It makes sense, as much as something like this could," Leran said. "If anyone is a god, it would be Asherah."

"Sibeal said much the same."

"I remember Torim," Leran continued. "I never knew she was also called Nyshanti."

"She is called Nyshanti still," I said. "She's in the mortal realm."

Ember shook her head. "All of this business with gods is enough to make my head spin," she said. "It's why elves don't worship any gods. We can't be bothered with such foolishness."

I smiled at my youngest daughter. "Spoken like a true Lady of Tingu."

***

While Finlay and the rest discussed Asherah's godhood, I returned to the infirmary to confront the goddess herself. I found her sitting next to Finn's cot, her hand resting on his uninjured shoulder. Mara sat on the other side of the cot, holding Finn's hand with both of hers. She was plainly exhausted, what with her red-rimmed eyes and how her body slumped against the wall, but she hadn't budged from Finn's side. I was struck by how much Mara reminded me of Aeolmar when he'd watched over me when I'd been confined to the healers ward in Teg'urnan. As I watched Mara stroke Finn's battered, bruised knuckles, I suspected she watched over him for the same reasons Aeolmar had stayed with me.

I approached Mara first, and brushed her hair away from her cheek. "I thought he was awake."

"He was," Mara replied, "but only for a few moments. He'll wake again."

I noted the dried tears on her cheeks. "I'm very proud of you, brave one."

"I'm not brave," she said. "Finn's the brave one. The way he climbed the wall and held off the orcs..." Her voice caught, and she began again. "Finn's the brave one."

I kissed her forehead. "You're both brave. Do you need anything?"

Mara shook her head. "I just need Finn to be well."

"We all want that." I gave her shoulder a final squeeze, then I found a chair, and brought it to the other side of Finn's cot. I sat, and faced Asherah.

"How are you?" I asked.

"I... I have no idea how I should answer that," she replied. "I shouldn't have left Finlay, not before explaining myself."

"Mar and Grelk are with him," I said. "As are Ember and Leran, and Caol'non and Tor."

"Is this something private?" Mara asked. "I can step away, if you need me to."

"What I need is for you to keep holding Finn's hand, for as long as you're willing." Asherah reached across Finn's body and placed her hand on top of Mara's. "I am so glad you and Ember were here for him."

Mara smiled, albeit weakly. "It was the least we could do."

Finn shifted, and Mara adjusted his blankets. As I watched Mara care for Finn, I said to Asherah, "I wish I had the slightest idea of what to expect next."

"You mean you didn't expect me possibly being a god?" Asherah countered.

Mara glanced up at us, eyes wary. "Please, Asherah," I said. "I knew you were a goddess the moment I met you."

"Kemen was right, then," Mara said. "You're The Deliverer."

"So it would appear," Asherah said. "The light that destroyed the orcs? That was me."

I nodded. "A useful trick, but perhaps next time deploy it at the beginning of a battle?"

"I'll do my best," she said. "Apparently, my war against Olluhm is not yet lost."

"What of the latter part of the stories, where you also wage war on his descendants?" I asked. "I'd rather not have you declare war on my children."

"But, you wouldn't mind if I declared war on Aeolmar?" she asked, her black eyes glinting.

"He would probably grumble and ignore you," I said, recalling how both Atreynha and Asherah claimed that Aeolmar favored his mother, the parent who was more closely linked to Olluhm. I shoved that thought away, and said, "Either way, I'd hate to have to defeat you."

Asherah scoffed. "You, defeat me? I'm a god!"

"I'm the deva'shi!"

"We have Ember, too," Mara added. "She killed the orc king."

"Did she?" I asked. "That's amazing."

"Perhaps now Aeolmar will retire his orc story," Asherah said, and we all laughed.

"That orc story will outlive us all," I said, and we laughed again. Once we'd quieted down, I asked, "What will you do next?"

"I don't know," Asherah replied. "There's much to do before I even consider what being Ish h'ra means to me. To all of us. I need to see to Finn, and get the lot of us back to Teg'urnan... Perhaps I should speak with the High Priestess."

"Perhaps," I said, recalling Atreynah's kind eyes and wise words. "Or, perhaps you should begin with Torim."

"My Nyshanti," she murmured. "It was only because of her we made any headway against Olluhm. She was so gentle, yet so strong."

"She was the sun, before Olluhm?" I asked.

Asherah shook her head. "She was the dawn. The sun was her father. He was called..." She shook her head again. "I can't remember, not yet."

"It will come to you," I said. "When you're ready, I can bring you to the temple in Gannera."

"It's a lovely place," Mara said. "It's built like a tiny version of Teg'urnan."

"Why has everyone been to this temple except me?" Asherah wondered.

"I think Torim was waiting for you to remember who you are," I said. "With any luck, once you're reunited with her, you'll remember the rest."

Asherah nodded, then she looked at her wounded son. "I hope these returning memories turn out to be a good thing." Asherah glanced at me, and added, "I don't know if I want to be a god."

"*I don't think you have much of a choice,*" I said. "*We can't run from what we are.*"

Asherah adjusted Finn's blanket. "*No, we certainly can't.*"

Chapter Sixty-Two

Mara remained at Finn's side for the rest of the night, until she collapsed from exhaustion and slumped half in her chair, and half onto Finn's cot. The last thing she remembered before sleep took her was Finlay setting his hand on Asherah's shoulder, and asking if their son had woken again.

When Mara woke, she was on a cot that was shoved right next to Finn's. As she blinked sleep from her eyes, she realized Finn was watching her.

"Hello," she whispered. "Do you need anything?" He responded with the barest shake of his head. "I'll get you something to drink," Mara began.

"No," Finn rasped. "Just stay here with me."

Mara found his hand amid the blankets. "A lot has happened while we waited for you to come back to us."

"Tell me everything."

"For starters, your mother is a god," Mara began. "All the orcs seem to be dead, the trolls funded a secret group of Parthians who have sworn to destroy Olluhm, and Kemen died." Her voice cracked at the end, and the tears she was too numb to cry earlier, now flowed freely.

"I'm so sorry," Finn said. "I know you loved him. He loved you, too, you know that, don't you?"

"I shouldn't burden you with this," Mara said. "You're hurt, and you saved us from the orcs, and—"

"Hush." Finn pushed himself up a bit, and held out his arm. "Come here."

Mara moved from her cot until she was on his, and Finn held her as she wept.

***

The next morning, Latera rushed to the infirmary to check on Finn and Mara. Aeolmar had been the last to check on them, and it was he who ordered Mara to be given a cot of her own. While Latera appreciated her daughter's empathy, she worried if Mara didn't get some real rest, she'd end up ill herself. She'd just reached the infirmary's entrance when Aldo approached her.

"My lady, you have a visitor," he said.

"I do?" Latera asked, as she followed Aldo into the receiving chamber. "Who in the nine realms even knows I'm here?"

"It's one of your sisters," Aldo advised, then he stepped aside and Latera saw Wren and Bron sitting at a table enjoying bowls of selka.

"Wren, Bron," Latera said, as she rushed to greet them. "Why are you all the way up here? And how did you get past the border?" she added, since it was well known that Parthians weren't allowed beyond Tingu's southern keep.

"I told those stationed at the border that I'm your sister," Wren replied with a shrug. "You're right, elves will do anything for the *deva'shi.*"

"We may have mentioned Asherah's name, as well," Bron added.

"That's all well and good, but why are you here?" Latera asked. She noticed that others were filing into the room; Aeolmar, Leran and Ember, Asherah and Finlay. Aldo must have gotten them after he told Latera about Wren's arrival.

Wren glanced about the room, and cleared her throat. "I looked into the information you sent me from Thurnda," she began. "What we found is that Dremmsvard, the village where Iruna's last estate stands, is also where Sarelle was born."

"Sarelle," Aeolmar muttered. "Will we never be done with her?"

"Apparently not," Wren continued. "What's more, the Northern Waste wasn't always a waste. It was once a green, lush land—"

"Until Olluhm destroy it," Grelk finished, having entered the room after everyone else. "Troll remember."

"Elves remember, too," Leran said. "One of the main reasons the trolls went underground was the blight on the land."

"Why did Olluhm do such a thing?" Latera asked. "Was it a punishment?"

"Evidently he didn't intend to cause such destruction," Wren said. "Dremmsvard had two very large shrines, one to The Deliverer, and one to the Dawn."

"Nyshanti," Asherah whispered.

Wren nodded. "Yes, Nyshanti. Olluhm tried to abduct Nyshanti from her shrine, but The Deliverer had already gotten her to safety. In his anger, Olluhm unleased the power of the sun on the surrounding lands and destroyed almost everything."

Everyone in the room fell silent. "There's more," Wren said.

"Please." Latera gestured for her to continue.

"I got two of the elfin scrolls you sent me somewhat translated," Wren began. "Apparently, the key to defeating Olluhm lies in Dremmsvard. The third scroll is older, and the language much more archaic. I'm having a hard time understanding it."

"Do you have the scroll with you now?" Leran asked, and Wren nodded. "Aldo," he called. "Would you mind reading something for us?"

"Of course." Aldo approached Wren, and unrolled the fragile scroll. After a few moments, he said, "The Deliverer will defeat Olluhm and restore the True Sun, but she must do it at her shrine in the north." Aldo paused, and said to Asherah, "I have a map of all the shrines in Tingu."

Asherah nodded. "Good. Is there anything else?"

"Yes. In order to gain entrance to the shrine, you will need the lodestone."

"A lodestone?" Latera repeated. "Will any lodestone do?"

"Not a lodestone, *the* lodestone," Aldo said. "It guided Nexa here from the mortal realm, and it guided Elvasla back there when she was destined to kill the *mordeth-gall*."

"Where is the lodestone now?" Finlay asked.

Leran shrugged. "No one knows. It was last known to be with Elvasla's daughter, Priya."

"Sibeal claims no one's seen Priya since shortly after Elvasla died," Latera said.

"Maybe Nyshanti knows where she is," Ember offered. "Someone should ask her."

Everyone turned to Asherah. "Agreed," Asherah said. "Someone should."

Latera leaned over to look at the scroll. Aldo handed it to her, and she scrutinized the unfamiliar language. "Dremmsvard," she said, pointing at one of the few words she understood. "Cerillia is from Dremmsvard. She put herself in front of Senan, and convinced him that he should take her as a mate, and that she should be the next Lady of Thurnda."

"And Cerillia traipsed around wearing that awful necklace that mirrored Iruna's symbol," Ember concluded. "Cerillia doesn't care about being the next Lady. She wants the lodestone, and she thinks it's in Thurnda."

Latera looked from the scroll, to Ember, to Asherah. "What should we do about Cerillia?"

Asherah threw up her hands. "Add it to the list of crises—however, my most important mission right now is seeing to Finn. Everything else can wait."

Everyone in attendance mumbled their agreement. No matter what was to come, Finn's recovery was their most pressing and important task.

"May I see Finn?" Wren asked. "I was told he suffered a head wound, and I've some experience with those."

"I will take you to him," Asherah said, and Wren followed her out of the room. Once they were gone, Latera approached her mate and Finlay.

"The more we learn, the more it seems we must return to Gannera," she said. Aeolmar pulled her against his chest.

"You don't want to see your home again?" Finlay asked.

"I didn't leave on the best of terms," she admitted. "Who knows what will happen when I go back."

"We can send someone else," Finlay offered, but Latera shook her head.

"No. I'll go. I just…" she looked up at Aeolmar. "It's hard to go home again."

Finlay nodded. "Asherah has said much the same."

Chapter Sixty-Three

The day after Wren and Bron arrived at The Seat, Leran's warriors, Graun and Diem, returned from Ysr. The Lord of Tingu greeted them along with his Lady. Latera and Aeolmar were also present. All were interested in the current state of the island nation.

"The island's inhabited, all right," Graun said. "The people are shy, and they did their best to avoid us."

"How do they live?" Leran asked. "Does the island have a city, or are the inhabitants in huts or caves?"

"There aren't cities or villages, so much as monasteries," Diem replied. "The complexes are as large as any palace I've ever seen, and everything happens within those walls—farming, smiths, you name it."

"Did you find the armory?" Aeolmar asked.

Graun shook his head. "It's either gone, or inside one of the walled complexes."

Along with their first-hand accounts, Graun had drawn maps of the island, and of the monasteries and shrines they encountered. He'd even secured a short letter from the leader of Ysr, a man called Dinnu. Leran broke the seal on the missive and scanned the page.

"What language is that written in?" Aeolmar asked.

"*Ahm'ri,*" Leran replied. "Perhaps it's the language of the old gods, as well."

Aeolmar frowned. "Does the letter mention Caol'non?"

"It does." Leran handed the letter to Aeolmar. "It says that Caol'non was with them for a very long time, and only left the sanctuary of the island to offer help to his family."

"Sanctuary," Latera repeated. "Then they did go there for safety."

"More importantly, we now know that Caol'non is who he says he is," Ember said. She was settling nicely into her role as Lady of Tingu, which was no doubt helped by her ready defense of The Seat. All of

Tingu's warriors viewed her as much of a leader as Leran. "We can stop wondering if he's a spy."

"Look at this symbol." Aeolmar turned the scroll around and pointed toward a drawing of a sun crossed with a spear. "It's the same as Kemen's amulet. According to Dinnu, the spear's tip is the lodestone."

"Then that disc is Olluhm," Latera concluded. They exchanged glances.

"We need to find that lodestone," Leran said.

"And figure out how to approach Olluhm," Ember added.

"Are we really contemplating killing a god?" Aeolmar asked.

"Before we do any of that," Latera said, "we need to get Finn home to Teg'urnan."

***

It was another two moons before Finn was deemed recovered enough to travel. While Tingu's healers were without equal, they were also without pride and lauded Wren's efforts to help Finn. She accepted their compliments gracefully, and shared all of her recipes and techniques for treating head wounds with them. Most grateful of all was Finn, who was thoroughly sick of being sick.

At last, the day came when they were about to set out for Teg'urnan. A carriage had its interior converted from seats to a bed, and Finn was to travel in it accompanied by two healers, and Mara, at all times.

"That's it, then," Finn said. Though his shattered bones were far from mended, the healers had splinted his leg so he could get around with a cane. "I'm going from flat on my back in The Seat to flat on my back in a carriage."

"It's only temporary," Mara said.

"Doesn't feel temporary," he grumbled.

"Soon we will be home, and then everything will be better," Mara said. "You'll have your own bed, and Wren has so many herbs and simples in her still room you'll be back on a horse in no time."

Finn glanced at her. "You think so?"

"I do." Mara looped her arm with Finn's, and helped him sit on a stack of trunks. "I believe in you, Finn, enough for both of us."

Finn squeezed her hand. "Dearest Mara, I truly don't know what I'd do without you."

A *saffira* approached them, and offered bowls of hot broth. Finn gladly accepted his, but Mara declined hers. "Aren't you hungry?" he asked.

"How can you drink that?" she countered. "It smells awful."

"I guess I'll just have to drink yours."

Mara rubbed her midsection, hoping it would quell her nausea. "Ugh. I hope it tastes better than it smells, for your sake."

"I can't have you starving," he said, as he held the bowl to her lips. "One sip, for me."

"For you." Mara dutifully took a sip, and fought the urge to retch. "Gods, Finn, I wouldn't have done that for anyone else."

"Really?" he asked, a hopeful gleam in his eye. They still hadn't talked about their kiss, or Finn's declaration of love, or that Mara had hardly left his side since he was pulled out of the battle. Mara wondered how much Finn remembered, and for the hundredth time she resolved to talk to him about that, and other things.

She opened her mouth to speak, and bile rose in her throat. Mara squeezed her eyes shut and took a deep breath, willing her belly to be calm.

"Mara?" Finn asked. "Is it really that bad? I'm sorry, I didn't want you to be sick."

"I'm not sick," she said. "I'll be fine, but you'll need to finish this for me."

Mara watched as Finn finished her broth, then his. She was happy he was doing well, and would be happier yet once they were home.

***

Latera observed Finn and Mara together, sipping broth as they watched the various trunks and chests get loaded onto the carts for the return to Teg'urnan. While Latera had enjoyed her time in the north, she hadn't expected to be gone for so long. Nor had she expected almost anything that had happened since they left for Thurnda.

"Homesick?" Aeolmar asked, as he stood behind her and slid his arms around her waist. Thanks to their bond, they always knew each other's mood.

"I am, but we'll be there soon," she said. "Then, I suspect I'll miss Tingu."

"I know I certainly will. Perhaps we can relocate to The Seat, and convince Mara and Tor to come with us. We do already own a nice bath house here in the north. Perhaps we can set up a full estate."

"Perhaps." Latera smiled, remembering the perfect afternoon she'd shared with her mate at the secluded hot spring. "Before we can think about any of that, I expect we'll need to go to the mortal realm, and Asherah's temple. What do you think we'll find there?"

"The lodestone, hopefully," Aeolmar replied. "But when is anything ever that easy?"

***

Asherah stood atop the grand steps of The Seat, beside Nexa's statue. It had never occurred to her how Teg'urnan's front courtyard mirrored The Seat's, what with its large public square and massive entrance. Now that she knew how much time Olluhm had spent fighting against the old gods in the north, she wondered what else had inspired him.

And when he was fighting in the north, he was fighting me.

Asherah had never felt a pull toward Olluhm or his temples. She'd long thought her indifference toward the gods was a result of her time as a prisoner, for what god of love would allow his people to be mistreated so? She now understood that Olluhm was not a god of love. He was a vain, capricious man, and his sole love was power.

Asherah resolved to teach Olluhm what true power was by removing the tyrant. That, she would love.

"What are you thinking?" Finlay asked, coming to stand beside her.

"Oh, about things," she replied. "The last time I left The Seat, I was the Lady of Tingu. Now, I'm no longer the Lady, but a goddess." She gave her mate a wry grin. "We certainly got more than we bargained for out of this journey."

"Everyone did," Finlay said, jerking his chin toward Leran and Ember. They would journey to Teg'urnan with the rest and stay on for a time, before returning to The Seat. To the populace at large, the Lord and Lady of Tingu were making a diplomatic journey to Teg'urnan. In reality, Leran would help search the archive for mentions of Priya, and the lodestone.

"I always hoped we would have a daughter one day," Asherah said. "Now, we have Ember."

"We do, but perhaps we could have another," Finlay said. "What say you, my goddess?"

Asherah swept her gaze across the bustle of the square, then she smiled at her mate. "I say that anything's possible."

Chapter Sixty-Four

Leran stood atop The Seat's grand steps, and grinned at his mate. "Today is a good day," he declared.

"You say that every morning," Ember said, as she slid her arm around his waist.

"Not so, beloved." He kissed her hair, and continued, "I've only greeted the mornings in such a manner for the last few moons."

"Really? And what changed to brighten your mood?"

"You know."

The Lord and Lady of Tingu watched as the final preparations were made for their journey to Teg'urnan. "I've never traveled so much in all my life," Ember murmured.

Leran glanced down at her. "Do you like traveling?"

"I do like seeing new places, and meeting new people," she began. "What I'll like even more is staying home with you."

He tightened his arms around his mate. "Yes. I will like that, too."

"How long will we stay on in Teg'urnan?" she asked.

"As long as you like," Leran replied. "I want you to say a proper goodbye to your home."

Ember swallowed the lump in her throat. "I never thought I'd have a different home, yet now I know I can and will protect The Seat with my life." She looked around the courtyard, noting that while most of the evidence of battle had been cleared away, scars remained. The biggest scar was the Gate, which remained a pile of rubble.

"Perhaps we should erect a new Gate before we leave," Ember suggested, but Leran shook his head.

"I need to rebuild it with The Sala," he replied, touching the armband Ember proudly wore. "It's how the original was made, only I'm not sure how to do it."

Ember understood what he left unsaid, that he'd never had the opportunity to learn how to properly wield the Sala and its many powers. "While we're traveling to Teg'urnan and back, let's practice building things with it," she said. "Then, by the time we return home, we'll be able to rebuild the Gate together."

"Together," Leran repeated. "My love, you're brilliant. We will do that, and then lead Tingu together through an age of peace and prosperity."

Ember leaned against his chest, and gazed at their people. "Yes, we will."

***

The story continues in...
Sunfall
The Chronicles of Parthalan, Book Six
Keep reading for a sneak peek!
Thank you so much! You, the reader, make all of this worthwhile.

***

Mara speaks...
It wasn't supposed to be like this.
I was supposed to hold myself chaste until I met my soul's true mate, then I would give him my one gift just as Cydia had given hers to Olluhm. After the claiming we'd be bound, share our lives, and have many, many children.
None of that happened.
I pressed my hand against my belly, feeling the small but firm curve that hadn't been present a few sennights past. While we were at The

Seat, and the elves had celebrated Madoc'na, I'd spent the night with Kemen. Mind you, I hadn't chosen him, but apparently such formalities were unnecessary. He claimed me, then he went off and died battling orcs and trolls in the Northern Waste while his seed sprouted in my womb. If I ever encounter his shade, I'll throttle him for leaving me.

And now we're in the last leg of our return journey to Teg'urnan, and I couldn't wait to have a bit of privacy and sleep in my own bed. We'd left Tingu almost two moons ago, and the size of our party, coupled with the many carriages for transporting the sick and wounded, had necessitated our slow pace. One of those carriages had been especially reserved for Finn, who'd been gravely injured while defending The Seat. Since I'd been caring for Finn all along, it was only natural for me to travel in the carriage with him. What I hadn't realized was that the carriage's constant rolling, bumping gait would agitate both my gut and my bones, making me a sick, sore, retching mess.

When we stopped for the night, and the tents were raised, I naturally followed Finn into his. The other healers followed him, too; I daresay he yearned for privacy more than I did. But while Finn was technically my charge, all I wanted was a quiet, non-moving bedroll where I could sleep away the exhaustions of the day. For the first few nights, that tactic worked.

Then the dreams began.

They weren't nightmares, or even unwelcome dreams, but they were vivid, and disjointed, and every day I woke more exhausted than the last. The only thing that calmed me, and the tiny life inside me, was Finn's presence.

Sometimes we woke lying in the same bedroll, and while I occasionally stirred when Finn came into mine, I never remembered going to his. During the day when we traveled in that merciless carriage he held my hand, and told me stories, and kept me from screaming and wailing and wanting to throw myself off a cliff. Soon enough it was plain that I was no longer taking care of Finn, and he was caring for me.

I often thought about the time he'd kissed me, moments before he went out—alone and armed only with a crossbow—to defend The Seat from the invaders, and when he told me he loved me. We hadn't kissed again, and we hadn't talked, and honestly that was for the best. Finn needed to work on his recovery, and not burden himself with me and my problems. Finn will be just fine once we return to Teg'urnan. As for me, and my baby, we'll also be fine. Somehow.

Gods, Kemen, I really do want to throttle you.

Chapter One

Finn adjusted Mara where she lay in the crook of his arm, and smoothed her hair back from her face. She'd fallen asleep shortly after the carriage started rolling, and it was the first peaceful sleep she'd had in days. What's more, they would be back home in Teg'urnan by nightfall, which meant she could sleep in a bed and not in a drafty tent.

He'd give anything for one more night of travel, and one more night with her.

Finn had loved Mara for as long as he could remember. The only reason he'd attended Madoc'na at The Seat was because he'd lost hope of ever being with her... Then The Seat was attacked, and since he figured he was going to die anyway he drew up his courage and kissed her goodbye. Not only had she kissed him back, he'd survived the battle and Mara had become his constant companion while he recovered. Once he'd recovered enough from his injuries he resolved to find the time to talk to Mara, but then she began getting sick.

Her symptoms were minor, at first; she was more tired than usual, and certain foods bothered her. Finn assumed her fatigue was due to her constant vigilance over him, and honestly he wasn't fond of elfin foods either. Then the trip home began, and one night Mara's nightmares worsened. A few sennights ago they were so bad she crawled into his bed for comfort. Finn had turned to her, his chest against her back, and thought the moment had finally come for him to tell her how he felt. When his hand moved over her belly he paused.

There was a curve, a swell that had not been present before.

Finn spent the rest of the journey staring at Mara's midsection whenever she was sleeping, which was often. When she slept flat or her back, or when she was outside and the wind flattened her clothes against her body, the swell was noticeable. What's more, it was growing.

Mara was with child, and Finn was certain no one knew but him.

The procession turned onto the royal road, and Finn saw the gray spires of Teg'urnan for the first time in more than half a year. He'd missed his home, but he had no idea what lay ahead for him or any of his family. His mother, Queen Asherah, had finally regained her memory, and her true identity as Ish h'ra, The Deliverer. She was once the leader of the old gods and the sworn enemy of Olluhm, the patriarch of the current Parthian gods. Finn laughed to himself; of all things he thought he might one day become, being the son of a god was not on that list.

Mara stirred at his laughter, and he soothed her. She'd no sooner settled against him when Elkin, the Second Hunter, rode out from Teg'urnan's gate. He stopped before Aeolmar and they exchanged a few tense words, then Elkin sought out the king and queen. While Finn wondered what was going on, Latera, Mara's mother, approached the carriage window.

"Is Mara awake?" Latera asked.

"She's just fallen asleep," Finn replied, moving away from Mara as he pulled back the curtain. "What's happening?"

"It seems we have some visitors waiting for us in Teg'urnan," Latera replied. "Or at least, I do."

"Who is it?"

"My sisters. They came here from the mortal realm, looking for me."

***

Latera watched as Finn woke Mara to tell her they were coming up on the palace, and almost wished he'd let her sleep. Mara had seemed perfectly healthy when they set out from Tingu, but she'd grown weak and pale during the journey home. Latera hoped Mara was merely showing the strain of caring for Finn, and that after a few nights spent in her own bed, eating good food rather than travel rations, would fix whatever ailed her.

Mara waved at her mother through the carriage window, and Latera put her latest worry aside as she urged her horse through Teg'urnan's dark iron gates. As she passed beneath the statues of the stag and doe, her gaze landed on a sight she never thought she would see in

Parthalan. Two of her sisters, Elia and Jannei, were standing in the palace square.

She waited a moment as Asherah and Finlay entered the square followed by Ember and Leran, with Finn's carriage rumbling behind them. As the royal members of the party entered Teg'urnan with all the associated pomp, Latera walked her horse toward her sisters.

"Girls," Latera called as she dismounted, then she paused. The women waiting for her were just that—grown women, not the children she'd last seen in Gannera. "What's happened?"

"You haven't seen us in half a lifetime, and the first thing you ask is what's happened?" Elia snapped. Jannei began apologizing, but Latera waved it away.

"It has been a long time," Latera conceded. "How are you?"

"Us? We're fine, I suppose." Elia eyed Latera. "You haven't returned home in all this time because of Father?"

"In a word, yes." Latera looked between the two of them, and asked, "Where is Sasha?"

"That's why we're here," Jannei replied. "No one knows. We thought she might have come here."

"What do you mean, no one knows?" Latera demanded, then there was a commotion near the palace steps.

"What's happening?" Elia asked.

"I don't know," Latera replied, then she reached out to Aeolmar with her mind.

Mar, what's going on?

Finn. He fell on the steps.

Is he all right?

He seems to be. Your sisters are here?

Two of them. Sasha seems to be missing.

I will be right there.

Bring Wren?

I will. It will be a Ganneran reunion.

"Aeolmar is on his way, along with Wren," Latera said. "How long has Sasha been missing?"

Jannei sighed. "We have much to tell you."

***

The story continues in Sunfall, available wherever books are sold, and here: https://books2read.com/sunfall

Homecoming
Winter's Queen, an urban fantasy set in Scotland and Elphame:
Touch of Frost
Giant's Daughter
Elphame's Queen
Changes, a contemporary romance:
Changing Teams
Changing Scenes
Changing Fate
Changing Dates

ABOUT THE AUTHOR

Jennifer Allis Provost is a native New Englander who lives in a sprawling colonial along with her beautiful and precocious twins, a dog that thinks she's a kangaroo, a parrot, a junkyard cat, and a wonderful husband who never forgets to buy ice cream. As a child, she read anything and everything she could get her hands on, including a set of encyclopedias, but fantasy was always her favorite. She spends her days drinking vast amounts of coffee, arguing with her computer, and avoiding any and all domestic behavior.

Find Jenn on the web here: http://authorjenniferallisprovost.com/

For up to the minute sale notifications, follow her on Bookbub here: https://www.bookbub.com/profile/jennifer-allis-provost
   For exclusive content, follow her on Patreon: https://www.patreon.com/jenniferallisprovost/
   Friend her on Facebook: http://www.facebook.com/jennallis
   Follow her on Instagram: @jenniferaprovost
   Happy reading!

9 798986 232331